D0594890

STORM TROOPERS

"I'm Gregory Mitsopoulas, NYPD. Mind if I ask who you are?"

"Aaron Fitzwater, Bureau Commandant, New York City Internal Security," the other replied.

"I figured it was something like that. And in your New York City, you guys are the only cops there are, right? So when you saw us lined up out there like that, you must have thought you had a goddamn revolt on your hands, right?"

Fitzwater stared silently for a moment, then asked, "*Your* New York City?"

"Don't you have reality storms where you come from? One dumped you here," Mitsopoulas explained.

"So," Fitzwater said, "you and your men were caught in a reality storm, and you found yourself in our world?"

"Hey, no," Mitsopoulas said. "*You* guys were caught. You're in *my* world."

He hoped.

By Lawrence Watt-Evans
Published by Ballantine Books:

THE LORDS OF DÛS
The Lure of the Basilisk
The Seven Altars of Dûsarra
The Sword of Bheleu
The Book of Silence

The Misenchanted Sword
With a Single Spell
The Unwilling Warlord
The Blood of a Dragon

The Cyborg and the Sorcerers

The Wizard and the War Machine

Nightside City

Crosstime Traffic

CROSSTIME TRAFFIC

Lawrence Watt-Evans

A Del Rey Book
BALLANTINE BOOKS • NEW YORK

"Paranoid Fantasy #1" first appeared in AMERICAN ATHEIST. Copyright © 1975 by The American Atheist. Reprinted by permission of the author.

"One Night At A Local Bar" first appeared in THE SPACE GAMER, under the title "Minus Two Reaction." Copyright © 1980 by The Space Gamer. Reprinted by permission.

"Why I Left Harry's All-Night Hamburgers" first appeared in ISAAC ASIMOV'S SCIENCE FICTION MAGAZINE. Copyright © 1987 by Davis Publications.

"Real Time," first appeared in ISAAC ASIMOV'S SCIENCE FICTION MAGAZINE. Copyright © 1988 by Davis Publications.

"Windwagon Smith and the Martians" first appeared in ISAAC ASIMOV'S SCIENCE FICTION MAGAZINE. Copyright © 1988 by Davis Publications.

"One-Shot" first appeared in ISAAC ASIMOV'S SCIENCE FICTION MAGAZINE. Copyright © 1990 by Davis Publications.

"A Flying Saucer with Minnesota Plates" first appeared in ISAAC ASIMOV'S SCIENCE FICTION MAGAZINE. Copyright © 1991 by Davis Publications.

"Storm Trooper" first appeared in ISAAC ASIMOV'S SCIENCE FICTION MAGAZINE. Copyright © 1991 by Davis Publications.

"New Worlds" first appeared in ISAAC ASIMOV'S SCIENCE FICTION MAGAZINE. Copyright © 1991 by Davis Publications.

"Science Fiction" first appeared in ANALOG SCIENCE FICTION/SCIENCE FACT. Copyright © 1991 by Davis Publications.

"Truth, Justice, and the American Way" first appeared in *Alternate Presidents*, edited by Mike Resnick. Copyright © 1992 by Lawrence Watt Evans.

"Watching New York Melt" first appeared in *Newer York*, edited by Lawrence Watt-Evans. Copyright © 1990 by Lawrence Watt Evans.

"An Infinity of Karen" first appeared in AMAZING STORIES. Copyright © 1988 by TSR, Inc.

"The Drifter" first appeared in AMAZING STORIES. Copyright © 1991 by TSR, Inc.

"The Rune and the Dragon" first appeared in DRAGON MAGAZINE. Copyright © 1984 by TSR, Inc.

"The Palace of al-Tir al-Abtan" first appeared in MARION ZIMMER BRADLEY'S FANTASY MAGAZINE. Copyright © 1989 by Marion Zimmer Bradley, Ltd. Used by permission.

"After the Dragon Is Dead" first appeared in MARION ZIMMER BRADLEY'S FANTASY MAGAZINE. Copyright © 1990 by Marion Zimmer Bradley, Ltd. Used by permission.

"The Final Folly of Captain Dancy" first appeared in *The Rebirth of Wonder*, by Lawrence Watt-Evans. Copyright © 1992 by Lawrence Watt Evans.

"Monster Kidnaps Girl At Mad Scientist's Command!" first appeared in PULPHOUSE: A FICTION MAGAZINE. Copyright © 1992 by Lawrence Watt Evans.

Sale of this book without a front cover may be unauthorized. If this book is coverless, it may have been reported to the publisher as "unsold or destroyed" and neither the author nor the publisher may have received payment for it.

A Del Rey Book
Published by Ballantine Books

Copyright © 1992 by Lawrence Watt Evans

All rights reserved under International and Pan-American Copyright Conventions. Published in the United States of America by Ballantine Books, a division of Random House, Inc., New York, and simultaneously in Canada by Random House of Canada Limited, Toronto.

Library of Congress Catalog Card Number: 92–90618

ISBN 0-345-37395-2

Manufactured in the United States of America

First Edition: November 1992

Dedicated to
Barbara Conroy
as explained elsewhere

CONTENTS

INTRODUCTION

Welcome to my book!

Maybe you're here because you've enjoyed my novels, or because you've seen some of these stories in magazines or anthologies and liked them. Or maybe the title piqued your interest, or the cover caught your eye. Whatever the reason, I hope you'll be pleased by the stories; I think there are some good ones.

I always wanted to see my name on a collection of short stories; I've always wanted to be a writer, always loved short stories. My novels have been appearing for over a decade, and much of the thrill has worn off, but short stories are still special for me, and a single-author collection like this—well, it's been something I've wanted for as long as I can remember, and I've finally made it.

It's taken a long time for it to happen, and I want to use this introduction to tell you how it came about. Let me start off with an explanation of how I wound up as a writer of fantasy and science fiction. After that I'll explain where the stories in this collection came from. It's going to be largely a shameless display of egotism, so nobody will be offended if you get bored and skip ahead to the stories.

Here's the beginning: I started reading science fiction when I was five. Honest. And I decided to write it when I was seven.

Both my parents read science fiction, you see. That meant my three older siblings read it as well. I don't remember ever not knowing what science fiction was; the concept had percolated into my consciousness by the time I was four, definitely.

It was about that age that I noticed my sibs reading comic

1

books, and I saw the nifty pictures of dinosaurs and space-ships and stuff and *I* wanted to read comic books, too.

And when I was five, I learned the letters of the alphabet in kindergarten and the sounds each one made. I still remember the flash of insight when the teacher wrote a song called "K-K-Katy" on the blackboard and taught us to sing it, and the connection between those three *K*s and the sound at the beginning of the song clicked into place somewhere in my head, and I began sounding out words.

I didn't know I was actually reading; I assumed that there was some trick to it I hadn't learned yet, but what I was doing seemed to work, so I tried it out.

I tried it not on Dr. Seuss or any of the kid stuff I was supposed to read, but on a coverless comic book, identified twenty years later as *Adventures into the Unknown #105*, that my sister Marian had picked up somewhere and left lying around the house. The lead story, "Last of the Tree People," involved a botanist who goes to the moon and finds intelligent trees and carnivorous dinosaurs. Another story was called "The Martian Mirage" and had this nifty domed city that appeared and disappeared. A third was "Born to Be A Grocer," about these weird disembodied intelligences that live among us—and who are about to take over the world.

I was hooked.

Not on science fiction, per se—on comic books.

Tarzan, Turok, Superboy, all of those. It was 1959. I'd missed the Golden Age of Comics; the gruesome horror and crime of the early 1950s had been stamped out; the great superhero revival hadn't really started yet. All the same, there were plenty of exciting comic books out there to read, and I loved them all. I had no money, but I had two older sisters who bought them and that was just as good.

I had an older brother, too, but I don't remember him ever having any money or buying any comic books. Fortunately, Marian and Jody weren't the stereotypical 1950s sissy-type girls—they didn't bring home romance comics, they brought home westerns and science fiction and superhero stuff. Also Little Lulu and Donald Duck, but those were great, too.

And there was a whole big box that had accumulated before I'd learned to read.

So I went on to first grade and discovered that I was reading the right way after all, and then I went on to second grade, where several very important events in my life happened.

First, I ran out of comic books. I'd worked my way through the box, and I was reading them faster than my sisters bought them, and my weekly allowance was only a dime, and even at the used-book store in those preinflation days that only bought two secondhand comics—four, if I got coverless ones.

I could go through four in an afternoon; what about the other six days each week?

My parents had been complaining all along that I should read something better than comic books, so in desperation I took them up on it. I'd had my fill of Dick and Jane and their kin in school—books, I am convinced, that were designed to teach kids that reading is excruciatingly dull. I wanted something *good*.

Well, my parents read books for fun, so I swiped two of those, and sneaked 'em up to my room, and even into school. The idea of reading an entire grown-up novel was too daunting to contemplate, so I picked two that were collections of short stories.

The first one was *The Green Hills of Earth*, by Robert A. Heinlein. The second one was *The October Country*, by Ray Bradbury.

That got me hooked on science fiction. And fantasy. And horror. I was thoroughly caught, even though I couldn't follow a lot of what the heck was going on in those stories—when I was seven, most of "Delilah and the Space Rigger" or "The Watchful Poker Chip of H. Matisse" went right over my head.

The next important event was my first in-class writing assignment. The teacher, Miss Conroy, gave us a title and told us to write something to go with it—a story, an essay, anything. The title was "Little Bird."

Most of the kids did stuff like "See the bird. It is a little bird. See the bird fly away. Fly, bird, fly." Dick and Jane strike again. *Bleah.*

A few got some rudimentary plot in there; I remember there were about three that I thought were okay.

Mine was a love story about two chickadees—it just about covered both sides of the sheet of paper we were given. When the teacher read it it sounded pretty dumb—but not as bad as the other kids, and Miss Conroy praised it and said something about maybe someday I'd be a writer.

I liked that idea. Writing it had been fun. Not much of what I did in school was fun, at that point. So I went home and showed my paper with the gold star on it to my mother and said, "I want to be a writer when I grow up."

Seven is an age when the subject of what you'll be when you grow up is a popular one. I'd previously talked about being in real estate—"a house seller"—or urban planning—"a city builder"—or the sciences—"an atom-bomb builder"—and my parents had always encouraged me.

But when I said I wanted to be a writer, my mother said, "Are you sure? That's a very hard way to make a living; you might not be able to do it."

I was astonished and baffled. I could be a rocket scientist, or a nuclear physicist, but not a writer?

So I tried it out on my father and got about the same reaction.

I'm still not quite sure why, even after thirty years. It wasn't just a bad day, or anything; from then on, right up until I sold my first novel, my parents encouraged me to write, if I wanted to, but as a *hobby*—making a career of it they seemed to consider impractical or downright impossible.

I took it as a challenge, though.

I read my third grown-up book not long after that—an anthology called *Fifty Short Science Fiction Tales*, edited by Isaac Asimov and Groff Conklin. The stories in there were a lot of fun, but not so spectacularly well written as Heinlein and Bradbury, and they were short, too. I could imagine writing as long and as well as some of these other guys—I *did* imagine writing as long and as well as some of these other guys.

So when I was eight, I wrote my first science-fiction story and hid it from my parents. I still have it. It's terrible, of course, but not bad for a third grader. It's in first person, told by a mutant lab mouse—I stole the idea of a super-intelligent rodent from "Barney," by Will Stanton, but making him the narrator was original with me.

From then on, I wrote stories off and on, and unless they were for school assignments, I never showed them to anybody. They weren't all science fiction, by any means; for one thing, in high school I discovered the distinction between science fiction and fantasy, and encountered the fantasy subgenre known as sword and sorcery, which I fell in love with for a time.

In 1972 I burned most of those old stories. Also in 1972 I first submitted one, to *The Magazine Of Fantasy & Science Fiction*.

It got rejected, of course. But it was a form rejection—there wasn't any letter telling me that if I ever again polluted their slush pile, they'd track me down and smash my typewriter.

I found this moderately encouraging.

Also in 1972 I sold a few feature articles to a local weekly paper—a very bad local weekly, but they paid me actual money. This was encouraging, too. And I published a sort of satirical underground newspaper called *Entropy*, using borrowed equipment, and sold it in my high school for a dime a copy and actually turned a profit. I wrote about half of each issue myself, including parodies of Conan the Barbarian and the like.

And it was *fun*. I'd never enjoyed making money before, when I'd shoveled snow or sold greeting cards or bagged groceries at the local supermarket, but I was getting paid for writing, which was what I did for fun anyway!

And people liked it!

I came to the conclusion that writing for money had to be about the best racket there ever was, and I was determined to get into it, sooner or later, somehow. My parents notwithstanding, I was convinced I could do it.

Not convinced enough to start immediately, though. Instead I went off to college on schedule, majoring in architecture.

I had a good time in college—too good a time. Early in 1974 I got kicked out—"asked to withdraw"—for what I think was officially termed "flagrant neglect of studies." Which means I was partying instead of going to class for much of my final semester.

Now, having been kicked out, I was faced with the problem of what to do next.

One thing I did *not* want to do was go home and face my parents—especially my father, who had graduated summa cum laude from the same university that I'd just flunked out of and had been the class salutatorian, as well. *His* father had taken his degree there cum laude. That was a lot of family history I preferred to avoid.

So I went to Pittsburgh and rented a furnished room, using borrowed money. Why Pittsburgh? Because my girlfriend was there—the one I'm married to now.

Another thing I did not want to do was to get a real job. I've always hated the very concept of holding down a real job, and I haven't been impressed with the reality, either, on those occasions when I've tried it. And I rather resented having been kicked out. It was my own damn fault, but I still didn't like it. I wanted back in.

Fortunately, the university had—and has, I believe—a fairly generous readmission policy. The theory seems to be that if you got in in the first place you can do the work; if you got kicked out, the problem was motivation, not ability, and that's something that can easily change. So you can be readmitted up to three times.

You have to apply for it, though, and prove you've been doing something with yourself other than sitting in a basement somewhere listening to Led Zeppelin over headphones for sixteen hours a day. And you are supposedly required to be gone for more than a year, though I knew people who had managed to get around that part.

That meant that I could apply for readmission in the spring of 1975, and theoretically, if I impressed the relevant bureaucrats, I could return to campus in September of '75 to take another shot at the semester I'd blown off.

I wanted something I could put in my readmission application that would make it look as if I were doing something interesting with myself, something conducive to personal growth and self-discovery and all that sort of thing. I also wanted something to do with my time that I could use as an excuse for not going full time flipping burgers somewhere. I had a year and a few months.

And I'd recently heard a story—I still don't know if it's true—about Larry Niven that I took as an inspiration.

According to the story, when Niven decided to be a writer, he gave himself a year. He holed up somewhere and wrote and did nothing much *except* write for a year. He collected lots of rejection slips and then, toward the end of the year, started selling short stories.

Sounded good to me. If I wrote for a year, I would collect lots of rejection slips that I could then enclose with my application for readmission. That should look sufficiently interesting to the people considering my case. It would be an excuse not to get a real job. And what the heck, the stuff might start selling.

So I started writing.

I didn't *just* write, in the event; I did a stint as a cook at Arby's, among other things. Mostly, though, I pounded away at the typewriter. I turned out reams of stuff, including fragments that are still in my "to be finished someday" pile; I actually finished about two dozen short stories and a couple of novelettes and submitted them to every market I could think of. Most of them were fantasy, some were science fiction, a few were mysteries, humor, or unclassifiable.

And in the spring of 1975, just a few days apart, two important pieces of mail arrived.

I'd been readmitted.

And I'd sold my first story.

The sale was for all of ten dollars, to a publisher I'd found in *Writer's Market* and submitted to almost as a joke; I went back to college.

That first story, though, has been reprinted a couple of times, earning several times the original ten bucks, and I rather like it. For historical reasons, I chose it to start off the present collection, so there it is: "Paranoid Fantasy #1." It was originally entitled, "Paranoid Fantasy #1, or, A Day in Whose Life?", but that was mercifully shortened the first time it was reprinted. The full-length version of the title hasn't been used since its original appearance in August, 1975. And yes, there were other "paranoid fantasies"; I got up to #4, at least. The others never sold, and deservedly so.

It's worth noting that there is a standard piece of advice to beginning writers, one that I hand out myself, that says you should never start off a story with, "The alarm clock rang . . ." It's a boring opening, and ninety-nine times out of a hundred it's the wrong place to begin the story.

I got away with it, though.

So I went back to college, and having actually sold a story, even so trivial a one as that, I was thought of as a Writer, by my classmates and myself. I'd learned a lot from all those rejections—about seventy of them, mostly form letters, but some more personal and detailed—and from reading *Writer's Market*, and from other books and magazines, and simply from the practice of writing that much.

One thing I'd learned—I'm not sure just where—was what the supposed odds were of selling a story through the slush pile. SF magazines, at that point, reportedly bought about one story out of every four hundred unsolicited submissions.

SF book publishers reportedly bought about one novel out of every forty unsolicited submissions.

One in forty is lousy odds, but it's a lot better than one in four hundred.

I therefore decided that my basic mistake had been writing short stories instead of a novel. When the summer of 1976 rolled around, and I was faced with the prospect of getting a summer job, I came up with a dodge—I'd write a novel instead.

I did, too. I made the mistake of finishing it in a mere ten weeks, though, so that I wound up with a job cleaning laboratory glassware for the last few weeks of summer.

The novel was called *Slant*, and it was terrible. It didn't sell.

In May of 1977, I gave up on college, dropped out, and moved to Kentucky, where my fiancée—we were married three months later, and we're still married—had just gotten a good steady job. I continued to try to write, rather than getting a real job—it was a habit by this time. I took one of those unsold novelettes, one that had gotten favorable comments from an editor—though it had still been rejected—and expanded it, rewrote it into a novel. This time I took fourteen months.

And this time, after a delay so long I'd given up and started looking for another line of work, it sold.

So I was a real writer, finally.

From then on, selling novels wasn't much of a problem. I wrote three sequels to that first one, rewrote *Slant* into the drastically improved *The Cyborg and the Sorcerers*, and forged steadily onward, with book after book.

Short stuff, though—I still didn't have the hang of that. I tried a few more stories, got a few more rejections.

A magazine called *The Space Gamer* contacted me early in 1980—the editor had read *The Lure of the Basilisk* and wanted to do an article on using overmen, creatures I'd described in the book, in role-playing games. I agreed and asked if they might be interested in buying fiction.

They were. I sold them two stories, an old one from my files and a new one that had come to me in a dream.

Honest. It did. I woke up one morning and there it was in my head. There's one description in it that I wrote only because it was important in the dream, and I still haven't figured out *why* it was important. *The Space Gamer* published it under the unintelligible-to-nongamers title "Minus Two Reaction"; I've included it here under its correct title, "One Night at a Local Bar."

Since the story came from a dream, I can't tell you much about it beyond the simple fact of its existence. It does have a point, but a good many readers seem to miss it.

I've spared you the other story that ran in *The Space Gamer*—the older one.

After those two, *The Space Gamer* seemed to have become disenchanted with me; they rejected a couple of stories, and I quit submitting to them. I was doing well enough with novels that I didn't care all that much.

Short fiction still happened occasionally, though—something would demand to be written, and I would write it, and it would go out gathering rejections. And every so often one would sell.

For example: I was living in Lexington, Kentucky. There was a shop in town called The Rusty Scabbard that sold games and gaming supplies, and some friends of mine were regular patrons there.

One day my wife said something about the place and got the name wrong—she couldn't remember the real name, so she made one up that sounded right and called it The Rune and the Dragon.

I liked that. It was obviously the title of a story. What's more, it was obviously the title of a story I had to write. And it should be done in a high-fantasy style.

I made a couple of false starts, but then the whole thing fell together, and I wrote "The Rune and the Dragon," and it got rejected a couple of places, both of which said, "This is a fine story, but we're not doing this sort of straight fantasy adventure right now." The first one suggested sending it to the second one; the second one suggested sending it to *Dragon* Magazine. *Dragon* bought it and published it in their November 1984 issue.

And that was the last place it appeared until now. Here it is again.

Now, for the next part of this account, we need some background.

In March 1982, Ace Books reissued Spider Robinson's short-story collection, *Callahan's Crosstime Saloon*, and I saw it displayed in the bookstores. I didn't read it, didn't even open it, just saw it. I liked the title. I'd always been fond of parallel-world stories, never thought they'd really been done right, and I assumed from the title that the book was about parallel worlds. I also like barroom tales, and the combination sounded like a good idea. That title stuck with me, somewhere in the back of my head.

In 1983, my wife and I drove from Kentucky to Washington, D.C. and to Baltimore for the World Science Fiction Convention. We stopped for lunch in a place called Sutton, West Virginia, and ate at a diner there that we liked—it's hard to say just why; there was just something about the atmosphere that appealed to us.

These two items percolated in my subconscious, tangled themselves up with parallel-world theory and certain attitudes, and came out as a story called "Why I Left Harry's All-Night Hamburgers."

It sold the first place I sent it, which was *Isaac Asimov's Science Fiction Magazine*—henceforth *Asimov's*, for short. It was my first sale to a real science-fiction magazine. It was the first time a short story of mine had sold on the first try.

It went on to be the first story of mine to win a Hugo and the first to be nominated for a Nebula and the first to win the *Asimov's* Readers' Poll Award. It's been anthologized, translated into Japanese and Polish, and adapted to radio.

After all that, I decided I'd finally gotten the hang of writing short stories.

And since then, while I still get rejections, I've been able to sell most of my short fiction.

Naturally, when one has a hit, one tries to follow it up, and the concept of "Harry's" obviously still had plenty of potential. Several other related stories have been planned; so far, I've only finished one. It's called "A Flying Saucer with Minnesota Plates," and it's here, right after the original story. It isn't exactly a sequel; it's just another story about the same place. It, too, appeared in *Asimov's* originally.

I'd had another idea about parallel worlds that was intended to be a whole series of short stories—the basic concept was that some sort of accident has created a permanent, stable opening connecting an effectively infinite number of alternate Earths. The series title was to be "The Hole Above the Parking Lot."

So far, though, I've only written one of the stories. My title for it was "Eurydice," and anyone who has a classical background will recognize the name and understand where the story came from. My agent protested, probably accurately, that 90 percent of the readers *wouldn't* have the necessary background, so it was retitled "An Infinity of Karen." It was first published in *Amazing* in 1988; this is only its second appearance in English.

Another variant on the parallel world theme occurred to me about ten years ago while I was walking to the supermarket one afternoon, thinking about vectors. No, I don't generally think about things like vectors when I'm out strolling; I have no idea why I did that day, I just did, and when I got home I wrote a story called "The Drifter"—but it's not the one that's included here. It was only about half as long, and although it had the same central concept, I'd approached it entirely differently, and it was a pretty lousy story. I sent it out several places, and eventually it wound up in my agent's files, gathering dust.

Then, just recently, he cleaned out his files. He sent me a whole package of old stories he had no particular use for.

Most of them I didn't have any use for, either, but when I reread "The Drifter" I said to myself, "I can fix this!" With the additional experience I'd acquired in the intervening years I could see immediately what I'd done wrong.

I just didn't fix it, though, I just about wrote an entire new story with the same title and premise, and I did it more or less in a single sitting. I don't think there's a single line from the original in the rewritten version, but it all poured right onto the page, as if it had been working itself out in the back of my head all that time.

And yet another angle on the parallel-world idea—I've come up with dozens, many still unused—was the possibility that experimenting with travel between different realities would have unforeseen side effects, effects that might be felt in worlds other than where the actual experimentation was being done. These might be very serious. Frederik Pohl came up with the same idea independently and used it as a subplot in *The Coming of the Quantum Cats*, under the name "ballistic recoil." I thought that he threw away some excellent story possibilities there—what if some of the affected parties had no idea what was causing it? Reality might seem to be coming apart, they would have no idea why, and they would have to just learn to live with it.

The result, so far, is the story "Storm Trooper," contained herein.

Related to the whole field of parallel worlds is the idea of alternate histories—what if some event had happened differently? How would the world be changed?

I'm not really all that fond of the subgenre, because there are just too many variables involved and there's a tendency for the stories to degenerate into fictional history lectures, but I've tried it a couple of times. One of them was a very short consideration of one of the classic time-traveler-changes-history scenarios, written at the suggestion of Laurence M. Janifer; it's called "One-Shot," and it's included here.

And then there was Mike Resnick's invitation to do a story for his *Alternate Presidents* anthology—the premise was to write alternate-history stories based on presidential elections turning out differently.

I picked 1932, studied up on it, and discovered that Al Smith came very, very close to declaring himself a third-party candidate, which might have split the Democratic Party and gotten Hoover re-elected in a squeaker—Herbert Hoover, "the most hated man in America," with a second term, a heavily Democratic Congress, failing health, and the interventionist Henry Stimson as his Secretary of State and effective second in command.

What would have happened with Henry Stimson running U.S. foreign policy in the 1930s, rather than Franklin Roosevelt?

My guess is called "Truth, Justice, and the American Way."

And while we're changing history, the idea of time police who prevent people from changing history isn't a new one at all; probably Poul Anderson's "Time Patrol" stories are the best-known examples. It's a fascinating idea. It's also sort of creepy—how mutable is the past? Fritz Leiber's "Change War" stories, about the Snakes and the Spiders, consider that. And one day, I sat down and wrote a little story about just how would a time patrolman know what's real and what isn't?

At least, I think that's what it's about. It's called "Real Time." It's about my favorite of all my short stories.

And one more final twist on the parallel-world theme— why do science fiction stories seem to focus on crosstime travel, or on space travel, but never on *both*? After all, if there are an infinite number of parallel Earths, then there must be just as many Marses and Alphas Centauri. I had that question kicking around my head for years, and then one day I came up with the clever idea of writing a story live on-line on the

GEnie computer network, as a publicity stunt—rather like Harlan Ellison's stunt of writing a story while sitting in a bookstore window. The idea I chose was the question of why either/or, and not both, and the result was "New Worlds."

I like stunts. I like doing things that aren't supposed to work, such as the first line of "Paranoid Fantasy #1" and some other things in this collection that I don't want to give away here. I like challenges, if they're the right sort.

I was in a discussion of all those old juveniles from the '40s and '50s—that's what they were called then, anyway; now we'd say "young adult novels"—where two kids build a spaceship in their backyard. It's an idea that even made it into the movies, in *Explorers*.

It was the consensus of the discussion, though, that SF readers are all too sophisticated for that sort of thing nowadays—you couldn't make it work. *Explorers* wasn't exactly a hit, so maybe it's not just readers, either.

It seemed to me there should be some way to *make* it work, to make people believe two kids could build a spaceship in their backyard.

So I did. I even sold it to *Analog*, that bastion of hard-core technological fiction—my very first sale there. And I had the audacity to call it simply "Science Fiction."

I know exactly where that story came from. Others just happen, for no reason that I know of. One that just happened was "Watching New York Melt," which was written with my wife's help—she suggested the characters' luncheon preferences and added a few other details. I think I'd been thinking about conceptual art—always a dangerous thing to do.

In much the same way that "Science Fiction" was a result of one of the ancient cliches of the SF field, another one brought forth "Monster Kidnaps Girl at Mad Scientist's Command!" The title alone should make it plain that I wanted to write a story that would actually *belong* behind one of those old pulp covers that depicted a tentacular monster carrying off a busty young woman. I also wanted to explain why a monster would *want* a woman.

I tried to put a new twist on the whole thing, of course.

This story was turned down for being too sexy, too long, too strange, and for various other reasons that struck me as silly, before finally selling to *Pulphouse Weekly*. It's one of my own favorites, it's been a hit at public readings, and I really don't understand why it took so long to sell.

One way to come up with a new twist is to put together two things that haven't gone together before. When *Locus* reviewed *On Stranger Tides*, by Tim Powers, the reviewer remarked on how Powers had done something that should have been obvious, by putting together two things the Caribbean is famous for—pirates and voodoo—that hadn't been put together before.

That got me thinking.

Mostly, it got me thinking, "Damn, why didn't *I* think of that?"

But then it got me thinking about what I could put together that obviously *went* together, but hadn't been done before.

I didn't come up with anything obvious, like pirates and voodoo, but I did eventually come up with an American folktale—one that happens to be based on an actual historical incident; Thomas "Windwagon" Smith was real—and some elements of Ray Bradbury's *The Martian Chronicles* that looked like a nice fit.

Bradbury and American legends seemed like a pretty good match, and I'd always wanted to write a real old-fashioned tall tale; I did a little research, sent the rough draft to Mr. Bradbury to make sure he didn't object to my story, and the result was "Windwagon Smith and the Martians," which won me my second *Asimov's* award and went on to various reprintings and adaptations.

Let me emphasize that I know what I derived from *The Martian Chronicles*; it was quite deliberate, and I would never have allowed the story to be published if Mr. Bradbury had not given his permission.

Thomas Smith, of course, is available for any author who cares to use him, like any other public figure of his day.

There is, by the way, a third source—it really only provided a passing reference. I'll leave it as a puzzle for the knowledgeable reader to identify what other (public domain) story I drew on.

So far, except for the first, these stories have been mostly science fiction, or at least borderline. After "Windwagon Smith and the Martians," though, we get into pure fantasy. Fantasy is the field I've been most successful in; I'm not quite sure why. I like it fine, you understand, but I like science fiction just as much.

Ah, well, no accounting for the vagaries of fate.

I have already, however, accounted for the origin of "The

Rune and the Dragon." Let me now explain "The Palace of al-Tir al-Abtan."

Remember those two dozen stories I wrote in 1974 and 1975 that didn't sell?

Well, one of them was called "The Palace of Llarimuir," and from the minute I started writing it, it felt special, better than anything else I'd done up to that point. I was very, very pleased with it; I had a feeling that here, at last, was the story that was going to break me into print. I mailed it off to an editor who shall remain nameless.

And he lost it.

I got a letter from the slush reader who had read it and passed it on to the editor with a strong recommendation; he really liked it. After that, nothing.

Eventually, I inquired and was told that they had no such story, the editor didn't remember any such story, and did the slush reader really say that, because they didn't believe me.

I still have the reader's letter. He said that.

The story was gone—and I didn't have a carbon. I'd run out of carbon paper just before writing it and didn't want to take time to get more, not while the writing was going so well. I figured it wouldn't hurt, just *one story* with no carbon.

I mean, of *course* that was the one they lost—of mine; I've heard from other writers that that editor lost a *lot* of manuscripts over the years.

Life is much easier in these days of cheap photocopies and writing on computers, where I can just plug in a disk and print a new copy as needed. Back then, though, it was typewriter and carbon paper. All I had left was the rough drafts— and they were rough, all right. The story had gone through several false starts and variations before reaching its final form. And by the time I was convinced the story was lost, I was on my way back to college.

So I put it aside and tried to forget about it, with the intention of someday digging it out and reconstructing it.

And for once, someday actually came.

Susan Shwartz was editing the second *Arabesques* anthology and invited me to submit a story. I didn't have any stories around that were appropriate, and a novel was nearing deadline, so I didn't have time to come up with an entirely new one. In a sudden inspiration, I pulled out the rough draft of "The Palace of Llarimuir," which was rather Oriental in setting and feel, and rewrote it into "The Palace of al-Tir al-

Abtan." The only change necessary to make it an *Arabian Nights* sort of story was to change the names from vaguely Celtic coinages to genuine Arabic.

In fact, the Arabic names fit the whole thing better than the originals.

It didn't really fit the anthology that well, though, and Susan didn't take it. *Marion Zimmer Bradley's Fantasy Magazine* did.

"The Final Folly of Captain Dancy" happened after watching the adventure movie *Nate and Hayes*. Throughout that, it seemed as if the heroes were making up elaborate schemes, risking their lives carrying them out, and not telling anybody what their plans were.

What would have happened, I wondered, if one of them had gotten killed? How could the rest of Bully Hayes' crew have carried on? All these complicated plots that depended on other people carrying out their parts in time . . .

The idea stewed for a while, then gradually started growing. I had no idea how long the story was going to be—for a while I thought it might be a novel, but it wrapped itself up neatly as a novella, the only one I've ever written. I like it.

And while I was always a few steps ahead of the characters, no, I did *not* know, while I was writing it, how it was all going to come out.

And finally, as a coda to these fantasy adventures, we have "After the Dragon Is Dead," which is a consideration of just what does happen after the final fade-out.

So that's the lot. These are not all my short fiction, by any means—I've left out most of my work in horror, series fantasy, and hard SF. And of course, I'm still writing more. All those will have to wait for some future volume or volumes. This time around I've focused on alternate realities and personal favorites.

I hope you'll enjoy reading them as much as I enjoyed writing them.

PARANOID FANTASY #1

The alarm went off, and Nathan woke up.

He glanced out through the bulletproof glass of the window by his bed; seeing no obvious danger, he unstrapped himself, sat up, and turned off the burglar alarm, muttering the charm, "Rabbit, rabbit," as he did so. He took the silver cross from around his neck and dressed for the day, starting with chain-mail undershirt and lead-lined jockey shorts.

After replacing the garlic at each window, he burned a cone of incense, with the appropriate prayers, to placate the gods. Carefully, his hands protected by rubber gloves, he took his defanged white mouse, Theodosius, from its massive cage, then headed down to the corner restaurant for breakfast, being certain to lock the door behind him, both the three regular locks and the special one the police couldn't open. Always watching for the things that come through the walls, he ate heartily, after feeding a little of everything to Theodosius to check for poison.

Shortly thereafter, Nathan, briefcase in hand, was off to his downtown office. As if from nowhere, his obnoxious neighbor Eddie appeared before him. Nathan had been too busy not stepping on the cracks in the sidewalk to see him coming.

Eddie cried out, "Hi, Nathan! How's business?"

Nathan made a sign to ward off the evil eye, glanced about for other menaces, then muttered something about being late.

"Aw, hell, Nathan, so you'll be a few minutes late! I missed the entire day, yesterday, and nothing's happened to me! You worry too much, you know that? Why are you always . . . hey! What's that? Hey! Help!" This last was said as several large trolls and assorted gargoyles suddenly leaped out of the nearby shrubbery. With nasty giggles and remarks

17

about foolhardiness, they grabbed Eddie, trussed him up tightly, and carried him off.

Nathan watched them go, then continued on his way to the bus stop, unconcerned. *He* was safe from *that* bunch. It was the Others that worried him, and *they* only come out at night.

WHY I LEFT HARRY'S
ALL-NIGHT HAMBURGERS

*H*arry's *was a nice place—probably still is. I haven't been* back lately. It's a couple of miles off I-79, a few exits north of Charleston, near a place called Sutton. Used to do a pretty fair business until they finished building the interstate out from Charleston and made it worthwhile for some fast-food joints to move in right next to the cloverleaf; nobody wanted to drive the extra miles to Harry's after that. Folks used to wonder how old Harry stayed in business, as a matter of fact, but he did all right even without the interstate trade. I found out when I worked there.

Why did I work there, instead of at one of the fast-food joints? Because my folks lived in a little house just around the corner from Harry's, out in the middle of nowhere—not in Sutton itself, just out there on the road. Wasn't anything around except our house and Harry's place. He lived out back of his restaurant. That was about the only thing I could walk to in under an hour, and I didn't have a car.

This was when I was sixteen. I needed a job, because my dad was out of work again, and if I was gonna do anything, I needed my own money. Mom didn't mind my using her car—so long as it came back with a full tank of gas and I didn't keep it too long. That was the rule. So I needed some work, and Harry's All-Night Hamburgers was the only thing within walking distance. Harry said he had all the help he needed—two cooks and two people working the counter, besides himself. The others worked days, two to a shift, and Harry did the late-night stretch all by himself. I hung out there a little, since I didn't have anywhere else, and it looked like pretty easy work—there was hardly any business, and

19

those guys mostly sat around telling dirty jokes. So I figured it was perfect.

Harry, though, said that he didn't need any help.

I figured that was probably true, but I wasn't going to let logic keep me out of driving my mother's car. I did some serious begging, and after I'd made his life miserable for a week or two, Harry said he'd take a chance and give me a shot, working the graveyard shift, midnight to eight A.M., as his counterman, busboy, and janitor all in one.

I talked him down to seven-thirty, so I could still get to school, and we had us a deal. I didn't care about school so much myself, but my parents wanted me to go, and it was a good place to see my friends, y'know? Meet girls and so on.

So I started working at Harry's nights. I showed up at midnight the first night, and Harry gave me an apron and a little hat, like something from a diner in an old movie, same as he wore himself. I was supposed to wait tables and clean up, not cook, so I don't know why he wanted me to wear them, but he gave them to me, and I needed the bucks, so I put them on and pretended I didn't notice that the apron was all stiff with grease and smelled like something nasty had died on it a few weeks back. And Harry—he's a funny old guy, always looked fiftyish, as far back as I can remember. Never young, but never getting really old, either, you know? Some people do that, they just seem to go on forever. Anyway, he showed me where everything was in the kitchen and back room, told me to keep busy cleaning up whatever looked like it wanted cleaning, and told me, over and over again, like he was really worried that I was going to cause trouble, "Don't bother the customers. Just take their orders, bring them their food, and don't bother them. You got that?"

"Sure," I said, "I got it."

"Good," he said. "We get some funny guys here at night, but they're good customers, most of them, so don't you screw up with anyone. One customer complains, one customer stiffs you for the check, and you're out of work, you got that?"

"Sure," I said, though I've gotta admit I was wondering what to do if some cheapskate skipped without paying. I tried to figure how much of a meal would be worth paying for in order to keep the job, but with taxes and all it got too tricky for me to work out, and I decided to wait until the time came, if it ever did.

Then Harry went back in the kitchen, and I got a broom

and swept up out front a little until a couple of truckers came in and ordered burgers and coffee.

I was pretty awkward at first, but I got the hang of it after a little bit. Guys would come in, women, too, one or two at a time, and they'd order something, and Harry'd have it ready faster than you can say "cheese," practically, and they'd eat it, and wipe their mouths, and go use the john, and drive off, and none of them said a damn thing to me except their orders, and I didn't say anything back except "Yes, sir," or "Yes, ma'am," or "Thank you, come again." I figured they were all just truckers who didn't like the fast-food places.

That was what it was like at first, anyway, from midnight to about one, one-thirty, but then things would slow down. Even the truckers were off the roads by then, I guess, or they didn't want to get that far off the interstate, or they'd all had lunch, or something. Anyway, by about two that first night I was thinking it was pretty clear why Harry didn't think he needed help on this shift, when the door opened and the little bell rang.

I jumped a bit; that bell startled me, and I turned around, but then I turned back to look at Harry, 'cause I'd seen him out of the corner of my eye, you know, and he'd got this worried look on his face, and *he* was watching *me*; he wasn't looking at the customer at all.

About then I realized that the reason the bell had startled me was that I hadn't heard anyone drive up, and who the hell was going to be out walking to Harry's place at two in the morning in the West Virginia mountains? The way Harry was looking at me, I knew this must be one of those special customers he didn't want me to scare away.

So I turned around, and there was this short little guy in a really heavy coat, all zipped up, made of that shiny silver fabric you see race-car drivers wear in the cigarette ads, you know? And he had on padded ski pants of the same stuff, with pockets all over the place, and he was just putting down a hood, and he had on big thick goggles like he'd been out in a blizzard, but it was April and there hadn't been any snow in weeks and it was about fifty, sixty degrees out.

Well, I didn't want to blow it, so I pretended I didn't notice, I just said, "Hello, sir; may I take your order?"

He looked at me funny and said, "I suppose so."

"Would you like to see a menu?" I said, trying to be on my

best behavior—hell, I was probably overdoing it; I'd let the truckers find their own menus.

"I suppose so," he said again, and I handed him the menu.

He looked it over, pointed to a picture of a cheeseburger that looked about as much like anything from Harry's grill as Sly Stallone looks like me, and I wrote it down and passed the slip back to Harry, and he hissed at me, "Don't bother the guy!"

I took the hint and went back to sweeping until the burger was up, and as I was handing the plate to the guy, there was a sound out front like a shotgun going off, and this green light flashed in through the window, so I nearly dropped the thing, but I couldn't go look because the customer was digging through his pockets for money, to pay for the burger.

"You can pay after you've eaten, sir," I said.

"I will pay first," he said, real formal. "I may need to depart quickly. My money may not be good here."

The guy hadn't got any accent, but with that about the money I figured he was a foreigner, so I waited, and he hauled out a handful of weird coins, and I told him, "I'll need to check with the manager." He gave me the coins, and while I was taking them back to Harry and trying to see out the window, through the curtain, to see where that green light came from, the door opened and these three women came in, and where the first guy was all wrapped up like an Eskimo, these people weren't wearing anything but jeans. Women, remember, and it was only April.

Hey, I was just sixteen, so I tried real hard not to stare, and I went running back to the kitchen and tried to tell Harry what was going on, but the money and the green light and the half-naked women all got tangled up and I didn't make much sense.

"I *told* you I get some strange customers, kid," he said. "Let's see the money." So I gave him the coins, and he said, "Yeah, we'll take these," and made change—I don't know how, because the writing on the coins looked like Russian to me, and I couldn't figure out what any of them were. He gave me the change and then looked me in the eye and said, "Can you handle those women, boy? It's part of the job; I wasn't expecting them tonight, but we get strange people in here, I told you that. You think you can handle it without losing me any customers, or do you want to call it a night and find another job?"

I really wanted that paycheck; I gritted my teeth and said, "No problem!"

When you were sixteen, did you ever try to wait tables with six bare boobs right there in front of you? Those three were laughing and joking in some foreign language I'd never heard before, and I think only one of them spoke English, because she did all the ordering. I managed somehow, and by the time they left, Harry was almost smiling at me.

Around four things slowed down again, and around four-thirty or five the breakfast crowd began to trickle in, but between two and four there were about half a dozen customers, I guess; I don't remember who they all were anymore, most of them weren't that strange, but that first little guy and the three women, them I remember. Maybe some of the others were pretty strange, too, maybe stranger than the first guy, but he was the *first*, which makes a difference, and then those women—well, that's gonna really make an impression on a sixteen-year-old, y'know? It's not that they were particularly beautiful or anything, because they weren't, they were just women, and I wasn't used to seeing women with no shirts.

When I got off at seven-thirty, I was all mixed up; I didn't know what the hell was going on. I was beginning to think maybe I imagined it all.

I went home and changed clothes and caught the bus to school, and what with not really having adjusted to working nights, and being tired, and having to think about schoolwork, I was pretty much convinced that the whole thing had been some weird dream. So I came home, slept through until about eleven, then got up and went to work again.

And damn, it was almost the same, except that there weren't any half-naked women this time. The normal truckers and the rest came in first, then they faded out, and the weirdos started turning up.

At sixteen, you know, you think you can cope with anything. At least, I did. So I didn't let the customers bother me, not even the ones who didn't look like they were exactly human beings to begin with. Harry got used to me being there, and I did make it a lot easier on him, so after the first couple of weeks it was pretty much settled that I could stay on for as long as I liked.

And I liked it fine, really, once I got used to the weird hours. I didn't have much of a social life during the week, but I never had, living where I did, and I could afford to do the weekends up in style with what Harry paid me and the tips I got. Some of those tips I had to take to the jewelers in Charleston, different ones so nobody would notice that one guy was bringing in all these weird coins and trinkets, but Harry gave me some pointers—he'd been doing the same thing for years, except that he'd gone through every jeweler in Charleston and Huntington and Wheeling and Washington, Pennsylvania, and was halfway through Pittsburgh.

It was fun, really, seeing just what would turn up there and order a burger. I think my favorite was the guy who walked in, no car, no lights, no nothing, wearing this electric-blue hunter's vest with wires all over it, and these medieval tights with what Harry called a codpiece, with snow and some kind of sticky goop all over his vest and in his hair, shivering like it was the Arctic out there, when it was the middle of July. He had some kind of little animal crawling around under that vest, but he wouldn't let me get a look at it; from the shape of the bulge it made it might have been a weasel or something. He had the strangest damn accent you ever heard, but he acted right at home and ordered without looking at the menu.

Harry admitted, when I'd been there awhile, that he figured anyone else would mess things up for him somehow. I might have thought I was going nuts, or I might have called the cops, or I might have spread a lot of strange stories around, but I didn't, and Harry appreciated that.

Hey, that was easy. If these people didn't bother Harry, I figured, why should they bother me? And it wasn't anybody else's business, either. When people asked, I used to tell them that sure, we got weirdos in the place late at night—but I never said just how weird.

And I never got as cool about it as Harry was; I mean, a flying saucer in the parking lot wouldn't make Harry blink. *I* blinked, when we got 'em—we did, but not very often, and I had to really work not to stare at them. Most of the customers had more sense; if they came in something strange, they hid it in the woods or something. But there were always a few who couldn't be bothered. If any state cops ever cruised past there and saw those things, I guess they didn't dare report them. No one would've believed them anyway.

I asked Harry once if all these guys came from the same place.

"Damned if I know," he said. He'd never asked, and he didn't want me to, either.

Except he was wrong about thinking that would scare them away. Sometimes you can tell when someone wants to talk, and some of these people did. So I talked to them.

I think I was seventeen by the time someone told me what was really going on, though.

Before you ask any stupid questions, no, they weren't any of them Martians or monsters from outer space or anything like that. Some of them were from West Virginia, in fact. Just not *our* West Virginia. Lots of different West Virginias, instead. What the science-fiction writers called "parallel worlds." That's one name, anyway. Other dimensions, alternate realities, they had lots of different names for it.

It all makes sense, really. A couple of them explained it to me. See, everything that ever could possibly have happened, in the entire history of the universe right from the Big Bang up until now, *did* happen—somewhere. And *every* possible difference means a different universe. Not just if Napoleon lost at Waterloo, or won, or whatever he didn't do here; what does Napoleon matter to the *universe*, anyway? Betelgeuse doesn't give a flying damn for all of Europe, past, present, or future. But every single atom or particle or whatever, whenever it had a chance to do something—break up or stay together, or move one direction instead of another, whatever—it did *all* of them, but all in different universes. They didn't branch off, either—all the universes were always there, there just wasn't any difference between them until this particular event came along. And that means that there are millions and millions of identical universes, too, where the differences haven't happened yet. There's an infinite number of universes—more than that, an infinity of infinities. I mean, you can't really comprehend it; if you think you're close, then multiply that a few zillion times. *Everything* is out there.

And that means that in a lot of those universes, people figured out how to travel from one to another. Apparently it's not that hard; there are lots of different ways to do it, too, which is why we got everything from guys in street clothes to people in space suits and flying saucers.

But there's one thing about it—with an infinite number of universes, I mean really infinite, how can you find just one? Particularly the first time out? Fact is, you can't. It's just not possible. So the explorers go out, but they don't come back. Maybe if some *did* come back, they could look at what they did and where it took them and figure out how to measure and aim and all that, but so far as any of the ones I've talked to know, nobody has ever done it. When you go out, that's it, you're out there. You can go on hopping from one world to the next, or you can settle down in one forever, but like the books say, you *really* can't go home again. You can get close, maybe—one way I found out a lot of this was in exchange for telling this poor old geezer a lot about the world outside Harry's. He was pretty happy about it when I was talking about what I'd seen on TV, and naming all the presidents I could think of, but then he asked me something about some religion I'd never heard of that he said he belonged to, and when I said I'd never heard of it, he almost broke down. I guess he was looking for a world like his own, and ours was, you know, close, but not close enough. He said something about what he called a "random-walk principle"—if you go wandering around at random you keep coming back close to where you started, but you'll never have your feet in *exactly* the original place, they'll always be a little bit off to one side or the other.

So there are millions of these people out there drifting from world to world, looking for whatever they're looking for, sometimes millions of them identical to each other, too, and they run into each other. They know what to look for, see. So they trade information, and some of them tell me they're working on figuring out how to *really* navigate whatever it is they do, and they've figured out some of it already, so they can steer a little.

I wondered out loud why so many of them turn up at Harry's, and this woman with blue-gray skin—from some kind of medication, she told me—tried to explain it. West Virginia is one of the best places to travel between worlds, particularly up in the mountains around Sutton, because it's a pretty central location for eastern North America, but there isn't anything there. I mean, there aren't any big cities, or big military bases, or anything, so that if there's an atomic war or something—and apparently there have been a *lot* of atomic wars, or wars with even worse weapons, in different worlds—nobody's very likely to heave any missiles at Sutton, West Virginia. Even in the realities where the Europeans never found America and it's the Chinese or somebody building the cities, there just isn't any reason to build anything near Sutton. And there's something in particular that makes it an easy place to travel between worlds, too; I didn't follow the explanation. She said something about the Earth's magnetic field, but I didn't catch whether that was part of the explanation or just a comparison of some kind.

The mountains and forests make it easy to hide, too, which is why our area is better than out in the desert someplace.

Anyway, right around Sutton it's pretty safe and easy to travel between worlds, so lots of people do.

The strange thing, though, is that for some reason that nobody really seemed very clear on, Harry's, or something like it, is in just about the same place in millions of different realities. More than millions; infinities, really. It's not always exactly Harry's All-Night Hamburgers; one customer kept calling Harry Sal, for instance. It's *there*, though, or something like it, and one thing that doesn't seem to change much is that travelers can eat there without causing trouble. Word gets around that Harry's is a nice, quiet place, with decent burgers, where nobody's going to hassle them about anything, and they can pay in gold or silver if they haven't got the local money, or in trade goods or whatever they've got that Harry can use. It's easy to find, because it's in a lot of universes, relatively—as I said, this little area isn't one that varies a whole lot from universe to universe, unless you start moving long distances. Or maybe not *easy* to find, but it can be found. One guy told me that Harry's seems to be in more universes than Washington, D.C. He'd even seen one of my doubles before, last time he stopped in, and he thought he might have actually gotten back to the same place until I swore I'd never seen him before. He had these really funny eyes, so I was sure I'd have remembered him.

We never actually got repeat business from other worlds, y'know, not once, not ever; nobody could ever find the way back to exactly our world. What we got were people who had heard about Harry's from other people, in some other reality. Oh, maybe it wasn't exactly the same Harry's they'd heard about, but they'd heard that there was usually a good place to eat and swap stories in about that spot.

That's a weird thought, you know, that every time I served someone a burger a zillion of me were serving burgers to a zillion others—not all of them the same, either.

So they come to Harry's to eat, and they trade information with each other there, or in the parking lot, and they take a break from whatever they're doing.

They came there, and they talked to me about all those

other universes, and I was seventeen years old, man. It was like those Navy recruiting ads on TV, see the world—except it was see the *worlds*, all of them, not just one. I listened to everything those guys said. I heard them talk about the worlds where zeppelins strafed Cincinnati in a Third World War, about places the dinosaurs never died out and mammals never evolved any higher than rats, about cities built of colored glass or dug miles underground, about worlds where all the men were dead, or all the women, or both, from biological warfare. Any story you ever heard, anything you ever read, those guys could top it. Worlds where speaking aloud could get you the death penalty—not what you said, just saying *anything* out loud. Worlds with spaceships fighting a war against Arcturus. Beautiful women, strange places, everything you could ever want, out there *somewhere*, but it might take forever to find it.

I listened to those stories for months. I graduated from high school, but there wasn't any way I could go to college, so I just stayed on with Harry—it paid enough to live on, anyway. I talked to those people from other worlds, even got inside some of their ships, or time machines, or whatever you want to call them, and I thought about how great it would be to just go roaming from world to world. Any time you don't like the way things are going, just pop! And the whole world is different! I could be a white god to the Indians in a world where the Europeans and Asians never reached America, I figured, or find a world where machines do all the work and people just relax and party.

When my eighteenth birthday came and went without any sign I'd ever get out of West Virginia, I began to really think about it, you know? I started asking customers about it. A lot of them told me not to be stupid; a lot just wouldn't talk about it. Some, though, some of them thought it was a great idea.

There was one guy, this one night—well, first, it was September, but it was still hot as the middle of summer, even in the middle of the night. Most of my friends were gone—they'd gone off to college, or gotten jobs somewhere, or gotten married, or maybe two out of the three. My dad was drinking a lot. The other kids were back in school. I'd started sleeping days, from eight in the morning until about four P.M., instead of evenings. Harry's air conditioner was busted, and I really wanted to just leave it all behind and go find myself a better world. So when I heard these two guys talking at one table about whether one of them had extra room in his machine, I sort of listened, when I could, when I wasn't fetching burgers and Cokes.

Now, one of these two I'd seen before—he'd been coming in every so often ever since I started working at Harry's. He looked like an ordinary guy, but he came in about three in the morning and talked to the weirdos like they were all old buddies, so I figured he had to be from some other world originally himself, even if he stayed put in ours now. He'd come in about every night for a week or two, then disappear for months, then start turning up again, and I had sort of wondered whether he might have licked the navigation problem all those other people had talked about. But then I figured, probably not, either he'd stopped jumping from one world to the next, or else it was just a bunch of parallel people coming in, and it probably wasn't ever the same guy at all, really. Usually, when that happened, we'd get two or three at a time, looking like identical twins or something, but there was only just one of this guy, every time, so I figured, like I said, either he hadn't been changing worlds at all, or he'd figured out how to navigate better than anyone else, or something.

The guy he was talking to was new; I'd never seen him before. He was big, maybe six-four and heavy. He'd come in shaking snow and soot off a plastic coverall of some kind, given me a big grin, and ordered two of Harry's biggest burgers, with everything. Five minutes later the regular customer sat down across the table from him, and now he was telling the regular that he had plenty of room in his ship for anything anyone might want him to haul crosstime.

I figured this was my chance, so when I brought the burgers, I said something real polite, like, "Excuse me, sir, but I couldn't help overhearing; d'you think you'd have room for a passenger?"

The big guy laughed and said, "Sure, kid! I was just telling Joe here that I could haul him and all his freight, and there'd be room for you, too, if you make it worth my trouble!"

I said, "I've got money; I've been saving up. What'll it take?"

The big guy gave me a big grin again, but before he could say anything Joe interrupted.

"Sid," he said, "could you excuse me for a minute? I want

to talk to this young fellow for a minute, before he makes a big mistake."

The big guy, Sid, said, "Sure, sure, I don't mind." So Joe got up, and he yelled to Harry, "Okay if I borrow your counterman for a few minutes?"

Harry yelled back that it was okay. I didn't know what the hell was going on, but I went along, and the two of us went out to this guy's car to talk.

And it really was a car, too—an old Ford van. It was customized, with velvet and bubble windows and stuff, and there was a lot of stuff piled in the back, camping gear and clothes and things, but no sign of machinery or anything. I still wasn't sure, you know, because some of these guys did a really good job of disguising their ships, or time machines, or whatever, but it sure *looked* like an ordinary van, and that's what Joe said it was. He got into the driver's seat, and I got into the passenger seat, and we swiveled around to face each other.

"So," he said. "Do you know who all these people are? I mean people like Sid?"

"Sure," I said. "They're from other dimensions, parallel worlds and like that."

He leaned back and looked at me hard and said, "You know that, huh? Did you know that none of them can ever get home?"

"Yes, I knew that," I told him, acting pretty cocky.

"And you still want to go with Sid to other universes? Even when you know you'll never come home to this universe again?"

"That's right, mister," I told him. "I'm sick of this one. I don't have anything here but a nothing job in a diner; I want to *see* some of the stuff these people talk about, instead of just hearing about it."

"You want to see wonders and marvels, huh?"

"Yes!"

"You want to see buildings a hundred stories high? Cities of strange temples? Oceans thousands of miles wide? Mountains miles high? Prairies, and cities, and strange animals and stranger people?"

Well, that was just exactly what I wanted, better than I could have said it myself. "Yes," I said. "You got it, mister."

"You lived here all your life?"

"You mean this world? Of course I have."

"No, I meant here in Sutton. You lived here all your life?"

"Well, yeah," I admitted. "Just about."

He sat forward and put his hands together, and his voice got intense, like he wanted to impress me with how serious he was. "Kid," he said, "I don't blame you a bit for wanting something different; I sure as hell wouldn't want to spend my entire life in these hills. But you're going about it the wrong way. You don't want to hitch with Sid."

"Oh, yeah?" I said. "Why not? Am I supposed to build my own machine? Hell, I can't even fix my mother's carburetor."

"No, that's not what I meant. But kid, you can see those buildings a thousand feet high in New York, or in Chicago. You've got oceans here in your own world as good as anything you'll find anywhere. You've got the mountains, and the seas, and the prairies, and all the rest of it. I've been in your world for eight years now, checking back here at Harry's every so often to see if anyone's figured out how to steer in no-space and get me home, and it's one hell of a big, interesting place."

"But," I said, "what about the spaceships, and—"

He interrupted me and said, "You want to see spaceships? You go to Florida and watch a shuttle launch. Man, that's a spaceship. It may not go to other worlds, but that *is* a spaceship. You want strange animals? You go to Australia or Brazil. You want strange people? Go to New York or Los Angeles, or almost anywhere. You want a city carved out of a mountaintop? It's called Machu Picchu, in Peru, I think. You want ancient, mysterious ruins? They're all over Greece and Italy and North Africa. Strange temples? Visit India; there are supposed to be over a thousand temples in Benares alone. See Angkor Wat, or the pyramids—not just the Egyptian ones, but the Mayan ones, too. And the great thing about all of these places, kid, is that afterwards, if you want to, you can come home. You don't *have* to, but you *can*. Who knows? You might get homesick some day. Most people do. *I* did. I wish to hell I'd seen more of my own world before I volunteered to try any others."

I kind of stared at him for a while. "I don't know," I said. I mean, it seemed so easy to just hop in Sid's machine and be gone forever, I thought, but New York was five hundred miles away—and then I realized how stupid that was.

"Hey," he said, "don't forget, if you decide I was wrong, you can always come back to Harry's and bum a ride with

A FLYING SAUCER
WITH MINNESOTA PLATES

Harry nodded. "Yeah, I'll take these," he said.

The customer smiled in relief. "Thanks," he said. "And thanks for the burger." He started for the door.

"Any time," Harry said, waving.

He glanced out the window, trying to decide whether the eastern sky might be starting to lighten a little.

What the hell, he couldn't tell with the lights on, and he wasn't about to turn them off, even if he didn't have any customers in the place just then.

He probably wasn't going to *get* any customers for at least an hour, either; the late-night oddballs who were his best customers, who had provided most of his income for years, wouldn't be coming anymore at this time of night, and it was still too early for the truckers catching an early breakfast. The day shift wouldn't be in until eight.

Harry wondered if any of the people who worked the other shifts for him had any idea what kept Harry's All-Night Hamburgers in business. They probably didn't.

He'd been in business for years before he figured out himself just what the story was on the late-night customers. He hadn't done anything to attract them, other than running a decent diner, serving good burgers, and never hassling anyone— but maybe that was enough, because they kept coming.

Harry's late-night customers were not your usual weirdos. Some of them, he was pretty sure, weren't even human.

As long as they paid for their meals, though, he didn't much care what they were.

The kid he'd had helping him on the night shift for a while had explained it, but Harry had already doped most of it out for himself. The weirdos were from other dimensions. "Parallel worlds," some of them said; "alternate realities," according to others.

"Other dimensions" suited Harry. They were from places that were still Earth but were *different*, in various ways. They had some way of traveling between worlds, and they came to Harry's because Harry never hassled anyone, because he'd take all sorts of weird trinkets in trade, and because there was a place like Harry's somewhere in this part of the West Virginia hills in millions upon millions of universes, so that they knew where to find him.

And they didn't want to be seen; that gave Harry's another advantage, being out in the woods in the middle of nowhere. Even isolated as the place was, they still only dared show up between midnight and dawn, and usually allowed an hour or so margin on either side.

That last guy had hung around later than most of them ever dared, but even so, Harry had an hour to kill.

Well, that hour would give him a chance to sweep up, maybe clean the grill; the grease was getting a bit thick.

He was out of practice looking after everything himself; he'd gotten spoiled having that kid working the graveyard shift with him for so long, and now that the kid had lit out for wherever the hell he was—he'd sent postcards from Pittsburgh and New York, so far—it was taking awhile to get back into the swing of it.

Maybe, he thought, he should see about hiring another kid—but there was always the question of how a kid would handle the late-night crowd, and just because the last one had done okay, that didn't mean the next one would.

The bell over the door jingled as he was pushing the broom along behind the counter, and Harry looked up, startled.

It was his last customer, back and looking worried.

"Something wrong?" Harry asked.

He hoped it wasn't about the payment; those little coins he'd accepted looked like the platinum the guy had said they were, and that meant they were worth several times what the burger should have cost. He didn't particularly want to give any of them back, though; after all, he'd have to take them up to Pittsburgh to sell them, and he deserved something extra to cover the overhead.

"Yes," the man said. "It's my . . . my vehicle. You know anything about . . . um . . . motors?"

"Well, that depends," Harry said. "What sort of motor are we talking about here?"

The traveler opened his mouth, then closed it again.

"Um ..." he said, "Maybe you had better come take a look."

Harry looked him over.

He looked ordinary enough, really. He was definitely human, and he was wearing pants and a shirt and shoes and a jacket, nothing particularly weird.

Of course, the shoes were cerise and appeared to be plastic, and the shirt couldn't seem to decide if it was white or silver, but the pants were ordinary black denim and the jacket was ordinary black vinyl—cut a little funny, maybe, but it could pass for European if you didn't know any better. The little display screen on the collar could pass for jewelry if you didn't look close.

The guy's head was shaved, but he didn't look like a punk, especially not with that worried look on his face.

Harry had seen a whole lot worse, in his late-night trade.

"Okay," Harry said, "I'll take a look."

He slipped off his apron and draped it across the counter, and the two men stepped outside into the cool of a late-summer night.

Harry blinked as his eyes adjusted, and the customer pointed and said, "There."

He hadn't needed to point or say anything. His vehicle was the only one in the lot. Harry stared.

Harry sighed.

The vehicle was silvery, with a finish like brushed aluminum that reflected the light from Harry's signs in broad stripes of soft color. It was round, perhaps twenty feet in diameter, six feet high at the center, but curving gradually down to a sharp edge. A section of one side had lifted up to reveal a dark interior where various colored lights glowed dimly. There were no windows, portholes, or other visible openings, but a band of something milky ran around the lower disk and seemed to be glowing faintly.

It was, in short, a classic flying saucer.

"Oh, Lord," Harry said, "What's wrong with it?"

"I don't know," the customer said, worried.

Harry sighed again. "Well, let's have a look at it."

The customer led the way into the dim interior of the thing

and showed Harry where the access plate for the main drive was.

Harry went back inside, collected his tool box from the furnace room in back, and went to work.

He had never seen anything like the "motor" in this particular vehicle; about half the components looked familiar, but they went together in ways that made no sense at all.

And the other half—Harry didn't even like to look at the other half.

After about fifteen minutes he emerged from the engine compartment and shrugged.

"I'm sorry, buddy, but I can't fix it. I think that . . . that thing on the right might be bad—everything looks okay, no loose wires or hoses, but that thing's got this black gunk on it that doesn't look like it should be there."

The customer stared. "What will I *do*?" he wailed. He turned and looked desperately at Harry. "Is there anyone in your world who knows such machines?"

Harry considered that long and hard, and finally replied, "No."

"No? I am *stranded* here?"

Harry shrugged. "Maybe somebody'll come in who can fix it. We get all kinds here."

"But you said . . ."

"Yeah, well, I meant that *lives* here, there's nobody can fix it. But my place, here, I specialize in you guys, I figure you know that or you wouldn't be here. Tonight, tomorrow, sooner or later we'll get somebody in who can fix your gadget."

"Someone from another time-line, you mean?"

Harry shrugged again. "Whatever. I don't know who you guys are that come here; I just let you come and don't hassle anybody. It's none of my business if you're from time-lines, whatever they are, or from Schenectady, but I do get a lot of you weirdos late at night."

The customer frowned and looked over the controls.

"You are not very reassuring," he said.

"Not my job to be reassuring," Harry said. "My job is selling burgers. Now, would you mind getting this thing out of sight, before the sun comes up?"

The customer turned and blinked at him.

"How am I to do that?" he asked. "Without the primary driver, the vehicle cannot move at all."

Harry's eyebrows lowered.

"You serious? I thought you couldn't do whatever it is you guys do, but you mean it won't go *anywhere*?"

"It will not go anywhere," the other affirmed.

Harry looked out the door of the craft; the sky was definitely getting lighter now. Early truckers might happen along almost any time now.

What would they do if they saw a flying saucer in his parking lot? This could be very bad for his daytime business. The late-night trade was important, but the daylight business didn't hurt any, either.

"Maybe we can shove it back into the woods?" he suggested, not very enthusiastically.

The customer shook his head. "I doubt it very much. The craft has a registered weight of seventeen hundred kilos."

"What's that in pounds?" Harry asked.

"Ah ... about, perhaps, four thousand pounds?"

Harry sat down on a convenient jump seat. "You're right," he said, "We can't shove it anywhere, unless it's got wheels. I didn't see any."

"There are none."

"Figures."

The two men sat, thinking.

"Can we not leave it here, until someone comes who can repair it?" the customer asked.

Harry glowered. "How the hell am I supposed to explain a goddamn *flying saucer* in my parking lot?"

The customer shrugged.

"I don't know," he said.

Outside, an engine growled. The first of Harry's daylight customers was arriving.

An idea struck him.

"Look," he said, "I gotta go, but here's what you do ..."

The saucer sat in the lot through the morning and the afternoon, while Harry finished his shift and went home to bed, leaving the day shift in charge. It was still there at about six P.M. when the county sheriff pulled in and saw it.

He got out of his car and looked the saucer over from every side. The door was closed, and the exterior was virtually seamless. He had no way of knowing that its driver was asleep inside.

Painted on one side, in big red letters, was the legend, HARRY'S HAMBURGERS—THEY'RE OUT OF THIS WORLD!

He smiled and went inside.

Twenty minutes later, Harry came out of the back room, yawning, and poured himself a cup of coffee. The evening crew, consisting of Bill the cook and Sherry the waitress, paid no attention to him; they knew, from long experience, that he wouldn't be fit company until he had had his coffee.

The sheriff knew it, too, but between bites of hamburger he said, "Cute gimmick, Harry, that saucer out front."

"Thanks, sheriff," Harry said, looking up from his cup.

"Is it permanent?"

"Nah, I don't think so," Harry said sleepily. "Takes up a lot of space. Thought I'd try it, though, see if it pulled in any customers."

The sheriff nodded and took another bite.

"Uh . . . why d'you ask?" Harry inquired, uneasily.

The sheriff shrugged and finished chewing.

"Well," he said, "I figured it wasn't there for good when I saw the Minnesota plates. If you keep it there more than a couple of months, you'll want to take those off."

"Oh, yeah," Harry said, weakly.

He hadn't noticed the license plates.

Three days later, just after dawn, a trucker pushed open the door.

"Hey, Harry," he called, "what happened to your flying saucer?"

"Got rid of it," Harry said, pulling a breakfast menu out from under the counter. "Wasn't doing any good."

"No? I thought it was a cute idea," the trucker said, settling onto a stool.

Harry just shrugged.

"So, Harry," the trucker asked, "where'd it go?"

Harry remembered the weird shimmer as the saucer had vanished, several hours before. He remembered all the snatches of conversation he'd overheard, all those years, about parallel realities and alternate worlds, places where history was different, where *everything* was different. He remembered all the strange coins and bizarre gadgets he had accepted in payment, thousands of them by now. He thought of all the stories he could tell this man about what he had seen, in this very place, late at night.

"Minnesota," he said, as he handed over the menu.

AN INFINITY OF KAREN

The approving officer had told him that his request was unusual, the first of its kind. He didn't know whether that had encouraged or delayed its eventual approval.

He remembered that clearly as the policemen led him to the waiting car. Had anyone here ever made such a request? Would they believe his story?

He had the entry tag the guards had given him, and he had done no real harm; at worst, they would simply throw him back into the Hole. As long as he didn't lose his bearings, he'd be no worse off than before.

After all, if they let him go, he would simply go back to the Hole on his own. He had seen all he had to see here, and again, he had not found what he wanted. If he had been strong, if he had followed his own rules, he would have already been gone, but he had been weak. The sight of her, alone, had broken down his resolve, and instead of the quick check he had intended, and had already made fourteen times in nightmarish repetition, he had followed her home and watched.

He remembered crouching in the all-too-familiar bushes, peering in through those familiar windows, as he watched her put away the groceries, heard, faint through the glass, her shouted conversation with her husband. He remembered how he had hated that husband, hated himself, and toyed with thoughts of killing him and taking his place.

He could not do that, though—at least, not yet. If the disappointments continued, world after world, he was not sure he would be able to resist that evil temptation. He told himself that his doubles had as much right to live—and to her—as he did himself, that it would still be cold-blooded murder whatever the circumstances, and that, worst of all, the deception couldn't work; he had lost five months out of their life together, months he could never recover, months she would remember and discuss that he knew nothing about. He would be out of place, out of time, with his business and their friends—and all that was in addition to whatever other divergences there might be between this reality and his native world, divergences not related to her death.

He climbed into the police car, grateful that the officers had not bothered to handcuff him. He thought they believed what he had told them of his story; certainly his face provided good evidence. Karen's reaction when they had brought him to the door had been proof enough of that. He had seen not the slightest doubt or hesitation on her face as she blurted, "Not him! That's my husband!"

Then her husband, her *real* husband, her husband of *this* world, had come up behind her, and her annoyance with the blundering police had dissolved into shock. She had stared first at one, then the other, and been able to distinguish them only by their clothes and by the prowler's unkempt hair.

The officer had seen the resemblance, of course, and had demanded, "Lady, are you sure which one's your husband?"

Karen had hesitated, a ghastly uncertainty in her eyes, and he had fought down that treacherous urge to lie, to try to win her by deceit. He could not bear that hurt confusion. "He's her husband," he had said. "I'm from crosstime. I came through the Hole, and I wanted to see my double." That was not exactly true—in fact, he had hoped above all else that he had no living double in this world. He had come to see Karen.

But that would be too hard to explain, there on the little porch with Karen staring at him, so he had lied and let the police lead him away.

He said nothing during the ride. When they reached the little station on Corrigan Street, he sat silently while one of the pair got out, came around, and opened the car door. Obediently, he slid out and stood up, then froze.

The old red Chevy was pulling in behind them, Karen in the passenger seat and his double driving.

"What are they doing here?" he demanded.

"They're the complainants," a policeman replied. "They have to decide whether to press charges."

"Oh, God," he said. He fought back tears at the thought of

Karen—not *his* Karen but still Karen—swearing out a complaint against him.

The doubles sat in the car, waiting for him to be led inside before they emerged, and he knew she couldn't hear him, but he shouted, "I'm sorry, Karen!"

The officers led him up the stone steps.

Inside he told the whole story, with Karen sitting and staring at him. He tried not to look at her as he described the accident, when the drunken idiot had lost control and sent his Mercedes smashing into the side of the old red Chevy, crushing her body, driving shards of glass into her face, but he glanced over involuntarily and saw her expression of horror, so like the one that had been frozen on his own Karen's face when they took him to identify the body. The undertaker had straightened her features and covered the wounds with makeup, but the result had not been Karen anymore, but a mannequin.

He didn't have to explain the Hole, of course, since it had appeared in their world as well, but he did explain the special commission that decided who was allowed in and out and how they had approved his request on humanitarian grounds. In this reality such a commission had never been appointed, and anyone who chose to could enter the Hole after listening to a few hours' instruction on the theory of parallel worlds, what was known of the Hole's history, the odds against ever returning to exactly the world one left, and what the greatest dangers were believed to be.

Incoming people were searched, questioned briefly, then allowed to roam freely. When they released him, as he had done fourteen times before, he had headed directly for his own house and looked it over.

The garage was empty, and no one answered the bell. He had taken out his key, but hesitated; even if it worked, if the parallelism extended that far, he would be guilty of breaking and entering if he used it.

And then, as he stood on the little porch, it didn't matter anymore because he saw himself come driving up in an unfamiliar blue sedan. There could be no doubt of the driver's identity.

He had turned away. He was not here to steal his double's wife. Somewhere, in one of the infinite worlds the Hole touched, was a world where Karen had lived and he had died; he was certain of it, believed in it with the same faith a Christian had in God. He was determined to find that world, a world where a Karen waited, as bereft as himself.

He had walked quickly away, before his double could be sure he'd seen anyone at the door, bound for the Hole and a sixteenth attempt. But then, two blocks away, the red Chevy had appeared with Karen driving in her slow, timid fashion, and he had stopped, mesmerized by the sight of her there, alone, returning home. She had been so very much like his own wife, with no husband there to spoil the illusion, and he had turned and followed, watched as she parked the Chevy in front of the garage, as she hauled the groceries from the back, as she stepped up on the stoop and fumbled with her keys, trying to open the back door.

He had slipped into the bushes—just to watch, he told himself, to see a little of her, of the life that that drunk had stolen from him. Just for a moment.

But the moment had stretched on and on, as he was unable to tear his eyes away, and he had grown careless, thought himself unreal, invisible. How could he be lurking in the shrubbery, when he was inside with Karen?

And they had seen him, and his double had called the police without his realizing it, and now he was explaining it all to them, and to the sergeant and two officers.

When he had finished, there was a moment of silence, and he looked up at Karen.

She was crying, and he could not hold back his own tears anymore, but she turned to her own husband and embraced him. He folded her in his arms and comforted her, staring over her back at his double with puzzlement, sorrow, and anger in his eyes.

"Ma'am?" the sergeant asked. "Do you want to press charges? If you don't, we'll take him back to the Hole, as an undesirable. If you do, he'll probably wind up there anyway, but it'll have to go to a judge."

"Let him go," his double said.

"Thank you," he answered.

The husband glanced down at his wife. "Good luck," he said.

"Thank you," the widower repeated. "Sergeant, if you could have someone drive me to the Hole, I'll be glad to leave."

The sergeant nodded.

Half an hour later he stepped through the door of the ramshackle inner barrier around the Hole, the plywood and scrap that had been thrown up in the first panicky confusion after the Appearance. He looked up at the Hole.

Sunlight poured through it from another cosmos somewhere, a world where no one had yet roofed it over. He leaned a few inches to one side and the sunlight vanished.

He had stood beside the Hole fifteen times before, read all the descriptions and theories, and he still didn't really understand how it worked or what he was actually seeing. He did know that the world he saw through the Hole now was not the one he would reach if he stepped through. Whatever that sunlit world was, it was very far away in crosstime, probably totally unlike any world he knew, and that was not what he wanted. He wanted his own world back, but with a single difference: a living, widowed Karen.

He stepped forward into the Hole. As always, he felt no transition, sensed nothing out of the ordinary, save that around him everything he saw shifted slightly, the visible aspect of the Hole expanding into vast confusion before him; but he knew that he had stepped out of that world forever, twisted himself sideways in time.

He turned around and stepped back, out of the Hole, knowing that he could not possibly have arrived in exactly the reality he left; in the Hole the worlds were crowded together in an infinite density, after all. To return, he would need to have stepped back through *exactly* that spot through which he had departed, down to the width of an electron or less.

He had come close, though, so this world should be similar. The barrier around the Hole appeared identical. He knocked on the door.

No one answered. He tried the latch; it worked. He swung it open and stepped out onto a parking lot.

There were no guards, no scientists, no one to interrogate him or search him for weapons; the prefabricated offices and laboratories that had surrounded the Hole in the last world he had visited—and most of the others he had seen—were gone without a trace. The inner barrier stood, untended and neglected, in the parking lot of a Holiday Inn, just as it had when first built.

He glanced around and shrugged. This neglect certainly made things simple. Apparently in this reality, nothing had been done about the Hole's manifestation.

He closed the door behind him and saw that a large sign

hung on it, reading EXTREME DANGER! ENTER AT YOUR OWN RISK! He smiled, and walked up the short slope toward the hotel.

He called a cab from the lobby and got a candy bar from the machine while he waited for the cab to arrive. His coins had worked the vending machine correctly, and he hoped that his paper money would be close enough to pass here.

The cab arrived, and he gave his home address as he settled into the rear seat.

He watched the scenery closely during the ride. There were differences—a billboard bore a different advertisement, a house hadn't been painted—but it was, generally speaking, all familiar. He had not stepped too far away from his own world.

The cab stopped at the curb; he paid the fare, and the cabbie accepted the bills without comment. A moment later he was standing alone on the sidewalk.

The bushes in front of the house had been cut back, far shorter than he had ever trimmed them. An unfamiliar porch swing was crowded in to the left of the front door.

He walked slowly up the path, wondering what significance these changes might have.

The living-room drapes were different, as well, and he was suddenly sure that in this reality he did not live in this house; no analog of himself could possibly allow those things in his home. He rang the bell anyway.

An unfamiliar woman answered, about thirty, short and slender, with beautiful red hair and a plain, bland face. "Yes?" she said.

"Ah ... I was looking for a Karen Criswell? Mrs. Karen Criswell?"

"Oh, that's the lady we bought the house from! Gee, I'm sorry, but she's gone; we've lived here for three months now."

"Gone? Gone where?"

"Well ..."

"Listen, I really need to find her; it's a family matter. About her brother-in-law." That seemed like his best approach. After all, wasn't he his own brother? If there was a Karen Criswell who had owned this house, then surely it was his wife—her maiden name had been Hoechst.

"I don't know; I don't think I can help you."

"Why not?" He had almost shouted. He fought himself under control again, then said, "I'm sorry. It's been pretty rough. Please, where did she go? Do you know why she moved?"

"Well, after her husband died she didn't want the house anymore—said it was too big for her, that it reminded her of him. Gave us a real good price, to get rid of it quickly—I don't know if we could have afforded a place this nice otherwise."

His throat tightened, and he felt as if a great weight had fallen from his back, as he remembered what hope was. "Her husband died?"

"Oh, about five months ago. Didn't you know?"

"No, we've been out of touch for a year now. Family argument."

"Oh, that's too bad. Well, he died—car crash. Hit by a drunk driver while he was running some errand for her."

"I'm very sorry to hear that," he said, forcing his lips not to smile, and inwardly wondering that he could be so delighted by news of his own death.

"Yes, well, so was she, I guess. She was about the sorriest woman I ever saw, Mrs. Criswell was. She said she just couldn't live in this world without him, so she wrapped up her affairs, sold her belongings, and went down to the Holiday Inn out on Route Four and jumped into that thing there, the Hole, they call it. Said she'd find him somewhere—that there had to be a world where he lived and she died, and she'd find it if it took the rest of her life. So you see, mister, I can't help you find her; she's gone."

Hope vanished, and he plummeted anew into desperation. He said nothing more, just turned and walked down the path. He had been so close, so very close! If only she had waited! He would find her yet! She was somewhere in the Hole, somewhere in the universes that the Hole could reach, searching for him.

He turned onto the sidewalk and began running, back toward the Hole, toward his only hope, running and crying like a lost child.

THE DRIFTER

*H*e *didn't really listen as the explanation droned on; he* had already made his decision. As soon as the scientist finally shut up, he said, "Sure, I'll do it."

The scientist blinked uncertainly at him. "You're sure? I mean, you understand that this will change your life *permanently*, if it works?"

"Yeah, I understand. That's no problem; my life could use some changes."

"We don't know how much, you understand—we can't calibrate it yet."

"I know; that's fine."

The scientist obviously thought the volunteer was crazy, but the volunteer didn't care. It was *his* life, after all, and he knew just how boring and crummy it was so far; the scientist didn't. Letting them push him into some other world sounded like as good an idea as any.

There was a chance he'd get killed, of course; they had told him that, insisted he sign papers attesting that they'd told him that. It didn't bother him. There was a chance he'd get killed every time he crossed the street, or drove down the block, or flew home to visit his mother in L.A. That was no big deal, and the odds here didn't really look much worse than everyday life. This traveling into other universes was certainly safer than walking through some parts of town after dark.

And there was a chance it would make him rich and famous, and that was a kick, no doubt about it, and it looked just as likely as getting killed, so he was willing to try it.

He didn't care about the technical stuff; they were writing all that out for him, so he didn't need to know any of it. He got the gist of it, the basic theory, and that was plenty enough to interest him. It wasn't anything all that unheard of—he'd seen the idea in stories, even in Hollywood movies. It was a staple in science fiction.

When he'd answered the ad for volunteers, though, was the first time he'd ever heard of anyone taking it seriously as science, rather than fiction.

They were looking for alternate realities. The theory was that rather than one universe, reality included an infinite number of universes, all rolling along side by side without touching—parallel worlds, the science-fiction writers called it, or diverging time-streams, depending on how they modeled it. The parallel theory said that all the universes were there all along; the diverging theory said that originally there was only one, but that each time an event could have gone two different ways, it *did* go two different ways, splitting the existing universe into two, one for each possibility.

The volunteer didn't see that there was really much of a difference between these theories, but the scientists considered it an important distinction, and he didn't argue.

Whichever it was, they intended to send him into another universe.

He thought that was a pretty nifty idea—him, Danny Royce, the first man to visit another universe!

Of course, the catch was that they didn't think he could come back.

The gadget they'd built—it filled most of the basement of the physics building, where the cyclotron used to be, but Danny still considered it a gadget—was going to push him into another world, but all it could do was push, not pull; in order to get back, he would need to land in a reality where there were people who had developed a machine of their own that could push him back.

And they didn't know how to aim, either, so even if his new universe *did* have a machine, he might not wind up back where he started.

Now, right there, Danny told himself with a smile, is where 99 percent of the volunteers would back out; live the rest of his life in *another world*? Fat chance.

But Danny had listened further; after all, what did he have to lose, besides his sick old bitch of a mother and a bunch of college loans he wouldn't be able to pay off, because with the grades he was going to get this semester he wasn't going to graduate?

And they'd gone on to say that they weren't going to push him very *far*, not on the first human trial; they were going to use the minimum power needed to overcome his temporal inertia—whatever the hell that was.

"The chances are good," the scientist had said, "that you won't see any obvious changes at all when you emerge. You may need to research extensively to find any differences. It may take weeks to be sure whether you've moved or not, because you should land in a universe similar enough that they'll have just sent out their reality's version of you."

And hey, that made it easy! Rich and famous, just for going through this machine and coming out someplace that he couldn't even tell the difference?

If it worked, and nothing went wrong.

If it didn't, if they'd guessed wrong, he could get killed, he could wind up in Nazi America, or World War III, or Orwell's 1984 ten years after.

But hey, really, what did he have to lose?

"Sure, I'll do it," he said.

So he signed more forms, and a doctor gave him a physical, and a psychiatrist talked to him for an incredibly boring hour, and at last they took him down into the basement of Palmer Hall and put him into the sphere at the center of the gadget, and threw switches.

The sphere closed around him, and he was alone in the dark, unable to hear anything but a faint hum, and something pressed on him from every direction at once, until he thought he could hear his bones creaking, and his heart was beating fast and so loud he could hear it over the hum, and he wondered if he would throw up, and then the pressure stopped, and the hum died away, and the sphere split open around him, light spilling in in a perfect circle that widened into a cylindrical view of the world around him. He stepped unsteadily out into his new world.

It looked exactly like the old one.

He blinked at the scientist—Dr. Hammond, it was, Hammond at the keyboard, like those Hammond organs, except that the keyboard was a computer. "Did it work?" he asked.

Hammond glanced at his associates, then back at the volunteer. "I don't know," he said. "Does it look any different?"

Royce looked around carefully. Gray metal boxes, silver conduits held together with baling wire and duct tape, servomotors in black, silver, and copper—the gadget looked the same, but he wouldn't notice any difference unless it was really major, because he had never looked that closely at the thing in the first place.

Bare brick walls with sloppy mortarwork, light bulbs in rusted steel cages, concrete floor with cracks running across it—the basement looked the same.

Three physicists in white lab coats, Hammond, Brzeski, and the one with the Middle Eastern name Royce hadn't caught, all of them with dark hair, Hammond and the Arab, or whatever he was, with mustaches, Brzeski needing a shave and a haircut, his glasses crooked—the scientists looked the same. The computers, the videocameras, all of that was just what he remembered from five minutes before.

He shrugged. "Looks the same to me," he said.

The physicists looked at each other, frowning.

"Did you bring anything with you?" Brzeski asked.

"Oh, yeah," Royce said. He held out the thick loose-leaf binder that contained the technical notes. "You gave me this."

Brzeski accepted the binder and thumbed through it, while Royce stood waiting.

"It looks the same," Brzeski said. "Let's check the numbers."

Hammond nodded and pulled another binder out of a desk. The three bent over the papers.

"Hey," Royce said. "What about me? What do I do now?"

Hammond looked up and pursed his lips. "Well, we'll want you to see Dr. Chin again," he said.

"We'd better do that right away," Brzeski agreed, closing the binder.

Hammond considered. "Here, you two go ahead and check the notes," he said. "I'll take Royce up and get this taken care of."

The others nodded agreement, and a moment later Hammond and Royce were climbing the stairs, on their way to get Royce another physical.

"So," Royce asked at the first landing, "did I go anywhere or not?"

Hammond didn't answer immediately; in fact, they were halfway across the drive, on their way to the campus infirmary, before he said, "We don't know yet."

"So when *will* you know?"

Hammond hesitated, but as they stepped up on the sidewalk

he said, "We may *never* know. If we find a difference, then we'll know, but if we don't find a difference, it won't prove anything; it could just mean that you landed in a universe where the only difference is, say, that some unstable radioisotope on some distant planet had atom A go poof, instead of atom B."

"Hell," Royce said, "if that's the only difference, for all you know people could go bopping about between universes all the time, without any million-dollar gadgets, and you wouldn't know a thing about it."

"That's true," Hammond agreed, as they climbed the infirmary steps. "And that might in fact be the case, that people *do* drop from one universe to another spontaneously. That might explain a great deal."

"You must have done animal experiments," he said. "Did you get any changes with them?"

Hammond hesitated again; they were in the infirmary lobby. He paused, instructed the nurse receptionist to tell Dr. Chin they were coming up, then led the way to the fire stairs.

"Yes," he said, "we did animal experiments. Hundreds of them. And the results were confusing."

"How, confusing?" Royce asked uncomfortably.

He should have asked this *before* the experiment, he realized. He stumbled as his toe hit a step that was higher than he expected, but caught himself on the railing and continued.

"Well," Hammond said, "we sent guinea pigs, mice, and rats, for the live-animal trials, and books and papers for inanimate object trials. Some of them didn't change at all, any more than you did—especially at minimum force. At maximum force they all just disappeared, and we never saw a trace of them again; we must have sent those so far away that any parallels sent toward us at the same power shot right through without stopping. In between, though—well, that was confusing."

"How?" Royce demanded, holding the handle of the fire door at the top of the stairs.

Hammond sighed. "Well," he said, "some of the animals vanished, some didn't change—and some *did* change. We sent out rats and got back hamsters, sent white guineas and got back brown, sent textbooks and got back novels. Sometimes we didn't send *anything*, and we got stuff appearing in the sphere, rats and books and once a slide rule with the numbers in Arabic."

"Arabic numerals?"

"*Real* Arabic, not the numbers we use."

Royce nodded. He opened the door and stepped through into the hallway beyond, Hammond close behind. "That doesn't sound so confusing," he said. "I mean, weren't those what you expected?"

"Well, yes," Hammond said. "Pretty much. The really confusing part came after we took things out of the sphere."

"Why?"

"Because some of them vanished later. Lab animals get loose, sometimes, and things get mislaid, but they've done so much more than usual on this project. It's got Dr. Brzeski a little spooked, I think. And sometimes animals have turned up in the wrong cage, or we've found animals we don't recognize in the cages—it's confusing, as I said."

Royce felt an uneasy chill. "You mean that this might not be entirely over for me?" he said. "There might be some sort of aftereffects?"

"There might be," Hammond admitted. "We just don't know."

Then they were in Chin's examining room, and Royce was obediently taking his shirt off.

The exam found nothing out of the ordinary. After the physical was done, Hammond and Chin asked Royce to stay for observation; he reluctantly agreed.

They were paying him, after all—ten dollars an hour, they'd promised.

A nurse brought him a magazine, and he sat and read. The magazine seemed oddly slippery, which he attributed to nerves; he couldn't see any shaking, but his hands did seem somehow unsteady.

It was tiring, reading the tiny print when it didn't want to hold still, so after awhile he put it down, lay back on the couch, and took a nap.

When he awoke it took a moment to remember where he was. He sat up and looked at the clock—he had slept through the night. He must have been much more tired than he had realized.

And he hadn't had any dinner; he was ravenous. He glanced around.

There was a magazine on the table, and at first he thought it was the one he had been reading, but that had been

Newsweek and this one was *Time*. He wondered why anyone would have switched it.

The door was closed; he stood up and opened it.

The hallway was empty and silent.

He hesitated, but then shrugged. What the hell, he thought, he wasn't a prisoner or anything, he was a volunteer. There wasn't any reason to bother anybody here or settle for infirmary food. He had his wallet in his pocket, after all.

He walked up the hill to the edge of campus and got himself a breakfast at P.J.'s Pancake House, then drifted back.

Just where to go was a good question; he could go back to his room, or to the infirmary, or to the gadget room in the basement of Palmer. If he went back to his room, Hammond and the rest would probably be pretty pissed, and there wasn't anything he wanted to do there in any case. If anything was happening, he'd miss it.

They probably expected to find him at the infirmary, but it was *boring*, sitting around there reading last week's news.

He headed for the physics lab.

Brzeski was asleep in a chair in the corner, his head down on the desk, the computer screen in front of him displaying an array of complex mathematics. Hammond and the other guy were poring over a stack of papers.

"Hey," Royce called. "What's happening?"

The two looked up, startled.

Royce looked back, startled.

"Hey," he said. "What happened to the mustache?"

The Middle Eastern guy's right hand flew to his face, feeling the bristly black hairs; Hammond turned to look at him.

"No," Royce said, "I meant *your* mustache, Dr. Hammond."

Hammond stared at Royce, his hand creeping up to feel his own upper lip.

There was no mustache there, only a faint dark fuzz that had resulted from not yet shaving that morning. "What mustache, Mr. Royce?" Hammond asked.

"*Your* mustache," Royce insisted. "You had one yesterday, a thin one sort of like Clark Gable. Made you look like ... well, you had a mustache."

Hammond and his associate looked at each other, then back at Royce.

"I have worked with Dr. Hammond for three years now,"

the other one said, "and I have never seen him wear a mustache."

"Are you quite sure I had one, Mr. Royce?" Hammond asked.

"Quite sure, yeah," Royce agreed.

"That was before the trial?"

"Before the experiment and after, yeah; you had it last night when you left me at the infirmary."

The two looked at each other again; then, abruptly, there were three of them, as Dr. Brzeski was simply there, standing beside them. Royce stared.

"I think," Dr. Brzeski said, "we have a problem."

The tools that gave them the final clue weren't any complicated pieces of laboratory apparatus, but the office photocopiers.

Included in the notebook Royce had carried was a page of random numbers, on the theory that this would provide an ideal way to check for small random changes. It was a photocopy of one that Dr. Hammond had kept on his desk, and the theory was that the two sheets of paper could be held up to a bright light, superimposed over one another, and any differences would show up immediately.

This had in fact been done immediately after the experiment, and no differences had been detected.

When Royce had appeared, inquiring after Hammond's mustache, the two were compared again, and no fewer than eleven digits had changed.

The two sheets were then taken upstairs to the office of the departmental secretary, where two photocopiers resided. The original was put in one machine, the copy that Royce had carried in the other, and both machines set to turning out copies one after another.

Every copy of the original was identical, from the first until the machine ran out of toner some seven hundred pages later.

The first copy of the copy was just as Hammond had recorded it moments before, with eleven differences from the original. So was the second, and the third.

Around the seventieth copy, though, there were twelve differences.

Around the hundredth there were thirteen.

By the time that machine ran out of toner, some eight hundred and fifty copies later, the page that Royce had brought with him was no longer even in the same typeface as the original, and some thirty digits, out of three thousand, were different.

To Royce, the one he had brought had not changed at all, but the others had.

To Hammond, the one Royce had brought had been steadily altering, while everything else remained constant.

And it wasn't just the paper; Hammond's mustache had disappeared, Brzeski had changed his shirt and shaved, and various other things had altered over time, while to the scientists none of these had altered, but Royce had—his clothing and hairstyle were no longer what the physicists remembered from before the experiment.

It was Brzeski who finally came up with a theory to account for this and explained it to Royce.

"Think of all those universes we talked about as parallel lines," he said, "and each version of you is like a ball rolling down the line, from past to future."

Royce nodded.

"Well, we had thought of those lines as little grooves, and we were going to nudge you up out of one groove and into the next."

Royce nodded again.

Brzeski grimaced. "It seems we got our analogy wrong, though; they aren't grooves, just lines on a flat surface. We gave you a push sideways, and you moved off your original line—but instead of dropping into the next groove, you've just kept on rolling across the surface, from one line to the next, at an angle. There are no grooves, nothing to stop you from sliding on across the different lines forever. You have the same futureward vector as you started with, but you've added a small crosstime vector, as well."

"So how do I stop it?"

Brzeski shrugged. "I don't know," he admitted.

Royce stared at him.

"There may be friction," he said. "In fact, there probably *is* some sort of friction, because after all, you interact with your surroundings—we gave a crosstime shove to what was in the sphere, and that's just a finite mass, made up of you and the notebook and a lot of air and miscellaneous particles, which means a finite momentum; as the molecules of your body are replaced with molecules that were not in the sphere, that momentum will be dissipated, and your average velocity as a system, if we can call it that, will be reduced. We have no way of measuring the reduction, though, no way of knowing when it'll slow you down to a stop."

Royce was glad that Physics 101 was a course he had *not* flunked—he thought he understood the explanation. "Well, can you put me back in the machine and shove me back the other way, cancel out the momentum?" he asked.

Brzeski hesitated before replying, "No."

After a moment he realized that wasn't adequate and explained, "We can't aim the thing; in fact, I think it's stuck pointing in one direction, so to speak. If we put you in it again and shoved, it wouldn't slow you down, it would speed you up. Didn't Hammond warn you about that, that we didn't think you could ever get back to your home universe?"

"Yeah," Royce admitted, "he said something about that."

"We'll work on it," Brzeski assured him. "Hang in there."

"Yeah," Royce said, "But how long is it going to take? Am I stuck here until you get it worked out? So far all the changes have been stupid little stuff, but what happens if something *important* changes? How often am I going to make these hops from one universe to the next?"

Brzeski swallowed. "I thought you understood," he said. "You're making hops, as you call it, *constantly*, every second, every instant. You're not in the same universe you were in five minutes ago, or ten seconds ago, or even when I started this sentence. You're falling, or rolling, or however you want to describe it, through one universe after another—but the transitions are instantaneous, and the differences are so minute and so scattered that you don't see most of the changes. The population in China could have gone up or down by a million in a single transition, and you wouldn't know, because it's outside your immediate area. Whole planets could vanish or appear, and you wouldn't notice. There must be millions, billions of changes happening every second, for there to have been any you observed directly in the . . ." He glanced at his watch. ". . . nineteen hours since you got your push."

Royce puzzled with this for a moment, then asked, "But then how can you talk to me? How can you even *see* me, if I'm only in your universe for an instant?"

"Because it isn't just a single you," Brzeski explained. "There were an infinite number of closely bunched worlds where this experiment was tried, where you were the subject, and where the results were the same. That means an infinite number of versions of you, all moving together through an infinite number of worlds." He sighed. "Think of two sets of parallel lines, set at an angle, crossing each other. The intersections of the lines form a line of their own, and *that's* the line we're interacting along. You aren't the same Dave Royce that I started explaining this to; you're just one of millions who have flashed through this universe and millions of adjacent universes, each of you hearing an instant of this in each of those different realities."

"*Danny* Royce," Royce said. "Danny, not Dave."

Brzeski blinked and looked down at his notes.

"The one we started with," he said, "was Dave. See?" He held up a sheet of paper, and Royce read the line near the top, "Subject volunteer David H. Royce."

A chill ran through him.

"So there are a million of us," he said. "Can you stop us, somehow? Or tell where we're going?"

Brzeski shook his head. "No," he said, "all we can do is hope that I'm right about friction slowing you down."

They tried anyway, of course; they measured everything they could think of to measure, ran dozens of computer models, and considered a hundred different ways to recalibrate the gadget.

Nothing held out any hope. For weeks, he lived in an uncomfortable world of constant small changes, a world all his own, moving at an angle to everyone else. Small objects moved about untouched, sometimes hopping instantaneously from one place to another as he watched; people did the same. Hair, clothing, and makeup could change at any instant; conversations sometimes shifted directions in the middle of a sentence or even a word.

And then came the day when he woke up on his cot in the basement of Palmer and found two people sitting nearby, not Hammond and Brzeski, but Hammond and Dave Royce.

He had reached the universes where the experiment had not been done, where no one had volunteered; Dave Royce, who was otherwise almost indistinguishable from Danny Royce, had considered it, and had backed down.

"You first appeared—that is, your analogs did—about six weeks ago," Dave explained. "It was pretty weird; at first everyone thought I had a long-lost twin brother turning up. Really gave me the creeps, seeing you."

Danny, staring at his doppelgänger in uneasy fascination, shuddered slightly and said, "I can understand that."

"Before you bother to ask—I mean, I guess you will, because all the others did, practically every five minutes—we can't do anything to stop your crosstime drift. Things are different here, yeah, but that's because the experiments didn't go as far as they did where you world. The equipadget got built, here, but I didn't volver tried it out on humans."

Danny blinked; the conversation was fragmenting more than usual. Perhaps that had something to do with being near a major transition, between universes that had done the experiment and universes that hadn't. There was no pattern to the changes that he could detect, but they did sometimes seem to come in bunches.

Then Dave was gone, and Dr. Hammond was saying, ". . . six weeks to study your situation, but as yet we haven't made much progress."

Then Dave was back.

He lived in the basement for another week. He no longer had a room, of course, since in these universes it was Dave Royce, not Danny, who was a student on the verge of flunking out. Danny Royce didn't exist at all, or at any rate had not existed prior to six weeks before.

The one encouraging piece of news, received in a rather fragmented conversation with Dr. Brzeski, was that his situation might actually have been improved by this doubling up.

"In all the universes where a Dave or Danny Royce was sent out," Brzeski explained, "that created a sort of vacuum, we think, that all the others, coming up behind, can move into easily. This may, in fact, be one reason that you're moving far more quickly than we would have expected—only the very first in the sequence had to overcome any significant resistance. Now that you're into universes where this didn't happen, though, friction should be much greater."

Royce frowned. "But I'm still following seven weeks' worth of myself," he said. "Aren't they all pulling me along?"

Brzeski frowned and scratched at his beard. "Maybe," he admitted, "but not as much as they were, I don't think."

Before Royce could say anything, the tail end of another conversation intruded, as Brzeski said, ". . . your best chance."

"What's my best chance?"

"Waiting it out," Brzeski said. "I just said looks bad, and I wish I could be be be be more timistic."

"What looks bad?" Royce hated this sort of thing, where attempts to communicate went in bizarre and unexpected directions without warning.

"Your situation. I mean, with the dead ones."

"Dead ones? What dead ones?"

Brzeski sighed. "Here we go again. I was explaining, for about the hundredth time, that the first few of you to arrive in our universe were dead. We don't know what killed them. It scared the hell out of us when the first live one arrived—having a dead body appear in the physics lab was bad enough, but when it sat up and started asking questions . . ."

Brzeski vanished.

By the end of the third month Royce was absolutely convinced that the changes were speeding up, not slowing down; the friction theory didn't seem to be working.

Dr. Brzeski no longer existed; the physicist with the Middle Eastern name was now Dr. Hamid, which Royce was fairly certain was not what he had heard originally; Douglas Royce had not been admitted to the university but had been waitlisted and not made the final cut; no Dave or Danny Royce had ever existed, prior to some forty days ago. The gadget had never been built; Hammond's work in parallel-world theory was entirely theoretical.

The fact that it was no longer six weeks since the first appearance worried him.

Then he found out about the body.

Or bodies.

"We don't understand what's happening, exactly," Hammond explained. "But dead bodies have appeared in the basement lab, and then disappeared again, and sometimes this coincides with a live Royce and sometimes it doesn't."

"A live Royce?" Royce asked. "You mean there's more than one?"

"I mean that you appear and disappear and even when you're here you flicker sometimes."

Royce could understand that; he had sometimes seen other people flick about or blink in and out of existence. He had not realized that he was doing it.

Upon consideration, though, he thought he could explain it. He was becoming an expert on the practical ramifications of crosstime travel, from firsthand experience combined with an urgent personal interest. Some of his other selves were diverging slightly as they moved through time. Some had died; some had moved about in different ways.

And the existence of more than one at a time—that needed more thought, but he had a guess.

"It's friction," he said. "When I move and eat and breathe, I interact with the air around me, and so on, and that increases the air resistance, sort of. Not air resistance, exactly, but . . ."

"Temporal resistance," Hammond suggested.

"Right, temporal resistance," he agreed. "So when some of me stop eating and breathing, or do so differently, then that changes the amount of resistance they encounter. So dead bodies ought to be moving faster across time than the live versions." He considered that. "So they're coming from behind me," he said. "I've slowed down more than they have, and they've zipped past me."

He looked at himself for a moment and then the duplicate was gone again.

"And I'll bet we're bumping against each other, too," he said. "Some of us would be slowed down by collisions and some would be sped up—whole chunks of the sequence, millions at a time. That would account for some of the flickering, too, as we get spaced out further. My part must be speeding up a little, because the changes have been coming more quickly for me. But it means there *is* friction and eventually I'll come to rest. Right?"

"I'm sorry," Hammond said, "but I couldn't make that out; your speech is deteriorating."

By the end of the first year, no Dr. Hammond or Dr. Hamid had ever existed, and no one he spoke to knew anything about any serious study of parallel-world theory. It was purely the province of science-fiction writers. He could find no Doug, Dave, or Danny Royce anywhere; his mother was not living in the house he had grown up in.

The world wasn't all *that* different, though. The United States was still there, history seemed unchanged in any significant way, the university was still there—though one quadrangle was drastically altered; he supposed a different architect had done it.

He survived by sleeping in campus lounges, eating anywhere he could sneak in, doing odd jobs for cash. He could no longer chart exactly how long his doppelgängers had been appearing, because appearances were scattered in both time and space. Mysterious corpses appearing and disappearing had been a frequent phenomenon in these worlds for months.

He tried to count changes as best he could but had no real way of doing so. Whether he was speeding up or slowing down he was not certain.

For three days, he found himself passing another section of the sequence, and the two versions of himself were able to compare notes, but nothing came of the comparison. Danny Royce was clearly drifting faster than Dave Royce in this particular pairing, which Dave found heartening and Danny depressing, but beyond that he learned nothing of any use.

In the third year he was caught by troops enforcing a curfew he hadn't known about and was shot while fleeing; he heard the rifle crack, saw the bullet coming toward him, and then it was gone, and he ran on.

One of his doppelgängers was dead, killed by that bullet, he was sure; probably millions were dead of millions of identical bullets. He, personally, was not.

His sense of self had suffered over the past two years; so had his grip on reality, since reality kept changing. The university was gone, the United States in the chaos of a second civil war that had begun twenty years before, and he knew nothing of any of it. Still, he knew that he was alive; he was not so far gone as to doubt that.

From then on, though, he found people starting at his appearance; he was frequently asked, "Where'd you go?" or "Where'd you come from?" and concluded that there was a gap in his existence now, a space of several seconds.

His life had become sufficiently disjointed that he no longer looked for any way to slow his drift; he only worried about surviving from one meal to the next, while he waited for friction to stop him.

It was a relief when he finally found himself in uninhabited forest. He had been avoiding people for years, ever since English had ceased to be the local language, and the utter absence of other human beings made that much easier. He could concentrate on finding food and water, without worrying about hiding—fortunately, the local predators, bears and mountain lions, didn't seem interested in him.

He sometimes wondered whether he had reached a world where human beings had never existed at all, or one where they had died out, or one where they simply hadn't found the Americas yet. He rather hoped it was the last of those three, because once he was sure he had stopped drifting, he intended to try to find a human society where he could fit in. He was lonely. It had been thirteen years since he had stepped out of that metal sphere, thirteen years since his life had had any pretense of normality.

He knew that he had not stopped yet, though, because every so often, perhaps once a week, or only once a month, something would change—a rock would be shifted, a branch unbroken, or some other sign that reality was still not constant.

With no one to talk to, he had no idea whether there were any of his other selves still in existence, but he theorized that there had to be.

He certainly hoped so.

The child stared and called for her mother. She came quickly, and together they gazed down at the huddled shape.

Royce awoke on a comfortable object—he had no name for it, though it was obviously furniture, something akin to a large beanbag chair and also to an oversized pillow, but not quite either one. He looked up at an arched, sand-colored ceiling.

He stretched, sat up, and looked around.

The mother and daughter were standing in the doorway, watching him.

He smiled, then thought better of showing his teeth—twenty-two years without a dentist had left them in sorry shape.

"Hello," he said, his voice cracking. "I don't suppose by any miracle you speak English?"

The pair simply stared.

Royce shrugged. "I didn't think so," he said. "So I'll learn your language. After all, I'm going to be here for a long time." He smiled again, keeping his lips closed this time. "You're probably wondering where the hell I came from, and I wish I could tell you; maybe someday I'll be able to explain it." He looked around the room, at the oval window and the various inexplicable furnishings. "So this is your village, huh? I've been watching you guys for months—I mean, I didn't want to just walk up and get a spear through my belly, or wind up in the community stewpot, you know? I guess I misjudged a little, though. You must have found me asleep, right? I thought I was farther away than that." He grimaced.

The silent watchers listened to the stream of strange, babbling noises from the creature, but made no response.

"And I've stopped drifting, haven't I?" Royce said, unable to repress a grin. "It's been six months since I spotted any changes and believe me, I've been looking. God, it was *so lucky* that I made it as far as you folks before I stopped! Living the rest of my life alone out there in the woods—well, I'm not as young as I was, y'know? And even though you people aren't anything like where I came from, I like your looks." He waved an arm at the room and its contents. "I like this place. Homey."

The daughter squeaked at her mother, who honked a reply. A yellow claw patted the daughter's scaly head.

"That's gonna be a tough language to learn," Royce said, considering.

Then, before the eyes of the two observers, he vanished.

STORM TROOPER

*T*he orange juice had more pulp than he liked and was warm, as well—one of the drawbacks of eating breakfast at his desk, that.

Of course, back when he ate breakfast at home, his ex-wife had usually gotten orange juice with too much pulp in it anyway. It had generally been good and cold, though.

Mitsopoulas put the little carton aside and used the space to unfold the paper.

No new storms were mentioned; the lead story was something about the Middle East. He skipped that—it wasn't his problem. A smaller item, near the bottom of the page, was more in his line; scientists had managed to keep alive a tissue sample from the "skywhale" that a storm had dropped in a Kansas cornfield last week and were optimistic about eventually cloning it and growing a full-sized specimen.

He snorted. What would they *do* with a two-hundred-foot, lighter-than-air whale? Oh, he supposed it might have some value as a source of methane, for fuel, but it would be an awfully awkward thing to have around. For his own part, he thought it was just as well that the poor creature had arrived dead. He couldn't imagine what its home reality might have been like.

The swinging door opened, and Orlando's back appeared, pushing it. He turned around and displayed a cardboard tray of styrofoam cups. "You like it black, right, lieutenant?"

Mitsopoulas looked up. "Yeah, black." He accepted the proffered cup and pried off the plastic lid but waited for the coffee to cool before sipping. His eyes wandered back to the newspaper.

Some fundamentalist preacher was calling for a national

63

moment of prayer at noon. "The Lord is testing us," he was quoted as saying. "He is reshaping His creation even as we watch, to show us His power. We must acknowledge Him, show Him that our faith in His Word is still firm, or He will destroy us all."

Mitsopoulas didn't buy that. If God wanted to send messages, there were easier ways than the reality storms. If the storms were a test of faith, the instructions were pretty damn unclear; what did a flying whale have to do with sin or salvation? How were the Nazis in the Bronx, or those poor weirdos on Coney Island, supposed to change his beliefs? It was the crazy suckers who were getting dumped who had to change their beliefs, not the ordinary people of the real world. He folded the newspaper and drank coffee.

Orlando was back after distributing the other cups.

"So, Orlando, what've we got today?" Mitsopoulas asked.

"Nothing for sure, lieutenant," Orlando said, shrugging. "You saw the paper."

"Nothing came in after deadline last night?"

"Not that we've gotten called on yet."

"No?" Mitsopoulas leaned back in his chair. "Funny," he said, "I thought I heard a storm last night; half woke me up."

"There *was* a storm," Orlando agreed. "About five this morning. They logged calls about some weird machines cruising over Forty-Third Street, and a lady called in about her cat turning into a vacuum cleaner or something, but the night shift didn't find anything. Must've just passed over without dumping anything, for once, the way they used to when they first started. Maybe they're slowing up again."

"We should both live so long," Mitsopoulas muttered, leaning forward again.

Orlando heard him and retorted, "Hey, they can't go on forever!"

"No?" Mitsopoulas looked up at him and grimaced. "How do you know? Nothing like this ever happened before."

"We don't know that, lieutenant," Orlando said contemplatively. "Maybe these things used to drive the dinosaurs nuts. Maybe it was reality storms killed the dinosaurs off, for all I know. Maybe all those stories about fairies and leprechauns were true, and they came from storms."

"Aah!" Mitsopoulas waved a hand. "That's garbage. The storms started two years ago, not back in the Dark Ages or whenever the dinosaurs lived. It's all part of the crazy times we live in, that's all."

Orlando shrugged. "Suit yourself."

"I will, just watch." He sipped coffee. "Hey, what was that about the lady's cat?"

"Oh, someone up in Turtle Bay Towers said her cat turned into a vacuum cleaner, or some piece of machinery that looked like one."

Mitsopoulas snorted. "Anybody check it out?"

"Not in person," Orlando replied. "A sergeant took the call, someone named Derring, and told her that if the machine did anything suspicious she should call again, or bring it to the station. That was the last we heard about it."

"I know Derring," Mitsopoulas said thoughtfully. "He's as lazy a son of a bitch as you're going to find on the force."

"Hey, lieutenant, come on!" Orlando protested. "She's probably just some old loony whose cat ran away. How could it turn into a vacuum cleaner?"

"How the hell do I know? How could three blocks in the Bronx turn into a concentration camp? How did those people in that castle out on Coney Island get in a solid stone room with no doors or windows, so it took six hours to jackhammer them out? How'd that castle get there at all?" He shrugged. "So this time it's probably just a nut with a missing cat; you want to sit around here all day? It's nice weather out there, and I could use a little drive uptown. We've got radio now, Orlando, you know that? If anything important comes up we won't miss it."

Orlando nodded reluctantly. "You're taking the whole squad?" he asked.

"Hey, that's what the rules say—we stay together as a unit, just in case. Did you boys have something better to do?" When Orlando hesitated, considering whether or not to answer, Mitsopoulas smiled and added, "On city time?"

"I guess not," Orlando conceded.

"What was it, anyway—penny-ante stud?"

"Nickel-dime, dealer's choice," Orlando admitted.

"So save your money. Get the equipment on the wagon and let's go."

They went.

Fifteen minutes later the DCS van stopped for a light at Forty-third and Third, and Mitsopoulas leaned forward, studying the streets around them. "I thought I felt something just then," he said. "Like an aftershock or something. Any of you guys feel it?"

Simons, at the wheel, shook his head, and Orlando called from the back, "Maybe it's heartburn, lieutenant."

"Very funny," Mitsopoulas retorted, as the others snickered quietly. He knew that he had felt something, as if gravity had shifted direction for an instant, as if the common, everyday reality around him had blinked. That the others had failed to notice it didn't mean it hadn't happened; he had gotten his post as commander of the DCS squad partly because he was unusually sensitive to such phenomena.

"This was where the storm was centered last night?" he asked.

Simons nodded. "So they told me."

"Hey, storm troopers!" someone called cheerfully from the sidewalk, waving at the van.

"Oh, jeez," Mitsopoulas said, sinking down in his seat.

"I wish they didn't call us that," Simons said.

"I know," the lieutenant agreed, "especially after the Bronx. But I guess you can't expect kids to yell, 'Hey, Discontinuity Control Squad!' "

"No, but my kid brother calls us reality cops, and I can handle that a lot better than 'storm troopers.' "

Mitsopoulas didn't answer; he was staring at the buildings on the north side of Forty-third. The light changed, and Simons started the van forward.

"Turn here," Mitsopoulas told him, pointing.

Startled, Simons obeyed, belatedly yanking the wheel around hard in order to make the corner. "I thought we were going up to Forty-sixth," he said when he had the van safely in lane.

Mitsopoulas was staring out at the building immediately east of the familiar facade of the Church of Saint Agnes. "I thought so, too," he replied. "But we're not; stop here."

Simons eased the van over, double-parking it in front of the indicated building. "What is it?" he asked.

"Look at the sign."

Simons looked and read, "New York City Internal Security, Midtown Boo-ro. B-U-R-O? I never saw 'bureau' spelled like that."

"And I never heard of the New York Internal Security," Mitsopoulas said.

"You don't think it's just some rent-a-cop outfit?" Orlando asked from the back.

"I don't know—but that's a damn big building for a rent-a-cop operation I never heard of, and besides, it wasn't here the last time I came past."

"That sign doesn't look new," Simons said doubtfully.

"I know," Mitsopoulas replied grimly.

"Are you sure it wasn't here?"

"Hey, don't argue, all right? I'm sure; it doesn't go right with the church."

"So they had a bad architect . . ."

"That's not what I mean; I mean I remember it being different. I don't know every block in the city, but I know Saint Agnes, and that's not the building that should be next to it."

Simons stared for a moment. "You mean it's part of a reality dump? The report was on Forty-sixth, wasn't it?"

"Yeah," Mitsopoulas said, "it was."

"That's another three blocks, lieutenant, and on the other side of Third Avenue; if it were that big, wouldn't we have gotten a lot more word on it already?"

"I'd like to think so," Mitsopoulas said quietly. "Maybe we got two separate spots. One way or another, though, we check this place out."

Simons shrugged. "Okay, lieutenant, but maybe it's just your memory playing tricks."

"My memory doesn't play tricks." Mitsopoulas opened the door and got out; on the other side Simons followed suit, and the rest of the team crept forward between the seats to follow.

In accordance with standard practice, four of the men, including Mitsopoulas, formed a line facing the building, spaced at arm's length; Mabuchi stood back a pace, scanning the opposite sidewalk and to either side. Orlando stayed in the van, sitting with one leg out the open door, the radio mike in his hand, ready to call for help, or to leap out to provide backup, or to jump back in and flee. All but Orlando had their guns drawn and pointed skyward.

In the center of the line, facing the door of "New York City Internal Security" 's midtown bureau, Mitsopoulas felt a rush of adrenaline; the palm that was wrapped around the butt of his gun was sweaty, and his throat was dry. It was always this way at first, when he faced a complete unknown that could be literally *anything*. Once he found out what was inside that building, once he knew something, he could be calm again, no matter how bizarre or dangerous it might be; it was the not knowing that affected him, not any actual threat.

He knew his men did not necessarily feel the same way; he thought that all of them must be calmer than he, and Simons, on his right, looked just as cool as if he were on the firing range back at headquarters.

Well, they didn't understand as well as he did. The people in the reality dumps could be complete wackos. There could be things in there that weren't people at all. The dumps might not come from the real world, but they were solid and dangerous all the same. Two men died capturing the camp in the Bronx.

He took the first step forward, toward the three low steps leading up to the door, but then he stopped and snapped his gun down into firing position.

The door was opening.

Mitsopoulas glimpsed a sleek black uniform, dark hair, a pale face, and then whoever had opened the door spotted the line of men outside, the six cops, the storm troopers, and he—or just possibly she—ducked back in, out of sight.

The door did not close again, however; a crack remained, too narrow for Mitsopoulas to see anything through.

"Look for cover," Mitsopoulas said, "but stand your ground for now."

From the corner of his eye, he could see Weinberg nodding an acknowledgment, and O'Donnell, on the other side, passing the order on to Simons.

"Orlando," he called, "pass the bullhorn."

Orlando obeyed, handing it to Weinberg, who passed it to Mitsopoulas. He took it, turned it on, and raised it.

As he did, he noticed that a crowd was beginning to collect on the sidewalks. "Mabuchi," he called over his shoulder, "keep those gawkers back."

Then, using the bullhorn, he called, "You in the building, the one that says Internal Security! This is the police! We want to talk—send someone out, unarmed!"

He lowered the loud-hailer and waited. On either side, his men waited with him.

A moment later a window on the second floor slid up, and an amplified voice called out, "Who did you say you were?"

"Damn," Mitsopoulas muttered. He raised the horn. "This is Lieutenant Gregory Mitsopoulas, of the New York Police Department. Who's in there?"

For a long moment there was only silence; then the amplified voice said, "We have you covered. Throw down your weapons, and we'll talk."

The barrel of a rifle, black and menacing, slid out across the second-story windowsill.

"Oh, shit," Mitsopoulas said. "Take cover!"

The men scattered, behind parked cars and a *Daily News* box. Mitsopoulas himself ducked back to the van and crouched by Orlando's knee, behind the open door.

"This is the police," he bellowed through the bullhorn. "Nobody's been hurt here, and we want to keep it that way. We just want to talk. No guns. Send someone out!"

"Listen," the voice from the building replied, "I don't know who you are really, but if you're the police, who the hell do you think is in here?"

Mitsopoulas blinked and read the sign again.

INTERNAL SECURITY.

Yeah, that might mean police somewhere, but in New York?

Besides, he knew perfectly well who the cops were here.

But then, there had been a reality storm last night, and it was clear that this building was from some *other* New York. Were the occupants unaware of what had happened?

Maybe, somehow, they were.

Well, then, someone had to explain it to them. That was simple enough.

And figuring out whose job the explanation was wasn't too tricky, either.

"This is Lieutenant Mitsopoulas," he called. "I'm going to leave my gun here and come inside to talk to you."

After a moment's hesitation, the voice replied, "Come ahead. Keep your hands where we can see them."

Mitsopoulas muttered to himself as he handed the bullhorn and his service revolver to Orlando.

"You guys be careful out here," he said. Then he stood up, raised his hands to shoulder height, palms out, and walked across Forty-third Street and up the three steps.

The heavy front door was still ajar; he pushed it open with one toe and leaned in.

"Hello," he called, "anyone here?"

Two men with drawn guns appeared at the opposite end of a small, dingy hallway. They wore sleek, one-piece black uniforms that didn't look much like any cop suits Mitsopoulas had ever seen—more like something athletic, though no bike racer or ice skater would have added the equipment-laden Sam Browne belts. The lieutenant wiggled his fingers. "I'm clean," he called. "See?"

One man frisked him while the other kept him covered. Neither spoke. They looked through his wallet and inspected his badge and kept them both, as well as the cuffs and a few other items he had been carrying.

When they were satisfied that he was unarmed, they took him to a small, bare room with three wooden chairs and a hanging light—Interrogation, obviously.

Mitsopoulas sighed and played along, taking the suspect's chair. One man stayed to guard him; the other stepped out.

A moment later another, older man entered, wearing a variant of the same black uniform, but trimmed in gold at the cuffs. He took a seat.

Mitsopoulas waited to see whether he would be offered a hand to shake. He wasn't.

"So," the questioner asked, "who are you?"

"I'm Lieutenant Gregory Mitsopoulas, NYPD. I assume you read the ID I had on me."

The other man nodded.

"I take it you don't believe it, for some reason," Mitsopoulas said.

The other smiled a tight, humorless little smile.

"Mind if I ask who you are?" Mitsopoulas said, smiling back.

"Aaron Fitzwater, Bureau Commandant, New York City Internal Security," the other replied.

Mitsopoulas nodded. "I figured it was something like that. And in your New York City, you guys are the only cops there are, right? So when you saw us lined up out there like that, you must have thought you had a goddamn revolt on your hands, right?"

Fitzwater stared silently for a moment, then asked, "*Your* New York City? Is there more than one, then?"

"Sure is. So I guess you guys didn't have reality storms where you came from? At least, not until the one that dumped you here?"

"Mr. Mitsopoulas," Fitzwater said, "you aren't making much sense."

Mitsopoulas sighed. "You don't have the storms. Okay, just

bear with me for a couple of minutes, all right? It's gonna sound stupid, but let me talk. That okay?"

Fitzwater nodded. "Say your piece," he said.

"Okay," Mitsopoulas said. He took a breath and began.

"Two years ago we started getting what we call reality storms—and when I say we, I don't just mean me, or New York, I mean the whole friggin' world. For anywhere from about half a second to a couple of hours, the whole world goes nuts in a certain area—things appear and disappear, or change shape, the air can change, the light, colors, everything. Sometimes gravity or even time itself is affected. The size of the storm can range from . . . well, we don't know the lower limit, but the smallest one anyone's confirmed was about the size of a breadbox. That one lasted about a minute and a half. The biggest one reported so far was over the mid-Atlantic, thank God, and was estimated at five miles long and two miles wide. We don't know what's causing them; nobody does, or at least nobody we know of. There are lots of theories, of course—that Judgment Day is approaching, that reality's coming apart at the seams, that it's all just illusions or mass hysteria. My personal favorite theory is that some scientist somewhere in some other universe is screwing around with space-time or something, and we're getting caught in the backwash, but we don't really know." He spread his palms. "So," he asked, "you heard about anything like that?"

Fitzwater calmly answered, "No."

Mitsopoulas shook his head. "Too bad," he said. "Then you probably think I'm nuts. I'm not, though—it's true. These weird storms are happening, and during them the whole world is warped out of shape—up can be down, or you can get heavier or lighter, light and sound do strange things, people see mysterious things in the sky. Weird stuff."

"Go on," Fitzwater said.

"Okay," Mitsopoulas said agreeably, "you're humoring me, that's good. It's a start, anyway. Thanks. So, anyway, sometimes, after particularly bad storms, there are bits of reality that have been changed permanently, and we get strange things left behind—bits and pieces of other worlds. And yeah, that means that parts of our world are gone, and no, we don't know where they went, and no, none of them have ever come back again. They're just gone, and we've got other stuff there instead, stuff that doesn't always make sense. Like a flying whale—a dead one, with all its gas sacs ruptured, turned up in a Kansas cornfield; that drove the science guys nuts. I don't know about you, but nobody in *my* world had ever seen a flying whale before, or any other animal that was lighter than air." Mitsopoulas shook his head. "Hell of a thing."

"Go on," Fitzwater repeated.

"Sure. Well, anyway, we get a lot of these in New York—maybe it's got something to do with population density, or maybe with all the electronics stuff around here. Whatever, New York gets more than its share, so the city put together a special team to deal with all the bits of other realities that get left behind. We call it the Discontinuity Control Squad, and me and my men, we're it."

Fitzwater nodded slowly.

"Lieutenant," he said, "I told you a lie a couple of minutes ago. We've had a few incidents such as you describe—not on the scale your world apparently has, assuming you're telling me the truth, but we've had a few. We don't call them reality storms; we call them illusion zones. The official doctrine is that the things in them aren't real. We, too, have a special team to deal with them—we call them Zone Police. The street name is the dream police."

Mitsopoulas grimaced. "They call us storm troopers," he said.

Fitzwater smiled his little smile again. "So I don't think you're crazy," he said.

Mitsopoulas smiled back. "That's a relief," he said.

"At least, not crazy in the usual way. I don't think you're real at all."

Mitsopoulas started. His smile vanished. "What?"

"Not real in *our* world, anyway. So you and your men were caught in one of these reality storms, as you call them, and you found yourself in our world?"

"Hey, no," Mitsopoulas said. "*You* guys, *you* were caught. You're in *my* world."

Fitzwater's smile vanished as well. "Nonsense, lieutenant," he said. "Look around you. This is *my* world, my bureau."

"Yeah, it's your bureau," Mitsopoulas said, "because your whole building got it, around five o'clock this morning."

As he spoke, though, a slithering uneasiness slipped into the back of his mind.

If the building had made the transition at five A.M., why was the full daytime crew here? Why hadn't any of them noticed the transition? And there had been that little twinge while waiting at the light on Third Avenue.

Fitzwater was definitely not smiling now; his face looked hard as granite, far harder than the acoustic-tile walls. "I'm afraid you're mistaken," he said. "You and your men are the strangers here—the invaders. Now, if you would kindly order them all to come in here, I'm sure we can make arrangements."

"Arrangements," Mitsopoulas said, feeling cold. "What kind of arrangements?" New York City Internal Security, they called it. Security, like the Committee for State Security—the KGB. Or the Rumanian Securitate. These weren't just cops, like himself and his men; he was sure of it. They were the secret police, the enforcers, the midnight knock on the door.

Dream police, illusion zones—so what did they do with the very real things that were left behind? And the very real people? In Mitsopoulas's New York, there were eleven people out in Queens who thought they were wizards, people who were being taught English and offered vocational training. There were three hundred survivors of the camp in the Bronx in the city hospitals, recovering. There was an exact double of a Wall Street broker who was trying to set himself up in a new line of work. There were half a dozen unidentified creatures in the Bronx Zoo, and a warehouse in Brooklyn half full of unidentified *things*.

Nobody called any of that stuff an illusion. Insane, maybe, but not illusion. How can you call it illusion when there's so much evidence?

You'd have to get rid of the evidence before you could say it was all an illusion.

"Come with me, Lieutenant," Fitzwater said, "and we'll get your men in here."

"Commandant," he said, "I think you're making a mistake. This is *my* world, my New York. I can prove it." To himself, Mitsopoulas prayed, Oh, God, I *hope* it's my New York.

"How?" Fitzwater demanded, his voice cold, and Mitsopoulas knew that this was life and death, that Fitzwater and the NYC Internal Security men were not playing games.

He had to escape, to get out of here somehow.

But if he did, then what? What if this really *wasn't* his familiar world?

He didn't know what happened to people who vanished in the storms, but he knew one thing—they never came back. In the two years since the storms began, none had ever come back.

His ex-wife, his daughter, the stenographer he'd taken out to dinner Saturday, he'd never see them again if he had been shifted into another reality. New York was still here, so the world couldn't be too different, but his job was gone, and who knew what else? Were the Mets in this world? Who was president, if anyone? What sort of a world *was* it?

Judging by the people he'd seen, not a good one.

"Well," he said, "seems to me a little drive downtown to look at the sights should settle the matter. If my office is still there at Police Plaza, it's my world, right?"

"Police Plaza?"

Mitsopoulas nodded. "Downtown," he said.

"Not in this world," Fitzwater said.

"You mean not in *your* world," Mitsopoulas replied.

"This *is* my world," Fitzwater snapped.

"Prove it," Mitsopoulas snapped back.

"This is a trick," Fitzwater said. "You're planning to escape somehow, once you're outside the building."

"Why should I escape?" Mitsopoulas retorted. "You don't mean me any harm, do you?"

"Of course not," Fitzwater replied reflexively. He stared at Mitsopoulas for a long moment.

It was Mitsopoulas who broke the silence.

"Listen," he said, "to hell with the bullshit. You kill your dump survivors, don't you? So you can keep up the pretense that it's all illusion and there's nothing seriously wrong?"

Fitzwater drew his gun and pointed it between Mitsopoulas's eyes. Mitsopoulas held up a hand.

"Wait a minute," he said, hoping his voice wouldn't crack, "just wait a minute, okay? Before you go shooting *anybody*, just wait a minute. Think it through. You don't want to kill me, not yet; my men out there are armed and know how to take care of themselves. They aren't going to listen to you unless I tell them to. And however sure you are which world we're in, what harm would it do to check? Call someone, will you? Just use the phone or the radio and call someone, see which world we're in. If it's yours . . ." Mitsopoulas heard his voice shake; he took a deep breath and continued, "If it's yours, I'll call my men in, we'll surrender, on condition you let us live. Exile us, send us to Australia or somewhere, anything you like, we'll keep our mouths shut, you don't need to

kill us. I swear you don't. But first, just check it out, okay?
Use the phone."

"The phones are out," Fitzwater snapped. "They've been
out all morning. The whole building—offices, barracks, officers' quarters, all of it. We figure a main must have broken."

Hope leaped in Mitsopoulas's chest.

The phones were out. And they *lived* here, in a barracks—
they hadn't commuted.

"Your phones are out—don't you see?" he said. "They've
been out since five, right?"

Fitzwater lowered the gun slightly. His jaw tightened.

"What about the radio?" Mitsopoulas asked.

"We don't use radio," Fitzwater said.

Mitsopoulas groped for a moment for the next idea and
said, "Hey, but *we* do! Listen, let me talk to my men—let me
tell them to call for backup. Don't you see? If anyone re-
sponds, then it's *our* world out there!"

Fitzwater brought the gun back to his shoulder. "And if no
one comes?"

"Then we'll surrender. If you'll guarantee our safety."

He almost hadn't bothered adding the condition; he
doubted that Fitzwater's promises would be worth anything.
If this was truly Fitzwater's world, then barring a miracle, he
and his men were as good as dead.

He prayed for a miracle as Fitzwater considered.

"All right," the commandant said at last. "Come on."

He led the way out of the room and down the dingy hallway; two of his men fell in behind, keeping their guns ready,
keeping a close eye on the prisoner—for there was no longer
any pretense that Mitsopoulas was anything but a prisoner.

At the door, Fitzwater stepped to one side and said, "Talk
to them—but if you take one step out the door, my men will
shoot."

Mitsopoulas nodded.

"Hey, Orlando!" he shouted, hands cupped around his
mouth, "call for backup! Lots of backup!"

He saw Orlando's head bob up, and a hand wave in acknowledgment. He thought he heard the crackle of the van's
radio.

And then there was nothing to do but wait.

He stood in the doorway, two drawn pistols at his back, and
waited.

"Hey," he asked after a minute, "take a look around—does

this look like your New York? You got Saint Agnes right there?"

"Of course we do," Fitzwater snarled, without bothering to look.

It wasn't until a few seconds later, when the first siren sounded coming up Third Avenue, that Fitzwater looked.

Another siren shrieked, this one somewhere to the west, probably coming across on Forty-second Street. Fitzwater stared.

The first of the familiar blue-and-white sedans pulled up and then a second and a third, lights flashing, and Mitsopoulas had to fight down an urge to giggle as Fitzwater's jaw sagged.

This was going to be rough, dealing with these people. They weren't harmless innocents, like the camp inmates or the magicians. They weren't criminals, like the camp guards who were up on charges of assault, battery, kidnapping, and a hundred other wrongs. They were dangerous—but they weren't technically criminals.

God, Mitsopoulas thought, the things the reality storms dumped!

"Don't worry," he said, "we don't kill anyone. Nobody here ever pretended the storms weren't real, and we're all a bunch of goddamn humanitarians compared to you guys. We're soft; you'll do fine, all of you."

Fitzwater made a strangled noise as car after car discharged New York cops with guns drawn.

"I'd suggest," Mitsopoulas said loudly, "that you put your guns down and come out with your hands up."

It took a long, long moment, but at last the three men in black did that, and Gregory Mitsopoulas walked down the three low steps onto the familiar pavement of his very own New York.

It felt good to be home.

Of course, he had never really left. It had been his own world all along.

"My world," he said to himself, savoring it. "My world."

Then he added, with a shudder, "This time."

ONE-SHOT

The FBI man turned the tiny calculator over in his hands, still marveling, as the prisoner said, "It took me this long to get up my nerve—sixteen months, is it? I'd meant to confess right away, but I couldn't, I was scared. But it's been eating at me. I had to show someone. I had to tell someone the truth."

The agent put the calculator down on the old green blotter, next to the yellowed newspaper clipping, and looked up. "All right," he said, "maybe you did come here from some alternate future. Maybe it's all true, crazy as it sounds. But it's still murder."

"I know," the prisoner said miserably, "but I *had* to. I couldn't let President Kennedy die."

The FBI man nodded. He glanced at the calculator and tapped the clipping with a finger. "Yeah," he said, "I can see that. The lab says this paper and ink are really, genuinely thirty or forty years old, not just artificially aged, but the date's just last year—so if this *is* a hoax, you've been setting it up for a long, long time." He read the headline.

JFK SHOT.

He shook his head.

"Damn," he said. "I don't know if we should give you the chair or a medal. I mean, so far, it's been hushed up, everyone's bought the suicide story, but sooner or later it's bound to leak, you know?"

The prisoner nodded miserably.

The FBI man stared at the clipping. "President Kennedy shot," he said. "And you prevented it. Still, did you have to *kill*? Couldn't you have stopped it any other way?"

The prisoner shrugged. "I had to be *sure*," he said. "When

77

you're dealing with someone that unbalanced, stopping one attempt might not be enough."

The agent shut his eyes and rubbed at his forehead, trying to stall off another headache.

"Excuse me . . ." the prisoner said.

The agent opened his eyes. "What?"

"I was just wondering . . . Has anyone talked to President Kennedy about it?"

The agent shook his head. "No. I've passed the word up to headquarters, and they're considering it. Maybe when the president gets back from Dallas next week." He grimaced. "He'll probably want you shot—they say he had a real thing for Marilyn."

TRUTH, JUSTICE,
AND THE AMERICAN WAY

"*Damn!*" *the Secretary of State said.*

His aide looked up, startled by the outburst. "What's the matter?" he asked.

"It's this man Rosenman," the Secretary said, flinging down the telegram. "The Japanese say they won't recognize him as our ambassador."

The aide blinked at him in astonishment. "Can they *do* that?"

"Well, why the hell not?" his superior said, swiveling his chair about so he could glare out the window more easily. The cherry trees were in full bloom on the Mall, but he couldn't see them from this particular window, which added to his frustration. "What are we going to do about it, go to war again? We did that already, nineteen years ago, and it doesn't seem to have done us much good, does it?"

"Maybe we should have done it more thoroughly the first time," the aide suggested. "I mean, if they keep making trouble like this, we may wind up fighting them again eventually."

"Oh, we might someday," the Secretary agreed, "but not today. And not over this Jew, Rosenman. No one's crazy enough to go to war over the Jews."

"Why should the Japanese even care?" the aide asked. "I mean, Japan isn't a Christian nation."

"Oh, they've been listening to the damn Germans again," the Secretary growled. "Or the British, going on about Zionism as a threat to world peace. World peace, ha! It's a threat to their damn Empire, that's what it's a threat to. They just want to make sure there's nobody in Palestine who knows how to point a gun."

He lapsed into moody silence. The aide picked up the telegram; it was signed by Undersecretary Sumner Welles and dated April 4, 1953.

"Damn!" the Secretary said again, under his breath.

"It's all Stimson's fault," the Secretary told the President. "If he hadn't gone so easy on the Japanese back in '37, they wouldn't dare do this. They took it as a sign of weakness."

The President sighed. "I suppose you think he should have gone ahead with the invasion of the Home Islands and dragged the war out another year or two and lost another million men? Fine shape we'd be in now if he'd done that. Look, you know as well as I do that Henry Stimson only started the war in '34 to get the country out of the Depression, since Hoover's programs weren't doing the job. He wasn't looking to stamp the Japanese into the ground."

The Secretary leaned back in his chair. "And I suppose that it didn't matter that the Japs were killing our people in China and walked out of the peace conference and repudiated the naval treaties?"

"Not much," the President replied. "If they really were."

"Oh, they were, sir—no doubt about it."

"Well, I don't think anybody here at home really cared—or at least they wouldn't have if Stimson hadn't stirred them up. Old Bert Hoover didn't think any of that was enough to start a war, did he?"

"No, sir, but Herbert Hoover was a Quaker pacifist. He wouldn't have started a war until the Japs were bombing Hawaii. If then."

"Then I guess it's a good thing that Stimson and the Congress hated him enough by then to declare war anyway, isn't it?"

The Secretary shifted uneasily in his chair. "I don't think Stimson hated Hoover. He was just trying to distract everyone."

"Or get himself elected president in '36," the President suggested sourly.

"How could he know Egg Curtis was going to drop dead a month before the primaries started and leave Hoover without a veep?"

The President almost sneered. "You think anyone would have voted for Curtis?" he asked. "You may know foreign affairs, but you don't know shit about getting elected—and I do, Mr. Secretary, I do. I may not know what's happening in every third-rate country in the Balkans or wherever the hell you've been sending people, but I know the American people. Roosevelt would have won easily against Curtis. Hell, Hoover only beat Roosevelt by two electoral votes in '32 as it was, even with Al Smith's third party messing up the Democrats, and Stimson didn't exactly get a landslide in '36."

"Nobody wants to change parties in the middle of a war, though," the Secretary ventured.

"Ha!" the President replied.

The secretary thought he saw a long lecture on domestic politics approaching, and he spoke quickly to head it off. "We're getting off the subject, sir," he said. "About this man Rosenman. The Japanese won't take him as our ambassador. So do we just apologize to him and tell him to go home?"

"No, damn it, we don't. He's earned a post somewhere—the man's brilliant, and he's been a good party man for years. He worked on all three of Roosevelt's campaigns, as well as both of mine, and damn it, we owe him a post." The President sat back in his chair, thinking. Then he leaned forward and said, "Look, you find him a place. It's your baby—do it."

"Yes, sir," the Secretary said, unhappily.

His wife gave a puzzled little frown. "I don't understand," she said. "What's the problem?"

"The problem is," the Secretary said, "that there's nowhere to send him."

"Oh, that's silly. There must be. Where are there vacancies?"

"Nowhere," the Secretary said, slumping into the chair by the radio. "We'll have to recall someone if we want to make Rosenman a full ambassador. Or more likely we'll just send him along as plenipotentiary somewhere and let him make up the job to suit himself. I don't want to recall anyone, though."

"Well, then, just make him a what-do-you-call-it."

"Okay, fine, maybe that'll do—but where do we send him?"

"*I* don't know," his wife said, throwing up her hands. "You're the Secretary of State."

The Secretary grimaced. "Well," he said, "I don't know, either. That's the problem."

"Well," his wife suggested, "his people came from Germany, didn't they? Can't you send him to Germany?"

"Oh, God, no! Of course not!"

His wife glared. "Why not?" she demanded. "They shot that idiot Hitler back in '38, and those generals are still running things?"

"Yes, of course they did—but the Nazis are still the biggest single party, and the generals don't want any trouble with them. Besides, the Nuremberg Laws are still on the books. I wouldn't dare send a Jew to Germany under *any* circumstances—not even for a day, let alone a regular posting."

His wife considered. "Pardon a stupid question," she said, "but if the Nazis are still the biggest party in Germany, then what on Earth did the Germans shoot Hitler for?"

"For invading Czecho-Slovakia," the Secretary explained. "Nobody in Germany except that one lunatic wanted a war—once Chamberlain and Daladier stood up to Hitler's threats, the generals knew the Czechs and the French and the British would beat the pants off 'em, even assuming the Soviets didn't get into it. I think France and Britain were almost looking for an excuse to fight—we'd made 'em look bad by whipping Japan and getting China back on its feet while they all just stood on the sidelines watching, and they'd probably have loved a chance to whip Germany." He paused. "But we might have had a second World War if they hadn't. Even so, the Nazis are still popular—while they were in power they got the economy going, pulled off the Anschluss with Austria, all the rest of it. The generals don't want any trouble with them. The Nazi leader's Hermann Goering now—a lot brighter than Hitler ever was, even if he's not half the orator."

"And they still don't like Jews?"

"Anti-Semitism is basic to their whole philosophy."

"And the Czechs and the French didn't do anything about it in '38?"

"No. Why should they?" asked the Secretary. "Roosevelt tried to make something of that in the 1940 campaign, actually—said it was our duty to fight the spread of Fascism, or some such thing—but nobody paid much attention. Didn't help him any at the polls, either. We'd had our war with Japan and that was enough; nobody was about to go to war over the Jews!"

His wife thought for a moment, her fingers busy with her crocheting, then asked, "I suppose the other Fascist countries are all out, too?"

The Secretary hesitated.

"Well," he said, "I don't think any of the rest are as bad as Germany, but in general, yeah. Which eliminates Italy and Spain and Hungary and Rumania and Portugal in Europe, and Argentina, Paraguay, and Brazil in South America."

She nodded. "And I guess I know why you don't want to send him to Russia or Poland or Lithuania or Latvia."

"It's not so much that he'd be in trouble himself, really," said the secretary, "but we don't want him making a fuss, protesting the pogroms. Wouldn't do any good, and it would just stir up a lot of ill feeling."

"If the Communists had stayed in power in Russia maybe things would be better—weren't a lot of them Jewish?"

"I don't really know," the Secretary admitted. "Hitler used to talk a lot about the Jewish-Communist conspiracy, but I don't know if there was anything in it. Doesn't seem as if anybody knows much of anything about what Communism was really about, not since they kicked Stalin out. No one but the Russians ever tried it—though there were rumors that Roosevelt was a Communist. Maybe we'd have found out if he'd gotten elected."

"Maybe that's why he was so anti-Fascist, if there really *was* some connection between Communists and Jews, and he was a Communist."

"Maybe—but he sure wasn't Jewish."

His wife nodded, and asked, "What about Estonia, or somewhere in Scandinavia? Nobody seems to mind Jews much there."

"They might do," her husband admitted. "But the idea is to *reward* Rosenman, not freeze his ass off."

"Scandinavia's supposed to be very pleasant . . ." she began.

"I don't think so," he said, cutting her off. "But maybe, if we can't find anything else."

"What about England, then? They even speak the same language."

"Well, sort of, they do," the Secretary admitted. "But they've got the whole anti-Zionist thing. They're obsessive about Jewish plots against their empire in the Near East."

"But Rosenman's not a Zionist, is he?"

The Secretary shrugged. "Not that I know of," he said, "but I don't think it matters. He's definitely a Jew."

"Maybe France?"

The Secretary sighed. "I don't know," he said. "It might be all right. But they're still talking about the Dreyfus affair, after all this time." He hesitated. "I wonder if we really need to send him overseas at all, though? Maybe we can find him something in another department." He sighed. "At least it would be out of *my* hands, then!"

"Sir," he asked, "couldn't you find him something here in the States? It'd be a lot easier."

The President swiveled his chair around to stare at the Secretary.

"Come on," he said at last, his voice cold, "you know better than that!"

"I didn't mean here in the White House, sir!" the Secretary said hurriedly. "I was thinking of a job with Interior, maybe, out west somewhere . . ."

"Don't be ridiculous," the President snapped. "A Jew out west?"

"I guess not," the Secretary admitted.

"If there were some way to keep him in New York, I suppose that would be workable," the President said, "but I don't have anything for him to do there. And for that matter, I'm not sure I want him where he's got so many of his own kind around to stir up."

"No, sir," the Secretary agreed, "I suppose not."

"And I sure don't want him here in Washington, where he might take it into his mind to come around every so often."

"Would it really be . . ."

"It would be a bad precedent, is what it would be," the President interrupted. "Rosenman's all right; I've talked to him now and then—but I don't want any of his people getting the idea they belong here."

"Yes, sir."

For a moment, both men were silent. Then the President spoke. "You can't find him anything?"

"Not very easily, sir."

"Well, neither can I," the President said. "Why do you think I waited this long before trying to post him to Japan? You need to pay more attention to domestic affairs, instead of spending all your time worrying about Europe and Asia. I did try to find him something stateside." He sighed. "I do have one possibility, but I don't like it. We could post him to the Philippines, on the governor's staff."

"That sounds fine, sir," the Secretary said, puzzled. "What's wrong with it?"

"Oh, nothing really—it's just that the governor there's a good man, and I hate to do this to him. But I guess the rest of the world's got plenty of Jews without taking any of ours."

"Sure," the Secretary said. "And with all this fuss down South the last year or two, you can tell the governor to look on the bright side—at least we aren't sending him a nigger."

REAL TIME

Someone was tampering with time again; I could feel it, in my head and in my gut, that sick, queasy sensation of unreality.

I put my head down and gulped air, waiting for the discomfort to pass, but it only got worse.

This was a bad one. Someone was tampering with something serious. This wasn't just someone reading tomorrow's papers and playing the stock market; this was *serious*. Someone was trying to change history.

I couldn't allow that. Not only might his tampering interfere with my own past, change my whole life, possibly even wipe me out of existence, but I'd be shirking my job. I couldn't do that.

Not that anyone would know. They must think I'm dead. I haven't been contacted in years now, not since I was stranded in this century. They must think I was lost when my machine and my partner vanished in the flux.

But I'm not dead, and I had a job to do. With help from headquarters or without, with a partner or without, even with my machine or without, I had a job to do, a reality to preserve, a whole world to safeguard. I knew my duty. I *know* my duty. The past can't take tampering.

They might send someone else, but they might not. The tampering might have already changed things too much. They might not spot it in time. Or they might simply not have the manpower. Time travel lets you use your manpower efficiently, with 100 percent efficiency, putting it anywhere you need it instantly, but that's not enough when you have all of the past to guard, everything from the dawn of time to the present—not *this* present, the *real* present—you'd need a million men to guard it all, and they've always had trouble recruiting. The temptations are too great. The dangers are too great. Look at me, stuck here in the past, for the dangers— and as for the temptations, look at what I have to do. People trying to change everything, trying to benefit themselves at the cost of reality itself—they need men they can *trust*, men like me, and there can never be enough of us.

I sat up straight again, and I looked at the mirror behind the bar, and I knew what I had to do. I had to stop the tampering. Just as I had stopped it before, three—no, four—four times now.

They might send someone else, but they might not, and I couldn't take that chance.

I had to find the tamperer myself and deal with him. If I couldn't find him directly, if he wasn't in this time period but later, then I might need to tamper with time myself, to change *his* past without hurting *mine*.

That's tricky, but I've done it.

I slid off the stool and stood up, gulped the rest of my drink, and laid a bill on the bar—five dollars in the currency of the day. I shrugged, straightening my coat, and I stepped out into the cool of a summer night.

Insects sang somewhere, strange insects extinct before I was born, and the streetlights pooled pale gray across the black sidewalks. I turned my head slowly, feeling the flux, feeling the shape of the time-stream, of my reality.

Downtown was firm, solid, still rooted in the past and the present and secure in the future. Facing in the opposite direction, I felt my gut twist. I crossed the empty street to my car.

I drove out the avenues, ignoring the highways. I can't feel as well on the highways; they're too far out of the city's life-flow.

I went north, then east, and the nausea gripped me tighter with every block. It became a gnawing pain in my belly as the world shimmered and shifted around me, an unstable reality. I stopped the car by the side of the street and forced the pain down, forced my perception of the world to steady itself.

When I was ready to go on, I leaned over and checked in the glove compartment. No gloves—the name was already an anachronism even in this time period. But my gun was there. Not my service weapon; that's an anachronism, too advanced. I don't dare use it. The knowledge of its existence could be dangerous. No, I had bought a gun here, in this era.

I pulled it out and put it in my coat pocket. The weight of it, that hard metal tugging at my side, felt oddly comforting.

I had a knife, too. I was dealing with primitives, with savages, not with civilized people. These final decades of the twentieth century, with their brushfire wars and nuclear-arms races, were a jungle, even in the great cities of North America. I had a knife, a good one, with a six-inch blade I had sharpened myself.

Armed, I drove on, and two blocks later I had to leave the avenue, and turn onto the quiet side-streets, tree-lined and peaceful.

Somewhere, in that peace, someone was working to destroy my home, my life, my *self*.

I turned again and felt the queasiness and pain leap within me, and I knew I was very close.

I stopped the car and got out, the gun in my pocket and my hand on the gun, my other hand holding the knife.

One house had a light in the window; the homes on either side were dark. I scanned, and I knew that that light was it, the center of the unreality—maybe not the tamperer himself, but something, a focus for the disturbance of the flow of history.

Perhaps it was an ancestor of the tamperer; I had encountered that before.

I walked up the front path and rang the bell.

I braced myself, the knife in one hand, the gun in the other.

The porch light came on, and the door started to open. I threw myself against it.

It burst in, and I went through it, and I was standing in a hallway. A man in his forties was staring at me, holding his wrist where the door had slammed into it as it pulled out of his grip. There had been no chainbolt; my violence had, perhaps, been more than was necessary.

I couldn't take risks, though. I pointed the gun at his face and squeezed the trigger.

The thing made a report like the end of the world, and the man fell, blood and tissue sprayed across the wall behind him.

A woman screamed from a nearby doorway, and I pointed the gun at her, unsure.

The pain was still there. It came from the woman. I pulled the trigger again.

She fell, blood red on her blouse, and I looked down at her as the pain faded, as stability returned.

I was *real* again.

If the man were her husband, perhaps she was destined to remarry, or to be unfaithful—*she* would have been the tamperer's ancestor, but *he* might not have been. The twisting of time had stopped only when the woman fell.

I regretted shooting him, then, but I had had no choice. Any delay might have been fatal. The life of an individual is precious, but not as precious as history itself.

A twinge ran through my stomach; perhaps only an aftereffect, but I had to be certain. I knelt and went quickly to work with my knife.

When I was done, there could be no doubt that the two were dead and that neither could ever have children.

Finished, I turned and fled, before the fumbling police of this era could interfere.

I knew the papers would report it the next day as the work of a lunatic, of a deranged thief who panicked before he could take anything, or of someone killing for perverted pleasure. I didn't worry about that.

I had saved history again.

I wish there were another way, though.

Sometimes I have nightmares about what I do, sometimes I dream that I've made a mistake, killed the wrong person, that I stranded myself here. What if it wasn't a mechanical failure that sent the machine into flux; what if I changed my own past and did that to myself?

I have those nightmares sometimes.

Worse, though, the very worst nightmares, are the ones where I dream that I never changed the past at all, that I never lived in any time but this one, that I grew up here, alone, through an unhappy childhood and a miserable adolescence and a sorry adulthood—that I never traveled in time, that it's all in my mind, that I killed those people for nothing.

That's the worst of all, and I wake up from that one sweating, ready to scream.

Thank God it's not true.

NEW WORLDS

*Dead leaves had accumulated against the fence at the north-*ern boundary of the Myers Starport. Sheltered by the overhanging trees, they had lain undisturbed through the changing seasons.

Now, suddenly, they whirled up from the tarmac and were flung aside. A squirrel that had long since learned to ignore the sound and vibration of the great ships that landed a hundred meters away fled in terror from this strange new phenomenon, scampering back down its tree, safely outside the fence.

Across the field the *Arthur H. Rostron* continued loading, her crew and the port workers oblivious to the tiny disturbance.

Nobody saw the cat-sized, turtle-shaped machine, its metal shell a pebbled matte black, that appeared out of nowhere. A camera lens formed its single eye, a foam-covered microphone projected where a nose should have been, and its tail was a thin black cable that ended in a curiously undefined way. The cable's length varied as the device moved, and an observer would have found it impossible to focus on just where it stopped. Half a dozen stubby antennae protruded from various places, as if sniffing the air.

The thing had no legs, but instead crawled forward on a single black plastic caterpillar tread, whirring softly to itself.

The lens swiveled, scanning across the asphalt and concrete, along the kilometers of chain-link fence and the drifts of brown leaves, along the line of sycamores beyond the fence, past the distant, blocky buildings. It stopped when pointed at the *Arthur H. Rostron* and the surrounding service complex, and adjusted the focus.

Machinery buzzed quietly.

Then the turtle turned and retreated, vanishing back into the air, pulling its tail-cable after it.

For a moment, nothing more happened. The squirrel leaped back up onto a fence pole and looked about warily; seeing nothing out of the ordinary, it dropped to the pavement again.

A white-booted foot appeared from the air behind it, and the squirrel fled again, for good this time.

The foot was followed by a leg and a body, both wrapped in baggy white material. Head and hands emerged, and the figure of a man stood on the tarmac, clad in a bulky protective suit and helmet, with a large pack slung on his back, tools and weapons held in place elsewhere with canvas loops and strips of Velcro. A small microphone was clipped to the base of his helmet, its cord trailing down behind his back and then stopping abruptly in midair.

He scanned the area, taking in the fence, the overhanging trees, the distant buildings, the *Arthur H. Rostron* and its attendants. He tapped at the microphone.

"Sugarman to Base," he said, his eyes fixed on the starship. "I'm through, and everything looks okay, just the way the probe showed. Definitely looks like an airport. Some people working, but they haven't noticed me yet. The airplane, or airship, or whatever it is . . . Well, first, I only see one on the whole field, and it's nothing like anything I've seen fly—I think we've got some new technology here. Could be big bucks." He glanced around, assuring himself that he had missed nothing important, and then added, "Lee, McDowell, Seibert, come on through, any time you're ready."

He took two paces forward, then turned to watch as three more figures appeared from the air, all clad in the bulky protective suits and broad-visored helmets.

As they looked about themselves with cautious interest, the first arrival spoke into the microphone again.

"Looks as if we all made it. I'll leave Seibert here with the mike while we scout around a little."

He unclipped the microphone and handed it to the shortest of the group, who clipped it to her own helmet. Sugarman then turned to another and asked, "How's the air?"

The other shrugged. "All the usual caveats, Mr. Sugarman. We're working from a small sample, we can't spot every virus that's out there, even the familiar ones could be mutated into something that'll kill us instantly—you know the drill.

There could be anything out there, and we wouldn't necessarily have found it yet. What we *have* found is plain old ordinary air, a bit high in ozone and carbon monoxide compared to what we might like, but no worse than you'd get any number of places back home." He held up a small wire cage, displaying the white mouse inside; the little animal looked no more skittish than any mouse might look when thus exposed. "Herman's breathing just fine, hasn't keeled over, lost his lunch, or even coughed," the man said. "It's your call."

Sugarman nodded. He scanned the area again.

One of the workmen seemed to be looking their way, Sugarman thought.

There were signs on the fence, probably warnings of some sort, but he couldn't read them from this side; they faced out. Nobody was carrying guns, so far as he could see. The fence wasn't electrified, and the single strand of barbed wire at the top didn't look very serious. The trees hadn't been cut back. This might be someplace people weren't supposed to be, but it wasn't any sort of high-security installation.

One had to be ready for absolutely anything, but one also had to know when to take risks and which risks to take. This world appeared safe enough and not too different from his own. Looking like invaders from Mars was probably not good policy, under the circumstances; it would draw attention.

"What the hell," he said, unzipping the neck-seal of his helmet. "Let's let 'em know we're human and not a bunch of bug-eyed monsters."

By the time he got the helmet off completely, the workman who had first spotted the strangers was pointing and shouting, and others were paying attention as well.

Sugarman took a deep breath; the air seemed just fine. He was almost sorry this particular version of Earth was inhabited.

Those people over there were buzzing about like angry hornets, he thought. Time, he judged, to make some provision for backup.

He turned and said, "Seibert, when I give the word, step back through the gate and wait in the air lock for ten minutes—by your watch, no rough estimates. Then step back through here and stay by the gate until you hear from us." That would split the party, since he was sure that he and the others would not still be here in ten minutes, but it would give them a contact; in an emergency they could radio Seibert, and she could phone through the gate.

Was there anything else?

"Oh, yeah," he added, as an afterthought, "and take Herman back; we're done with him."

Seibert nodded and accepted the caged mouse from McDowell. She hung it from a clip on her belt, then glanced back along the microphone cord to see where the opening was.

"Lee, McDowell, you'll stay with me," Sugarman ordered. "And all of you, keep radio silence until *I* tell you otherwise, even if we get separated. There's no privacy on radio, remember that."

The others all nodded in acknowledgment. Sugarman turned back to face the *Arthur H. Rostron*, and the others followed his gaze.

A small, wheeled vehicle was approaching across the broad expanse of pavement. It was open, with a flat windshield— Sugarman might have called it a jeep in his world, but he knew not to assume that similar appearances meant anything here.

Two men were riding in it, one driving, the other holding something that looked distinctly like a weapon.

"Seibert," Sugarman said without looking back, "Now. Tell 'em what's happening."

Seibert stepped back and vanished.

Sugarman and the others stood, waiting. Lee and McDowell had kept their helmets on, so their expressions didn't matter, but Sugarman pasted a smile on his own face and held it as the vehicle came to a stop, about three meters away.

Always make a friendly first impression, Sugarman reminded himself—an important rule in these preliminary contacts. In most situations, a smile on his face could make up for any number of weapons on his belt.

The driver sat in the vehicle, leaning forward over the steering wheel, and Sugarman noticed a gun—or something very like one—held loosely in one hand.

The passenger stood on a structure that wasn't quite a running board, holding a larger and more obvious gun, and called out angrily, "All right, this is private property. Who the hell are you people supposed to be, and what are you doing inside the fence?"

Sugarman smiled and held a hand up in a friendly wave, pleased that the natives spoke recognizable English. "Hi," he said. "I'm Neil Sugarman and I'm a representative of the New Worlds Corporation."

"Never heard of it," the passenger snapped. "And I'd suggest you three put up your hands while we talk and keep them well away from those belts."

Sugarman glanced back at McDowell and Lee and nodded, then put his own hands atop his head. Behind him, the others followed suit.

"Now then," the standing native said, a bit less belligerently, "what are you people doing here?"

"Exploring, I guess you'd say," Sugarman replied. "Just where are we, anyway?"

"You don't know?" the man asked, glaring suspiciously.

Sugarman shook his head, still smiling.

"You're on the outer north blast apron of the Myers Starport."

Sugarman's smile slipped somewhat. "Starport?" he asked.

That couldn't mean what it seemed to. Maybe the language was slightly different here after all, or the name was figurative.

"Starport," the man repeated. "That's the *Arthur H. Rostron* over there, outbound for Epsilon Eridani IV. She's taking off at 1600, whether you're still here or not, and if you *are* here, and you get fried, United Starways isn't responsible, because you're all trespassing."

"Well, now," Sugarman said, trying to gather his wits. The threat of frying didn't worry him, since the sycamores just beyond the fence didn't look scorched, but he was still trying to consider all the ramifications of a ship bound for Epsilon Eridani.

Definitely new technology here, he thought.

"We aren't trying to cause any trouble," he said, "but I think we need to talk to someone in charge. I think we've got ourselves some important business possibilities to discuss."

Any place where an installation like this was private property, and people spoke of corporations not being responsible for damages, was clearly set up along economic lines similar to Sugarman's home reality, and that meant they could do business.

"Business?" The passenger looked puzzled; the driver sat up slightly, evincing renewed interest.

"Yes, business," Sugarman repeated. "I think United . . . United Starways, was it?" There it was again—these people had starships. But how could they? A flight would take decades; as a government project that might be feasible, but how could anyone make a profit?

It had to be something entirely new and potentially valuable to New Worlds. Sugarman tried not to think about how big a bonus he might get for this one.

"Yes," he said, "I think United Starways may be very interested in learning more about the New Worlds Corporation." Not that they would learn all that much, of course—just enough to arrange a trade deal. New Worlds would trade any information they had or could get—except, of course, for their own company secrets, which were what everybody most wanted.

The passenger glared silently for a moment, then said, "You're trying to sell something? A little corporate espionage, or something like that? Maybe the location of a promising planet?"

Now, even with starships going out, how could anyone know the location of a promising planet? That added to Sugarman's confusion, but he mentally shelved the question for the moment. There was no point in thinking about it before he had any hard data. He replied, "I'm not about to talk business out here on a whaddayacallit, blast apron, with my hands on my head."

He stared at the passenger, still smiling.

The standing native chewed his lip, then called, "All right, into the car."

Sugarman led the way.

The starport's spokesman carefully collected all the more obvious weapons—knives, guns, nunchaku—before herding the strangers into the back of the "jeep."

The vehicle was designed to hold six people in all, but the bulky protective suits and backpacks more than made up for the fact that only five were aboard, and the three explorers were uncomfortably crowded during the short drive to the starport offices. Lee used the time to take off her helmet, since Sugarman had as yet shown no ill effects from his exposure to the local environment. McDowell was more conservative and kept his own helmet on until ordered to remove it by a blue-clad security guard, at the building entrance where they disembarked.

As they clambered from the vehicle and were ushered inside, with their helmets in their hands, Sugarman peered back for as long as he could at the looming silver form of the *Arthur H. Rostron.*

A starship, was it? How had these people made such a thing economically practical, when the stars were years, or decades, apart? Was the thing designed for multigenerational voyages?

After some discussion among the security staff, the three explorers were required not only to leave behind their helmets and their gear, but to strip off their protective suits in front of what appeared to be video cameras. This was to be done before they entered the port manager's office.

They obliged—but even so, after further delays, Lee and McDowell were ordered to wait in an anteroom while Sugarman entered the innermost sanctum alone.

At the door, a security guard told Sugarman to wait for a moment while he was announced. Sugarman stood, waiting politely, and looked about.

The antechamber was utilitarian and uninteresting, except for something sitting in the corner that Sugarman couldn't identify. At first, despite the absence of a pot and the bluish color, he thought it was a plant, but when he saw it move slightly he guessed it was a machine, and finally he decided it was some sort of modernist sculpture.

He certainly couldn't think of anything else it could be, given its location. It had to be the local version of office art.

Interesting that that sort of highly abstract art existed here, he thought, as the guard emerged and beckoned him through the inner door. There might be trade possibilities in that as well as in new technologies.

Once the visitor was safely inside the inner office, the guard departed, and Sugarman found himself facing a heavy-set man seated behind a desk. The nameplate on the desk read STEPHEN APPERSON.

"Hi, Mr. Apperson," Sugarman said, holding out a hand and hoping that he wasn't making a fool of himself by the standards of this particular society.

Apperson glared and did not take the hand; Sugarman immediately concluded that this culture was more restrained than his own about handshaking, probably about physical contact of any sort. He quickly tucked the hand into a pocket of his jumpsuit.

"Just what the hell are you people supposed to be?" Apperson demanded. "What's with the suits? And who are you, anyway? Make it quick!"

Sugarman smiled. His host was speaking, anyway, and not using any fancy ritual greetings. Maybe the locals weren't all that friendly, but that was no big problem. They hadn't tried to kill him yet, which was something.

"Fair enough," he said. "I'm Neil Sugarman and I'm a scout working for the New Worlds Corporation—and Mr. Apperson, I'm not from your world at all."

Apperson glared, then pulled open the lap drawer of his desk, took out a roll of candy, and threw a mint into his mouth.

He did not offer Sugarman one. Instead, he said, "Sit down," and pointed to a chair against the far wall.

The mint crunched.

Sugarman pulled the chair over and sat down. For a moment the two men sat silently, studying each other. Sugarman maintained a facade of polite calm, while Apperson made no attempt to hide his annoyance.

Sugarman wondered if the candy was just that, or if it were an antacid, or a drug of some sort. If it was supposed to cheer the port manager up, it didn't appear to be working.

It was Apperson who finally spoke.

"All right," he said, "what's going on? You claiming to be an alien? We don't usually get nuts in groups unless they're protesting something, and they don't usually have all the fancy equipment my people said you had, so I figure it's a scam, and I might as well hear your pitch. What's the story? You supposed to be from Lambda Aurigae or something?"

Sugarman hesitated; some of the slang was unfamiliar, and Apperson's accent—one not quite like anything Sugarman had heard before—didn't help.

He got the gist of it, though.

"No," he said, "I'm from Earth. But not *your* Earth. I don't know if your civilization has the concepts I need to explain this, but let me try: Have you ever heard of parallel worlds?"

Apperson chewed on his mint some more before answering.

"You supposed to be from a world where the Nazis won World War II or something?" he asked at last.

Sugarman smiled a bit more genuinely than usual at this proof that the concept *was* known here.

"Nope," he said. "In fact, the Nazis never came to power at all, where I come from. Adolf Hitler—was that the name?" He looked questioningly at the port official.

Apperson nodded.

"Well," Sugarman continued, "he was killed by a thrown beer bottle in 1923, where I came from. But we've found worlds where he and the Nazis *did* win—and we stayed out of them. Nasty places. Not worth the risk, not when there are a million others to explore."

Apperson grimaced sourly.

"Parallel worlds aren't real," he said. "They're just something sci-fi writers made up."

"*What* writers?" Sugarman asked, startled.

"Sci-fi writers—you know, science fiction."

"Oh," Sugarman said, "science fiction. We don't call them . . . whatever you said."

"Yeah, well, whatever you call them, parallel worlds are just something they made up."

"Sure—like starships," Sugarman said, grinning.

Apperson didn't reply.

After a moment, recognizing that the next move was his, Sugarman said, "Listen, I can't *prove* anything to you sitting here in your office, but in my equipment pack I've got a pocket video on Schenck's discovery of the crosstime gate and some of what New Worlds has done with it. I think you'd be interested, and short of taking you back through the gate with me and showing you everything firsthand, I can't think of any better way to convince you."

Apperson thought that over, then nodded. He touched a button on his desk and said, "Carl, bring in Mr. Sugarman's backpack, will you?"

Sugarman gave him a friendly smile; Apperson considered it, then pressed the button again and added, "And have your gun ready when you bring it in. I don't trust this guy."

Sugarman's smile turned wry.

A moment later, a security guard dumped Sugarman's pack on the desk. At Apperson's orders, he kept Sugarman closely covered.

"Get your gadget," Apperson said.

Sugarman gave the gun a good look and then pulled a black object, roughly the size and shape of a cigar box, from one of the side pockets on the pack. By the time the guard had hauled the rest of the pack back out of the office,

Sugarman had shown Apperson how to work the tape—play, fast forward, rewind, and freeze-frame—and the port manager was studying the display with interest.

Half an hour later he clicked off the power; the screen went dark, and Apperson shoved the little black box away.

"All right," he said, "I'm convinced, for now—I'm no scientist, I just handle administration here, but it looks good to me. Now what?"

"Well," Sugarman said, leaning back, "now we need to talk about whether it would be profitable for our two worlds to trade with one another. You saw on the video about some of the deals we've made—and some we didn't make, for that matter. You know more about our worlds than we know about yours, so I think it's time for you to tell me a little."

"What's to tell?" Apperson asked, with a shrug. "I can't describe the whole damn universe in fifty words or less. It looks to me as if our world is a lot like yours—but different, too. I can't tell what the differences are from a twenty-minute tape."

His words were calm, but Sugarman thought Apperson was worried about something. There was no overt sign, but Sugarman had had plenty of practice in reading people.

The tape was designed to reassure people. It emphasized the limits of the crosstime gates—how they couldn't be aimed, how no two had ever come out in the same reality, how one couldn't be reopened once it was closed. It was supposed to convince potential customers that they didn't need to worry about Sugarman's people invading them, or spying on them, or opening gates into places they had no business going.

So why was Apperson worried?

Well, the man was confronting a whole new reality—a little nervousness was understandable. Particularly if he didn't believe everything on the tape.

"True enough," Sugarman agreed. "So let me start with something simple. That ship out there, this whole field—this isn't anything I've seen before."

"The ship? You mean the *Arthur H. Rostron*?"

Sugarman nodded. "It's a starship? Bound for Epsilon Eridani, someone said? That's what, eleven light-years?"

"Something like that, yeah. It's a three-week run. She leaves in . . ." He glanced at a digital clock on his desk. "Eight minutes."

Sugarman blinked. "Three weeks?".

Apperson nodded, obviously thinking about something else.

"Twenty-one days to another *star*?" Sugarman asked, struggling against disbelief. He had encountered some amazing things in his crosstime travels, but this was a whole new order of unlikelihood.

Had he reached a universe where the very laws of physics were different?

"Yeah," Apperson said, becoming more interested. "You people don't have a stardrive?" His expression shifted, became calculating.

"Nope. No more than you have crosstime gates."

The two men stared at each other for a moment.

"Listen," Sugarman said, "how is that possible? I mean, faster-than-light travel? Didn't Einstein prove it was impossible here?"

"Sort of," Apperson said. "In normal space. But there are loopholes, ways around that. How'd this Schenck person ever come up with that crosstime stuff?"

"She's a genius," Sugarman answered, shrugging. "How do I know how she did it? But listen, are there other habitable planets out there? I mean, it's not all just rock and ice like the rest of our solar system?"

"Oh, there are plenty of good worlds and most of them aren't even inhabited. Besides, so far all the extraterrestrials we've found have been harmless enough, anyway. About these parallel worlds, though—that tape said that a gate costs millions of dollars, but once it's operating, you just *step through*? I mean, instantaneously?"

"Sure," Sugarman said. "There's no distance involved, after all. But . . . extraterrestrials? You're serious?"

"Of course I am. You didn't see Tcheeb on the way in, in the corner there? I didn't think it had had time to move anywhere. Look, about these gates—do you sell that technology?"

"No, that's a trade secret, I'm afraid, but we have plenty of other things we can sell." He glanced toward the door to the antechamber. "That thing in the corner's an *alien*? I saw it, but . . ."

The conversation was interrupted by a weird, high-pitched shriek, like nothing Sugarman had ever heard before. It rose quickly to a crescendo, then died away again.

"The ship," Apperson explained. "The *Arthur H*. She's off."

"And the stardrive . . ."

"Company secret."

The two men stared thoughtfully at each other.

"I think," Sugarman said slowly, "that I need to consult with my superiors on this. I mean, we've found new technology before, but a *stardrive* . . ."

"Yeah," Apperson agreed. "I'm just a bureaucrat, I don't make policy. And you could still be faking, somehow— maybe that videotape was all computer-synthesized or something. I need to call corporate in New York."

"Sure." Sugarman wondered whether Seibert, out on the blast apron, had actually been in any danger. He hoped not.

But then, they were all in danger, he realized, remembering the guards' guns.

"Listen," he said, "can you send me and my two people back to the gate for a few minutes? Radio doesn't transmit through it, and we've got to go back and report in person."

Apperson mulled that over while he ate another mint. He watched Sugarman's face, while Sugarman tried hard not to give anything away. He tried to ready explanations in case Apperson asked to know why all three had to go; he gave serious thought to what he should do if Apperson demanded to keep Lee or McDowell as a hostage.

Of course, neither Lee nor McDowell knew anything about transtemporal theory. They couldn't tell Apperson's people anything, no matter what happened.

"Okay," Apperson said at last, and Sugarman breathed more easily.

Fifteen minutes later, in the back of the starport jeep, Lee leaned over and whispered in Sugarman's ear, "What's going on? We're not going back, are we? We left all the gear . . ."

Sugarman held up a hand to hush her.

Reluctantly, Lee obeyed. McDowell scanned the horizon, apparently disinterested.

The *Arthur H. Rostron* was gone; the patch of concrete where it had stood seemed to shimmer oddly.

Sugarman wondered if Seibert was all right and what she had seen.

She was waiting for them at the gate, watching uncertainly, but apparently unhurt; Sugarman supposed she was trying to decide whether or not she should vanish back through again.

Well, he intended to make that quite clear.

Even before the jeep came to a complete halt, Sugarman leaped from his seat and took her by the arm. "Come on," he called to McDowell and Lee.

"Where are you going?" called their driver. "Mr. Apperson didn't . . ."

"It's all right," Sugarman said, with a reassuring wave. "We'll be right back." He shoved Seibert back along the microphone cord and through the gate before she could protest.

McDowell was next, and then Lee, and then Sugarman himself. He took a last look at the Myers Starport and saw the driver climbing from his vehicle, a worried expression on his face.

Probably thought he'd catch hell for this, Sugarman thought. He didn't need to worry, though; Sugarman was quite sure that Apperson wouldn't mind.

Then Sugarman was through the gate and back in the reassuringly familiar airlock on the home-world side. He herded his team toward the exit and slapped at the red emergency button.

"Blow the gate!" he called. "Blow it!"

He was barely through the Number Two hatch when the transtemporal field collapsed with a roar of displaced air, and the opening to the Myers Starport closed forever.

Amanda Brewer, the project director, called down to him from the observation balcony, "That's eight million bucks we just threw away on your say-so, Sugarman!"

His teammates were standing before him; Lee and Seibert were staring at him.

"Neil," Lee said, "I don't get it. It looked fine to me!"

"Yeah," Seibert said. "What was wrong with it? And did you see that ship take off? What *was* that?"

"That's all proprietary information, as of right now," Sugarman said. "And I can't tell you."

"Was it something that Apperson told you?" Lee asked.

"Sorry, I can't . . ." Sugarman began.

"So come and tell *me*, Sugarman!" Brewer called down. "I want you in my office five minutes ago."

Five minutes later Brewer and Sugarman were seated on opposite sides of Brewer's desk.

"We've blown gates before," Brewer said, "because of crazies like the Nazis, or environments like that one where they'd nuked everything with cobalt bombs. You know that.

But I think you forget sometimes, Sugarman, that we don't *like* blowing them. So why'd we shut *this* one down? What was the threat to human civilization in this world?"

"It wasn't a threat to human civilization," Sugarman admitted, "only to *us*—to New Worlds."

"Go on," Brewer said. "What kind of a threat?"

"Economic," Sugarman said. "These people had interstellar travel."

Brewer tapped a felt-tip pen against her desk. "Sugarman," she said, "you better explain that."

"They have faster-than-light travel, Ms. Brewer. Three weeks to Epsilon Eridani."

"So?"

"So which would you rather have, Ms. Brewer—a way to reach other Earths, the way we do, or a way to reach really *new* worlds? Which do you think is more valuable, a way to find all the mirror images of ourselves we could ever want, or a way to find entirely new intelligences? They've got *aliens*, Ms. Brewer—extraterrestrials. We've found new societies, but they have whole new *species*. Who needs the competition?"

Brewer frowned. "Would we have to compete?"

"You know the regulations we work under—we couldn't have kept a stardrive under wraps. We'd have to let this United Starways expand into our reality, or license the technology—and you can bet we wouldn't get the license! Sure, we'd still have the gates for ourselves—but who's going to want to pay us to use the gates if they can build starships and find whole new planets?"

Brewer considered that.

"I'm not sure," she said. "It might have been worth the risk."

"It was a judgment call," Sugarman admitted.

"You may have just thrown away the biggest new technology we've found yet," Brewer pointed out.

Sugarman shrugged. "Maybe I did," he agreed. "But hey, now that we know it can be done, maybe we can find it for ourselves and not have to share it."

Brewer nodded thoughtfully.

In his office in the Myers Starport, Stephen Apperson listened carefully as his men swore they could find no trace of the strangers or the aperture that they had vanished through.

Finally he nodded. "Good," he said. "I was afraid we might have to ... *dispose* of them, somehow, but apparently they got scared and ran. Cowards, I'd say—they've done it before. According to this," he said, with a wave at the black video box that Sugarman had left on the desk, "they can't re-open the path once it's gone. Which world they hit each time they open a gate is supposedly random, can't be controlled. So if the gate's gone, *they're* gone, for good.

"Which means we don't need to worry about competition from a system with zero travel time, instead of weeks aboard ship, and where most of the worlds found are habitable, not dead rocks."

He threw another mint into his mouth and considered the video box.

"Of course, now that we know crosstime travel is *possible* . . ." he said.

He didn't finish the sentence.

ONE NIGHT AT A LOCAL BAR

Hanging half a meter out from the top of the glossy black facade, glittering Stardust™ spelled out THE ORIGINAL OLD-TIME JOE'S BAR AND GRILL. Below, five fuzzy-edged spots of depolarized transparency chased one another across the obsidianlike surface, giving passersby tantalizing glimpses of the dim, red-lit interior. Xahh paused and peered longingly; the ruddy, warm glow was painfully reminiscent of his far-off home.

Varkles, he thought, why not? He wasn't due back aboard ship for five hours yet, and the door stood invitingly ajar just a meter away. He'd never been in a joint like this before and had heard discouraging tales of their hazards, but that friendly glow made him dismiss such stories as xenophobic fabrications.

The door swung open as he approached, admitting him freely.

The place was bigger inside than he had expected; one wall was covered with game machines, half the opposite wall with dispensers, and the remainder by a huge, old-fashioned, solid-wood bar with ornate brass and crystal trim. The rear wall was totally invisible, lost in the smoke and darkness. Close at hand there reared up a large brass serpent, polished to a ruddy gold in the crimson gloom; where its snout should have ended in a pair of slit nostrils, there were instead three upward-curving horns, each capped by a solid-brass ball, and its mouth gaped open impossibly. A sniff in its direction told Xahh's sensitive nose that it was dispensing pure oxygen, for those who chose to start the evening's intoxication with an oxygen jag.

Psychbeat music filled the room, blending subtly with the hum of conversation from the two dozen occupied tables;

Xahh relaxed as its soothing effects reached him, and crossed to the bar. Clambering awkwardly onto an empty stool, he glanced around at the other patrons while waiting for the bartender to notice him.

To one side were three unoccupied seats and the end of the bar; to the other side, a single stool separated him from an immense green lizard-creature, looking almost black in the red light, which sat contemplating a half-empty glass of some viscous purple fluid. Beyond it—or probably him, but Xahh was uncertain—were arrayed three identical young pure-human women, presumably free clones, sniffing cocaine; they struck Xahh as being slightly misshapen, with far more chest than seemed reasonable. There was a gap after them, and then, at the far end of the bar, there sat a withered old man with chocolate-brown skin, wearing a tattered and archaic pressure suit but no helmet; the bartender was talking to him, though Xahh couldn't hear a thing at that distance.

Behind him, at the tables, he saw a representative sampling of the port's groundling population: naked loading androids, human administrators in uniform, gleaming metal mobile AIs, inhumanly graceful cyborgs, and all the other specialized or purebred people that one found in Terra's greatest starport.

"What'll it be?"

The bartender's voice startled him, distracted as he was by his study of the bar's patrons; he turned back around and said, "Ah, whiskey and water, please." It was the only local drink he was familiar with; he had been too timid to do much adventuring in his brief stay on Terra, but one of the old hands among his crewmates had introduced him to this concoction that was both cool and fiery at once. It didn't have the same intoxicating effect on him that it did on humans, but a few of them would give him a slight feeling of euphoria.

He had only seen the bartender reach below the counter, without mixing anything, but here his drink was; obviously an automatic dispenser at work. Some "old-time" authenticity! He barely restrained a snort as he handed the bartender his credit card. Well, at least they had a human bartender; probably most bars had gone completely modern.

Assuming, that is, that the bartender *was* human; Xahh peered at him suspiciously but couldn't decide. There were no visible signs that the bartender was anything but pure, but they made convincing cybers and androids of even his own rather small people these days; a thing the size of that bartender, a portly two meters tall, could hold any intelligence around with room to spare.

The man, if he was a man, returned the card, and Xahh restrained another snort as he saw his new balance registered on the display; at these prices, they could sure afford a human! Tucking the card away, he sipped his drink and was pleasantly surprised; it was *good*, almost worth what it cost. Whatever else they might stint, the bar's owners didn't scrimp on their booze; no wonder it was a popular local hangout.

He sipped again and glanced up at the mirror behind the bar; his eyes met the reflected gaze of the lizard-thing, who seemed to be blearily studying Xahh's image. Xahh turned away, looking instead at a cobwebbed bottle below the mirror, as the stories of beatings and robberies at these dives came back to him.

"Hey, Shorty."

The unsteady voice came from the lizard-creature, who was now studying Xahh himself rather than his reflection.

"Yeah?" He hoped his voice didn't give away his nervousness.

"You new 'round here?"

"Passing through."

"Oh." The green creature turned back to its purple goo long enough to suck some up through a hollow tongue, then went on, "Wha's yer name?"

"Xahh."

"Kha?"

"Close enough; Xahh."

"Khah, right. Please t'meet yer. I'm called Argonath; Argo for short."

Xahh nodded politely.

"Gonna be 'round long?"

"No; my ship leaves tonight."

"Ship? Oh. Never ridden one, myself."

That caught Xahh by surprise; his crest twitched as he took another sip of his drink. He looked up at the creature. "You're from around here?"

"Yeah. From the plant down the road." Holding its drink in one three-clawed hand, it motioned vaguely with the other, then hiccupped; Xahh saw sparks scattering from the thing's mouth. He would have liked to dismiss it as an illusion, but he couldn't imagine why he might be hallucinating; had he gotten the wrong drink? Maybe whiskey had effects he hadn't noticed before.

He said, "Oh," politely, and took a gulp of whiskey and water.

"Yeah, I'm a, I'm . . ." The creature tittered drunkenly, then abruptly stopped and whined, "I'm a factory reject, tha's what I am. S'posed to be a dragon, for some ennertainmen' or somethin', but I didn' come out like they wanted."

"Too bad." Xahh was honestly touched by the creature's pitiful expression, but he was also increasingly nervous of his own safety.

"Where you from?"

Xahh shrugged. "Nowhere special."

"Ah, c'mon; you sure aren't a purebred, you must be from somewhere."

"I'm second pilot on a starship."

"Oh, so *tha's* why yer so small! Save weight!"

Xahh nodded.

"Where y'from originally?" Xahh could smell the creature's acrid breath; it was leaning toward him, and he knew he couldn't avoid answering much longer. He considered lying but knew he wouldn't; it would be worse to be caught in a lie than to admit the truth, and he didn't know enough terrestrial geography to lie convincingly.

"Arcturus III."

"Arc . . . ?" The dragon-thing sat up straight. "You're an *alien*?"

"Yeah." He might brazen it out yet, he thought.

"An *alien*?! In *Joe's Bar*?"

He wasn't going to get away with it, he knew; with a gulp, he finished his drink, as conversation died and the occupants of the bar all began to stare in his direction. One of the big-chested clones pulled a needlegun from somewhere and leaned past the dragon toward him, weapon raised and pointing at the mirrored ceiling; the dragon itself was still too astonished to do much but gape. She said nothing, merely glared, letting the weapon speak for itself.

"Hey, buddy, this is a nice joint." It was a naked, sexless android that spoke.

"Yeah, we don't need you here," a glittering golden cyborg said.

"This is a Terran bar, freak." The monotone voice came from the wheeled box of a cryogenic artificial.

"An alien!" The dragon still gaped.

Xahh knew when he wasn't wanted; he slipped from his stool and walked, with all the dignified calm he could manage, out the door. Behind him he heard a clone saying, "Damn foreigners! C'mon, Argo, I'll buy you a drink."

SCIENCE FICTION

Jim looked up as Sandy poked his head in.

"What're ya doing?" Sandy asked.

"Reading," Jim said, holding up the book.

"Reading what?" Sandy demanded as he climbed into the old packing tube that served the boys as a refuge from their families and the outside universe in general.

"Science fiction," Jim said. "It's a real old book my mother found somewhere, about two kids who build a spaceship in their backyard and fly to the moon."

Sandy blinked. "What would they want to go to the moon for? And how would they get home again?"

"The ship takes them both ways, of course. It's got some sort of special nuclear drive—it's called 'atomic propulsion.' "

"Sounds fake to me," Sandy replied. "As if the author was making it up."

Jim shrugged. "He probably was."

"So what did they want to go to the moon for?" Sandy asked.

"Well, 'cause no one had ever done it," Jim answered.

Sandy stared. "Aw, come on," he said.

"Hey, I *told* you it was a real old book. *Real* old."

"It must be a hundred years old, if no one had gone to the moon!"

Jim nodded solemnly. "About that, yeah."

Sandy was silent for a moment in awestruck silence. "You're reading a book a *hundred years old*?"

"Yeah."

"How'd it get here?"

"*I* don't know; my mother just found it somewhere. I guess somebody brought it along when they built the place."

Sandy started to accept this, then stopped. "Wait a minute," he said. "If this book is from before anybody even went to the moon, then where are these two kids who build the space-ship in their backyard?"

Jim grinned. "On Earth," he said.

Sandy stared at him in disbelief for a moment, then snick-ered.

Jim snickered back, and in a moment both boys were rolling around the tube, hysterical with laughter.

"On *Earth*?" Sandy gasped. "Two *kids* . . . build a *space-ship* . . . in their *backyard* . . . on *Earth*?"

Jim managed to stop laughing long enough to reply, "That's what it *says!*"

"But Earth's at the bottom of the biggest gravity well in the inner system! Except the sun, anyway."

"I *know*, I *know!*" Jim replied, chortling.

A new wave of hysterics swept over them.

It took the boys several minutes to calm down, but at last they managed it and lay quietly side by side, getting their breath back.

"Y'know," Sandy said, as he stared at the curving steel overhead, "I bet we *could* build a spaceship in my backyard."

"Sure," Jim replied. "If we wanted to. *We* aren't in any gravity well!"

"We could even launch it—my yard's right above the Number Three emergency lock."

Jim considered. "We'd need to put it on maglev or wheels or something to get it to the lock, though," he pointed out.

"That's no problem," Sandy said. "We couldn't go to the moon, though. Or if we did it'd be a one-way trip and prob-ably a rough landing."

"No," Jim agreed. "But if we had maneuvering jets we could probably go to one of the other colonies."

Sandy nodded. "If they'd let us in. They probably wouldn't."

"'Course not. We wouldn't have clearance from ISA. They don't allow direct flights between colonies."

"Why not, anyway? I never understood that."

Jim shrugged. "Me, either. My dad says it's just politics. He's been to one of the other colonies—Shepard, I think it was. Had to go to Earth first, then back up. Seems stupid."

They lay quietly for a moment, and then Sandy said, "*I've* never been to any of the other colonies."

"Neither have I," Jim said. "I've never even been to Earth. But I was outside once."

Sandy lifted his head and stared at his friend in surprise. "You were?"

"Sure—just out on the shell, though. Mom took me along on an inspection tour once."

"Wow, neat."

"Yeah, it was."

"I'd like to see outside," Sandy said, lowering his head again.

Another silent moment followed, and Jim recovered his antique volume. Before he could find his place, Sandy remarked, "If we *did* build a spaceship, we could just cruise around a little, maybe do a single orbit, and then come back aboard. They'd *have* to let us aboard our own colony!"

Jim put the book down and considered.

"It'd be a neat thing to do," Sandy pointed out.

Jim had to agree.

At first Jim had hoped they would be able to use the old book as a sort of guide, but that didn't work out; the descriptions in it were insufficiently detailed, and most of the equipment described was either fanciful or hopelessly outdated.

Still, he read it cover to cover twice. His father, in a moment's distraction from his work, noticed the flamboyant little volume.

"Where'd you get that?" he asked.

"From Mom," Jim told him.

His father picked the book up and looked it over curiously. "From Earth," he said. "Someone wasted part of his lift weight allowance on *that*?" He shook his head. "What an idiot."

This gratuitous remark rankled, and Jim made it a point from then on not to mention the spaceship project to anyone.

Work proceeded. The packing tube, hauled from the empty lot where it had been ditched to Sandy's yard, made a fine main hull. Jim bought a bubble of polarizing plastic from the colony's salvage dump; that would close off the open end when the time came.

Emergency oxygen tanks were easy to come by; the colony had them in every room and on every walkway corner, far more than the present population would ever need. The colony had been designed for a much larger population, but Earth had stopped sending volunteers, and natural increase still hadn't come anywhere near filling the available space.

It wouldn't any time soon, either, since the colony was short on necessities other than air and space, and meanwhile no one was going to miss an oxygen tank or two.

Jim had an old algae tank his sister had built as a school project two years before; he cleaned it out and restocked it. That would help with the air and provide a backup food supply.

Both had their own pressure suits, of course. Everyone in Havel Colony had a suit. Jim and Sandy were well aware, as they sat on Sandy's back lawn, that under the oxygen-producing grass lay a few centimeters of topsoil, and below that about a half-meter of metal hull, and below that—nothing.

Nothing but the emptiness of space, emptiness where the occasional meteor or chunk of space rubbish stood a finite chance of whacking into the colony.

So everyone in Havel Colony had a suit.

Neither boy was willing to risk his personal AI to provide an on-board computer, so Sandy's old nursery computer was brought out of storage and installed, with the operating system hot-rodded and with navigational software off the public net. Wheels, for maneuvering inside the colony, were provided by the simple means of bolting the boys' outgrown toy wagons to the handling loops on the packing tube.

The hardest physical labor in the entire project was levering the tube up high enough to work the wagons underneath; it took most of an afternoon.

Propulsion and steering were the big problems, though.

"All we need is something under pressure," Sandy said, as he lay in the partially finished hull, his feet propped up on the algae tank.

Jim snorted. "Sure. Like what? We don't dare swipe any more oxy bottles, and those wouldn't last long enough to do any good, anyway—this thing we're building must weigh a tonne!"

Sandy didn't argue with that; instead he suggested, "Maybe we could *make* something."

Jim didn't bother snorting again. "Like what?" he asked.

"*I* don't know," Sandy admitted.

"We don't need pressure, anyway," Jim pointed out a moment later. "All we need is reaction mass and some way of throwing it. Doesn't have to be pressurized."

"How *else* are you going to throw it?"

"I don't know, but it seems as if we ought to be able to rig up *something*," Jim replied. "Look, if we don't need to pressurize it, we can use any old thing—we can just take all the junk from the salvage dump that nobody wants, the stuff that would be going into the furnaces anyway. Then we just throw it away when we need to steer."

"Yeah," Sandy said, "but we're either going to need a lot of mass or a lot of speed, if we want to move the whole ship! Pressure's real good for building up speed. Stuff comes out fast."

"There are other ways, though. Suppose we put a piece of scrap on a big flywheel and spun it up? I mean, we're planning to use the colony's spin to launch in the first place, right? Why not do the same thing to steer?"

"I dunno," Sandy said. "How would it work? I mean, how would you control what direction it went? How would you get something to stay on while you spun it up?"

Jim rolled over, blinking, then got to his knees. "Let's see," he said. "Well, suppose you had strings, with pieces of scrap tied to them, and when you needed to turn you tied the other end of the string to rim of the flywheel. Then you'd spin it up fast as you want and then cut the string as it went by."

"When you spin the flywheel, the rest of the ship's going to turn the other way, you know."

"Yeah, I know," Jim admitted. "You'd have to allow for that. Shucks, you could *use* it—you could get yourself pointed in the right direction that way."

"And how are you going to cut the string at exactly the right instant? How do you know the mass of the scrap you're using?"

Jim stopped and considered that with mounting annoyance.

"All right," he said. "It wouldn't work. Not with anything the two of us could build."

"Nope," Sandy agreed. "I like the flywheel for rotating the ship, though—I think we should do that."

"That's easy enough. A bike wheel with weights along the rim should do fine, and it can go inside with us."

Sandy nodded.

For a moment they sat, thinking silently.

"What about a crossbow?" Sandy said, suddenly. "Or a catapult? Something with a spring in it? We can put a winding motor on it, and load it with a remote grappler—tie a big bag of scrap alongside, and when we need propulsion we just haul a piece out of the bag with the grappler, load it in the catapult, and let fly."

"We couldn't put them on every side, though!"

"No, of course not. We mount one big one, on a swivel. Then we use the flywheel to rotate the ship to the right direction, the grappler to load the catapult and point it the right way, and there we are!"

Jim blinked and tried to imagine such a thing.

"No," he said. "You'd need at least two, because if there's only one you'll just wind up spinning around. You'd need to fire off two at once, on opposite sides."

Sandy struggled with the physics for a moment, then nodded. "I guess you're right," he said. "So we build two."

"They'd need to be balanced."

"So?"

Jim had no direct answer to that. "Even if it worked, it'd be awfully slow and clumsy," he remarked.

"So what?" Sandy asked. "We aren't going anywhere, just around the colony. Who needs speed? And we'll take a radio and call for help if it breaks down."

Jim nodded and grinned.

"It's going to look *really* stupid," he said, "but I don't see why it wouldn't work."

It did look stupid. When the catapults were built, a tangle of machinery projected from either side of the hull at a ninety-degree angle. It looked stupid, and it also took months to scavenge the parts that could be scavenged and save up enough to buy the parts that couldn't. Two radio-controlled remote grapplers with video hookups cost a good bit, and spring steel was also at a premium aboard Havel Colony just then.

When Jim first heard the prices for the steel and the grapplers, he balked.

"I don't want to waste all my money on this! I mean, what good's this ship gonna be, really?"

"It'll be neat, Jim," Sandy said. "Really! Something to tell your grandkids, y'know? How you built your own spaceship?"

Jim relented, reluctantly.

Assembling the whole contraption was, like most engineering jobs, much more complicated and difficult than expected.

The project kept the boys busy enough that they didn't worry about the latest ISA rulings; they were probably the only people in the colony old enough to understand what was happening who didn't worry. They noticed that dinners were getting smaller and less interesting and that prices on everything were rising, but with the self-centered confidence of youth, they assured each other that everything would work out all right.

"It always does," Sandy pointed out. "I mean, nobody blew up the world back in the Cold War, did they? And the biocrisis got fixed up by the genetic engineers, right? It'll turn out okay."

"Sure," Jim agreed, remembering, but not mentioning, plenty of cases where things had *not* turned out okay for one group or another. Yes, the human race as a whole survived and flourished—but did Carthage? Or the Polish Jews?

Or course, those were a long time ago. Nobody had attempted genocide in half a century.

Not that wiping out the orbital colonies would necessarily even constitute genocide. And nobody wanted to wipe them out, Jim's father assured him. The ISA just wanted to bankrupt them, not kill them—force most of them to go back to Earth. The colonies were profitable, and the ISA wanted all that money for itself. If the colonists were to give up and go home, the factories and farms aboard could be automated and made far more profitable.

Jim didn't really worry about it, though—not when he was welding the grapplers onto the hull, or loading the bolted-on wagons with netbags of scrap, or testing the winding motors, or building catapult frames around their precious strips of spring steel.

He was far more concerned with getting the catapults to work. His test shots sent various debris sailing every which way, once putting a marble clear into the zero-gee zone overhead, so that it never came down at all, so far as the boys could see.

And Sandy wasn't even as worried as Jim. He paid no attention at all as he mounted the flywheel he had constructed out of an old bicycle, with lead scrap mounted along the rim where the tire used to be, or while bolting Jim's catapults onto their swivels.

It came as a shock, therefore, when Sandy's mother announced at dinner one night, "We'll have to leave."

Sandy looked up from his burger. "Leave what?" he asked.

"Leave the colony," she said. "Go back to Earth."

"Back?"

She frowned. "All right, go to Earth, then. I know you've never been there. But it would be going back for me and your father—we grew up there."

"I know that. But why should we?"

"Because we can't afford to stay here anymore, that's why. Look at what you're eating!"

Sandy looked. He didn't see anything very unusual about it. The burger didn't have any cheese on it, and there weren't as many french fries on the side as usual, but it looked okay. "What about it?" he asked.

"What about it? Sandy, this is the third night in a row we've had nothing but those damned fake burgers for supper!"

"Is it?" Sandy tried to see why this was important.

"Yes, it is! Because they're all we can afford! Maybe if we had our own garden we could scrimp a little and get by, but I don't have time to work a garden, and we don't have enough money for seeds or topsoil or fertilizer anyway, and what could we grow in the five centimeters of sod they gave us?"

"The Wangs have a garden," Sandy mentioned, and immediately wished he hadn't.

His mother exploded, and he excused himself and slipped out before she could work herself up to sending him to his room, or even slapping him.

He didn't make out much sense in the explosion, but apparently his mother had talked to the Wangs, and they weren't interested in sharing their garden.

He went to the spaceship in the backyard and crawled in. There wasn't anything in particular to work on in there, but it was somewhere to go.

He sat down on one of the cushions they had recently installed and began idly working one of the winding motors, cranking the catapult back and then letting fly, while he tried to think.

Leave Havel Colony?

That was a scary thought. He'd always lived here, after all. He was born in the very house he still lived in. And Earth? With the open sky, and the dirty air, and that stuff that fell out of the sky—rain and snow and wind? Where it got colder than a freezer some places and hot as blood in others?

He didn't think he would like that.

And he particularly didn't think he would like living there *forever*, never going anywhere else.

Could you see the stars from Earth?

Oh, of course you could—half the time, anyway. Some of them.

He looked around at the bizarre, jury-rigged spacecraft he and his buddy had assembled. They hadn't had a chance to fly it yet, but it was just about done. All that was left was a little debugging—there were bound to be plenty of bugs.

Speaking of bugs—they had bugs on Earth, not just the planned and engineered ones in the agricultural areas, but wild ones that could bite or sting. And they had diseases there, where your body would stop working right because there were parasites inside it trying to eat you alive—yuck!

He wanted to take the ship out for its maiden voyage before he had to leave, to get a good look at the stars. Would there be time? Or did Mom mean to leave right away?

Why did they have to leave, anyway? Just because the ISA had raised prices? "Cutting the subsidy," they called it on the vid news—"passing on transportation costs."

Well, who asked the International Space Agency to do all the transporting in the first place?

Mr. le Beau, two doors over, always said that if the ISA didn't insist on doing all its own transportation and supplying all the colonies from Earth that there wouldn't be any problem. If they let private companies launch stuff up unmanned, instead of putting everything on the shuttles, or if they let the colonies trade directly with each other . . .

But that wasn't allowed. The ISA didn't want the colonists getting out of hand. They didn't really want the colonists here at all.

Sandy spun the flywheel. It whirled smoothly, with only the very faintest whirring sound.

Jim's dinner was more peaceful. Nobody shouted or ran off. Instead Jim's father held forth in a long, heartfelt lecture, while Jim, his sister, and their mother listened.

They'd heard most of it before, of course.

There was one new element, though.

"They're cutting off our supplies of fuel, did you know that?" Jim's dad said, slapping a hand on the table. "They say it's too dangerous, storing large quantities of volatile materials up here. Dangerous! And it isn't dangerous having short fuel supplies for the stabilizing rockets? It isn't dangerous being so shorthanded all the time, because they won't send up more people? They don't care about the danger, anyway—they're just worried that we'll start building our own ships up here and break their monopoly!"

Jim looked up, interested. Building ships?

Dad was off onto something else already, though, something that didn't interest the boy.

Jim pushed back from the table. "Excuse me," he said. "I'd like to take a walk while my food settles."

"Go ahead," his mother said.

His father didn't seem to notice.

Jim wandered out the front door, then paused and looked around.

The prefab house shells stood in neat rows along the street, curving up in either direction until the circle closed overhead—at that distance they didn't look much like houses, just like little boxes. Half of them were empty and unfinished. Way off in the distance, he could see some of the framework of the colony's solar reflectors, but the bright light made it hard to make out any details. The other end of the cylinder, with its offices and elevators and the access to the zero-gee zone in the colony's center, was much closer than the mirrors.

It looked very solid and comfortable, each house set in its lawn of genetically engineered grass, designed and bred for maximum oxygen production. Someone had told Jim once that natural grass, back on Earth, was a different color, a much less intense shade of green, but he wasn't sure he believed it.

Under that grass were a few centimeters of earth, a fraction of a meter of steel, and then all the infinite void, spattered with stars and other bodies—and except for that one brief trip out onto the shell, long ago, he had never seen those stars with his own eyes. What good was living in an orbital colony if you never even saw the stars?

The kids in that book had certainly been eager enough to go adventuring, no matter how dangerous it was. And they hadn't had the advantages of a hundred years' experience in building spacecraft.

He turned and headed for the ship.

He was startled to find Sandy already there, crouched inside, playing with the flywheel.

"What's up?" he asked.

"Hi, Jim," Sandy replied. "It's my mom."

"What about her?"

"She says we have to go to Earth, that we can't afford to live here anymore."

"What?" Jim exclaimed.

Sandy shrugged.

"Really? You're going to Earth?"

"I guess so, yeah."

"When?"

"I dunno; soon."

"Hey, that really sucks!"

"Yeah. And we didn't even get the ship out yet."

Jim looked around.

"We could do that, you know. It's almost ready."

Sandy blinked. "I thought you were still having trouble aiming the catapults."

"Not really; I've gotten pretty good." Jim flushed slightly. "I was just nervous, you know? Launching this thing's a big experiment. It could be dangerous. We could get killed."

"Yeah," Sandy agreed, "I guess so."

"If you're going to Earth, though—well, that sucks. I think we should take it out for a spin before you go."

"Yeah," Sandy said, thoughtfully. Then, more enthusiastically, "Yeah! Yeah, let's do it! Right now!"

Jim hesitated.

"Now?" he said. "Right now?"

"Sure, why not?"

Jim had no answer to that.

In point of fact, though, there were several last-minute things to be done beforehand—tying nettings across the heaps of scrap so they wouldn't come loose during launch, hauling stocks of food out from the boys' respective kitchens, and a great deal of checking things over.

Then they pushed the contraption across twenty meters of lawn onto the Number Three emergency airlock; it bumped down onto the bare metal of the air-lock door, rolled a few centimeters, and stopped. The boys donned their pressure suits and set their throat mikes to feed to external speakers, external pickups to feed to earphones. They ran through a final systems check—and discovered a small problem.

"How do we work the airlock from inside the ship?" Sandy asked.

Jim considered the situation, gauging distances by eye.

"If we set it right in the corner, here, and run the setup routine, and put everything on automatic," he said, "I think I can hit the cycle switch with the starboard grappler."

He fit actions to his words, typing the appropriate commands onto the airlock control panel; then he climbed aboard the makeshift spaceship and closed and sealed the hatch.

Sandy was already at the grappler's controls.

"Hey," Jim protested, "I was gonna do that!"

Sandy shrugged. "You did the preset, so I get to push the button."

He did just that.

With a rumble, the airlock cover began to slide out from under them.

At first it carried the boys' spaceship with it, but in a moment the craft bumped up against the edge and stayed there, the wheels turning and squealing as the door slid along underneath. The wheels were not aligned exactly at right angles to the door's movement, which created the squealing and also caused the ship to creep slowly along, sideways along the edge of the airlock.

Then the edge of the door passed the first of the eight wheels, and the ship wobbled slightly.

Another wheel, and a shudder ran through the vessel.

"I just thought of something," Jim said, his expression worried.

"What?" Sandy asked, grabbing at the flywheel for support as a third wheel came free and the ship began to lean noticeably.

"We're going to drop down into the airlock at the equivalent of just over one gee, aren't we?"

"Um . . ." Sandy said, "yeah, I guess we are."

The fourth and last wheel on the forward wagon came free, and the ship toppled over until it hung from the next pair of wheels. Every loose object aboard, including the two-man crew, plummeted into the plastic bubble that served as a nose. The algae tank sloshed noisily, but the seals held, and it and its contents stayed put.

The entire assembly then hung, swaying back and forth, as the door continued to retract.

Then the door vanished into the frame and the converted packing tube tumbled down into the body of the airlock.

It crashed against the outer door with a deafening metallic noise that left Sandy and Jim unable to think or hear as they tumbled about.

The craft did *not* land on its wheels or right itself; it struck nose-first, bouncing on the plastic bubble, rocking for a moment, then falling heavily onto its back.

Fortunately, no catapult or grappler had been mounted on what had been the ship's top.

The boys lay in their tiny cabin, stunned, as the inner door began to slide closed again above them.

"Uhh . . ." Sandy asked, still slightly dazed, "what did you set the auto cycle for?"

"Ten seconds," Jim answered, holding the side of his head where it had whacked against the inside of his helmet when the helmet struck the hard metal of the tube.

"Shit," Sandy said.

"Why?" Jim inquired, without looking at his comrade.

"That's not time enough to get out and abort it."

Jim glanced out through the bubble and saw nothing but the metal walls of the airlock; the door overhead was almost closed, and most of the illumination now came from the airlock's own internal lights—which were a dull orange color, not the natural bright sunlight of the colony's interior.

"I guess not," he said. "Why would you want to?"

Sandy let out an exasperated sigh. "To see if anything busted when we fell," he said. "Like the seal on the hatch."

Jim looked at the bubble again. "It *looks* okay," he said uneasily.

A loud hiss came from outside as the lock's atmosphere was either pumped out or vented—neither boy knew which. It faded quickly to silence.

"I guess we'll find out in a minute," Sandy said.

With a rumble, the outer door began sliding away beneath them.

This time the ship wasn't on its wheels, so it didn't roll; instead it was pulled to the side of the lock, where it clanged against metal. As the door continued to pull, the ship was twisted around until it was flush against the airlock wall; again, fortune favored the enterprise, and the catapults and grapplers weren't crushed. The airlock door dragged its way under the little ship's hull with a shuddering vibration that Jim feared would shake loose every bolt or wire that hadn't been jarred loose in the crash.

"We didn't plan this very well," he remarked.

Before Sandy could answer the door slipped away, and with a final bump of uncertain origin, the tiny spaceship fell out and away from Havel Colony.

The instant contact with the airlock was lost, the instant of that final bump, silence fell, total and startling. To each boy it seemed as if he had suddenly gone deaf—and then a moment later realized he hadn't, that he could hear his own breathing, the blood beating in his veins.

"Well, nobody thinks of everything," Sandy said. "Except maybe the guys in that book you read."

Before Jim could reply, the view outside the bubble caught his gaze, and he stared out at the stars, stars brighter and more numerous than he had ever seen them, ever imagined them.

Then he started giggling, just slightly at first, but finally in uncontrollable gusts.

Sandy, without knowing why, joined in.

Jim reached up to wipe his eyes and found himself slapping the faceplate of his suit instead, triggering a whole new round of hysteria. It also sent him bouncing around the ship, since they had been weightless from the instant they left the airlock.

Weightlessness was not new to either boy—they'd both taken several trips to the hub over the years—but it added to their hilarity.

Finally, however, the two boys managed to calm down.

"We not only didn't think of everything," Jim said, "we hardly thought of *anything*! I mean, we didn't even name our ship!"

"That's right!" Sandy exclaimed. He looked around the tube, at the algae tank glued to one section of wall, the flywheel bolted to another, while tools, cushions, their on-board radio, the controls and video monitors for the grapplers, the computer, and dozens of other objects drifted freely and randomly about. A haze of dust and debris filled the air. A conic section of sunlight blazed across one side, pouring in through the bubble at an angle; it moved around the cylinder, shortening and lengthening, showing that their little craft was tumbling through space. The boy thought he could hear a faint hissing, as if some of their air were escaping, but it might have just been the sound of his suit's systems going about their business.

"I hereby dub thee the I.S.A.S. *Mistake!*" he announced.

"Hey, no," Jim protested. "We're not I.S.A.S., we're an independent—the I.S.S. *Mistake*, Independent Space Ship!"

Sandy grinned. "Right!" he said. "My mistake!"

Jim smiled back but did not laugh. Their previous bout of hysterics had been sufficient, and besides, the reality of their situation was beginning to sink in.

"Okay," he said, "I.S.S. *Mistake*, James Iovino and Szandor Bardossy, co-captains, current location—where? Where the hell are we?"

Sandy shrugged. "I don't know," he said. "Somewhere near Havel Colony, in cislunar space, I guess. Take a look."

Jim looked but could make no sense of the starscape wheeling past the bubble. He located a grappler console, snared it, and turned on the video.

That gave him a lovely view of the portside catapult but nothing else.

He worked the controls and swung the little claw outward; all that gave him was a view of stars sailing by far too quickly to be identified.

"Use the flywheel," he said. "See if you can slow us down."

"Right," Sandy agreed. He thought about removing his pressure suit, for ease of work, but decided to play it safe—even if the seals had held so far, that didn't mean they always would.

He looked out the bubble, checked the drive chain to make sure the flywheel would be spinning the right way, and began working the crank that had once held a bicycle pedal.

The parabola of sunlight gradually slowed in its movement around the interior of the ship but did not stop, even when Sandy had worked the flywheel up to the maximum speed its bearings would permit.

Sweating inside his suit, he released the crank.

"Best I can do," he said, apologetically. The cylinder was still turning at more than half its initial speed.

Jim nodded. He was already at work with a grappler, trying to load an irregular chunk of steel scrap into the bucket of the portside catapult. "That was a rough take-off," he said. "I'll try and reduce the spin and the wobble, and then you can take a look out the bubble, see if you can spot the colony so I can head us back."

He turned the catapult on its swivel, doing the best he could to judge the direction of the ship's movement, and then hit the release.

The spring steel whacked against its frame, sending the chunk of debris off into the void, and with a slight jar the ship's motion changed. Sandy looked at the bubble; the sky beyond was still turning, but he thought there was some improvement.

"Hey, Jim," he said uneasily, "what if one of those things hits somebody?"

Jim looked at him, then back at the grappler's video monitor. "Um . . ." he said. "Well, it isn't very likely. If they hit Earth they'll just burn up in the atmosphere, which I guess won't hurt anybody, and there's an awful lot of empty space out there. I doubt they'll hit anyone." He shrugged. "I guess we'll just have to hope they won't. I mean, it's no worse than meteors or the debris from all those old probes, is it?"

Sandy nodded. "I guess you're right."

Jim didn't answer; he was reloading the catapult.

It took twenty-two shots, by exact count, and another cranking of the flywheel, before the ship's rotation was slowed to a manageable level.

Jim looked about uneasily.

"What's the matter?" Sandy asked.

"That took a lot of junk," Jim replied. "About a fourth of what we started with. I must have underestimated the ship's mass pretty badly, or overestimated the catapults' force." He shoved at the flywheel crank in annoyance. "Find the colony, will you? I think we'd better head straight back."

Sandy nodded and launched himself gently toward the nose, catching himself just before his faceplate smacked against the plastic.

He looked out at the universe.

To one side he could see the Earth, a gigantic blue crescent, the dark within the crescent's curve sprinkled with yellow dots of light that he knew were cities, though he had trouble imagining just what a city could be like.

About 150 degrees around from that was the moon, a half circle white as death.

And the sun was out there, too, at an angle he couldn't judge, because he dared not look directly at it. The bubble had no shielding, and he didn't trust his suit's faceplate to handle the full radiation.

Nowhere could he see Havel Colony, or for that matter anything man-made except those tiny golden lights.

He knew what the colony looked like; he'd seen plenty of pictures of the outside, the great cylinder with its docking complex at one end and its intricate array of solar mirrors at the other.

He didn't see anything like that out there now.

"I don't see it," he said, feeling his chest tighten as he spoke.

"Let me look," Jim said, scudding forward.

Sandy dropped back out of his companion's way and hung more or less motionless, waiting.

Jim looked for a long, long time before admitting, "I don't see it, either."

"What do we do now?" Sandy asked.

Jim chewed his lip. "It might be off that way," he said, pointing astern. "We couldn't see it then."

"So we should turn the ship around."

"Yeah," Jim said, "but that's not gonna be easy."

Sandy's nerve broke. "Oh, shit, Jim," he said, his eyes tearing up. "We're gonna die out here, aren't we?"

"Nah," Jim said, his own voice not terribly steady. "I mean, we brought a radio; we can call for help."

Sandy brightened, his tears stopping, at least for the moment. "That's right!" he said. "Why aren't we using it?"

"Because if they have to send a rescue party out after us we're gonna be in really big trouble, that's why! I want to get us back under our own power, if I can."

Sandy looked at the radio, and then at the bubble, where the stars continued to move in slow arcs.

"Maybe we could use it to home in on the colony, without telling them we're out here?" he suggested. "See, when we're pointing one direction the signal would be stronger?"

Jim glanced at the bubble and then shrugged. "It might work," he said. "I don't know. Won't hurt to try."

He turned on the radio, receive only, on the colony's exterior traffic frequency.

". . . oh, damn it, they're not listening. They probably didn't even take a radio, those fool kids!" someone was saying.

Jim and Sandy looked at one another.

"Does he mean *us*?" Sandy whispered.

The radio muttered for a moment as someone spoke outside the effective range of the microphone on the other end. Then the voice returned.

"Jim, Sandy, if you're listening, can you signal? We've got you on radar, but we don't know your condition. Jim, Sandy, are you listening?" The voice let out a loud sigh. "Damn fool kids."

"They know it's us," Sandy said, his eyes wide.

Jim frowned. "Yeah," he said. "I guess they must have gotten some kind of signal when we went out the airlock, and it wouldn't be hard to figure it out after that."

"What are we gonna do?" Sandy's moment of panic had passed; he was no longer worried about dying, only about staying out of trouble with the colony authorities.

"Maybe we should call, tell 'em we're all right," Jim said, looking about as if hoping to find useful information somewhere in the drifting dust.

"Yeah," Sandy agreed, "I think we should."

Hesitantly, Jim pressed the SEND button.

"Havel Colony, this is Jim Iovino, co-captain of the I.S.S. *Mistake*," he said. "We're both fine, but we're having a little navigational difficulty."

"A *little* . . ." Sandy began, but Jim shushed him.

For a long moment there was no answer, but at last the voice replied, "I'll be damned. You're okay?"

"Yeah, we're fine," Jim said. Before he could say anything more, the voice on the other end interrupted.

"Navigational difficulties? What kind of navigational difficulties?"

Jim looked at Sandy, who shrugged. Jim shrugged back and said, "Well, frankly, Havel Colony, we had some trouble when we launched, and we don't know where the heck we are."

After another pause, the voice replied, "That figures." She sighed again. "You're about forty kilometers away, with a relative velocity of about eight meters per second; your current course will put you in a long elliptical orbit around Earth, about a forty-hour period. You'll get low enough at perigee for braking effects, so the orbit's not stable."

Jim and Sandy looked at one another.

"I never thought about that," Jim said.

"There's a whole *bunch* of stuff we didn't think about," Sandy replied.

"Maybe we should give up and ask them to send out someone to get us."

Sandy looked around.

The air in the ship was dirty; the spin had thinned some of the particulates out of the air for a time, but since they had slowed the spin down and bumped the ship around in doing it, all manner of dust and slime and crud was now drifting about. The algae tank appeared to be leaking slightly; a thin mist was emerging from one corner, adding to the mess. Sandy saw now why real spaceships always had vents and filters and blowers, and wished they had some way to move the air around. A regular household air cleaner, like the one in his mother's kitchen, would have done fine. Without it, the shipboard environment was not very pleasant.

They had undoubtedly forgotten other things, as well.

The kids in the book hadn't forgotten any little details like that—but that was science fiction, Sandy reminded himself, not real life.

One of the grapplers was pointed toward the wagonloads of debris that served as fuel, and the video screen showed a distressing empty space where some of that fuel had been before they threw it away.

And the view out the bubble didn't include the colony, even though it was only forty kilometers away.

"Yeah," he said, "I think we should."

Jim pressed the SEND button. "Hello, Havel Colony," he said. "I think we're in trouble out here. Can you send a rescue?"

"Negative, *Mistake*," a new voice said, a masculine one this time. "You're on your own for the moment. We have nothing spaceworthy aboard, and no reserve fuel."

Jim looked up from the radio; Sandy's expression was grave.

"Now what?" Sandy asked.

Before Jim could respond, the radio said, "*Mistake*, do you boys have maneuvering capability?"

"Yes, sir," Jim answered. "But it's not very precise."

"Hm. I was thinking that maybe you could intercept Atanasoff Colony, but . . . How are you fixed for air and water?"

Jim and Sandy exchanged glances.

"I'm not sure, sir," Jim admitted. "We're not running short of anything yet." He hesitated. "Please, sir," he said, "we'd like to come home, but we can't *see* it. We ought to be able to, if we're only forty klicks out!"

"You sure ought to. Take another look, all around."

Sandy tossed himself into the nose and did just that. "Still nothing out this way," he called.

Jim frowned and swung a grappler to point astern. He wished the video lens had a wider angle. He studied the starscape.

"If it's any help," the voice from the radio said, "we're in Earth's shadow right now, so it's probably pretty dark. We went in about an hour ago."

That information was what Jim needed; he swung the grappler and shrieked, "I see it!" Then he calmed and said, "At least, I think I do. There's something occluding a patch of stars there." He left that grappler where it was and reached for the other set of controls.

A moment later he had both catapults cranked back and loaded, and aimed directly forward. He knew he would need to adjust course later, but right now he just wanted to make a start.

He tripped the releases, and two chunks of metal sailed off into empty space.

He started to reload, then paused. "Havel Colony," he asked, "are you tracking us?"

"Of course we are, Jim," the voice answered, the original female one again. "What kind of stupid question is that?"

Jim ignored the annoyance and said, "We just fired our main drive, such as it is—you guys see any change?"

A moment later the radio said, "Not much. Possibly a slight decrease in relative velocity."

Jim frowned and reloaded.

A dozen shots later the woman on the other end acknowledged, "You've killed about half your relative speed, but you've added a little drift, too—your trajectory's changed."

Jim continued loading, aiming, and shooting. The aft wagon was now almost empty, and he began to use the forward fuel supply instead.

An hour later Sandy was curled up in midair, trying to sleep, and the *Mistake*'s fuel supply was reduced to half a dozen large chunks and a scattering of little bits. Jim was hot and sweating, despite his suit's temperature controls, as well as hungry and very thirsty.

And the *Mistake* was on course to intercept Havel Colony, or at least pass very close—but with a relative velocity of scarcely two meters per second, with fifty kilometers of intervening space.

That meant seven more hours of travel time. Jim didn't dare use any more fuel. It was becoming impossible to match the loads in the two catapults, which meant each shot was likely to make the craft wobble or spin, and they might need to maneuver later.

He looked around and checked his suit readouts.

The helmet sipper was empty; the water recirculation wasn't working properly. And they hadn't brought any plain old water.

Their supplies did include boxes of synthetic fruit punch, though. Jim considered the fog of debris and concluded that the ship must be holding air just fine; he found a punch box and then popped his faceplate.

Hot air blasted in at him, and the accumulated stench made him gag. The ship was obviously gaining heat from the sunlight much faster than it could dissipate it, and Jim realized they hadn't even thought to bring a thermometer. Their suit refrigeration systems must be working near capacity, which would, of course, be adding to the heat in the ship.

He had never thought about heat buildup, all those weeks they were assembling the ship. The kids in the book thought of everything—but he and Sandy were only human.

Something stank horribly, probably something that had leaked from the algae tank—or perhaps some of the food supplies had gone bad in the heat. He almost lost interest in the punch, but he forced himself to jab the pointed straw into the foil circle.

Punch squirted out, adding to the floating mess, and Jim quickly clamped his lips around the straw.

When he had finished, he stuffed the empty box into the food bag, wiped away sweat, closed his faceplate, and joined Sandy in trying to sleep.

"Hey, boys, wake up!"

Jim started, an arm flying out and bumping a wall, sending him spinning in the opposite direction. He steadied himself and looked around, remembering where he was and what his situation was.

The sunlight was gone; the ship was dim, lit by starlight, the grappler video screens, and various gauges and pilot lights.

Sandy was stirring, rolling and bouncing along one side of the tube; Jim didn't worry about him. He made his way to the radio as the voice called, "Can you hear me, out there?"

Jim punched SEND.

"We hear you," he said. "What's up?"

"Not you," the voice said. "You're coming down fast. We estimate you'll make your closest approach to the colony in about twenty minutes, and we thought that you might want to try and adjust your aim. We've got people suiting up, and they'll come out on tethers to try and bring you in, but you'll have to get within a hundred meters or the lines won't reach. We estimate you'll be about a hundred and twenty out if you don't change course."

"Oh," Jim said, a bit sleepily. And then, *"Oh!"* as the situation sank in.

He began working the grapplers.

The colony was now plain on the video screen for the portside grappler; it gleamed pale blue in the scattered starlight, a gigantic cylinder so big that only a small fraction would fit on the screen at a time. As Jim watched, a row of golden lights blazed, sharp and clear and perfect in the vacuum of space; an airlock was opening.

He had both catapults loaded; he tripped the switches.

The loads weren't even; the ship turned toward the colony, but it was rotating anew, a slow, graceful roll.

Jim hissed air through his teeth and began reloading, making sure that the heavier load went on the starboard side, so as to slow or reverse the spin.

When he had the catapults loaded again, he swung the grapplers out and looked for the colony.

There it was, and he could see tiny figures emerging, their helmet lights white, the brightest things on the screen.

Then the *Mistake*'s new rotation carried the video pickup around, and Jim concentrated on his aim.

The catapults fired, and the ship had a new motion, a sort of corkscrewing.

It was also headed more directly toward the colony.

Jim hit SEND as Sandy studied the video screens. "How're we doing?" Jim asked.

"Better," the now-familiar voice said. "We estimate pericolony at 105 meters, and too far around the curve for the lines we're using. Keep trying."

Jim swung a grappler down and looked in the fuel bin that had been his express wagon.

Two more lumps of scrap—and they didn't even match. After that, nothing but steel shavings and plastic shards.

The kids in the book never had problems like this.

Damn that book, anyway. He should have known that any book that talked about building a spaceship in a backyard on Earth was nonsense right through.

He loaded and fired, and then waited, doing his best to keep both the video pickups pointed toward the colony as the *Mistake* rolled crazily through space. The spacesuited figures had grown from dots into human beings, and he could even see the writing on their helmets, glimpse bits of face through the transparent faceplates.

"Pericolony, eighty-five meters, in two minutes," the radio said.

Sandy drifted up to the nose to see what he could make out. Jim glanced after him, his pulse racing and his skin crawling with sweat; when he looked back at the video screens, the portside view was of an immense hand reaching toward him, like a shot from an old horror movie, and he let out a startled yip.

Then he felt the whole ship lurch slightly as the hand closed firmly around the grappler's "wrist." Another hand grabbed the catapult frame.

"Got you!" a new voice said over their suit intercoms.

Jim let his breath out, realizing for the first time that he had been holding it.

"That was an incredibly stupid thing to do," Jim's father said, as he and the boys stood at the mouth of the airlock, looking down on the battered I.S.S. *Mistake*. One grappler had been crushed and a catapult frame bent getting her back aboard the colony, and the plastic nose bubble had had to be smashed to get the boys out.

"I know," Jim agreed.

For a long moment the three of them stood, silently considering.

"On the other hand," his father said, "I'd say that it did serve as a good, practical demonstration that spaceflight's possible without rocket fuel, if you're not at the bottom of a gravity well."

Jim and Sandy both looked up at him, startled.

"This is just me making guesses, you understand," Iovino continued, "but I think that the ISA is going to have a few surprises in store for it, when people have had time to think this over. I've been thinking about it for eight hours now, ever since I found out you two idiots had gone out that airlock. I'd guess that in a few months, maybe a year, we'll see intercolony trade established, without any necessity for trips down to Earth, now that you boys have shown us we don't need Earth-built equipment to survive out there."

"Won't the ISA object?" Sandy asked.

"Probably," Iovino replied. "They might even cut us off, and we could have some rough times up here. These colonies were deliberately designed not to be completely independent—the Earthpeople were playing politics, scared what might happen up here. But the colonies are all different, and I think what each one lacks, another can make up—if we have some way to reach each other."

"I don't know, Dad," Jim said. "The catapults didn't really work that well."

"So maybe we won't use catapults. Maybe we'll use solar sails or some other system. People have dreamed up plenty of ideas over the last century; it's just a matter of finding which one works." He shrugged. "Not your problem anymore, boys."

He gave the *Mistake* one last look, then turned away.

"Let's go home," he said.

WATCHING NEW YORK MELT

A gobbet of molten glass spattered and sizzled across the sidewalk as I turned the corner; I stepped around it and glanced up. The saucer was still hanging there, right above the next block, and the building there—I didn't know the name—was down to about the fifteenth floor, the red-glowing ends of exposed beams like blown-out birthday candles.

I didn't have time to watch, though; I had to get lunch and get back to the office. I pushed past the guy selling souvenir pieces of the Empire State Building and went into the coffee shop.

Harry was already at the counter; I took the stool beside him and picked up the menu he had just put down.

He sipped coffee and said, "So what do you think?"

"About what?"

"Those saucers melting the city."

I shrugged. "Not my problem," I said.

"True enough, but it's a shame, all the same. I didn't mind when they got the World Trade Center, but I'm going to miss the Empire State."

"Could be worse," I said. "The Chrysler is still there. Maybe they're art critics and they'll leave the good ones."

"I thought of that," Harry said. "Sort of, anyway. I thought when they first started that maybe it was all some cockeyed conceptual art project, like when they wrapped that island in plastic, y'know what I mean?"

I nodded. "It's a thought," I agreed.

"That can't be it, though; they'd never get the city to go along this far. One building, maybe two, but not this."

I put down the menu as the waitress came along.

Harry ordered the grilled Reuben; I got a club sandwich.

134

"What I want to know," Harry said, as the waitress stomped away, "is who's going to clean up the mess? The souvenir hunters will get bored eventually, and you can bet that the garbagemen aren't going to do it. Against union rules, probably. The city'll have to hire a demolition crew to break up the bigger pieces and haul everything away. And do you think the city can *pay* for something like that? Of course not! And you can bet that the damn feds won't want to help—not in New York."

I nodded. "You're right; that stuff'll probably be lying around for months, maybe years, all over the city."

"Damn right," he said.

We didn't talk much after that, just ate, then ran. I had to get back to the office.

Outside the saucer had moved on, toward the West Side, and I could see two more in the distance. A pair of fighter planes roared past without doing anything.

My manager met me on the stairs. "Get your stuff cleaned out of that pigsty you call a desk." he said. "We're moving."

"What?"

"Some damn expert came by, says that the saucers will be taking down this building by Thursday or Friday—maybe over the weekend if we're lucky. I've got us a temporary place up on East Fifty-fifth; we'll probably need to move out to the suburbs eventually."

"Oh, jeez," I said.

"Not my fault," he said. "Get with it. The boxes are over by the coffee machine."

I nodded, and he went on past me down the stairs.

I went to my desk and started pulling open drawers.

"Damn," I said as I yanked the lap drawer open and spilled pencils on the carpet. "Stupid aliens. That's New York for you; if it's not one thing it's another. All we need now is for the movers to go on strike!"

MONSTER KIDNAPS GIRL AT MAD SCIENTIST'S COMMAND!

It slithered up to the bar and settled onto the stool beside me.

"Gin and tonic," it told the bartender.

The bartender gave it the eye. "Got any ID?" he asked.

The thing writhed around for a moment and produced a battered wallet from somewhere. It flipped the billfold open, extracted a folded paper, and handed it to the bartender.

"What's this?" he said warily, picking it up. "This ain't no driver's license."

"I can't drive," it said apologetically. "That's my genetic-experiment authorization form."

The bartender unfolded the paper and looked it over.

"Hmph," he snorted. "Looks okay. Where's the date?"

It extended a pseudopod and pointed.

"Oh, I see it," the bartender said. He blinked at it and then grinned. "Hey, kid," he said, "happy birthday!" He dropped the paper on the bar and reached for the bottle of gin.

"Thanks," the thing said.

It looked like about four hundred pounds of tentacles and slime. Two stalked eyes projected from a scaly purple lump that didn't have enough of a neck to be a head, and the rest of the face consisted of slit nostrils, a big sloppy maw, and a row of tendrils. The dominant color, overall, was a bilious green.

It looked familiar, but I couldn't place it at first.

A tentacle retrieved the paper from the bar. I watched, trying not to be blatant about it, and saw where it went—a belly pouch.

The bartender set the gin and tonic on the bar, and the thing picked it up gingerly in one tentacle. The eyes drooped down to focus on the glass, and it took a tentative sip.

I smiled. "Just turned twenty-one, huh?" I asked.

The eyes swung around to look at me, and then the mouth stretched into a grin bigger than my head. "That obvious, huh?" it said.

I recognized that grin.

"Hey, I know you!" I said. "You were in the remake of *Return of the Jedi*, right? In Jabba's throne room?"

The grin grew wider. "Yeah," it said, "that was me."

"Hey, you were great!" I said. "Really!"

"Thanks," it said, eyestalks dipping modestly.

"Hey, drink up—next round's on me!" I said. "I don't meet very many famous movie actors." I raised my glass and took a slug of bourbon.

It raised its own glass and took another sip, a little larger this time. I signaled the bartender and laid my MasterCard on the bar. "Keep 'em coming," I said, indicating the monster and myself.

"You don't have to do that . . ." it began while the barkeep was running the card through the reader.

"No, it's okay," I said. "I've got the money—I can afford it."

"Well," it said, "if you're sure . . ."

"I'm sure," I said. "Drink up!"

It drank.

"You always been in movies?" I asked.

It nodded. "Oh, yeah," it said. "I was made for the movies. Ever see an oldie called *Pets*?"

I sat back and thought for a minute, and it came back to me.

"I think I did," I said. "Big-budget horror movie, right? Tom Cruise as the crazy old hermit? Jennifer Bacon as the Marine sergeant?"

"That's the one," it agreed. "I was one of the extras, when all the monsters start coming out of the attic. I was six months old, could barely crawl. They ordered me up special for that film."

I nodded. "You remember working on it?"

It stared at me. "What, are you nuts? I was *six months old*! What do *you* remember that far back?"

"Nothing," I admitted.

"Well, I don't either," it said, miffed. "You think I'm some kind of freak?"

I hesitated and then pointed out, "Well, you *are* a monster."

"Sure I am," it said. "And proud of it, too! But that doesn't mean I'm not human."

"Ummm . . ." I began.

"Legally," it said warningly. "I'm human."

I shrugged. "Okay," I said, "you're human. No offense. But come on, how am I supposed to know how different you are? You've got to admit, you aren't exactly just another face in the crowd! I'm sorry if I offended you, but I've never had a chance to talk to a movie monster before."

"All right," it relented. "Apology accepted."

I gulped bourbon. "So," I said, "you started out in *Pets* when you were a baby. Then what?"

"Well, the studio put me up for adoption, but got no takers, and then the Artificial Child Welfare Act went through and the producer of *Pets* found himself playing Daddy to *fifteen* of us little monsters and farmed most of us out to relatives and ex-wives. I got lucky, I guess; Mom was ex-wife number two, and far too good for that son of a bitch. She raised me like her own son." It—or rather, "he," going by that last sentence—sniffled a little and slurped gin.

I nodded. "So was the *Jedi* remake your next role?"

"Naw," he said, "of course not! Mom needed money to support me—we eat a lot—and why shouldn't I help earn my keep, when it's so easy for me? I was in *Arms Race*, and *Ms. McGillicuddy on Mars*, and a couple of others—*Jedi* was my sixth. I was nine."

"Nine?" I marveled. "I'll be damned; that was a hell of a performance for a kid your age!"

"I know," he said. "I was *good*. I could always get work, even when half us monsters were on welfare." He drank gin, and I realized he was on his third or fourth; the bartender had been refilling them so smoothly I hadn't even noticed. I'd only had one before the kid came in and was working on my third over all.

I was just far enough gone not to worry about what might happen if I got a four-hundred-pound monster, a monster unfamiliar with alcohol, good and drunk.

"So if life's so good," I asked, "how come you're here drinking alone on your birthday?"

One eye had wandered off; the other had drooped somewhat. Now it rose up straight again and stared at me, though the other one was still looking somewhere in the direction of the video.

"You don't want to hear it," he said at last.

"Sure I do!" I said.

The other eye wheeled back around. "If you're so damn curious," he asked, "then what are *you* doing here drinking by yourself?"

I shrugged. "I've got nothing better to do."

Both eyes were trying to focus on me and not quite managing it, and a fifth gin and tonic was in a nearby tentacle. "Who are you, anyway?" he demanded.

I held out a hand. "Ryan Tewary," I said. "And what do you go by?"

It reluctantly held out a tentacle, and we shook. "They call me Bo," he said. "My real name's Genex HW 244-06."

"Pleased to meet you, Bo," I said. "Call me Rye."

He nodded.

"You haven't said what you're doing here," I remarked.

I think he glowered at me, but with his anatomy it was hard to be sure. "I just turned twenty-one," he said. "I shouldn't buy myself a legal drink to celebrate?"

"You've had a lot more than one," I pointed out—the fifth glass was empty. "And besides, isn't it sort of traditional to party with friends, not by yourself?"

"What makes you so snoopy?" he asked.

I shrugged. "Just curious. Scientific curiosity."

"You're a scientist?"

I nodded.

"Microbiology?"

I didn't like the tone he used to say that, and I was glad I wasn't a genetic engineer. "No," I said. "Flavor chemistry."

Bo nodded. He looked at the barman and held out his glass. "Fill 'er up," he said.

"Kid," the bartender said, "I think you've had enough for now."

Even in my own less than entirely sober condition I could see his point, so before it could turn into an argument, I said, "Come on, kid, let's find someplace friendlier."

Bo's eyes swiveled a little unsteadily, looking over the bartender, the bar, and me, and then he nodded. "Right," he said. He slithered off the stool. I signed the tab and got up.

"I'm still buying," I said as we headed for the door.

"Hey, you don't have to," he said. "I've got money. Truth is, I'm stinkin' rich, y'know. Movie work pays."

"That's okay," I said. "I'm stinkin' rich, too."

He stopped in the doorway and looked me over.

"You said you're a chemist?"

"A flavor chemist," I agreed.

"That pays well?"

I motioned for him to stop blocking the door as I said, "What're your three favorite flavors of ice cream, Bo?"

He blinked at me, puzzled. "You talking shop? I'm no chemist."

"Just tell me your three favorite flavors."

"Uh . . . vanilla, coffee, and creamberry, I guess," he said as he worked his way out onto the sidewalk.

"Well, I invented creamberry."

He stopped dead and stared at me. "You *did*?" he said.

I nodded and pointed at the drifting Stardust™ up the street. "Let's try that place," I said.

"Okay."

We walked on in silence for a moment—at least, I walked; I'm not sure how to describe what Bo did, but it moved him along. It wasn't *really* slithering.

Then he asked, "So if you're a rich, famous inventor, why don't you have anything better to do than go out drinking with me?"

"If you're a rich, famous movie monster . . ." I began.

He wiggled a tentacle at me. "Okay, I get the idea. I'll tell my story if you tell yours first."

"It's a deal. Mine's real short. About a year after creamberry hit the market, I had a little industrial accident—my own damn fault, I'm not blaming anybody. I got careless. Nothing all that serious, by most standards—just minor nerve damage."

"Uh . . . what kind of nerve damage?"

"Nothing much," I said bitterly. "I lost my sense of smell, that's all."

"But . . . oh. You're a flavor chemist."

"I *was*, anyway. But now . . . well, I can still run the computer, but that's about it."

"Jeez," he said. "That's rough!"

I didn't answer at first, except by pushing open the door of the bar, but then I burst out, "Damn *right* it's rough! I get so damn *mad* about it! One stupid little mistake and my whole career is gone!"

We sat down at the bar; the bartender was busy down at the other end.

"So you lost your career," he said. "I can see the drinking, I guess. But don't you have any friends to party with?" He seemed to realize he'd been a bit blunt, and he turned his eye-stalks away, ostentatiously examining the decor.

"Not anymore," I said. "People get tired of drinking with somebody who just gets morose about it."

The eyes drifted back in my direction, and he might have nodded a bit—or maybe that was just swaying. He'd been drinking a lot, after all, and he was new at it. "Um," he said.

"So what's *your* beef?" I said.

That huge mouth of his sort of pursed up for a minute; then he leaned over toward me and whispered, "It's sort of embarrassing."

"Spit it out," I said. "I'm hardened."

He blinked and spat it out.

"I'm still a virgin."

I blinked at that.

"You're a virgin," I said stupidly.

He nodded. "Twenty-one years old and I've never gotten laid. Never even gotten close."

I thought about that for a second and then said, "Um . . . pardon my asking this, Bo—but just what else did you expect, given your, ah . . . your appearance?"

"I don't know what the hell I *expected*, but I sure know what I *wanted*," he said bitterly, "and this ain't it!"

"But . . . Bo, your anatomy, I mean . . ."

"I know what you mean," he said. "Look, I don't know that much about it, I don't think anyone does, but Rye, I've been interested in girls since I was twelve, and I've got the equipment—maybe not exactly like most guys, but it works. I've been whacking off since I was thirteen—and I'm *still* just whacking off."

"Ah . . . what *kind* of girls?" I asked.

"*Girl* girls, stupid! You think because I look like this that I only want to screw monsters? Hey, you don't look like Valerie Bertinelli yourself, y'know."

"What about female movie monsters?"

He snorted, a truly disgusting sound. "Bleah!" he said. "Maybe they don't look as bad to me as they do to you—I mean, I'm used to what I see in the mirror, and I'm happy with it—but they sure don't have any sex appeal, either. I mean, would *you* want to make it with a movie monster?"

I had to admit I had never considered the idea and didn't find it very appealing.

"Besides," Bo went on, "there are only about sixty of us, all together, and because of all the legal trouble they aren't making any more and almost all of us are male. A couple I think are neuter. I don't know why they did that, but they did."

I knew why they did that, actually—I was old enough to remember when the point was brought up in the papers. They didn't want anyone taking chances on maybe producing a *fertile* female monster that could be the mother for whole new generations of monsters. I decided not to mention that.

The bartender came up about then, and Bo shut up. I gave the barkeep my card and told her, "It's all on me. I'll have bourbon and ginger. My friend here will have a Coke."

"Hey," Bo protested.

"You don't think you've had enough?" I asked him.

"Hell, no! Look, I told you why . . ."

I held up a hand. "Okay," I said, "what'll it be?"

He considered. "Get the Coke," he told the bartender, "but put rum in it."

"Right," she said.

While she was getting the drinks, I asked, "So are *all* you guys frustrated, then?"

He shrugged, an awe-inspiring sight. "I don't know," he said. "I mean, it's not that easy to talk about. I get the impression that a lot of us, especially the younger ones, just aren't interested."

The bartender arrived with his drink; he took a slurp and said, "I sure am, though."

The barkeep left, and I asked, "You ever date anyone?"

He snorted again, and his rum-and-Coke foamed up.

"You ever *try*?" I asked.

He hesitated and then he admitted, "Well, yeah. There was this girl in high school who got used to me, and I thought she liked me. Her name was Ashley, and she was a cute little blonde, and she'd say hi to me every day in the halls. So one day I met her after school and asked if I could take her out to a movie or something, and she just stared at me, and then she started to giggle, and then she just burst out laughing, and

I said something stupid, I forget what, and she was practically rolling on the ground, laughing at me ..."

I thought he was going to start bawling, but he gathered himself together and took a deep breath—*that* was something to see!—and then went on, "So after that I never even asked again. And I sort of avoided girls in general. And then I started avoiding guys, too, because they'd all talk about their dates, or how hot their sex lives were, or later on they'd even be talking about their *wives*, and I haven't even gone on my first damn *date*!"

He slammed the glass of rum-and-Coke down on the bar with that last word, and it shattered. He looked at it stupidly and said, "Oops."

"No problem," I said, mopping up the mess with a stack of paper napkins and waving to the bartender with my free hand.

She came, and we got the mess cleaned up and added to our bill, and a twenty-dollar cash tip let us stay where we were and go on drinking.

"Maybe I *have* had about enough," Bo admitted as he sipped his replacement Coke—no rum this time.

I nodded.

"You know," I said, "you shouldn't let that one girl, Ashley, ruin your whole life, Bo. I mean, she was just a kid, and you caught her by surprise. You're older now, you're not a kid, you're a little more self-assured—you should try again."

"Yeah, but I'm not in school anymore, either—where am I supposed to find someone to ask?"

"Anywhere," I said, with a sweeping gesture that left me a little dizzy. It began to register that I'd been drinking a little more than was good for me, but I didn't let that interfere with my speech. "Right here in this bar, maybe. The world's full of beautiful women, Bo, and they aren't *all* unreachable. You're a nice guy, you're rich, you're famous—you aren't handsome, but you can't have everything, and hey, you're *different*, right? There's gotta be a girl for you somewhere! All you need to do is find her—and you'll never find her if you don't *look*! Right?"

He stared at me with drooping eyes. "Right," he said, a bit doubtfully.

"And you've gotta let them know you *mean* it, Bo! That girl Ashley probably thought it was a joke—I mean, she probably didn't realize you were serious, that you've got the same

needs and desires as any other guy. You need to make a girl
know you really want her—you have to sweep her right off
her feet!"

I was losing the thread of what I was saying and wasn't
sure I was making sense any more, but it took a real effort to
shut myself up.

I was so busy gathering my wits that I didn't realize at first
that Bo was staring at me. His eyes weren't drooping any
more.

"You're right, Rye," he said. "You're *damn* right!"

Then he got off the stool, and I tried to get off my own, but
my feet got tangled and I went over sideways, and by the time
I was untangled I'd forgotten why I wanted to get up in the
first place, and it seemed like an awful lot of effort when
there was a perfectly good floor there for me to lie on.

Then the bartender was there leaning over me, which was
a very interesting sight indeed, and I enjoyed that for a minute before I realized she was trying to get me back on my
feet.

I was glad to cooperate, once I knew what she wanted, but
even so, it took both of us to get me upright.

And once I was upright, the first thing I did was to sit
down again—not on a stool this time; the bartender got me to
a booth.

"No more drinks for you," she said. "You want some coffee, or something to sober you up?"

"No coffee," I said, "but I could use something, I guess."

She brought something, a little green pill and some orange
juice to wash it down, and I swallowed it all and sat back,
while she went back to her duties. The stuff began to work in
a minute or two, or maybe the booze was just wearing off on
its own, and I was able to lift my head and look around and
realize that I didn't see Bo anywhere.

"Hey," I called to the bartender. "Where'd Bo go?"

"Who?"

"The guy I came in with—the movie monster. Where is
he?"

She shrugged. "He . . ."

That was as far as she got, because she was interrupted by
an ear-piercing shriek.

We turned just in time to see Bo weaving his way out the
door with a chunky redhead in his tentacles.

I don't mean walking alongside—Bo was carrying her, and

she didn't look at all happy about it. She was kicking and struggling, and she was the source of the shriek we'd heard.

Bo seemed oblivious to her reaction; his eyes were waving about wildly, and he was staggering—at least, I think it was staggering, but since I never figured out his means of propulsion in the first place I can't be sure. Let's just say his path was not a straight line.

"I'm calling the cops," the bartender said, and she slipped away.

I got to my feet, wavered for a moment until the floor steadied itself, then staggered out the door after Bo.

It wasn't hard to spot him—a four-hundred-pound monster carrying a screaming woman down the middle of an otherwise quiet street does sort of stand out from the background.

I tried to run after him, but with all the liquor sloshing in me, it wasn't much of a run, and he was really moving. I hadn't realized he could go that fast. He'd gone three blocks before I got close, and by then I was too out of breath to yell at him; I just tottered along behind him, trying to suck in enough air to be heard over the redhead's hollering.

Then we heard the sirens.

"Oh, shit," I said.

Bo stopped where he was and looked around, puzzled, still holding the girl.

She stopped yelling and looked around, too.

A moment later the first cop car pulled up in front of us, and two cops climbed out, one on either side. One had his revolver out, and the other had a riot gun.

"All right, hold it right there!" the one with the shotgun called.

Bo blinked, and I thought I'd never seen so stupid an expression on anybody's face, human or otherwise.

"You mean me?" he said, in a tiny little voice.

Another car pulled up, and some idiot in civilian clothes stuck his head and a camera out the window and started shooting.

"Put the lady down!" the cop called.

Bo looked down at her in surprise, as if he'd forgotten he was carrying her.

"Jeez, miss, I'm sorry," he said. "I guess I got carried away." He lowered her gently and stood her on her feet.

"*I* was the one who got carried away!" she snapped. She

tugged her purse free from where it had snagged in Bo's belly pouch.

I figured the crisis was over, so I stepped up and put a hand on Bo's tentacle.

"Freeze!" the cop with the revolver shouted, and I froze, startled.

"Put up your hands!" the other one yelled.

I put up my hands, saying, "Officer, it's okay, really, he's harmless!"

Bo raised his tentacles, too. On him it didn't look much like a gesture of surrender, though—more like he was getting ready to pounce. Fortunately, the cops didn't take it that way.

"You okay, lady?" one of them called.

"Yeah, I'm fine," she said, and she started to walk away, back toward the bar.

"Hold it!" the cop called, and she stopped, startled.

Then about three dozen other cops started arriving, and we were all bundled into a police van and taken to the station.

They put cuffs on me and tried to put them on Bo, but they wouldn't stay, just kept sliding off. He tried to look sheepish about it, but it didn't really work.

One cop even went up to the redhead with a pair of cuffs, but she snarled at him and said, "I'm the victim, bozo!"

The guy with the camera followed us.

At the station they checked our ID, and after a few minutes of standing around looking confused, the cops got us into a quiet little room, where a cop in plainclothes asked, "What's the story?"

Bo and I looked at each other, unsure who should say what, and the redhead took the opportunity to say, "This stupid monster kidnapped me!"

"I did not!" Bo burst out.

"You did too!" she shouted at him.

The cop held up his hands for quiet, and they subsided. Then he pointed at me.

"You," he said. "Who are you?"

"Dr. Ryan Tewary," I said.

"What do *you* say happened here?"

I sort of shuffled uncomfortably, then said, "I didn't see all of it, but I think it was just a misunderstanding. My friend here, Bo, was a little drunk, and he wanted to ask this lady for a date, and . . . and I don't know what happened after that."

"He kidnapped me, that's what!" the redhead announced.

The cop turned to her. "Tell me about it," he said, "and start with your name."

"Sheena Dubois," she said. "I was sittin' in the bar when this monster comes up and says hello and asks if he can buy me a drink, and I was sort of surprised, but I said yeah, and then he asks if I'd like to go somewhere for a bite to eat or something, and I looked at him and figured it had to be some kind of a joke, so I said ... ah ..."

Her voice trailed off for a moment, but the cop prompted her, "Go on."

"Well, I said, you know, where he's a monster, I said, you look more like you'd like to eat *me*, and he grinned at me and said sure, if you want, then he picked me up and carried me out of the bar, and then you guys came and stopped him. I guess it was supposed to be a joke, but it went a bit too far for me, you know?"

Bo had been staring at her during this speech, his eyes widening and his mouth coming open with surprise. "I thought ..." he began.

The cop turned to him. "You thought what?" he asked.

"I thought she meant like ... like oral sex, you know? I thought she was ..."

The cop stared at him. Ms. Dubois blushed crimson. "Oh," she said. "I was ... I didn't think of that."

Bo said, "Hey, I'm not a cannibal! You think I'd be walking the streets if I were dangerous? Come *on*!"

The cop just stared.

"It's not *my* fault the way I look!" Bo said to him.

The cop sighed. "I suppose not," he admitted. "But I'd have thought you'd be used to dumb jokes about it by now."

Bo shook his head. "You never get used to it," he said mournfully. "Maybe if I ... I don't feel too well."

"He's been drinking a lot," I volunteered, "and he's not used to it. We were celebrating his birthday—he just turned twenty-one."

The cop stared at me this time.

"So what did *you* have to do with all this?" he asked.

"Nothing, really. I mean, I do feel a little responsible, because I'd been buying Bo's drinks, and we were talking about women, you know, and I said he should be a little more forceful when he asked women out, and I guess he took that wrong, and ..." I let that trail off and then offered helpfully, "I was drunk, too."

The cop turned to Ms. Dubois and asked, "Do you want to press charges? We can call it battery, or kidnapping, or attempted rape, or we can just forget the whole thing as a simple misunderstanding. What'll it be?"

She blushed again and then said, "Oh, forget it. It was a misunderstanding. I didn't know ... I mean, he ... Never mind."

"Fine," the cop said. "We've got your name and address—tell the clerk where we can get hold of you if we need you, and you can go." He waved her away, and she marched out.

When the door opened I saw the guy with the camera standing right there, listening.

The cop asked a few more questions, then booked us as drunk and disorderly, and the night-court judge let us plead guilty and take a fine and a night in jail to sleep it off, which we did. I didn't feel like going home, anyway.

They put us in the same cell and kept us there until noon. It was nice and quiet and we slept well. No video—not in a local jail like that.

I woke up around ten, feeling a little rocky but not too bad, and called a guard, who brought us breakfast and, for an additional ten bucks, a morning newspaper, one of the tabloids. I opened it out and saw the headline—MONSTER KIDNAPS GIRL AT MAD SCIENTIST'S COMMAND!

I blinked and looked at the photo of Bo standing there in the street holding Sheena Dubois and looking stupid, with me crouched just behind him. It was easily the worst picture of me ever taken—I looked completely demented.

I started reading.

"Dr. Ryan Tewary, famed scientist and inventor who suffered brain damage in a laboratory accident two years ago, appears to have been the instigator of a wild late-night rampage by the monster known as Genex HW 244-06 ..."

I resented that; it wasn't brain damage, just nerve damage. I wondered if I should sue for libel.

The whole article was quite something—the writer seemed to alternate between describing Bo as a blood-crazed monster running amok and a poor, pitiful, misunderstood creature who just wanted a little love.

I, on the other hand, was consistently described as a lunatic.

I was just folding the paper when Bo stirred.

"Good morning," I called.

An eye curled around in my direction and opened.

"It wasn't all a bad dream after all, was it?" he asked.

"Afraid not," I said, thoughtfully sitting on the newspaper. He was clearly not ready to deal with it.

The guard heard his voice, I guess, because he came back and said, "Hey, Bo, your agent's on the phone, and I told her you weren't awake yet, but I can't get her to take no for an answer. You want to come talk to her?"

He blinked and sort of shrugged and said, "Sure, I guess so. I wonder how she knew where to find me, though?"

I bit my lip and didn't say anything, and Bo followed the guard down to the phone.

He talked for a long time, while I ate my breakfast and read the funnies.

When he came back Bo was clearly puzzled.

"What's up?" I asked, as the guard let him back into the cell.

"She says it was a great stunt," he said slowly, "and why didn't I tell her what I was going to do, and will I take two mil for the rights to my life story, and do I want to play myself? Oh, and there are some other offers, too." He looked at me. "Rye, what's she talking about?"

I showed him the newspaper. He sat down on his bunk to read it.

He made an unhappy noise when he got to the paragraph about thoughtless genetic engineers failing to consider the sex drives of their creations, but other than that he didn't say anything.

"They make me sound like a real freak!" he said when he'd finished it.

I just nodded.

"You know what my agent said, on the phone? She said they wanted to make a movie about me. They even have the advertising campaign worked out."

"Really?" He didn't sound pleased about it, so I didn't say anything more than that.

"Yeah," he said. He stood up and struck a dramatic pose. "They made him a monster," he declaimed, "but his heart was human—until an uncaring world drove him to acts of monstrous defiance!" He turned and spat at the sink. "What a lot of garbage!" he said, in his usual tones. "I mean, they're really making me sound as if I'm a complete psycho, or something." He shook his head sadly.

"It's a lousy world," I agreed.

"They must've seen the article," he said, picking up the tabloid and starting to read through it again.

He was just finishing it for the third time when the guard came to let us out.

"Noon," he announced. "Use the pay phone out front if you need to make any calls." He took the breakfast tray, then herded us out of the little cell block.

We collected our belongings, such as they were, and headed for the front door. As we approached, though, we both slowed down.

The doors of the station were glass, and we could see the little crowd out front, waving their homemade signs about.

OUTLAW MONSTERS! one said. END GENETIC EXPERIMENTS NOW! another said. MAKE OUR STREETS SAFE! a third said. All in all, there were twenty or thirty people milling about in an angry, unsettled way.

We stopped, our noses to the glass, and stared. Bo's eyes drooped in dismay.

Something caught my eye, and I pointed off to one side, where a smaller group stood, a little apart from the rest—three or four young women who weren't carrying any signs or marching about. They were standing and staring at us. They didn't look as hostile as the others.

"I wonder what they're doing here," I said. "They don't seem to be part of the demonstration."

Bo shrugged. "Just curiosity seekers, probably," he said. "I *am* in the movies, after all." He snorted derisively.

I nodded.

A sky-blue limo pulled up just behind the smaller group. A door opened, and a plump, dark-haired woman got out and stood there, looking at the protestors. Bo pointed and said, "That's Jenny, my agent. I asked her for a lift. Can we drop you somewhere?"

"Thanks," I said. "I could use a ride."

We both looked out at the mob again, and I said, "I don't think they'll hurt us, but it doesn't look as if they're going to leave, either."

Bo agreed.

"I guess we'd better just make a dash for it," I said.

He agreed again and opened the door.

We didn't run, but we walked quickly. None of the demonstrators touched us, but a few of them yelled insults, most of them obscene.

We were almost to the limo when one of the smaller group, a cute little brunette, jumped forward and grabbed Bo's tentacle.

"Bo," she said, "you can eat *me* if you like—and I'll eat you right back. I've never made it with a movie monster."

Bo's mouth fell open; so did mine.

Three other girls were right behind her, making similar offers either verbally or with body language.

Jenny was in the car, motioning for us to hurry up. The motor was running. I got into the limo and pulled Bo in after me.

Two of the girls managed to climb in before the door closed. We pulled away from the curb as they climbed onto Bo's ample lap.

He stared at them for a minute, then grinned and threw a tentacle around each. They cuddled up to him, squealing, and the tentacles slipped down a little lower.

I told the driver where to drop me off.

Jenny the agent ignored everything and just sat staring at the street ahead.

A few minutes later the car pulled over to the curb, and I reached for the latch. Then I paused. I leaned over and whispered in his ear, "They're just using you. They just want to try something kinky. They don't really care about you."

He looked up from the brunette's cleavage and asked, "So what?" Bo grinned at me. "Hey, Rye," he said, "true love would be nice, but up until now I've had nothing at all. Kinky sex has to be a heck of a lot better than nothing."

I didn't know what to say. I climbed out of the car and closed the door. As I was about to step away, the window slid down and Bo's eyes emerged.

"Hey, Rye," he said. "Thanks for everything! You were right—I just needed to be more forceful!"

He waved a tentacle as the car pulled away.

WINDWAGON SMITH
AND THE MARTIANS

I reckon most folks have heard of Thomas Smith, the little sailor from Massachusetts who turned up in Westport, Missouri, one day in 1853, aboard the contraption he called a windwagon. He'd rigged himself a deck and a sail and a tiller on top of a wagon and just about tried to make a prairie schooner into a *real* schooner. Figured on building himself a whole fleet and getting rich, shipping folks and freight to Santa Fe or wherever they might have a mind to go.

Well, as you might have heard, he got some of the folks in Westport to buy stock in his firm, and he built himself a bigger, better windwagon from the ground up, with a mainmast and a mizzen both, and he took his investors out for a test run—and they every one of them got seasick and scared as the devil at how fast the confounded thing ran, and they all jumped ship and wouldn't have more to do with it. Smith allowed as how the steering might not be completely smooth yet, though the idea was sound, but the folks in Westport just weren't interested.

And last anyone heard, old Windwagon Smith was sailing west across the prairie, looking for braver souls.

That's the last anyone's heard till now, anyways. A good many folks have wondered whatever became of Windwagon Smith, myself amongst them, and I'm pleased to be able to tell the story.

And if you ask how I come to know it, well, I heard it from Smith himself, but that's another story entirely.

Here's the way of it. Back in '53, Smith headed west out of Westport feeling pretty ornery and displeased; he reckoned that the fine men of Westport had just missed the chance of a lifetime and all over a touch of the collywobbles and a bit of wind. Wasn't any doubt in his mind but he could find braver men somewheres, who would back his company and put all those mule-drawn freight-wagons right out of business. It was just a matter of finding the right people.

So he sailed on and stopped now and then and told folks his ideas, and he was plumb disconcerted to learn that there wasn't a town he tried that wanted any part of his wind-wagon.

He missed a lot of towns, too, because the fact was that the steering *was* a mite difficult, and he didn't so much stay on the trail as try to keep somewhere in its general vicinity. He stopped a few times to tinker with it, but the plain truth is that he never did get it right, not so as one man could work it and steer small. After all, the clippers he'd learned on didn't steer with just a tiller but with the sails as well—tacking and so forth. If Smith had had more men on board, to help work the sails, he might have managed some fine navigation, instead of just aim-and-hope.

After a time, though, he had got most of the way to Santa Fe but had lost the trail again, and he was sailing out across the desert pretty sure that he was a good long way from where he had intended to be, when he noticed that the sand was getting to be awfully red.

The sky was getting darker, too, but there wasn't a cloud anywhere in it, and it wasn't but early afternoon; it just seemed as if the sun had shrunk up some, and the sky had dimmed down from a regular bright blue to a color more like the North Atlantic on a winter morning. The air felt damn near as cold as the North Atlantic, too, and that didn't seem right for daytime in the desert. What's more, Smith suddenly felt sort of light, as if the wind might just blow him right off his own deck, even though it didn't seem to be blowing any harder than before. And he was having a little trouble breathing, like as if he'd got himself up on top of a mountain.

And the sand was *awfully* red, about the color of a boiled lobster.

Well, old Windwagon Smith had read up on the West before he ever left Massachusetts, and he'd never heard of anything like this. He didn't like it a bit, and he took a reef in the sails and slowed down, trying to figure it.

The sand stayed red, and the sky stayed dark, and the air stayed thin, and he still felt altogether too damn light on his feet, and he commenced to be seriously worried and furled the sails right up, so that that windwagon of his rolled to a stop in the middle of that red desert.

He threw out the anchor to keep him where he was and had a time doing it, because although the anchor seemed a fair piece lighter than he remembered, it almost took him with it when he heaved it over. Seemed like he had to be extra careful about everything he did, because even the way his own body moved didn't seem quite right; of course, being a sailor, he could keep his feet just about anywhere, so he got by. He might have thought he was dreaming if he hadn't been the levelheaded sort he was and proud of his plain sense to know whether he was awake or asleep.

Just to be sure, though, he pinched himself a few times, and the red marks that left pretty much convinced him he was awake.

He stood on the deck and looked about, and all he saw was that red, red sand, stretching clear to the horizon whichever way he cared to look. The horizon looked a shade close in, at that; wasn't anything quite what it ought to be.

He didn't like that a bit. He climbed up aloft, to the crow's nest up above the main topsail, and he looked about again.

This time, when he looked to what he reckoned was west, he saw something move, something that was blue against the blue of the sky, so he couldn't make out just what it was.

It was coming his way, though, so he figured he'd just let it come and take a closer look when he could.

But he wasn't about to let it come on him unprepared. After all, there were still plenty of wild Indians around and white men who were just as wild without any of the excuses the Indians had, seeing as how they hadn't had their land stolen, or their women either, nor their hunting ruined. They could be just as wild as Indians, all the same.

He slid down the forestay and went below, and when he mounted back to the maintop, he had a six-gun on his belt and a rifle in his hand.

By now the blue thing was closer, and he got a good clear look at it, and he damn near dropped his rifle, because it was a ship, a sand ship, and it was sailing over the desert right toward him.

And what's more, there were three more right behind it, all of them tall and graceful, with blue sails the color of that dark sky. Proud as he was of his work, old Windwagon had to admit that the ugliest of the four was a damn sight better looking than his own windwagon had ever been, even before it got all dusty and banged up with use.

They were quieter, too. Fact is, they were near as silent as clouds, where his own windwagon had always rattled and clattered like any other wagon and creaked and groaned like a ship as well. All in all, it made a hell of a racket, but these four sand ships didn't make a sound—at least not that Smith could hear yet over the wind in the rigging.

He was pretty upset, seeing those four sand ships out there. Here he'd thought he had the only sailing wagon ever built, and then these four come over the horizon—not just one, but four, and any of them enough to burst a clipper captain's heart with envy.

If they were freighters, Smith knew that he wasn't going to get anywhere near as rich as he had figured, up against competition like that. He began to wonder if maybe the folks back in Westport weren't right, but for all the wrong reasons.

The sand ships' hulls were emerald green, and the trim was polished brass or bone white, and above the blue sails they flew pennants, gold and blue and red and green pennants, and they were just about the prettiest thing Smith had ever seen in his life.

He looked at them, and he didn't know what the hell they were doing there or where they'd come from, but they didn't look like anything wild Indians would ride, or anything outlaws would ride, so he just watched as they came sailing up to his own ship—or wagon, or whatever you care to name it.

Three of the sand ships slowed up and stopped a good ways off, but the first one in line came right up next to him.

That one was the biggest and the prettiest and the only one flying gold pennants. He figured it must belong to the boss of the bunch, the commodore or whatsoever he might be called.

"Ahoy!" Smith shouted.

He could see people on the deck of the sand ship, three of them, but he couldn't make out any faces, and none of them answered his hail. They were dressed in robes, which made him wonder if maybe they weren't Indians after all, or Mexicans.

"Ahoy!" he called again.

"Mr. Smith," one of them called back, almost as if he were singing, "come down where we can speak more easily."

Smith thought about that and noticed that none of them had any guns that he could see and decided to risk it. He climbed down, with his rifle, and he came over to the rail, where he could have reached out and touched the sand ship if he stretched a little.

He was already there when he realized that the strangers had called him by his right name.

Before he could think that over, the stranger who had called him said, "Mr. Smith, we have brought you here because we admire your machine."

Smith looked at the strangers and at the great soaring masts and dark-blue sails and at the shiny brass and the sleek green hull, and he didn't believe a word of it. Anyone who had a ship like that one had no reason to admire his windwagon. He'd been mighty proud of it until a few minutes ago, but he could see now that it wasn't much by comparison.

Well, he figured, the strangers were being polite. He appreciated that. "Thanks," he said. "That's a sweet ship you have there, yourself."

While he was saying that, he noticed that the reason he hadn't been able to make out faces was that the strangers were all wearing masks, shiny masks that looked like pure silver, with lips that looked like rubies. The eyes that showed through were yellow, almost like cat's eyes, and Smith wasn't too happy about seeing that. The masks looked like something Indians might wear, but he'd never heard of any Indians like these.

He said, "By the way, I'd be mighty obliged if you could tell me where I am; I lost my bearings some time back, and it seems as if I might be a bit off course."

He couldn't see which of the strangers it was that spoke, what with the masks, but one of them said, "My apologies, Mr. Smith. It was we who brought you here. You are on Mars."

"Mars?" Smith asked. He wasn't sure just how to take this. "You mean Mars, Pennsylvania? Down the road a piece from Zelienople?" He didn't see any way he could have wound up there, and he'd never heard tell that Pennsylvania had any flat red deserts, but that was one of the two places he'd ever heard of called Mars, and he didn't care to think about the other one much.

"No," the stranger said, "the planet Mars. We transported your excellent craft here by means that I am unable to explain, so that I might offer you a challenge."

Now, Smith knew something about the planets, because any

sailor does if he takes an interest in navigation, and he knew that Mars was sort of reddish, and the red sand would account for that nicely. He looked up at that shrunken sun and that dark-blue sky and then at those sand ships like nothing on Earth and decided that one of three things had happened.

Either he'd gone completely mad without noticing it and was imagining all this, which didn't bear thinking about but which surely fit the facts best of all; or somebody was playing one hell of a practical joke on him, which he didn't have any idea how it was being done; or the stranger was telling the truth. For the sake of argument, he decided he'd figure on that last one, because the second seemed plumb unlikely and the first wasn't anything he could figure on, never having been mad before and not knowing just how it might work. Besides, he'd simply never judged himself for the sort of fellow that might go mad, and he wasn't in any hurry to change his mind on that account.

So he figured the stranger was telling the truth. Whether it was magic, or some sort of scientific trick, he didn't know, but he reckoned he really was on Mars.

And he didn't figure he'd ever find his way back to Earth by himself.

"What sort of a challenge?" he asked.

He sort of thought he saw the middle stranger smile behind his silver mask.

"I," the middle stranger said, "am Moohay Nillay, and I am the champion yachtsman of all Teer, as we call our planet." Smith wasn't any too sure of those names, so I may have them wrong. "I have the finest sand ship ever built, and in it I have raced every challenger that my world provided, and I have defeated them all. Yet it was not enough; I grew bored and desired a new challenge and sought elsewhere for competitors who could race against me."

Smith began to see where this was leading, but he just smiled and said, "Is that so?"

"Indeed it is, Mr. Smith. Unfortunately, our two worlds are the only two in this system bearing intelligent life, and your world has not produced many craft that will sail on sand. I am not interested in sailing upon water—our planet no longer has any seas, and I find the canals too limiting. I might perhaps find better sport on the seas of your planet, but the means by which I drew you here will not send me to Earth. I have been forced to wait, to search endlessly for someone on your planet who would see the obvious value of sailing the plains. To date, you are only the second I have discovered. The first was a man by the name of Shard, Captain Shard of the *Desperate Lark*, who fitted his seagoing ship with wheels in order to elude pursuit; I drew him here and easily defeated his clumsy contrivance. I hope that you, Mr. Smith, will provide a greater test."

"Well, I hope I will, Mr. Nillay. I'd be glad to race you." Smith didn't really think he had much of a chance against those sleek ships, but he figured that it wouldn't hurt to try and that if he were a good loser, Mr. Nillay might send him back to Earth.

And of course, there was always the chance that his horse sense and Yankee ingenuity might just give him a chance against this smooth-talking Martian braggart.

Well, to make a long story a trifle less tiresome, Smith and the Martian agreed on the ground rules for their little competition. They would race due south, to the edge of a canal—Smith took the Martian's word for just where this canal was, since of course he didn't know a damn thing about Martian geography. Whoever got there first and dropped a pebble into the canal without setting foot on the ground would win the race.

The Martian figured it at about a two-day race, if the wind held up, and he gave Smith a pebble to use—except it wasn't so much your everyday pebble as it was a blue jewel of some kind. Smith hadn't ever seen one quite like it.

If Smith won, he was to have a big celebration in the Martian's hometown and would then be sent back to Earth, if he wanted. If he lost, well, he wouldn't get the celebration, but if he had put up enough of a fight, made it a good race and not a rout, the Martian allowed as he might consider maybe sending him back to Earth eventually, just out of the goodness of his heart and as a kind gesture.

Smith didn't like the sound of that, but then he didn't have a whole hell of a lot of choice.

"What about those other folks?" he asked, figuring he needed every advantage he could get. "I'm sailing single-handed, and you've got two crewmen and three other ships."

The Martian allowed as how that might be unfair. Captain Shard had had a full crew for his ship, and Mr. Nillay hadn't been sure whether Smith had anyone else aboard or not, but since he didn't, since he was sailing alone, then Mr. Nillay would sail alone, too. And the other three ships were observers, just there to watch and to help out if there was trouble.

Smith couldn't much quarrel with that, so after a little more arguing out details, the two ships were lined up at the starting line, Smith's windwagon on the left and the Martian sand ship on the right, both pointed due south.

One of the other Martians fired a starting pistol that didn't bang, it buzzed like a mad hornet, and the race was on.

Old Windwagon yanked the anchor aboard and started hauling his sheets, piling on every stitch of canvas his two little masts could carry, running back and forth like a lunatic trying to do it all by himself as fast as a full crew, all the while still keeping an eye on his course and making sure he was still headed due south.

Those sails caught the wind, and before he knew it, he was rolling south at about the best speed he'd ever laid on, with nothing left to do but stand by the tiller and hope a crosswind didn't tip him right over.

When he was rolling smooth, he glanced back at the Martian sand ship, and it wasn't there. He turned to the stern quarter, and then the beam, and he still didn't see it, but when he looked forward again there it was, a point or two off his starboard bow, that tall blue sail drawing well, full and taut, and that damn Martian yachtsman standing calm as a statue at the tiller.

And although it wasn't easy over the rattling and creaking of his own ship, Smith could hear the Martian sand ship make a weird whistling as it cut through that red sand.

Well, seeing and hearing that made Smith mad. He wasn't about to let some bossy little foreigner in a mask and a nightshirt beat him *that* easily, no sir! He tied down the tiller and ducked below and began heaving overboard anything he thought he could spare, to lighten the load and help his speed.

Extra spars and sails, his second-best anchor, and the trunk with his clothes went over the after rail; he figured that he could come back and pick them up later if he needed them. When the trunk had hit the ground and burst open, he turned and looked for that Martian prig and was about as pleased as you can imagine to see that he was closing the gap, gaining steadily on the Martian ship.

Then he hit a bump and went veering off to port and had to take the tiller again.

Well, the race went on and on, and Smith gained on the

Martian little by little, what seemed like just a few inches every hour, until not long after sunset, while the sky was still pink in the west, the two ships were neck and neck, dead even.

It was about at this point that it first sank in that they weren't going to heave to for the night, and Smith began to do some pretty serious worrying about what might happen if he hit a rock in the dark or somesuch disaster as that. He hadn't sailed his windwagon by night before.

He wasn't too worried about missing a night's sleep, as he'd had occasion to do that before, when he was crewing a clipper through a storm in the South Pacific or spending his money ashore in some all-night port, but he *was* worried about cruising ahead under full sail across uncharted desert in the dark.

It helped some when the moons rose, two little ones instead of a big one like ours, but he still spent most of that night in a cold sweat. About his only consolation was that the crazy Martian was near as likely to wreck as he was himself.

It was a mighty cold night, too, and he wrapped himself in all three of the coats he still had and wished he hadn't been so quick to throw his trunk over.

About the time when he was beginning to wonder if maybe the nights on Mars lasted for six months, the way he'd heard tell they did way up north, the sun came up again, and he got a good look at just where he stood.

He'd pulled ahead of the Martian, a good cable's length, maybe more. He smiled through his frozen beard at that; if he just held on, he knew he'd have the race won.

So he *did* hold on, as best he could, but something had changed. The wind had died down some, and maybe the Martian had trimmed his sails a bit better, or the wind had shifted a trifle, but by the middle of the afternoon, Windwagon saw that he wasn't gaining anymore, and in fact he might just be starting to lose his lead. He wasn't the least bit pleased, let me tell you.

He started thinking about what else he had that he could throw overboard, and he was still puzzling over that when he topped a low rise and got a look at what lay ahead.

He was at the top of the longest damn slope he'd ever seen in his life, a slope that looked pretty near as big as an ocean, and down at the bottom was a big band of green, and in the middle of that green was a strip of blue that Smith knew had to be the canal.

And it was downhill almost the entire way!

The green part wasn't downhill, he could see that, but that long, long red slope was. It wasn't steep, and it wasn't any too smooth, but it was all downhill, and that meant he didn't want to lighten the ship any more at all.

He tied down the tiller again and hung down over the side, pouring on the last of his axle grease so as to make the most out of that hill.

When he got back up on deck and looked back, he could see that he was gaining quickly now, pulling farther and farther ahead of the Martian's lighter ship. And that canal was in sight, straight ahead! He figured he just about had it won.

And then the wind, which had been just sort of puffing for a while, up and died completely.

By this time he was rolling hell-for-leather down that hill, at a speed he didn't even care to guess, and he didn't stop when the wind died—but that flat stretch of green ahead suddenly looked a hell of a lot wider than it had before.

He pulled up the tiller entirely, to cut the drag; after all, the canal stretched from one horizon to the other, so what did he need to steer for? He could still maneuver the sails if he had to.

He went bouncing and rattling down that hill, thumping and bumping over the loose rocks and the red sand, praying the whole way that he wouldn't tip over. He didn't dare look back to see where the Martian was.

And then he was off the foot of the slope, crunching his way across that green, which was all some sort of viney plant, and his wagon went slower and slower and slower and finally, with one big bounce and a bang, it came to a dead stop—a hundred feet or so from the canal.

Smith looked down at those vines and then ahead at that blue water and then back at the Martian sand ship, which wasn't much more than a dark spot on the red horizon behind him, and he just about felt like crying. There wasn't hardly a breath of wind, just the slightest bit of air, enough to flap the sails but not to fill them.

And what's more, the vines under his wheels weren't anywhere near as smooth as the red sand or the prairie grass back on Earth, and he knew it would take a good hard tug to get the old windwagon started again.

If he could once get it started, he figured that he could just about reach the canal on momentum, without hardly any wind; the vines sort of petered out in about another twenty feet, and from there to the canal the whole way was stone pavement, smooth white stone that wouldn't give his wheels the slightest bit of trouble.

But he needed a good hard push to get off those vines and get moving, and the wind didn't seem to be picking up, and that Martian was still sailing, smooth and graceful, closer and closer down the slope.

And thinking back, Smith recalled that the sand ship had a blade on the front. He hadn't seen much use for it back on the sand, but he could see how it would just cut right through those vines.

He looked about and saw that a dozen or so Martians, in their robes and masks, were standing nearby, watching silently. Smith wasn't any too eager to let them see him lose. If there was ever a time when he needed some of that old Yankee ingenuity he prided himself on, Smith figured this was it.

He looked down at the vines again and thought to himself that they looked a good bit like seaweed back on Earth. He was stuck in the weeds, just like he might be on a sandbar or in shoal water back on Earth.

Well, he knew ways of getting off sandbars. He couldn't figure on any tide to lift him off here, but there were other ways.

He could kedge off. He hauled up the anchor and heaved it forward hard as he could—and the way his muscles worked on Mars, that was mighty hard. That anchor landed on the edge of the pavement and then slid off as he hauled on it and bit into the soft ground under the vines.

That was about as far as he could haul by hand, though. For one man to move that big a wagon, even on Mars, he needed something more than his own muscle. He took the line around the capstan and began heaving on the pawls.

The line tautened up, and the wagon shifted and then inched forward—but he couldn't get up any sort of momentum, and he couldn't pull it closer than ten feet from the pavement, where it stopped again, still caught in the vines. When he threw himself on the next pawl, the anchor tore free.

He hauled it back on board and reconsidered. Kedging wasn't going to work, that was pretty plain; he couldn't get the anchor to bite on that white stone. So he was still on his sandbar.

He thought back and back and tried to remember every trick he'd ever heard for getting a ship off a bar or freeing a keel caught in the mud.

There was one trick that the men o' war used; they'd fire off a full broadside, and often as not the recoil would pull the ship free.

The problem with that, though, was that he didn't have a broadside to fire. His whole armory was a rifle, two six-guns, and a couple of knives.

He looked back up the slope, and he could see the sand ship's green hull now, and almost thought he could see the sun glinting on Mr. Nillay's silly mask, and he decided that he was damn well going to *make* himself a broadside—or if not a broadside, at least a cannon or two.

The wind picked up a trifle just then, and the sails bellied out a bit, and that gave him hope.

He went below and began rummaging through everything he had and found himself his heavy iron coffeepot. He took that up on deck and then broke open every cartridge he had and dumped the charges into the pot; he judged he had better than a pound of powder when he was through. He took his lightest coat, which wasn't really more than a bit of a linsey jacket anyway, and folded that up and stuffed it in on top of the powder for a wad. He put a can of beans on top for shot and then rolled up a stock certificate from the Westport and Santa Fe Overland Navigation Company and rammed it down the coffeepot's spout for a fuse.

The sails were filling again, but the wagon wasn't moving. Smith figured he still needed that little push. He wedged his contraption under the tiller mounting and touched a match to the paper.

It seemed to take forever to burn down, but finally it went off with a roar like a bee-stung grizzly bear, and that can of beans shot out spinning and burst on the hillside, spraying burnt beans and tin all over the red sand. The coffeepot itself was blown to black flinders.

And the wagon, with a creak, rolled forward onto the pavement. The sails caught the wind, feeble as it was, and with rattling and banging the windwagon clattered across that white stone pavement, toward the canal.

And then it stopped with a bump, about ten feet from the edge, just as the wind died again.

Smith just about jumped up and down and tore at his hair at that. He leaned over the rail and saw that there was a sort of ridge in the pavement and that his front wheels were smack up against it. He judged it would take near onto a hurricane to get him past that.

He looked back at the Martian sand ship, with its long, graceful bowsprit that would stick out over the canal if it stopped where he was, and he began swearing a blue streak.

He was at the damn canal, after all, and the Martian was just now into the vines, and he wasn't about to be beat like that. He knew that he had to *drop* the pebble, not throw it, so he couldn't just run to the bow and heave it into the water. He was pretty sure that that old Martian would call it a foul, and rightly, if he threw the confounded thing.

And then that old horse sense came through again, and he ran up the rigging to the main yard, where he grabbed hold of the starboard topsail sheet and untied it, so that it swung free. Hanging onto the bottom end, he climbed back to the mizzenmast, up to the crosstrees, still holding the maintopsail sheet, and dove off, hollering, with the pebble-jewel in his hand.

He swooped down across the deck, lifting his feet to clear it, and then swung out past the bow, up over the canal, and at the top of his swing he let the pebble drop.

It plopped neatly into the water, a foot or two out from the canal wall, while that Martian yachtsman was still fifty feet back. Windwagon Smith let out a shriek of delight as he swung wildly back and forth from the yardarm, and a half-dozen Martians applauded politely.

By the time Smith got himself back down on the deck, Mr. Nillay had got his own ship stopped on the pavement, and he was standing by the edge of the canal, and even with his mask on Smith thought he looked pretty peeved, but there wasn't much he could do.

And then a few minutes later the whole welcoming committee arrived, and they took Smith back to their city, which looked like it was all made out of cut glass and scrimshaw, and they made a big howdy-do over him and told him he was the new champion sailor of all Mars, the first new champion in nigh onto a hundred years, and they gave him food and drink and held a proper celebration, and poor old Mr. Nillay had to go along and watch it all.

Smith enjoyed it well enough, and he had a good old time for a while, but when things quieted down somewhat, he went over to Mr. Nillay and stuck out his hand and said, "No hard feelings?"

"No, Mr. Smith," the Martian said, "no hard feelings. However, I feel there is something I must tell you."

Smith didn't like the sound of that. "And what might that be, sir?" he asked.

"Mr. Smith, I have lied to you. I cannot send you back to Earth."

"But you said . . ." Smith began, ready to work himself up into a proper conniption.

"I did not believe I would lose," the Martian interrupted, and his voice still sounded like music, but now it was like a funeral march. "Surely, a sportsman like yourself can understand that."

Well, Smith had to allow as how he *could* understand that, though he couldn't rightly approve. It seemed to him that it was mighty callous to go fetching someone off his home planet like that, when a body couldn't even send him back later.

Old Nillay had to admit that he had been callous, all right, and he damn near groveled, he was so apologetic about it.

But Smith had always been philosophical about these things. It wasn't as if he'd had a home anywhere on Earth; all he'd had was his windwagon, and he still had that. And there on Mars he was a hero and a respected man, where on Earth he hadn't been much more than a crackpot inventor or a common seaman. And the food and drink was good, and the Martian girls were right pretty when they took their masks off, even if they weren't exactly what you'd call white, being more of a brown color, and those big yellow eyes could be mighty attractive. What's more, what with Martians being able to read minds, which they could, that being how they could speak English to Smith, the women could always tell just what a man needed to make him happy, and folks were just generally pretty obliging.

So Windwagon Smith stayed on Mars and lived there happily enough, and he raced his windwagon a few more times and mostly won, and all this is why he never did turn up in Santa Fe and why he never did find any more investors after that bunch in Westport backed out.

And I know you may be thinking, well, if he stayed on

Mars, then how in tarnation did I ever hear this story from him so as I could tell it to you the way I just did, and all that I can say is what I said before.

That's another story entirely.

THE RUNE AND THE DRAGON

When we came down from the hills of Lakar, the plains lay before us hot and green in the summer sun. The very air shimmered in the heat of the day, and the walls of the city of Taki'il flickered on the horizon like a mirage.

I turned back toward the cool blue of the hills, looked up, and saw the dragon wheeling in the sky. Far above us, so high that it looked no larger than a bird, it soared in the warm air, black against the light of day.

"Still it follows us," my comrade Pelirrin remarked, and I nodded in agreement.

"And still," Pelirrin added, "it does not attack."

"For that," I said, "we may be grateful." I had had my fill of watching the monster; I turned to face the plains again and saw that my brother Derenneth, the third and final member of our party, had moved on ahead into the tall grass.

I called him to wait, but he paid me no heed; so I ran to catch up with him. Pelirrin wasted no breath on calling but hurried to join us. We dared not be parted from Derenneth: it was he who carried the crumbling parchment that bore the golden rune.

We had come down from Lakar to learn the secret of that symbol and to rid ourselves of the dragon's presence. The legends we had heard since our earliest childhood spoke of the wise men of the plains—the magicians who guarded the cities—and we were seeking a mage or seer who might explain to us the mystery that had befallen us and the meaning of that strange sign. Our own people have no patience for tricks or befuddlements, for the elliptical speeches of dubious soothsayers. We had no time to spare for the reading of books or for the learning of ancient tongues. Life is hard in

Lakar, hard and fierce, and the men of the hills become themselves hard and fierce, with little taste for the decadent pleasures of the cities or for any wonder less direct than the edge of a fine blade.

That made it all the more curious that we had found the rune where we had, for we had been roaming the heights of the mountains beyond Lakar, where no child was ever born and cowards dare not venture. The winds are harsh and cold, even in the midst of summer, and the ground is broken stone.

I had seen sixteen winters; my brother, two more; and our friend Pelirrin fell between us in age. We were young and eager, and we set out to find adventure in the mountains. We dreamed of peaks scaled, of caves explored, of monsters slain, their hides brought back for our kin to marvel at. Derenneth boasted to Pelirrin's sisters of our planned exploits and basked in the warmth of their admiration.

When we had truly reached those mountains, though, we found that we had not planned as well as we had thought. The upper cliffs were too steep to scale without spikes and rope, both of which we had neglected to bring. We found no caves save for crevices too narrow to enter, and found but hollows that led nowhere. There were neither monsters nor, for that matter, any of the ordinary beasts we had thought to hunt for food; and after three days, we had eaten all we had brought. Our clothes were not warm enough for comfort; it had been impossible to believe, sweltering in the sun on the hills around our village, that these slopes could be so cold as we had been warned, and we had brought nothing beyond our ordinary leathers and light hide jackets. We had neither furs nor heavy woolens to protect us from the night winds.

On the fourth day, the winds grew worse, and, hungry and thirsty and tired, we sought any shelter that could be found. Pelirrin went to look in one direction, and I in another, while Derenneth stayed where we had last camped, guarding our meager supplies.

It was Pelirrin who found the hut and called for us to join him.

We arrived, coming around a shoulder of bare rock, to find Pelirrin backing out of the open doorway as if in horror of what lay within.

We stopped where we were and looked at one another for guidance. Seeing no answers in my face, Derenneth called, "What is it?"

"A man," Pelirrin told us. "A man in the hut. I think he's dying."

Derenneth turned to me once again, and I to him, but for a moment neither of us knew what to say. Pelirrin ceased his retreat and stood staring at the door of the hut. I called, "Is it plague, then?"

Pelirrin shook his head. "I cannot say," he replied. "It is no sickness I have ever seen, if sickness it be."

"Let us chance it, then," Derenneth said. "Perhaps we can help him, and we do have need of shelter."

I nodded my agreement, and cautiously we advanced. My own heart throbbed like a drum in my chest; I cannot speak for my comrades, but I am sure they were as frightened as I was.

The inside of the hut was dark: hides covered the windows, and the door faced away from the sun. Still, as the three of us entered—first Derenneth, then myself, and then Pelirrin—we could see the shape that lay on a rough bed against the opposite wall.

It was an old man, perhaps as old as my own grandfather, and his right arm was thrust up, clutching a roll of parchment. He groaned softly and turned his head toward us at the sound of our approach.

There was no covering; he wore the remains of leather breeches and a fur-trimmed tunic, but both were blackened and crumbling. We could see that much of his flesh, too, was black.

"Is it plague?" Pelirrin asked, leaning over my shoulder.

"No," Derenneth replied. "See his clothing? He's been burned."

"Burned?" Pelirrin and I exclaimed.

"How could he be burned so badly, though?" Pelirrin asked. "And how could he have lived through such a burning?"

"How should I know?" Derenneth replied.

"Perhaps he fell into a camp fire," I suggested.

"No camp fire was e'er so hot," Derenneth replied. "'Twas more likely a blacksmith's forge."

"There is no smithy in these mountains," I retorted, and we all fell silent for a moment.

The man on the bed moaned again and let his head sink back, no longer watching us. Curiously, though, he still held his right forearm upright, still with the parchment firm in his hand.

"We might ask him," Pelirrin suggested.

I nodded, and Derenneth moved to the bedside.

"I give you greetings, sir," he said. "Is there any manner in which we might aid you? I fear we have nothing with us to soothe your burns—no balm or salve, not even bear-fat—but is there anything else we can do to ease you?"

I drew up behind Derenneth and peered over his shoulder. I saw then why Pelirrin had fled: the man's body was horrible to see, the flesh bubbled up in oozing burst blisters and the skin blackened. I turned away, hoping that I would not disgrace myself before my brother by being ill.

The man did not seem to pay my brother's words any heed; instead, he said, in speech so slurred we could barely understand him, "'Ware the dragon."

"Your pardon, sir," Derenneth replied. "We do not understand. What dragon?"

Pelirrin suggested, "Perhaps he refers to old man Death as the dragon; it seems to me I've heard such usage."

"No, no," the old man said, rousing somewhat.

"'Twas not Death, but only a dragon that seared me. I found his treasure hoard, and I robbed it ere he woke and found me." He paused to catch his breath; his voice had sunk to a whisper after the first few words, and we all bent close so that we might hear.

"He caught me there and burned me, but I took the rune; he could not burn me again for fear of it. I escaped him and came here."

"Did not the beast pursue you?" Pelirrin asked. "I have heard that dragons are most persistent in recovering lost treasures and in slaying those that took them."

"So they are, boy, so they are," the man said in his fading whisper. "He waits outside."

We turned upon each other suddenly at that, looking at each other's eyes in fright and wonder. I turned away from the bed—and glad I was to look no more at the poor man's blackened body—and thrust my head out the door.

At first I did not see it, as from long habit I looked first ahead and to either side, but then I gazed upward and saw that great dark shape soaring overhead. It saw me as well and spat a tongue of yellow flame. I ducked back into the hut.

"The dragon is there," I said.

"How is it that we did not see this dragon as we approached?" Derenneth asked.

"Who looks to the skies when the wind is so strong?" I answered him. "The beast is high up in the air, higher than most birds dare. Yet it saw me and breathed fire; it must have the eyes of an eagle."

"And so it does," the old man said, having overheard my words.

"How, then, can we leave?" Pelirrin asked.

We looked at one another but had no answer.

We stayed that afternoon in the hut and did what we could to make the old man comfortable, giving him the little water we had hoarded; he, in turn, allowed us to eat his small remaining stock of salt beef and cheese. I think we knew from the first that our ministrations would be of no use, and it was scarce past sunset when he breathed his last breath. We had not had the heart to trouble him with our questions, and indeed, I do not think he knew much more than he had told us at the first.

We sat awake through the gathering of the darkness and into the night, not daring to sleep lest the dragon slay us where we lay. Midnight was approaching, and the old man's corpse was cold to the touch, when Pelirrin whispered, "Perhaps the dragon has gone."

Derenneth replied, "And perhaps it has not."

"Surely, it must sleep," Pelirrin persisted.

Derenneth shrugged. I said, "I have heard that dragons sleep for weeks or even months at a time and then do not rest for a year thereafter."

"I think we should try," Pelirrin said.

Derenneth shook his head.

"Have you a better idea, then?" Pelirrin demanded. "Or do you plan to starve here?"

"I don't intend to starve," Derenneth said. He held up the parchment that the old man had held, then unrolled it where the light of our lone lantern—the dead man's lantern, in truth—fell upon it. "We have the rune."

I had not given the parchment much thought nor heeded greatly the man's words, but now I looked at the rune and marveled.

It was all of gold as if gold leaf had been laid onto the paper, but it did not peel or chip as does gold leaf, though the sheet had been rolled and folded and wrinkled. The design was all of one piece, a single symbol incredibly intricate. A web of curving strokes led inward toward a central crossing, in an elaborate interweaving that reminded me of the seashell my great-grandmother brought with her from the Great-Water-Called-Ocean. Looking at it made me dizzy, as if I were in danger of falling into it, and it was immediately obvious that this was a magic of great power.

Pelirrin looked at it, then turned away. "We know nothing about it. We do not know how to use it."

"What of it?" Derenneth asked. "What do we need to know? This is plainly a strong magic; we need merely command it to slay the dragon, and we can be safely away."

Pelirrin snorted. "What do we know of magic? Only a wizard can use such charms without hazard. For all we know, this rune may summon a demon that will eat our souls."

"The old man used it against the dragon."

"Aye, and the beast still lives, does it not?"

"He was hurt and had no time to use the rune's full power."

"Derenneth, we know nothing about the rune!"

"We know what the old man said, that the dragon did not kill him for fear of it."

"Do we need this rune?" I asked. "Perhaps the dragon has gone; perhaps it cares nothing for us, but waits only for the old man. I think we should try to leave."

Pelirrin agreed with me; faced with us both, Derenneth gave in. That decided, Pelirrin and I crept to the doorway while Derenneth hung back.

"We should bury the old man," he said.

"We have no tools, and we know nothing of his tribe or faith," Pelirrin replied.

"Better we should leave him where he is, then," I said, "and tell whom we can of him so that others may decide what to do."

Derenneth made to object again but saw that we were determined not to be swayed, and said nothing.

Pelirrin put his head out the door and looked up. "I see nothing but stars," he reported.

The cold wind blew around the door frame, and I shivered as I, too, leaned out. A half-moon hung in the sky, and as I looked toward it, a black shape blotted out most of it.

"Look!" I exclaimed, pointing.

Pelirrin and my brother looked and saw the shape that rode

down the moonlight toward us. Flame, so bright in the midnight darkness as to seem white, blossomed from its jaws, and it drew quickly closer.

I ducked back inside, and my companions did likewise. We crouched in the feeble glow of the lantern, looking at one another. Derenneth's jaw moved, but he said nothing.

Reluctantly, Pelirrin said, "Very well, then. The dragon is not asleep. We will try the rune."

"When?" I asked.

Derenneth said, "Why not now?"

I shook my head. "I think not. It is night, when the powers of darkness reign. Better by far to wait for daylight, when the sun's light keeps away many of the evil spirits."

Pelirrin agreed with me, and Derenneth, too, after some thought. That decided, we sat in the hut, pretending to sleep, with the winds howling outside, the cold digging into our flesh, a corpse keeping us company, and a dragon waiting without. Never had I spent a worse night.

At dawn we rose, abandoning our pretense, and gathered at the doorway.

"Now what?" Pelirrin asked.

Derenneth looked about until he found the dragon, circling far overhead; then he unrolled the rune and held it up above his head while he proclaimed, "Spirits and powers, by this rune I command you: strike dead the dragon that flies above us!"

We waited, expecting we knew not what—a bellow of agony, perhaps, or a clap of thunder or swirling clouds. There was nothing. My brother stood, clutching the parchment, while we knelt at his side and the dragon soared calmly, untroubled by any magical dooms.

We stayed thus for a long time, jammed together in the doorway. Then Pelirrin suggested, "Perhaps the dragon must see the rune, or the rune must face the dragon."

I nodded, and Derenneth agreed that that made sense.

"Then you must step outside and confront the dragon," Pelirrin said.

Derenneth admitted unwillingly that that seemed to be the case. He gathered himself together and strode out of the hut, putting on a bold face.

Immediately, the dragon broke off its gentle looping and dove toward him.

He held the parchment up with both hands, displayed before him. "Dragon, begone!" he cried. "I command you to vanish!"

The dragon did not vanish, but with an earthshaking bellow, it veered to one side and turned away before it came within a hundred yards. We saw it clearly in the morning light: a great scaled beast that glittered green, with huge, batlike wings and short legs tipped with long, curving talons. Its tail whipped about like that of an angry cat as it turned aside. Smoke trailed from its muzzle, but it did not spew flame upon us.

We all took note of that at once, that the beast had not burned us to ash where we stood, and took heart from it. True, it had not vanished, yet we still lived. That was the greatest part of our concern.

"I have done it!" Derenneth cried. "I have driven it away!"

"No," Pelirrin said, "you have only turned it aside."

"You certainly have not destroyed it, as you sought to do," I agreed—though in truth, I was glad enough of Derenneth's result.

"Very well, then, I have turned it away; is that not enough to please you, O great one?" Derenneth was angered by our quibbling. "I am no scholar who knows the precise words that direct this rune's power most effectively."

"True," I said, "and I meant no harm. You have done well; let us flee, then, whilst the rune's power still holds."

On that we could all agree; we fled, making our way down the mountainside as quickly as we could and turning our steps back toward our home village. We had had our fill of adventure and had with us, we knew, enough glory for any three youths such as we were. We had slain no monsters, yet we had found a treasure, and a great one, though we knew nothing of its nature or how it might best be used.

For the first hour we simply fled, moving as quickly as we dared across the stony slopes, without converse or complaint. Then for the second hour we bantered with one another, boasting of our courage in facing the dragon, and belittling one another with remembered or imagined acts of timidity on each other's parts.

The morning was half over when we paused for a rest, and for the first time we looked up at the sky in the direction whence we had come.

The dragon was there.

We had thought it far behind us, up on the mountain; it had

not followed us openly, and we had lost sight of it when we first rounded a shoulder of the rock that shielded us from its gaze.

But we had underestimated its intelligence and determination. Now we saw it, circling, far, far above us, a misshapen black cross against the sky.

Our jesting ended, and again we fled silently, still downward, away from the mountains, toward our own familiar hills.

Whenever we paused and looked back at the sky, the dragon was there, circling above us like a hawk waiting its moment.

All that day we fled, and all that day the dragon followed. Yet it never attacked, never came down to earth, but hung always far up in the sky, watching and pursuing us.

That night we took shelter beneath a grove of stunted pines, still high in the mountains but well below the worst of the wind and cold. Sleep did not come easily; we all feared, though we did not speak of it, that the dragon was waiting until we slept to strike. We took turns standing watch, but even so, what could one youth do if the dragon should come roaring down from the night sky, belching flame and smoke?

No attack came. When I was awakened for my watch, relieving Pelirrin, I suggested that perhaps the dragon had itself gone to ground somewhere, to sleep.

Pelirrin did not reply in words but pointed at the moons that hung in the sky to the east like the twin halves of a broken plate. I looked and saw the black shadow of the dragon glide silently across the higher of the two orbs.

I saw no need to speak but took my post as Pelirrin, shuddering with cold and worry, wrapped himself in his coat and tried to sleep.

The next day passed much as had the day before, save that Derenneth, becoming emboldened by the dragon's continuing reluctance to approach us closely, took to holding the rune aloft and spouting incantations of his own devising, in hopes of chancing upon one that would drop the monster from the skies.

We alternately derided him and cheered him on as our own hopes dwindled or grew, but none of his spells had any discernible effect.

The second night passed much as had the first, save that the cold was less; and the third day began.

It was midmorning of the third day, and the sun was warm and comforting in the eastern sky, when Pelirrin came to a dead stop. Derenneth, who had the lead, walked on unknowingly at first. I, who brought up the rear, halted at Pelirrin's side and called to my brother.

Derenneth turned and joined us as I asked, "What troubles you, Pelirrin? Why do you stop?"

"What troubles him? What else but the dragon?" Derenneth said. "The poor fellow has obviously broken beneath the strain."

I turned to reprimand my brother, but it was Pelirrin who spoke first.

"And are you so very bold, then, Derenneth, that you have no fear of the beast? Is your heart calm in your breast? Have you slept soundly these past two nights? Tell me that you have slept through the night, and I will call you a liar to your face, for I've seen you lying awake, watching the dragon above us." He paused, and Derenneth made as if to speak, but Pelirrin continued before the first word left my brother's lips.

"I have not broken beneath the strain any more than you or Elsen," he said. "Rather, I am thinking clearly for the first time since I found the old man in the hut. I know why the dragon follows us rather than slays us, and it is because of that knowledge that I have stopped here and will go no further toward our home."

"What are you saying?" I asked him.

"Have you not wondered what the dragon might want of us, if not our deaths?"

"It had not occurred to me," I replied, "that it might want anything else."

"Do you think, then, that Derenneth's babbling over that parchment has protected us?"

I hesitated, and Derenneth spoke up in his own part. "Of course, the rune has protected us! If not the rune, then what? Why would the dragon spare us if it could slay us and destroy or take back the rune?"

"Why does it follow us, then? Why does it not let us go in peace if it knows it cannot slay us?"

"It seeks the rune, of course," Derenneth answered. "It seeks to regain the thing that has the power to destroy it."

"I thought at first that it was as you say, Derenneth, but another thought has come to me. What if it seeks, instead, to destroy not merely the three who took the rune but also all their people so that it will be troubled no more by adventuring youths or avenging kin? What if it seeks to follow us to our home so that it may destroy the entire village?"

Derenneth considered this, and after a moment of silent thought, began, "If we were to split up—"

"And what if you were right to begin with, Derenneth?" I asked. "What would become of the two who do not carry the rune?"

"Then what else would you suggest?" he demanded.

"We mustn't go home," Pelirrin said. "We must find some way of driving the dragon away so that it can no longer follow us."

"And how do we do that, O wise one?" Derenneth asked mockingly.

Pelirrin had no answer; it was I who said, "There are wise men and magicians on the plains, it is said. Surely, there must be a mage somewhere who can tell us what the rune is and how it may be used against the dragon."

Derenneth conceded the wisdom of my words, and Pelirrin could offer no better course of action; so, we set off in a new direction, turning our footsteps to the southeast, toward the open plains and away from our homes.

None of our people had ventured out of Lakar in many long years, and of the three of us, none had left the hills since early childhood. We knew very little of what we might find or how far we must travel. Finding the way was the easiest part of it, for we needed only to head southeastward, across the ridge, taking our bearing from the sun.

So we went, then, and had it not been for the dragon, always hanging over us like an unpaid debt, the journey might have been pleasant indeed. Game was plentiful, as it had not been in the mountains, and we ate well on most nights. Runnels and rivulets supplied us with enough water, and on occasion we would come across streams large enough that they had to be forded rather than leaped. The sun was warm, the nights cool, and the trees provided shade and shelter. We crossed roads at times, following a few for some distance, but never meeting anyone. Perhaps people we might have encountered glimpsed the dragon from afar and avoided us.

The walking grew steadily easier, and the days warmer, as the mountains sank to hills and the hills in turn grew lower until at last, twelve days from the mountain hut, we came down from the final ridge into the broad green plain, where the trees no longer grew, but only the tall grasses. We glimpsed Taki'il in the distance, recognizing it from descriptions and Pelirrin's fading childhood memories; Derenneth turned his steps toward it, and we followed him, thinking that so great a city must surely have within its walls many scholars and mages.

Taki'il was still indistinct in the distance, however, when Pelirrin pointed out a small house, built of yellow brick, to one side of our intended path. He suggested that we might ask the inhabitants whether they knew of a wizard or scholar who could help us.

Eager for the sight of another human face, Derenneth and I readily agreed, and we all headed for the house.

As we neared, we saw smoke rising from the chimney and thus knew the house to be occupied—a good sign. Then, when we were able to see it more clearly, we saw the charm painted upon each gable, as well as the talisman that hung above the door, and hurried toward the house, sure that we had happened upon the object of our search.

A woman sat by the doorway, leaning back comfortably, with a cat upon her knee and a stick of candy in her mouth; and we hailed her vigorously. She was older than we were, but still young, having seen perhaps thirty winters pass; and I know that I, at least, was sure that she could not be the mage we sought, being as young as she was, whatever signs there might be upon her house. Still, she would know where the person responsible for the charms might be found.

She opened her eyes when she heard our cries and looked us over as we drew closer. She looked also at the sky behind us, and we knew that she had seen the dragon. I felt uneasy and waited to see if she would flee into the safety of her home, locking us out.

She showed no sign of alarm, however, but coaxed the cat from her lap onto the ground and arose, the stick of candy still in her mouth.

We ran into the clearing around the house and stood, panting, before her.

"I give you greetings," she said, taking the candy from her mouth. "What brings you hither, strangers?"

We glanced at one another, and Pelirrin stepped forward to act as spokesman. He made formal introductions and politely asked our hostess her name.

She said that she was called Harril and made us welcome; then she repeated her query.

Pelirrin recited the tale, with Derenneth and I speaking whenever he seemed to hesitate, correcting his omissions or mistakes. The woman who called herself Harril listened to it all carefully, asking no questions, but waiting until we had finished.

Pelirrin described our journey down from the mountains, and his thoughts upon the third day, and our search for someone who might aid us; then he concluded by asking, "Know you, then, of someone who could explain to us what this rune might be and how we might use it to free ourselves of the dragon's pursuit?"

"Let me see the rune," Harril replied. "I have some experience in such matters."

My companions were as startled as I was to hear so young a woman thus proclaim herself a scholar, and it was only reluctantly that Derenneth produced the battered parchment and passed it to her.

She unrolled it and studied it for a moment.

"This is no rune of destruction," she said at last.

"Is it not?" Derenneth asked, startled.

"No."

"Then what is it?" Pelirrin asked. "Why has the dragon pursued us, if not to preserve its life?"

Harril passed the parchment back. "I cannot say. I know little of dragons. My studies have been in the workings of our own world, and dragons, it is said, come from another. Certainly, this rune you have brought is no rune I know, and such signs have been my special interest these past ten years. I can tell you, though, that it bears none of the foci of power that must be in any destructive rune. Rather, it seems more like a protection or a shaping."

Pelirrin stared at the parchment for a long moment, and Derenneth watched the plainswoman suspiciously; I could see that he doubted her words. He was obviously recalling the tales we had heard of the treacheries of the plainsmen and the ancient rivalries between our two peoples.

For my own part, I looked from one to another, and then at the dragon that still circled above us.

"If the rune is a protective spell," I said, "then that would explain why we have not been harmed."

"Yes," Pelirrin said. "But why, then, would the dragon

have pursued us? Surely, it would know that the rune would protect us."

"Would it?" Derenneth said. "I think you credit the beast with more intelligence than it possesses."

"Do you think it stupid, then? It has followed us all this time without fail. Would not a mere beast have abandoned the chase before this?"

Derenneth had no answer to that.

"Harril," Pelirrin said, "need a protective rune be as complex as this one? I have heard tales of men drawing protective runes in the dust, and surely no one has so steady and quick a hand as would be needed to produce something like this so swiftly as the stories tell."

"The tales exaggerate," she replied. "But no, no protection need be so intricate as that. Furthermore, that rune that you carry has not protected you, for the spell it carries has not been awakened; I can see that much."

"Ah," Pelirrin said.

Derenneth and I stared at him.

"If the rune has not protected us," Derenneth said, "then what has? Why has the monster not devoured or scorched us?"

Pelirrin held up the parchment. "I think I see," he said. "The rune *has* in truth protected us—not with its magic, but by its fragility. The dragon has followed us because it wishes to recover its magic, but it has not dared to harm us lest the rune be damaged in the struggle. Think what a burst of the creature's breath could do to so ancient and dry a parchment!"

I needed but an instant to see that such an explanation would indeed account for the dragon's actions, but Derenneth was less easily convinced. He protested, "How could a monster know the use of the rune?"

"The dragon is no mere beast, Derenneth, can you not see that?"

Derenneth's face clouded with anger; before he could speak further, perhaps saying words that we might all come to regret, I interrupted.

"If the dragon has feared for the safety of the rune and sought nothing but its return, then perhaps we need only to give it back the parchment to be free of pursuit, free to return home," I ventured.

Even as Pelirrin nodded agreement, Derenneth exclaimed, "Madness! If we give it the rune, it will destroy us, surely!"

"No," Pelirrin said, "why should it? It will have what it wanted. Why should it be so vindictive as to harm us? We have been guilty of a misunderstanding, no more; it was not we who robbed its hoard. I think returning the parchment will be amends enough. After all, Derenneth, would it not fear the rune's destruction fully as much once it holds the parchment as it does now, while we hold it?"

"We will have nothing to show for our adventure," Derenneth protested.

"We will have a tale to rival the best," Pelirrin replied.

"I say you have gone mad, Pelirrin."

"And I say we must give the beast the rune. How say you, then, Elsen? Yours is the deciding vote. Do you feel as you did when you set forth the idea, or have you seen the error of your judgment and changed your mind?"

I was not happy to be put in a position where I must choose between my brother and my friend, between two courses of little appeal; presented with such a situation, I could only select the course I thought the wiser.

"Give it the rune, Pelirrin."

Satisfied, Pelirrin took the rune and walked out onto the plain, away from the house.

"Pelirrin!" Derenneth shouted, and I leaped up behind him and grabbed my brother's arms.

"Stay there!" Pelirrin called back.

Derenneth struggled, but not strongly. I felt a brief urge to release him, to run after Pelirrin myself. After all, whatever the exact circumstances, was he not taking away the only thing that had protected us from the dragon? I looked up and saw the beast hanging in the sky, watching us intently.

As Pelirrin walked away from us, he held the rune displayed above his head, where the dragon might see it; and as we watched, the monster turned his attention away from Derenneth and myself, focusing solely on our comrade.

Pelirrin came at last to a small clearing in the grass, where he knelt and placed the rune upon a small rise in the ground. Then he arose, turned about, and walked calmly back toward us.

I fully realized then that we had forsaken our only defense, and Derenneth seemed to have the same feeling as he went partially limp in my grasp. Then my hold on him slackened altogether as we beheld what unfolded before our eyes.

We watched—Harril as well as the three of us—and saw

the dragon, green and shining, swoop down from the sky. It landed gracefully in the tall grass, reached forward with one taloned claw, and touched the rune with what I can only call reverence. It turned and looked at us from blazing golden eyes for a moment, then looked back at the rune, and then, to our utter astonishment, it spoke.

Its voice was deep and resonant, with a sound like the roaring of flames, but there could be no mistake that it was speech. It was speaking in a tongue that we had never before heard. What was more, it seemed to be chanting as if speaking an incantation.

"It is waking the rune," the woman said.

Derenneth glanced at her.

"Pray, woman," he said, "that you have not lied to us about the rune's nature. If it does carry destruction, you will perish with us."

"I did not lie," she replied calmly.

Pelirrin paid no heed to the conversation; he was watching the dragon closely. "Look!" he called. "See what it does now!"

We turned and watched in bewilderment.

The dragon was forcing its way *into* the rune as if the parchment were not parchment but an opening in the ground. It had thrust both its foreclaws into it, though we would have judged the rune smaller than either one alone; and now, as we watched, it slid forward with wings folded, tucked its smoking snout between its legs, and dove.

It was impossible to say whether the rune stretched to accommodate it or whether the dragon shrank; the air wavered with the heat and with something more, and our vision seemed to be distorted as well. Still, impossible though it obviously was, the dragon forced itself down, into the rune, and out of our sight.

We watched in confoundment.

Pelirrin glanced at the witch. "You said that dragons were not of our world?"

She nodded. "So I have heard."

The dragon's body and wings were gone; all four of its legs, vanished; and as we watched, its tail slid down into the rune like a snake slides into a hole.

Then, abruptly, one of its foreclaws reappeared, rising up out of the rune; it reached out, gripped the edge of the parchment, and pulled it down over, and then into, itself. It shrank down out of sight and then vanished, leaving no trace of its existence.

"I don't understand," Derenneth said, as we all stared at the empty clearing. "Where did it go?"

"I am not sure," Pelirrin said, "but I could venture a guess. If it came from another world, as this woman says, then, surely, the reason it pursued us so relentlessly is obvious."

Pelirrin paused for a heartbeat and glanced toward the woman, who was smiling faintly as if she knew what he was going to say.

"We had taken its only way home."

THE PALACE OF
AL-TIR AL-ABTAN

This is a tale of the wizard al-Tir al-Abtan, when he dwelt in the ancient city of Tahrir, on the shore of the southern sea.

The palace of al-Tir al-Abtan stood, of the wizard's choice, in the poorest quarter of Tahrir. To reach it, a determined traveler would find himself required to pass through alleys that were little more than tunnels through crumbling piles of brick and down streets that were no more than mud-filled gaps between one decrepit tenement and the next. The Most Profound Tir, the greatest magician of the age, had raised his palace here to avoid the petty intrigues of lesser wizards and the maddening importunities of nobles and kings upon his time and talent. He did not care directly to refuse the lords of the earth admission to his palace, for that would mean constant harassment by those seeking exceptions or an end to the ban; but instead, he put the palace where no self-respecting nobleman would dare approach it, and where those who did approach it could be freely dealt with.

The Most Profound Tir made it impossible for any save himself to find a gate in the outer wall of his residence. Whether the gate was concealed somehow or moved about or did not actually exist at all was a matter of much debate among the people of Tahrir. Certainly, when he chose to enter or leave, a gate appeared, but no one else could ever find it again afterward or remember just where it had been.

Thus did the wizard guard his privacy, and for fully a century his palace remained inviolate, while he grew in necromantic prowess and those about him lived and died; and in all those years that passed without touching his citadel, no man or woman other than al-Tir al-Abtan saw the inside of the marble walls that separated the palace grounds from the remainder of the city. Even when the magician himself was away about the world, the palace was said to be guarded by a demon or ghoul that none saw but all feared. It was said, also, that other creatures, equally terrible, patrolled the gardens.

As tales grow in the telling, it was soon rumored that Tir used djinni and afrits as his household slaves, and his palace was shunned as an unholy and fearsome place, even when unrest came upon the city.

And unrest did come, for it happened that, many years after al-Tir al-Abtan completed the construction of his vast edifice, a foolish and evil man ascended the throne as Sultan of Tahrir, one Selim ibn Jafar. This sultan so oppressed his people that those who could fled the city, leaving behind only the poor and wretched, who knew that they would be no more welcome elsewhere.

Thus, while the magician's palace remained untouched, the condition of the city about it grew ever worse. The loathsome stench of poverty spread across the city, as beggars, thieves, whores, and cutthroats played an ever-larger role in the life of Tahrir.

The city became as a stinking swamp about the foot of the Sultan's throne, and like a rising tide about a seaside rock, the decay closed in, as more and more of the wealthy fled the city, allowing their homes to be overrun by the starving beggars and bloody-handed thieves. The rot came ever nearer to the Sultan's palace, as if to surround it as it already surrounded Tir's palace.

The Sultan Selim ibn Jafar was not totally insensible to this situation, and in the fourth year of his reign he could no longer stand the idea of his home being lost amid filth and poverty. He did not see that his own actions were the cause but rather cursed Allah, in his folly, for sending this blight upon his city. He declared open war upon his own people, accusing them of treason in their failure to maintain his city despite the burdens he placed upon them and the mistreatment and injustice he perpetrated. His men were sent out with torches, instructed to burn the tenements and brothels to the ground; but most of these soldiers simply disappeared forever in the maze of streets, either through desertion or because the unhappy citizens had ambushed them and cut their throats. The fires that began were short-lived and ineffective.

The only outcome was the incitement of the populace, and

it was then that the Sultanate of Tahrir ended, as the Sultan's subjects stormed the palace and tore it stone from stone and treated all those within its walls in barbarous fashion, leaving none whole enough to be recognized.

When the Sultan's corpse lay sprawled upon the floor of his own throne room and his head adorned a spike on his own gate, the beggar king who had led the mob and usurped the throne looked about himself and was well pleased with what he saw. His ragged followers had slaughtered every noble and man of wealth left in the city, staining the floors of the remaining great houses with their blood; he was absolute ruler of everything in Tahrir.

Everything, that is, except the palace of al-Tir al-Abtan.

That, the beggar king saw, would not do. He did not intend to let anyone remain who might interfere with his rule.

He knew that the palace was the work of a mighty magician, and he did not care to face such a foe himself. Instead, the new overlord of Tahrir determined to send a single expert thief into the palace, to see whether the enchanter, whom no one had seen in years, still lived.

Chosen for this task was a lad of twenty, whose name was Abu al-Din; this name was known throughout much of the city as the most promising housebreaker of the time. He was a bold and brash fellow, and when news of his selection reached him, he proudly accepted the commission as his due. The king summoned him to the royal presence and charged him as follows:

"You will enter the palace of the wizard al-Tir al-Abtan, by surmounting the wall that guards it, since there is no gate to be found. You will explore the grounds, taking careful note of all traps, pitfalls, and sentinels; you will enter the palace, and learn as best you can its plan and arrangement, once again taking note of all safeguards. Should you be spotted by any resident, slay him; should you find the necromancer, alive or dead, bring back his head. Do you understand?"

Abu al-Din nodded and said, "I understand, and I obey." He bowed low, with perhaps a touch of mockery in his action, and then took himself quickly home to his little attic to prepare.

Perhaps thirty enthusiastic fellow citizens followed him, calling advice and encouragement, and waited outside his window to see if he would actually do as he had promised and enter the demon's lair.

Abu ignored them. He ate a fine meal, but not a heavy one, while he considered what to bring.

He knew nothing of what he would face, and therefore could not prepare for any specific dangers. Since all other magicians of degree had departed Tahrir, he could not obtain any magic to aid him.

At last he decided to equip himself as he would for any ordinary housebreaking, and trust in luck and the will of Allah to see him through.

He wore a robe with a stout quilted front that would turn a light blow. He wrapped a long, strong rope about his waist and tied its end to a heavy iron hook that he hung on his left shoulder. He bore a good, long dagger on his belt. Nothing else.

He was followed through the streets by a small crowd of well-wishers, but when he came at last to the avenue that ran along the palace wall, when he faced that black marble barrier, he was suddenly alone. His entourage had faded into the shadowy alleys, terrified of the legendary power of the archmage beyond.

Whistling loudly, to show any watchers he knew were there his lack of fear, Abu flung his hook, trailing rope, over the wall; on the second toss, the barbed iron hook caught and held.

He clambered quickly up the line. At the top of the wall he turned and waved briefly and bravely to his unseen audience; then he turned and looked down at the palace grounds.

He saw nothing. Though the sun was bright overhead, it was as if he peered into a deep, dark cave.

Puzzled, he gathered up the rope and peered into the gloom, trying to make out any detail at all.

He could not. The blackness was impenetrable.

Cautiously, he freed his hook from its lodgement on the wall's inner edge, and then lowered it slowly down into the dark.

After a moment's descent he heard it strike ground with a muffled thump; as he handed down more rope the line grew slack.

Something, he knew, was down there, something that seemed to support the iron hook without difficulty.

A shiver of apprehension ran through him, and he glanced back out at the surrounding streets.

He saw no one, but he knew that he was being watched. He

would not, he swore silently to himself, show himself a coward so quickly as this!

He pulled up the hook, secured it solidly to the wall's outer edge, and then with a prayer and a gulp of air lowered himself down into the blackness.

His feet and legs vanished, yet he felt no different. Then his body was gone. And finally, as his head fell below the top of the wall, he was engulfed in darkness—but only for an instant, and then he was below the blackness and able to see a fine grassy sward just below him, no more than a man's height away, surrounded by flowering bushes.

He looked up and saw the blue sky and bright sun, and he smiled.

"A conjuror's trick, no more!" he told himself quietly. He quickly pulled himself back up onto the wall, freed the hook, and then, gathering up the rope once more, he dropped down inside. To the watchers in the alleys, he was gone, and did not return, and gradually, as the sun descended the western sky, they grew bored and drifted away.

Inside the wall, Abu landed catlike, crouched and ready for anything—or so he thought to himself.

When he saw his surroundings, however, his alert eyes glazed slightly. He was in a garden, a garden like none he had ever imagined.

Raised in the streets, he had rarely seen any gardens save those scraggly patches of vegetables and herbs in back lots and on rooftops that some of the frugal citizens of Tahrir cultivated. Now he faced a garden like no other anywhere; even the late Court Gardener to Selim ibn Jafar would have been amazed. Blossoms were piled high on every side, a profusion, a myriad of flowers, all vividly colored, varied in size from tiny pinpricks of gold and scarlet to vast parasols of azure and white with petals each as broad as a man's height. All about the thief, save only behind him where the black marble wall stood, were flowers; it seemed as though he had landed in the only clear spot to be found, and that was only a tiny patch of grass scarce big enough for him to stand upon.

He marveled that he had somehow not seen this fantastic beauty when he clambered down his rope and could only guess that it was somehow connected with the wizard's illusory darkness.

After a few moments, with a shake of his head, Abu recov-

ered his senses. He was not to be put off by a bunch of flowers! He stepped forward, and his leg brushed a nearby blos-
som, a yard-wide whorl of purple and black; and, as though
released from long bondage, there burst forth all about him
the perfume of the flowers, like all the incense of all the
world's mosques and temples in one place, pouring out on all
sides. He was breathing in thick clouds of scent, such sweet
scent as cannot be described. He could not catch his breath,
for the perfume so filled him that his lungs could not take in
air. In desperation, he drew his blade, flinging his arm out as
far as he could, and slashed at the mockingly beautiful blossoms. Then he was spinning, and the world went dark.

He came to later, he never knew how much later, and found
himself lying on the sward, green and smooth, untroubled by
the flowers. He could still smell their perfume but was no
longer overpowered by it. Looking up from where he lay,
he could see no blossoms nor leaves.

He stood up warily. Before him, twisted hideously, the
purple-and-sable flower that he had first touched lay on the
grass. Its thorny stem was slashed through where his dagger
had cut it, and from the slash flowed fresh red blood.

The lower portion of the stem did not end in a rooted stalk
but in a narrow green body with a whiplike tail, four short
legs, and scaly feet, like those of a great lizard.

Shuddering, he wiped his blade on the lawn and looked
about him.

Behind him was the marble wall; to either side was empty
grass, and the dreadful gardens stood beyond. Abu realized
even these strange and magical flowers are delicate things.
The death of one had frightened away the other plants.

He was sure he had nothing more to fear from the gardens
if he kept his wits about him. He looked on to the next obsta-
cle.

Ahead of him was another wall, a dozen paces away across
the green, not the wall of the palace but another line of defense, this one only a little taller than his head and surely no
higher than his reach. It appeared to be made of ivory, though
he could make out little detail from where he stood. The sun
was very low in the west, and already the day's light was fading.

He looked down at the plant-creature he had slain and
kicked at the dead thing, wondering if perhaps he should dis-

pose of it; a sharp pain in his foot informed him that a nee-
dlelike thorn as long as his index finger had passed right
through his leather boot into his flesh. Upon pulling his foot
away, he saw that behind the petals the entire upper part of
the plant was a ghastly mass of dull-green thorns, all razor
sharp and strong as steel.

After removing his boot, bandaging the wound as best he
could with a strip torn from the hem of his robe, and slipping
the boot back carefully so as not to dislodge the cloth, he
limped across the grass to the ivory barrier.

Beyond this inner wall he could see the glistening crystal
and stone of the palace itself, its tiled domes flashing and
bright in the slanting sunlight.

The ivory wall proved not to be completely solid; there
were small openings between the carved figures. A curious
feature was the nature of the carvings themselves, for each
was a different variety of serpent; Abu saw among them vi-
pers, adders, cobras, and a thousand others. Some were such
as are not known any longer among men.

That was nothing to Abu. Undaunted by the fearsome appearance of the wall, and seeing that the openings made excellent handholds, he leaped up to climb it; but scarce had he
left the ground when he felt the ivory writhe beneath his
hands. He almost began to drop back but then thought better
of it, and instead, with all his strength, he vaulted over, to
land rolling upon a stone-paved terrace. Behind him, the
carved serpents hissed, twisting venomously about each other;
for one terrible instant he thought they were preparing to follow him. At last, though, they stilled and were again only
lifeless ivory.

Trembling, Abu lay upon the flags; then, slowly, he got
again to his feet, wincing as he put pressure on his wounded
foot.

He was on a broad, paved terrace, bounded on one side by
the ivory barricade, on two sides by decorative pools and
fountains, and on the last by the palace that was his goal. The
palace wall was blank, however; there were no doors, no windows, no opening of any sort. High above colored tiles
adorned the roof edge, but otherwise the wall was sheer and
flat and featureless. Abu saw no hope of gaining entry there.
Instead, he turned to his right and limped to the little stone-
rimmed ponds that edged the terrace.

He saw hundreds of good-sized pools, scattered as irregularly as the stars in the heavens for as far as he could see, each with a fountain in its center, and paths of translucent golden bricks, like amber, wound between them. Each pool was lit from beneath by some means the thief could not fathom, and each glowed a different hue. Abu watched the fountains dance and play in the gathering dusk; they were, like the flowers, much more beautiful than anything in his previous experience. He wondered if they, too, held some hidden menace; their gentle hissing began to seem somehow ominous to him. Still, he had to go on, for he had a task to perform and did not care to go back over the ivory serpents into the gardens of the poisonous lizard-legged flowers. He could do nothing with the blank walls of the palace; an attempt to scale them, even if successful, might do no good, since he had no reason to believe that there were openings in the roof. He could see no end to the expanse of fountains; it seemed to continue forever. He had already noticed that the grounds inside the wall seemed to be much more extensive than the length of the wall, as seen from outside, could contain, but after all, this palace had been raised by magic, and he had already seen, coming over the wall, that its master was not above the use of illusions. Surely, the water garden did not, in truth, go on forever. If he walked steadily in one direction, he would surely come to an end, in time. With a shrug, he set out along one of the walks.

He strolled easily along, his dagger loose in its sheath; his wounded foot hurt only a little, as he learned how to walk smoothly without putting his weight on the injured area. The fountains whispered on every side as he walked, and their light drew his gaze. He wound on among them, listening to their liquid voices, imagining that they were murmuring secrets to one another; he even thought, absurdly, that he could catch their words. Yes, he thought, there was a word, most certainly, a very clear word, "death." A soft chill ran through him, but he still listened, and again he heard the words of the spilling fountains. "Death," they said, "death," and "sleep." Sleep—yes, he thought, he had come far, he wanted to sleep . . .

He caught himself suddenly as a sharp pain ran up his leg; the thorn wound had slammed into the low rim of one of the pools, and the sudden jolt brought him back to alertness. He looked about, wildly asking himself what he was doing. He had, he saw, been about to fall headlong into a great silver-blue pool of light, where a towering spray of vivid wine-colored light danced madly. The susurration of the fountains had mesmerized him; had he woken a moment later, it might have been too late, as he would have been well into the enchanted liquid that filled the pool.

He had no idea just what that liquid might do, and a powerful urge to dip his hand in it, perhaps to taste it, came over him, but he fought it off. That, he told himself forcefully, was the fountains' spell, making a final try for his mind and soul. He stepped back, well clear of the enticing, luminous water.

Shaking his head to clear it of the mistiness left from his trance, he looked about him. It abruptly occurred to him that he had no idea how long or far he had wandered among the fountains while enthralled; he could see nothing that gave him a clue. Far to the right, between the flashing columns of liquid, he glimpsed carven ivory; and far to the left, he saw the polished stone and tile of the palace. Behind him, though, the fountains seemed to go on forever; and before him was the same.

Seeing no point in continuing further through the forest of pools, and perhaps risking fresh ensorcellment, he turned left and made his way toward the citadel itself, with the intention of scaling it. At least from the roof he might be able to see some way in.

As he walked, he realized he no longer heard mysterious whispers in the sound of the water; it seemed that by breaking his trance, he had lost forever the influence of that soft, soft murmur.

The renewed pain in his foot, he thought, might also help. His limp was back, worse then ever despite his best efforts.

A few minutes' hobbling walk brought him to a narrow plaza between the water garden and the palace, and to his astonishment he found himself before a pair of great gem-encrusted golden doors. He paused to stare up at them dumfounded; from a single step back, the portal had been invisible, the palace wall blank.

Another illusion, of course—but which, he asked himself, was real? Was the blank wall an illusion, or were these doors?

Well, he answered himself boldly, there's one easy way to find out.

He crossed the polished red marble of the plaza and mounted three steps to the portal.

There, however, he had to halt, for he saw no latch or han-

dle; not so much as a knocker marred the expanse of glittering gold, studded irregularly with rubies and sapphires. For
that matter, he realized he could see no hinges; there were
simply two huge golden panels, set flush in the stone wall,
with only hairline cracks marking their edges.

He stepped back down to study the situation but could see
no solution. Returning to the top step, he pushed with all his
strength against the metal, but there was no give or play whatsoever; he could not budge it. He then tried to get a grip on
the projecting gems, to pull the door open, which likewise
had no effect. At last, disgusted, all caution lost, in frustration
he cried out an oath.

The doors trembled expectantly.

He froze. Nothing more happened. Hesitantly, he said, "Allah?" The doors quivered.

Cursing himself for not trying the obvious means for opening enchanted portals, described in any number of old tales,
he cried out, "Open, door of al-Tir al-Abtan, in the name of
Allah, the great, the merciful!"

Slowly and majestically, the golden portals swung inward,
revealing a vast reception hall walled with jade, a vaulted
ceiling almost out of sight above him, and a floor of green
marble. It was bare of all furnishings and all but empty; the
only thing in all that great chamber was al-Tir al-Abtan's
guardian.

Abu had his dagger out in a twinkling, upon seeing the
dark, twisted form of the demon; it was indeed a ghoul, a
loathsome twisted creature, a travesty of human shape with
grey skin and long, greasy ropes of black hair. Fangs jutted up
from its lower jaw; its eyes had no iris nor pupil but glowed
a fiery yellow. Across one side of its face, an oozing, leprous
growth clung. The demon was naked and grotesquely male.
Although no taller than Abu al-Din, it must have weighed
twice what he did, for it was as thick around as a barrel. It
was armed with two-inch claws on every finger.

The thief could see the monster clearly, for a soft light em-
anated from the jade walls. Rather than be caught outside, he
sprang inside and attacked first.

The ghoul fought like a mad dog, snarling and tearing at
Abu without thought, its only aim to hurt and weaken its opponent. Abu, on the other hand, concentrated on dodging,
only occasionally thrusting at the creature with his knife. He
realized quickly that his blade could not pierce the thick hide

of the demon; but still he kept stabbing at it, hoping against all evidence that it had some vulnerable spot.

Only when the blade snapped off did he recognize how badly he had erred. His only other equipment being his rope, he struggled to bring that into play; at last, he managed to break free for a moment and dash across the chamber. When the ghoul came after him, it met a hard-flung iron hook, which, as Abu had hoped and aimed for, took him in the eye.

The eerie golden orb burst with a blinding flash; the thief was staggered. An instant later the demon's roar of pain and hatred brought Abu back to full alertness, and taking quick advantage of his opponent's shock, Abu proceeded to swing the deadly hook into the other blazing eye. The flash was expected this time, and he recovered immediately from its effects.

The demon roared again, horribly, sat still in the center of the chamber; then, in a burst of motion, he sprang at his tormenter. Abu dodged to the side, and the ghoul followed; blind as it now was, it could still track him by sound.

Although he had improved his chances, Abu realized he was still facing a formidable enemy; he fled desperately, hampered by his injured foot and a dozen gashes from the demon's claws, trying to keep out of reach of the maddened monster.

As he fled, he continued to swing the iron hook at the ghoul, annoying it, but failing to wound it, until at last it grabbed the rope out of his hands, tearing the skin from his palms. The rope coiled and whipped about as he released it, and to the surprise of both combatants, it wrapped itself about the demon. Abu saw his chance; and snatching up the loose end, he began to run around the room, winding the cord about his assailant until the creature was unable to move.

By the time the blinded monster had freed itself, Abu was out of range of even a demon's sensitive ears.

Now, at last, the thief was loose in the palace, free to roam; prowling like a cat, he made his way through endless corridors and countless chambers, losing himself hopelessly in the maze of rooms.

He saw wonders like none he had dreamed of before. He saw peacocks that sang sweet songs and glistening fish that swam in the air. He saw books written in blood and scrolls of human skin. He saw fountains that burned and found a fire that cooled his wounds; strange fragrances filled the air, and stranger sounds and musics. It seemed to him that he wandered for days among the magician's playthings.

And then, at last, he came upon the magician.

This was in a tower room, far above the body of the palace. The walls were polished crystal, yet black as death, and the stairs that he climbed to reach the chamber were lit from within, yet seemed as opaque as coal.

It was at the top of these stairs that he entered the wizard's laboratory, cluttered with ghastly talismans and dusty books. Amid the clutter stood a tall, thin old man—very tall, with white hair that flowed to his waist and a silvery beard almost as long. He wore an absolutely plain black robe that shimmered eerily, and he was bent over one of the larger and dustier of the tomes.

Remembering the king's instructions and seeing his intended victim thus absorbed, Abu crept up behind him, the heavy hilt of his broken dagger in his hand; all strength abruptly ebbed from his limbs, and he collapsed helplessly, to lie unmoving on the floor.

The wizard finished reading the page, closed the book, and put it atop a pile nearby, then came and stood looking down at the paralyzed thief.

"You have disturbed me," the Most Profound Tir said. "This is not to be permitted. Further, I see in your eyes that all of Tahrir now wishes me ill, and that others will be sent after you. I will not have it." The dry, ancient voice seemed to fill everything, although Abu knew it wasn't really very loud. He tried to speak but could not.

"What will I do with you, you ask?" Al-Tir al-Abtan stroked his beard. "I don't know. You do bear examination, having gotten this far into my palace, don't you? But I'm too busy to bother with you just now; you'll have to wait."

He waved a hand, and Abu felt himself lifted by unseen hands. Then he was dropped roughly into a small trunk, and the lid fell closed.

It was a very small trunk, and very cramped, but Abu al-Din had nothing to say about the accommodations or anything else. He could not move, could not speak, and soon realized that he was not even breathing any more—yet still he lived.

He waited, unwillingly, for al-Tir al-Abtan to find the time to deal with him.

Within a matter of hours, he felt certain that even death could be no worse than continued imprisonment.

As he lay there, events went on without him.

Outside the palace, in the city of Tahrir, Abu al-Din had been given up as lost, and as the Most Profound Tir had said, another was to be sent; but then, word came to the beggar-King of a strange stirring of the sea at the docks. Curious, he put off other matters to investigate and made his way to the waterfront, so that he was the first man in all Tahrir to be engulfed by the first great wave that washed over the city. In quick succession, a dozen immense waves broke across the stinking mass of Tahrir, washing it into the sea. The land itself sank, and by the time peace had returned to the churning ocean, the city of Tahrir was utterly gone, lost forever, save for a single building, the Palace of al-Tir al-Abtan, which through all the tempest and flood remained untouched, as though a great glass wall encircled it. And when the seas stilled, the palace stood alone on a sheer-sided island, half beneath waves that broke harmlessly against that same invisible barrier, while inside, al-Tir al-Abtan worked on, paying scant attention to his handiwork. In his many long years of life and study, he had gained knowledge and power of an incomprehensible order; the destruction of Tahrir had been no more to him than squashing a bug.

Thus did the Island of al-Tir al-Abtan come into being, and thus it remained, for many, many years, until at last, one quiet night, al-Tir al-Abtan went away and took his palace with him. Now the seas wash lightly over the island when the tides are high, and gulls perch there calmly when the waves withdraw. All of Tahrir is long dead—save for Abu al-Din, who is still in that trunk, waiting for al-Tir al-Abtan to remember him.

THE FINAL FOLLY
OF CAPTAIN DANCY

1.

I was right there beside him when it happened, and I saw the whole thing. It wasn't anything but pure bad luck, such as could happen to anyone—but it had never happened to the captain before, and I'd guess he wasn't ready for it.

We had just come out of Old Joe's Tavern, where the captain had beaten the snot out of three young troublemakers, and we'd left by way of the alley, since the troublemakers had shipmates of their own, and that alleyway wasn't any too clean. I didn't see exactly what it was the captain stepped in, but it was brown and greasy, and when his foot hit it that foot went straight out from under him and he fell, and his head fetched up hard against the brick wall, and there was a snap like kindling broken across your knee, and there he was on the ground, dead.

It was pure bad luck and the damnedest thing, but that's how it happened, and Captain Jack Dancy, who'd had three ships shot out from under him, who'd come through the battle of Cushgar Corners—where only three men survived— without a scratch, who'd sired bastards on half the wives in Collyport without ever a husband suspecting, who'd stolen the entire treasury from the Pundit of Oul and got away clean, who'd escaped from the Dungeon Pits of the Black Sorcerer on Little Hengist, who was the only man ever pardoned by Governor "Hangman" Lee, who'd climbed Dawson's Butte with only a bullwhip for tackle—that man, Jolly Jack Dancy, lay dead in the alley behind Old Joe's Tavern of a simple fall and a broken neck.

And that meant that me and the rest of the crew of the good ship *Bonny Anne* were in deep trouble.

We didn't know the half of it yet, of course, but even then, drunk as I was, I knew it wasn't good.

I saw him fall, and I heard his neck break, but I was muddled by drink, and I didn't really believe that the captain could die, like any other mortal, and most particularly not in such a stupid and easy fashion, so I judged that he was just hurt, and I picked him up and tried to get him to walk, but a corpse doesn't do much walking without at least a bit of a charm put on it, so then I swung him up across my shoulders and I headed down that alley, swaying slightly, and in a hurry to get back to the *Bonny Anne*, where either Doc Brewer or the captain's lady, Miss Melissa, could see about reviving him.

I think somewhere at the back of my mind I must have known he was dead, but sozzled as I was, I probably thought even that wouldn't necessarily have been entirely permanent. I've seen my share of zombies, and I know they aren't of much use and don't remember a damned bit of what they knew in life, but I'd heard tales of other ways of dealing with the dead, one sort of necromancy or the other, and I won't call them lies as yet.

I had enough sense left to stay in the alley as much as I could, and halfway to the docks I ran into Black Eddie driving a freight wagon, and I hailed him and threw the captain's carcass in the back, and then climbed up beside him.

It took me two or three tries to get up to the driver's bench, what with the liquor in me, but I made it eventually, and Black Eddie had us rolling before I had my ass on the plank.

"Head for the ship," I told him, and he nodded, as he was already bound that way. He snapped the reins and sped the horses a mite.

Then he threw a look behind him and turned to me.

"Billy," he said, "what's wrong wi' the captain?"

"Broke his fool neck," I said.

He looked at me startled, then looked back at that corpse, and then asked, "You mean he's dead?"

I started to nod and then to shrug and then I said, "Damned if I know, Eddie, but I'm afraid so."

"Damme!" Eddie said, and he flicked the reins again for more speed.

That brought our situation to my attention. "Eddie," I said, looking around in puzzlement, "what're ye doing with this wagon?"

"Damned if *I* know, Billy," he said. " 'Twas the captain's order that I get it, and have it at the docks by midnight, but he didn't think to tell me why."

"Oh," I said, trying to remember if the captain had said anything about a wagon and not managing to recall much of anything at all. The captain had mostly been on about the usual, whiskey and women and the woes of the world and hadn't spoken much of any special plans. A moment or two later we rolled out onto the dock where the *Bonny Anne* lay, and I hadn't come up with a thing.

"Well," I said, "Mr. Abernathy will know."

We'd tied up right to the dock, as the harbor in Collyport is a good and deep one, with a drop-off as steep as a ship-chandler's prices; no need to ride out at anchor and come in with the boats, as there would be in most of the ports we traded in. About a dozen ships were in port, at one place or another, and the *Bonny Anne* was one of them, right there at hand, and we could see the lads aboard her watching as we came riding up.

Looking up at them, the thought came to me that perhaps there were things we had best keep to ourselves, at least until we'd had a chance to talk matters over with our first mate, Lieutenant John Hastings Abernathy, who had the watch aboard and was Captain Dancy's closest confidant. It seemed to me I recalled a few things I hadn't before.

"Eddie," I said, "give me a hand with the captain, would you? And let on he's just drunk, or been clouted, and let's not say any more of it than we must, shall we?"

He gave me the fish-eye, but then he shrugged. "What the hell, then," he said. "Let it be Mr. Abernathy what spreads the news, if you like."

"It'd suit me," I said. I was thinking of a deal the captain had made, six years before, with the Caliburn Witch.

So the two of us hauled that corpse out of the wagon with a bit more care than was honestly called for, and we got it upright between us, me with my hand at the back of the head so the crew would not be seeing it loll off to one side too badly, and we walked up the gangplank with the feet dragging between us, and we headed straight back to the captain's cabin.

Old Wheeler, the captain's man, was pottering about, and we shooed him away and dumped poor old Jack Dancy's mortal remains on the bunk, and then Black Eddie sent me to fetch Mr. Abernathy.

I found Hasty Bernie on the quarterdeck, just where he should have been, and had little doubt in my mind that he'd watched us every inch from the wagon to the break in the poop, but he didn't let on a bit, he just watched me walk up, and stood there silent as a taut sail until I said, "Permission to speak, sir?"

"Go ahead, Mr. Jones," he said, and I knew we were being formal, as he didn't call me Billy, but I didn't quite see why, as yet.

"Mr. Abernathy," I said, "I'd like a word with you in private, if I might, regardin' the captain."

He lifted up on his toes, with his hands behind his back, the way he always did when he was nervous about something, and he said, "And what is it that you can't say right here, Mr. Jones? Who's to hear you?"

I wasn't happy to hear that at all. He must have thought I was getting out of line somehow, and I remembered as he'd asked me especially to keep a close eye on some of the men, as they might be thinking the captain wasn't looking out for them proper.

I wasn't too concerned about mutiny brewing, not just then, in particular as I *had* been keeping an eye out and hadn't seen a man aboard who didn't have faith in the captain. They might not think much of the rest of us, but they all admired the captain and trusted in him to do right by them.

Which made my news that much worse. "Mr. Abernathy," I said, "you know as well as I do that any word said on this deck can be heard by any as might care to listen from below the rail, either on the halfdeck or on the docks, be they crewmen or townsfolk or any others that might chance by, not even mentionin' the possibilities of sorcery and black magic as might be involved. You were with the captain at Little Hengist, weren't you?"

He blinked at me and looked about as if he expected to see the Sorcerer's creatures climbing up the rigging, and then he turned back to me and said, "Very well, Mr. Jones, lead the way, then."

I led him straight to the cabin, where the poor captain's body lay and Black Eddie stood guard, and we closed up the sliding trap on the skylight above the map table, and we checked the stern windows and made sure they were tight, and

Black Eddie went from one cabinet to the next and made sure that there was nobody tucked away in any of them, neither a crewman tucked small nor the Sorcerer's homunculi, not as we really thought the Sorcerer still gave a tinker's damn for any of us aboard the *Bonny Anne*, but you never know.

And when we were sure that the place was as private as we could make it, I turned to Hasty Bernie and said, "He's dead."

The night air on the ride down to the ship and the business of getting the corpse aboard and getting ourselves alone and private with Bernie had given my head time to clear, and there wasn't any doubt any more. I'd heard that snap I'd heard, and I knew it for what it was.

Bernie snapped his head around as if to break his own neck and stared at that lump on the bunk. "Dead?" he said. "Captain Dancy?"

"Dead as a stone," Black Eddie said. "Whilst Billy was fetchin' you down, I took a look at 'im and listened for his heart and felt for his pulse, and the man's dead if ever a man was."

"Good Lord," Bernie said, staring at the corpse. "Now what are we going to do?"

I blinked and looked at Black Eddie, who looked back at me.

"We were hopin'," Eddie pointed out to Bernie, "that *you* could tell *us* that."

"Me?" Bernie looked from one of us to the other and back, with a look on him as if we'd just suggested he bugger the governor's pet penguin.

"You *are* in command," Eddie said mildly.

Bernie looked at us each, desperately, and then crossed to the bunk and knelt. "You're *sure* he's dead?" he asked.

We both nodded, but Bernie bent down and checked for himself, feeling for a breath from the nose and mouth, listening for the heart, feeling for a pulse, and finding nothing at all.

It was just then that someone knocked at the cabin door, and we looked at one another as if we were schoolboys caught with the maid and her bloomers down, and Black Eddie stared at Hasty Bernie, and Hasty Bernie stared around the room, and after a moment I called, "Who is it?"

"Got a letter for the captain," someone answered.

"Slip it under the door," I said.

The fellow hesitated and then said, "I don't think I can do

that, sir; I was told to give it to Captain Dancy and no other, or it'd be my neck in a noose."

I glanced at the others, but they just shrugged, so I went to the door and opened it.

There stood Jamie McPhee, with the letter in his hand, and I saw the red seal upon it and knew it wasn't just a bill from the chandler nor any such trifle.

"The captain's ill," I said. "Got a clout on the head in a fight and that atop a bottle of bad rum, and he's in no shape for readin' a letter. If you'd care to come in and put it in his hand, you'll have done as you were told, but you needn't wait for him to wake; he's dead to the world, and it might be noon before he rises again."

Or it might be Judgment Day, I added to myself.

The boy looked past me at the body on the bunk, and the situation seemed mighty plain, so he shrugged and said, "Well, I done my best, Mr. Jones, and with both you here and Mr. Abernathy there watching I reckon it's right enough. Here's the letter then, and I'm shut of it." And he handed me the letter.

Parchment, it was.

Jamie hurried off, and I closed the door tight and took the letter to Hasty Bernie.

I held it out to him, but he looked at it as if it were a hungry piranha and at me as if I were straight out of Bedlam. "That's for the captain," he said.

"And that's you, sir," I said. "Seein' as Captain Dancy's dead."

He stared at it for a moment longer, and I stood there, waiting.

"Oh, all right, damn you," he said, and he snatched the letter away and looked at it.

His face went white.

"Oh, Lord," he said. "It's from Governor Lee."

"Open it," Black Eddie said. "Let's hear the worst."

2.

His hands shaking, Bernie broke the big red seal and opened it, and he read it aloud, and what it said was this:

Dear Captain Dancy, As you will recall as well as do I, when I granted you Pardon for your Crimes this three years past, there were certain Terms agreed upon by us both. Though we have not always seen eye to eye on every Detail, I have, I feel, fully lived up to my end of the Arrangement, and I confess you have done well enough on your own. However, one Provision of our Agreement remains in Doubt. You must surely know to what I refer. Having seen Mistress Coyne twice this fortnight past, how could you not? I trust you will remedy this Oversight forthwith. Should you fail to satisfy me of your good Will by this coming Dawn, either by completing our Arrangement or by suitably demonstrating your Intent, I fear I will be required to consider the entire Agreement void, your Pardon revoked, and your Ship forfeit to the Crown. Signed, Geo. Lee, Governor.

When he'd read that, Bernie stared at the paper for a long moment. Then he looked up at Eddie and at me and said, "Good Christ, whatever is *this* about?"

Eddie and me, we shook our heads, as we hadn't either of us any more idea than a duck.

"Who's this Mistress Coyne, then?" Eddie asked.

"I have no idea," Bernie said.

"Nor do I," I said.

"An' what do we do *now*?" Eddie asked.

"Your ship forfeit to the crown, it says," I remarked. "Seems to me that we'd want to avoid that. I'm not overly concerned about losing the captain's pardon, as that was for a sentence of death, and he's clear of that, but I'm not eager to lose the ship."

"Could he take it?" Bernie asked thoughtfully. "We've men and guns, after all. We could fight."

"Aye, that we could," I said, "but we'd lose. The governor's got men and guns himself, aboard the frigate just across the harbor."

"The *Armistead Castle*," Bernie said. "I'd forgot her."

"Aye," I said, "that's the one."

"And the *Castle*'s ready for sea," Eddie pointed out. "I saw meself, they've a full crew aboard, standing a proper watch tonight, not a port watch."

"The governor must ha' meant that to fright the captain," I said. "He's lettin' us know he's serious in his threats."

"I don't know about the captain, but it frightens me right

well," Hasty Bernie said. "That frigate's sixteen guns a side; we couldn't possibly stand up to her."

"Aye," Eddie said. "Well then, shall we fetch the men and raise anchor to run? We can be over the horizon by dawn, if we're brisk about it."

"Nay," I said, "for then we'd be fugitives and shut of Collyport forever, not to mention having all the rest of the Royal Navy after us."

"Well, and aren't we fugitives now?" Eddie asked.

"Not here," I said. "Not with the governor's pardon."

"But that runs out at dawn," Eddie said.

"Not if we show our good intent," I told him.

Bernie was still staring at the parchment, but he said, "Maybe if we just went to the governor and told him what happened . . ."

"Would he believe us?" I asked.

"We've got the bloody corpse to prove it, ye blidget!" Eddie said. "How could he not?"

"Are ye plannin' to drag the captain all the way up to the governor's palace, then, and haul it in with us when he agrees to see us—*if* he agrees to see us?"

Black Eddie had to think about that one for a moment.

"We might could try it," he said at last, but we knew by the tone that his heart weren't in it. I was ready to mention the Caliburn Witch, and her promise to live and let live only until she heard that Jack Dancy was dead, but I could see Eddie wasn't going to argue, so I held off.

"Why'd the governor want to be so bloody cryptic in his letter, anyway?" Bernie snapped.

"And why'd the captain not tell us what in hell he wanted with that wagon, and what he'd promised the governor?" Black Eddie retorted.

"And when," I said, "did the captain *ever* tell us what he was up to?"

That silenced them both, for the truth was that Jack Dancy had always been close with his counsel. As he told me once, "Billy," he said, "if you don't tell people what you're planning, they won't worry about what might go wrong." And sure enough, he'd always pulled off everything he'd put his hand to; no matter how bad it looked, no matter how bad it *was*, he'd always pulled it off. Sometimes he only survived by the skin of his teeth, but he always survived, as if all the gods of luck owed him heavily and had interest to pay.

Well, his luck had run out tonight.

And we were standing there looking at one another, the three of us, when the cabin door opened. We heard the hinges creak, and the three of us spun about, and Black Eddie's dirk was out, and my own hand seemed to be on the hilt of me own dagger, and there we all were, staring at Miss Melissa, who was by her face just as surprised to see us as we were to see her.

"Good evenin' to ye, gentlemen," she said. "Is the captain in?"

Eddie and I looked at one another and then at Hasty Bernie, who swallowed and said, "Miss Melissa, there's bad news."

"Oh? Is he drunk, Mr. Abernathy?" She looked at the body on the bunk and stepped into the cabin.

Bernie looked at the two of us, but we were no help to him, and his face twisted up. "Worse," he said.

Miss Melissa gave him a look such as I hope I never have to endure. "He's hurt, then?" she asked, closing the door behind her.

"Dead," Black Eddie said.

"Dead?" She was at the bunk before I could blink, tipping the corpse's head back for a good look.

For a moment, we all just stood and watched her, as she saw what we'd all seen. Then she let out a great sob.

"Damn you, Jack Dancy!" she said, her back still to us, and her voice weren't steady at all. "What the hell did you go and die for? Eddie, go get Doc Brewer—he was down in the after hold last I saw, counting those masks we got at Pennington's Cay."

Black Eddie threw a look at Hasty Bernie, who nodded, and then Eddie trotted out the door.

Miss Melissa turned, and we could see the tears running down her face, and it seemed I felt my own throat thickening and my eyes going damp. All that strong drink must have numbed me, a bit, for surely the captain's death was enough to make a man cry, but it wasn't until I saw Miss Melissa weeping that it came home to me.

"How did it happen, Billy?" she asked me.

I shrugged and said, "He fell. Hit his head on a brick wall, and his neck snapped."

She stared at me, and the tears stopped.

"That's *all*?" she asked.

I nodded. "That's all," I said.

"That son of a bitch!" she said. "You mean it wasn't the governor's men? Nor the Sorcerer? Nor the Pundit? Nor the *Amber Lassie*? Nor 'Tholomew Sanchez?"

"No," I said, "wasn't any of those. He slipped and fell while drunk, and that's all there was to it."

"Well, I'll ... a man like Jack Dancy, dead like that?"

I nodded.

"That's not fitting. It's a damn poor ending to a life like that!"

"I'd agree with that," I said, and Bernie nodded.

For a moment the three of us stood silent, thinking about the captain. It was Miss Melissa who broke the quiet.

"What were his last words, then?" she asked me. "Did he leave us with a fine speech to remember him?"

I had to think about that. We'd been in Old Joe's, and we'd just beaten those sailors and were on our way out through the back, and Jack Dancy had turned to me, smiling and drunk.

"His last words," I said, "were, 'Billy, I'm going to need five guineas later tonight; have you got 'em?' "

Miss Melissa glared at me as I'd belched in church. "That's a hell of a way to go out, asking for money!"

I didn't argue any. Instead, I said, "I think there's something you'd best be seein', Miss Melissa." I pointed to the governor's letter.

Bernie handed it to her, and she read it, and then she looked up and asked, "Who's Mistress Coyne?"

"We don't know," I said. "That's just what we were askin' amongst ourselves when you came in."

She squinted at me suspiciously, and I looked her in the eye because I wasn't doing anything but telling the simple truth. "D'ye think Jack was bedding her?" she asked me.

I shrugged. "I don't know, Miss Melissa," I said. "I truly don't. I never heard her name until this letter arrived, not half an hour ago."

"Miss Melissa," Bernie said, "while I understand your concern with the mysterious Mistress Coyne, might I point out that it's rather more urgent that we discover just what promises Captain Dancy had made to Governor Lee, than whether he'd been ... ah ..."

"Than whether he'd been tomcatting about again," she finished for him. "You mean you don't *know* what the promise was?"

"No," Bernie said.

She looked at me, and I shook my head.

"Nor I," I said.

"Well," she said, looking at the letter, "we can't ask the governor, for he'd not have the likes of us in his palace."

I threw Bernie a glance and shook my head as he started to open his mouth. There was no need for her to know that we'd been in the palace half a dozen times with Jack Dancy, going in by way of the caves round the other side of Collins Island that led into the wine cellars. Nor did she need to be told that Captain Dancy had once walked in the front gate at the governor's invitation. The circumstances for that one didn't bear telling to the captain's lady.

"So that means we'll have to see this Mistress Coyne," Miss Melissa announced.

I blinked.

"Beggin' your pardon," I said. "but how are we to do that? We don't know who she is, or where, and we've no more than five hours to dawn, I'd judge, when the governor's said the ship's to be forfeit."

"Well," Miss Melissa said, "it seems plain to me that *somebody* knows who she is and where she's to be found. You tell me that you two don't know, but someone aboard might—did Jack go alone when he saw her, without word to any? And even if he did, there's the governor who knows who and where she is, and the governor's spies who told him that Jack had been to see her; can't we ask them?"

"Well, we can't ask the governor, can we?" I said.

"And half the crew's out carousing," Bernie pointed out.

"Well, then, what about the governor's spies?" Miss Melissa asked.

I had to think about that. Something seemed familiar there.

"Mr. Abernathy," I said, speakin' slowly so as to think about what I was saying, "wa'n't it one of the governor's men what brought you that bottle on Sunday?"

The bottle I referred to had had an imp in it once, and the captain had wanted it for a deal he was making with the vengeful brother of the harbormaster's first wife, but that's beside the point.

"Aye," Hasty Bernie said, "it was. What of it?"

Miss Melissa looked at me. "D'you think, then, that this man might know where we can find the wench?"

I shrugged. "He might, and what better have we got to do, than to ask him?"

"D'you know where he's to be found, then?" she asked.

"No," I said, "but I know who does."

It was at that moment that Black Eddie flung open the door and stepped in, with Doc Brewer close on his heels—and Peter Long the bo'sun right behind Doc Brewer.

"Here, you can't come in!" Bernie called at Peter. "The captain's ill!"

"Oh," Peter said, taking in the lump on the bunk and noticing who he was following. He stopped with his toes on the sill. "Well, then, tell the captain I've got his parrot."

Hasty Bernie blinked in surprise, and Miss Melissa stared, and I asked, "*What* parrot?"

"The one he sent me after, Billy. He told me to go up to the Hightown Market and buy the big parrot from the one-eyed bugger in the red and gold tent, and I did, and I've got the damn bird in the fo'c'sle, and it like to bit me nose off."

"All right, Peter," I said. "If he didn't hear that himself I'll be sure to tell him, you've my word on it."

"Thank ye, Billy. I've no fancy to keep the bird myself." He tipped his cap and turned away.

Black Eddie and Doc Brewer had been standing in the cabin listening to this, and when Peter was gone and Doc was closing the cabin door, Black Eddie said, "A *parrot*?"

"I've no more of it than you, Eddie," I said.

"Doctor," Miss Melissa said, paying no attention to Eddie and myself, "the captain's dead, and there's no doubt of it, so it's not your medical skills that we wanted. It's necromancy, and you're the man aboard that knows most of magicks, so I sent for you."

"Dead?" Doc Brewer started and turned to the bunk.

"Yes, he's dead, damn him!" Miss Melissa snapped, with her hands on her hips and fire in her eye. A pretty thing, she was then.

"Miss Melissa . . ." Bernie started to say, but at a glare from her he thought better of it.

Doc Brewer wasn't listening. He was inspecting Jack Dancy's remains, poking at the neck with his fingers and muttering to himself.

"Whacked his head, he did," he said. "Snapped the third cervical vertebra, and the severed edge went right through the spinal cord, by the look of it. He probably never felt a thing."

That was some comfort to me, hearing that.

Doc muttered on for a moment, whilst the rest of us gradually lost interest in talking and got to watching and listening. Finally, Doc straightened up and said, "He may not even know he's dead, it was so quick. If that's the fact, then the chances are good that his ghost is still back where he died, trying to ascertain what's happened to him. A witch might be able to locate the spirit and converse with it, but earthbound souls aren't anything I can handle."

Miss Melissa started to protest, but Doc Brewer held up a hand to silence her. "On the other hand," he said, "Jack Dancy was a sharp man and a realist, and he may have seen what happened and know he's dead. In that case, there's no telling what's become of him, whether he's earthbound or on to his final rest or somewhere in between. If he's yet in limbo, I can bespeak him, and if he's in hell, which I pray he's not, for rogue that he was I liked the man and I thought well of him ... well, if he's in hell, I may be able to reach him but it's not sure. If he's gone to the reward of the blessed, alas, though *he'll* be happy, *we* won't, for if that's the case he's beyond all earthly concerns and can't be reached by any means known to mortal man save direct divine intercession—and I've no knack for that, let me tell you! The pope himself can't rely on it!"

Hasty Bernie snorted. "Of course he can't," he said. "He's an old fraud, no holier than I am, and his whole church ..." He caught sight of our faces and stopped.

Black Eddie's a Papist, of course, and we all knew it, and Hasty Bernie had no call to speak ill of the Bishop of Rome in front of Eddie that way, but his own faith had got the better of him for a moment.

We didn't hold it against him, though, and Miss Melissa carried on, asking the doc, "So you might be able to reach him and ask him what his agreement with the governor was?"

Doc was puzzled by that. "The governor?"

Miss Melissa handed him the letter, and he read it.

"I don't know," he said, handing it back, "but I'll see what I can do. I'd best prepare my spells—the sooner the better."

We could none of us argue with that, so we stood politely as the doc left.

When the door closed behind him, Miss Melissa turned to me and said, "You were sayin' that you can find the governor's man, who might lead us to this Mistress Coyne?"

"Not I," I replied, "but Jamie McPhee, as he handles errands like that for the captain."

"Let's get on with it then," she said. "Have him in here and get *on* with it!"

"Couldn't we wait until the doctor . . ." Bernie began, but Miss Melissa cut him off with a glare.

"Now, Mr. Abernathy," I said, "you heard what Doc Brewer told us; it's as like as not he can't contact the captain. And we've no time to waste in trying. Eddie, can ye call the lad?"

Black Eddie nodded and stepped out, and the rest of us stood about fiddling our thumbs, staring each at the other and thinking on what we should do.

3.

We had none of us come up with anything when Jamie arrived, of himself, without a sign of Black Eddie. We sent him to talk to the governor's man and find out who this Mistress Coyne might be.

"Why?" he asked.

Hasty Bernie started to say, "Well, lad, the captain . . ."

Miss Melissa hushed him. "It's not your concern, boy," she said, "and we've no time to explain. You just go and ask and come back here quick!"

He nodded and hurried out.

We all looked after him as he left. Hasty Bernie remarked, "Collyport's a rough place by night; I hope he'll have no problems."

"Ah, the lad knows the town," I said. "There's nothing to worry about."

"Nothing to worry about!" Hasty Bernie shouted, glaring at me. "The governor's about to claim the ship, the captain's dead, and not one of us even knows what's happening, and you'd tell us not to worry?"

"Well," I said, "and what good did worry ever do a man? There's naught more to be done until we hear from the lad or Doc Brewer, is there? Then there's nothing *we* can do, and no reason to worry!"

"An odd philosophy," Hasty Bernie said.

"A fool's philosophy," Miss Melissa retorted. "How do we know there's naught can be done? What if the doctor can't reach the captain, nor the boy find this Mistress Coyne? Are we to give up the ship without a fight and starve in the streets?"

"Oh, we'd not starve," I said. "A man who'd sailed with Jack Dancy can surely find another berth! But I'd as soon keep the ship, I'll agree with that."

"Is it ours to keep, though?" Hasty Bernie asked, suddenly thoughtful. "Did the captain own it? Who are his heirs?"

"*We* are," Miss Melissa snapped. "Who else could there be?"

"I thought his family," Bernie began, "his children . . ."

"*What* family?" Miss Melissa shouted. "He swore he'd never married!"

"Nor did he," I told her.

"Then what children?" she demanded triumphantly.

"Miss Melissa," I said, "you must know better than that. By last count he knew of thirty-one, he told me this Sunday past, and he's been the sole support of the seven whose mothers aren't presently married. And there's a sister back in Weymouth, the captain spoke of her often—she's married to a chandler by the name of Wiggins, I understand."

Her mouth fell open, and she stared wide-eyed at me.

"I suppose that Mrs. Wiggins would be the heir of record," Bernie said, "given the lack of a marriage. But did Captain Dancy truly own the ship himself, or did he have a backer?"

"Thirty-one?" Miss Melissa squeaked.

"Or thereabouts," I told her. "You'll understand, the captain often took the lass's word, and I'll not swear they were all of them entirely truthful. But then he may have missed a few, as well, so I'd judge as it might balance out."

"*Thirty-one bastards?*" she shrieked at me.

"Or thereabouts," I repeated.

She stared at me, and Hasty Bernie asked, "Do you think Mrs. Wiggins would know if there were a backer? I'll need to send her a letter in any case, so I thought . . ."

"*Who cares?*" Miss Melissa screamed, turning to Bernie. "Who cares about any sister, or backer, or the thirty-one bleeding bastards that son of a bitch left? *We're* the ones who *have* the ship, and I don't intend to let the governor or anybody else take it away! Call the men to their stations—we'll take this ship out and sink anyone who tries to stop us!"

I looked at Bernie, but he was looking helplessly back at me. "Miss Melissa," I said, "I don't want to lose the *Bonny Anne* any more than you do, nor will we if we can help it, but there's no need for all that, now. The doc's trying to bespeak the captain, and Jamie's gone to find us Mistress Coyne, and there's still a fine hope that we'll be able to keep the governor's pardon *and* the ship, safe here in Collyport. If ye must do *something*, you'd be better to see if you can think what the captain promised the governor, not sending the men to stations."

"Well said, Mr. Jones," Hasty Bernie said. "Though I still think that determining the ship's rightful owner . . ."

"Can wait," I said, interrupting him. "Whoever owns her surely won't be wantin' her forfeit to the Crown, and if we can hold her free we'll be in a position to bargain when the time comes. First, though, we've to hold her free."

"Aye," Bernie admitted.

"And to do that, we've to know what the governor wants."

"Or to get out of Collyport," Miss Melissa said.

"And go where?" I asked her, as sweetly as I could. "In a ship forfeit to the Crown, every English-speakin' port will be closed to us as fast as the word can reach them—and every *other* port is *already* closed to the *Bonny Anne!*"

"All right, then," she said. "What does the governor want?"

"I've no idea," I admitted. "But the captain did, and he'd made arrangements, it seems."

"What arrangements?" she asked.

"Well," I told her, "Black Eddie was to have a freight wagon at the ship by midnight, and it's there on the dock now. Peter Long was to fetch a particular parrot, and he's got it in the fo'c'sle. It might be there are other things as well that I've not happened on yet."

"A freight wagon?"

I nodded. I didn't mention that we'd used it to fetch the captain's corpse in.

"And a parrot?"

I nodded again.

There was a knock at the door.

We looked at one another, and then Miss Melissa called, "Come in!"

The door opened, and there was Black Eddie with a scrawny little ape of a man I'd never clapped eyes on before. Before Eddie could speak, the stranger barked at us, "If ye'd changed yer damned plans, ye might 'a' had the courtesy to ha' told me!"

"See here, man," Hasty Bernie said, "who are you talking to that way?"

"I'm talkin' to *you*, ye pompous twit," he sputtered. "You and yer damned captain, what told me to wait for 'is bloody signal that was due at midnight and he ain't gimme yet! And there he is, sleepin' off a bottle or two, ain't he? Damned if I shouldn't 'a' known it. Bloody idiot. Bloody hell!"

He turned and would have stamped away, save that Black Eddie was in his way, which gave Miss Melissa time to ask, "What signal?"

The stranger turned back and squinted at her, then snapped, "A red light on the mizzen. Didn't the damned fool tell ye?"

She shook her head, and Bernie and I just stood there.

The little man looked over at the captain's mortal remains and snorted. "Reckon he passed out before he got that far. Well, then, d'ye want me to fire that warehouse, or don't ye?"

Bernie and I looked at each other. Miss Melissa started to ask, "*What* warehouse?" but I tapped her shoulder before she'd got a good start on the second word, and she hushed up nicely.

"We're runnin' a little late tonight," I said. "As ye said yourself, the captain's been no help to us." I looked at Bernie.

"Aye, if you could bear with us yet for a while, we'd appreciate it," he said.

The little man looked us all over and was about to snort again when I said, "Listen, man, you go back to your post and gi' us ten more minutes beyond. If the red light's not up by then, belay the whole job and go home to your bed with our blessings. There's an extra silver guinea for your trouble. Fair enough?" I fished the coin from me purse and held it up. Didn't leave me much, but he didn't look the sort to settle for a shilling.

He squinted again, then said, "Fair enough. Hand it over."

I obliged him, and he tucked the guinea away, and Black Eddie led him back to the rail.

Miss Melissa watched him over the side, then slammed the door and spun on us.

"What in hell was *that* about?" she asked.

Hasty Bernie shrugged.

"Seems to me," I said, "as the captain had a diversion planned. A big one. And I'll wager I know what warehouse it is, too, as Jack Dancy was always a man to get the most for his efforts."

Bernie blinked. Miss Melissa stared at me for a moment, and then a smile spread across her face.

"Sanchez?" she asked.

I nodded. "He's out to sea now, but he's got a good lot of his booty tucked away where he didn't figure it to be shot up if he meets an unfriendly ship. Wasn't worth our while doin' a thing to it in the ordinary course, but if it's a diversion we need anyway, why, there 'tis ready to go."

"But what do we need a diversion *for*?" Bernie asked, his face troubled.

"I don't know," I said, "but we have ten minutes to decide whether we need one at all."

"If Jack arranged it, we'll probably need it," Miss Melissa said, and I had to agree that that was generally true.

"There's a freight wagon," I said, "and this letter from the governor, and visits to Mistress Coyne, and now a fire to be set as a diversion just as the freight wagon was to be here."

"And a parrot," Bernie added.

"And a bloody damn parrot," I agreed. "With all that, then, does either of you have any notion of just what might be goin' on?"

They looked at each other and then back at me.

"No," Bernie said.

"Seems to me," I said slowly, "that a diversion over at the warehouse is meant to draw attention away from the ship. If it were a diversion elsewhere that the captain wanted, he could have made it himself ready enough right here, or any number of ways."

"If it really *is* a diversion," Miss Melissa suggested.

I considered that, while Bernie protested, "Captain Dancy wouldn't burn down that warehouse just for spite! And why on a signal from the ship, if he just wanted it done?"

"Maybe not a *diversion*," I said, "so much as *cover*. Now, the captain must have planned on being here aboard ship at midnight, so as to give the signal and to do whatever was to be done with the freight wagon. Suppose that you're aboard your ship, and you see a fire over there on the great wharf—what do you do?"

"I put out to sea, of course," Bernie said, "to get clear of sparks."

"D'ye think, then, that Jack was going to run?" Miss Melissa asked. "He was no coward!"

I shook my head. "No, not Jack Dancy. He wouldn't ha'

run from Governor Lee, nor from the *Armistead Castle*, nor from the devils of Hell. Nor would he give up Collyport so easy. So if he'd knowed what the governor was on about in that letter, and that this was the night he had to deliver, he'd ha' done his damnedest to deliver. So he planned on doing it from the sea, somehow."

"What about the wagon?" Bernie asked. "Maybe he figured on sending the ship to sea, so that everyone would think he was gone, and all the while he'd be about his business with the wagon."

"No, Mr. Abernathy," I said. "For then he'd want the *Bonny Anne*'s departure noted, and he'd 'a' had us sail out in broad daylight, not put out at midnight to escape a fire. No, the fire's to give us a reason for leaving harbor at night, I'm sure of it."

I had an idea, then, of where the captain might have had in mind to go, but I didn't know the why of it yet at all.

There'd be no point in leaving at midnight if we were to be bound for another island; we couldn't reach another that night, and if we'd a need to reach another at a particular time it would be easier to make the time right along the way than by sailing out in the dark—even in a harbor we knew as well as that one, sailing out at night is a bit of a risk.

So we were going somewhere else on Collins Island, somewhere that was best reached by sea, and where he didn't want us to be seen, and where we *would* have been seen if we'd sailed there by day, and somewhere that wasn't close enough to row there easy in the ship's launch.

I knew what that meant, plain enough. The captain had meant to sail around to the caves.

But why?

If he'd meant to meet with someone there, then we were bound to miss it entirely, as it was more than an hour after midnight and we hadn't even got most of the crew aboard, as far as I knew.

But then, if someone was waiting in the caves for us, he weren't about to go much of anywhere in any hurry, as the cliffs above and to the sides were a mighty rough climb, and the cliff below led nowhere but the sea.

There was the other end of the cave, of course, but there weren't many as knew about that.

All the same, if we were to have met someone there, he might be there yet by the time we could reach him, or he might not, and I'd have been much happier if I'd have known just what to expect.

I wished as Jamie McPhee would hurry back.

Someone knocked at the door, and I thought as my wish had been granted, but then Black Eddie called from without, "It's been nigh on ten minutes."

"Aye," I said, and then I called, "Send up the signal! And prepare for sea!" Boldness, Captain Dancy used to tell me, boldness will win sooner than wit.

"*What?*" Miss Melissa shrieked at me, and I looked at her quite reproachful, as it hurt my ear.

"Mr. Jones," Bernie said, "Billy, do you know just what you're doing?"

"Not entirely," I confessed, "but I have a fair to middlin' idea."

"What about Jamie?" Miss Melissa asked, still shouting, but not half as loud.

"I'll send a man to fetch him," Bernie said.

"I'd not waste the time," I said. "Beggin' your pardon, Mr. Abernathy. But what you might do is put a boat over and leave it by the dock with a couple of men aboard, to row the lad out to us when he arrives."

Bernie stared at me thoughtful for a moment, then nodded, and he left the cabin to see to it.

That left me and Miss Melissa and the corpse, and when I realized I was the only living man there with her, my tongue dried out and of a sudden I found nothing to say.

She hadn't the same problem, though.

"And who do you think you are, Billy Jones, to be ordering about Mr. Abernathy and doing what you please?"

"I'm second mate of this ship, Miss Melissa," I answered her, "and I'm just doin' what I can to see us all safe, now that the captain's not here to do it."

She looked me in the eye for a moment, and I didn't blink. Then she turned away and looked at the captain's body and whispered, "Damn you, Jack Dancy!"

Then she turned again and marched out.

4.

I covered up the captain and tried to make him look natural, just in case someone should chance to look in, and as I was about to go up on deck there was old Wheeler coming in, about to whine about somewhat or the other, and thinking quick I held up a finger to hush him.

"The captain's bad tonight," I told him. "Don't you touch him, unless you want to kiss the gratings tomorrow!"

Wheeler nodded and went about his business, throwing a glance over his shoulder every so oft but not going near the corpse.

I just hoped the captain wouldn't start to stink too soon. Maybe Doc Brewer could do something about that.

Then I went up, and at first I thought that dawn was breaking and we'd wasted the whole night, but then I saw as this light was orange, and not the pink of dawn at all, and I realized as it was the warehouse on fire.

Around us, other ships were casting off, their crews running about and shouting. I could see the *Armistead Castle* spreading canvas already—she had a good crew, that ship.

And there aboard the *Bonny Anne* about me were the men and boys hanging in the rigging and watching the fire and chattering amongst themselves like so many gulls and the ship still at the dock!

I looked about and saw Hasty Bernie on the quarterdeck, staring up the streets of Collyport, and I was as angry with him as I'd ever been. "Hey!" I called, "you bloody damn fools, that's a fire over there, and there'll be sparks in the air, and our sails could catch! Cast off! Get us out to sea!"

I saw Peter Long throw a look at Hasty Bernie, but Bernie just nodded, and a moment later we were making way, pulling away from Collyport on the westerly airs.

I saw that at least Bernie had put down a boat, with Black Eddie in it, lest Jamie should happen along. And I saw that those other ships were putting out, as well—the *Bonny Anne* would be second or third out of the harbor, behind the *Armistead Castle* and maybe a merchantman off to starboard.

And the sparks *were* blowing in the wind and coming after us, and I didn't like it at all, and as I called the orders to work the sails I made sure to send a boy below for buckets and lines. It was just like the captain, to have come up with a diversion that could burn the ship!

It was only when we were safe out at sea that I took the time to think about anything but getting the *Bonny Anne* clear, and looked about.

There was Bernie on the quarterdeck—as I was myself, I noticed, having come up and taken the wheel without thinking

about it. Miss Melissa was beside Hasty Bernie, and the two
of them were arguing in whispers—I didn't trouble myself
about just why, as yet. The rest of the crew, those as were
aboard, were going about their business as they should, despite it being the middle of the night and near as black as the
Sorcerer's soul.

Now it seemed to me as the time had come to decide what
to do. The captain's plan called for sailing around the island
to the caves, I was sure, but did we really want to do that?

Well, I supposed we did, as why else were we at sea?

I looked over at Mr. Abernathy and the captain's lady and
decided that I'd best not bother them about it, as it would
only mean more argument. I turned the wheel and put her on
the starboard tack.

She was turning sweetly when I heard a hail from the masthead.

Our boat was coming out from the harbor, with Jamie
McPhee and Black Eddie and, the lookout swore, a woman in
the bow.

"Heave to," I called, "and bring 'em aboard!"

The men went to it with a will, and that boat seemed to
skim right up to us in a mighty pretty piece of rowing, so it
wasn't but a few minutes before we had the boat up out of the
water and Jamie and Eddie and the woman on the halfdeck.

And sure enough they had a woman with them, a tall,
comely thing, with red hair free to her waist and wearing a
red and gold gown to go with it. She had a wide-brimmed red
velvet hat on her head, with a veil all around, and white
gloves to her hands, which seemed a little more than was
purely necessary for the weather.

I called the orders to get us under way again whilst Jamie
and Eddie brought her up to the quarterdeck. They took her
over to Hasty Bernie, as he was the senior officer aboard, but
I caught Eddie's eye and gestured for him to take the wheel.

"We're bound for the caves," I whispered to him. "Fast as
we can get there without riskin' the rocks."

He nodded and grabbed the spokes, and I slipped over toward the others.

"Mr. Abernathy," Jamie was saying, "this is Mistress
Annabelle Coyne."

Hasty Bernie took her hand and bowed and smiled his best
formal smile and then stood there staring at her and looking
stupid. 'Twas plain to me that the poor man had no idea what

to do. I thought back on the watchbill and realized that he'd most likely been without sleep for nigh onto thirty hours, while I hadn't missed but an hour or two's sleep as yet, so I stepped forward.

I smiled and tipped my hat, once I remembered I was wearing it, as it happens I was, and said, "I'm Billy Jones, Mistress Coyne. Welcome aboard the *Bonny Anne*."

I could see Miss Melissa out of the corner of my eye, and she looked somewhat put out, both with Bernie and myself, but I didn't worry about that as yet.

"Thank you, Mr. Jones," Mistress Coyne said.

"My apologies, Mistress Coyne," Bernie said. "It seems I need Mr. Jones to remind me of my manners. Welcome, indeed, and thank you for coming."

Miss Melissa glared at Bernie, and I knew that Mistress Coyne saw it; wasn't no love lost between those two women, be sure of that!

"Thank *you*, Mr. Abernathy," she said. "But I must confess, I'm not sure why I am here."

Bernie blinked at that, and he and I both looked at Jamie.

"She wouldn't say a thing to me," Jamie blurted out, "so's I brought her."

"Ah," Bernie said.

Miss Melissa suggested, "Jamie, tell us what happened."

He glanced about, but there wasn't any there as didn't want him to speak, so he spoke. "Well, you sent me to talk to a man I know and ask as to who Mistress Coyne was, and I did that, and he told me as he didn't know a thing about her, save where she lived and what she looked like, and that she was at the governor's palace every so often, and that the governor was at her place on occasion, and as the two of them sent notes back and forth. And I figured as that probably wasn't all you'd wanted me to find out, so I asked for more, and he swore as how that was all he knew, but he could show me her place, and I said as I'd be pleased if he did, so he did, and there she was, and I was looking in the door—it's a little tearoom that she runs. Anyway, I was looking in the door, and she saw me and asked me what I wanted, and I didn't know as what I should say, and she asked who I was, and I told her, and she asked as who sent me, and I said that I was from the *Bonny Anne*, and she asked as whether Captain Dancy had wanted something of her, and I allowed as how I hadn't any idea, and then she asked if the ship was in port, and I said of course it was or I wouldn't be there, and next thing I knew she was coming with me back to the ship to see what was happening, and here we are."

He stopped as if the words had run out sooner than he'd expected, and had surprised him in doing it, and he sort of blinked at us in confusion.

"Thank you, lad," Bernie said. He turned to Mistress Coyne and asked, "It seems to me, mistress, that you came here of your own will, and that you know why better than we."

"I'll tell you what I know, Mr. Abernathy," she replied tartly. "I know that Captain Dancy had told me his ship would be leaving port at midnight, and here it is after that when a boy turns up at my shop saying that the *Bonny Anne* is still in port, and with a tale of being sent to find out who I am, when Jack Dancy has known me well these several months past. So I came to see what's become of the captain. I'd hoped to see him here on his own quarterdeck, and instead I find you in command. Could you tell me why?"

Bernie harrumphed—did a fine job of it, too, rocking back on his heels. "Well, mistress," he said, "as it happens, the captain is indisposed. Very much so, I'm afraid. Our ship's doctor, Emmanuel Brewer, is tending to him now."

Mistress Coyne said, in a very quiet voice, "I'm sorry to hear that."

"So were we," Bernie replied. "And after he was taken ill, we had word from Governor Lee that he was concerned over some agreement he had made with the captain. The message was not at all clear, I fear, but it did let us know that the governor took the matter, whatever it is, very seriously. Being loyal subjects of the Crown, we wanted to do our best to carry on despite the captain's temporary inconvenience—but I'm afraid the captain had neglected to inform any of us of just what it was the governor wanted. However, your name was mentioned in the governor's message, so we thought perhaps you could shed a little light on the situation."

"I see," Mistress Coyne said. I looked away for a moment to judge our position—the cliffs to port loomed up black and appeared a good bit closer than I really cared to see them.

When I looked back, Mistress Coyne was lifting her veil, and the light from the mizzen lantern caught her face full. I swallowed and tried not to stare.

It was plain to me in that instant why she had worn a veil;

a face like that isn't to be risked parading openly through the streets of Collyport at night.

"Jack Dancy didn't tell you *anything*?" she asked.

We all shook our heads—Bernie, Miss Melissa, myself, even Jamie.

"Jamie, run along and get some sleep," I said, now that I'd recalled he was there.

The others turned to stare as Jamie started a protest, and when he met all those eyes he thought better of arguing. He shuffled away, disappointed.

"You've not mutinied, have you?" Mistress Coyne asked, once Jamie was clear.

Bernie and I were honestly shocked, but I saw as how she could think it might be. We both spoke at once, but I think we made it plain we'd done no such a thing.

Mistress Coyne looked about and asked, "Where are we? Where are you taking me?"

Bernie started to say something about how it wasn't her concern, but I spoke up and said, "We're bound to a place we know of around the other side of the island. The captain told us that much, though we were late on gettin' a start."

"Do you know what you're to do there?"

"No."

She nodded. "I see." She studied us, and then looked Miss Melissa straight in the eye and asked, "And who might you be?"

Miss Melissa took a deep, angry breath and turned red as a boiled lobster. Bernie spoke up before she could shout, though.

"This is Mistress Melissa Dewhurst, a good friend of Captain Dancy and aboard the *Bonny Anne* at the captain's personal invitation."

"I'm delighted to meet you, Mistress Dewhurst," Mistress Coyne said with a nod, "but I fear that you must be bored by all this chatter."

Miss Melissa drew another breath, but this time 'twas myself who stopped her.

"Miss Melissa," I said, "I'd take it as a great favor if you would go below and see whether there's been any change in the captain's condition." And I pointed to the cabin skylight.

She nodded and gave Mistress Coyne a look such as I hope I never receive from any woman and then marched off the quarterdeck.

Once she was gone, I kept an eye on the cabin skylight, lest Miss Melissa be clumsy in opening it to hear, while Bernie asked, "Now, Mistress Coyne, if you don't mind, is there anything you can tell us?"

She looked about dubiously and saw that the only people on the quarterdeck were herself and Bernie and me, and Black Eddie at the wheel. She could hardly expect the helmsman to leave his post, and Bernie and I were the captain's two senior officers and two of his closest friends. None of the men in the rigging were close to hand.

"I don't know the details of Captain Dancy's plan," she said, "but I do know what Governor Lee wants of him. He's to remove Madame Lee."

Bernie looked puzzled. "Remove Madame Lee?" he repeated.

Mistress Coyne nodded.

"Remove how?"

"Alive."

That was some relief, in any case; I'd no particular desire to kill a woman, and besides, it hardly made sense to hire a man like Jack Dancy as a mere assassin. There's many a simpler way for a man to kill his own wife, should he care to.

There'd been that fellow on Pennington's Cay, for one—but no, that wasn't all that much simpler at that and not relevant to the present case.

I tried to recall what I'd heard of Madame Lee.

The governor had brought her back from another island five years before and had held a wedding that was still the subject of many a barroom tale or boast, though there wasn't but two people actually killed that day, and at least one of them clearly deserved it. I'd no idea what her maiden name might have been or which island she'd come from, nor for that matter of much else about her. I'd never laid eyes on her, nor had any man I knew of, not to swear to. I knew precious little about her, if the truth be known.

There were rumors, of course, but I'd not put faith in rumors, after some as I'd heard where I knew the truth of the matter. Why, the rumors would have it that Jack Dancy . . . well, they lied, and enough of that.

But as to the discussion we were having with Mistress Coyne, the next word spoken came from Mr. Abernathy.

"Why?" Bernie asked, and in my heart I cursed the man for a fool. Hadn't he heard what Jamie had said? Hadn't he seen

Mistress Coyne's face? It was as plain to me as I might want that the governor had it in mind to keep company with Mistress Coyne, and for that sort of entertainment the presence of a previous wife can hamper one a mite.

"Why alive, do you mean?" Mistress Coyne asked, and I realized perhaps Bernie wasn't the fool I thought, as it was a sound question. As I said, there's many a simpler way for a man to kill his own wife, and in particular when the man is the governor and chief magistrate of a Crown colony, and none's to argue if he says his wife fell from a cliff and wasn't pushed, or that the meal she died of was rotten but not poisoned.

But then I saw Bernie's face and knew that he *was* a fool. He started to say, "No, I meant—" but I cut him off.

"Aye," I said. "It seems to me as that's a sound question."

"Well, because . . . well, there are reasons that . . ." She stopped, cross with herself, and started over. "I don't know for certain why the governor wants her taken alive, but I do know something about her that might have something to do with it."

I nodded. "And what might that be?"

Mistress Coyne grimaced. She said, "Madame Lee is a witch."

5.

Hasty Bernie and I looked at each other, and we each saw the dismay in the other's eyes.

We had both battled the Black Sorcerer with Jack Dancy. We were both beside him when he fought the devil-kites at Bethmoora and when the night thing came aboard in Dunvegan Sound. Bernie was there when he outwitted the Pundit of Oul. I was there when he sweet-talked the ship and the lives of a dozen men, myself among them, away from the Caliburn Witch. We'd both seen Doc Brewer work a few little spells, and even those could be enough to terrify any sane man. And we'd both seen enough of other magic to know that neither of us cared to see more.

The prospect of kidnapping a witch was not exactly one that cheered the either of us.

And here we were with little choice, when it came right down to bottom, but to do that very thing. In fact, we were already asail toward the caves, and I knew now why. It wasn't to meet anyone, there was no rendezvous we'd missed; it was because through the caves we could get into the governor's palace and catch Madame Lee and bring her out the same way without being seen and without stumbling across the palace guards, as we might have done by any other route.

That is, unless the captain had been planning something complicated, as he might have been; but we had no way of knowing.

I thought about it for a moment.

The warehouse fire was to get us out to sea without arousing suspicion—and so as to provide an alibi, as well, for later on, should anyone be looking into the matter of Madame Lee's disappearance, Jack Dancy could swear that he and his ship weren't even in the harbor at the time, so how could he be involved?

And Mistress Coyne and the governor's letter fit in, as well—I judged that Mistress Coyne and Governor Lee had got a mite impatient with the impediments they'd been encountering and wanted the captain to get on with it.

After all, if Governor Lee had made his arrangements with the captain *three years ago* . . .

The patience of the man would fair qualify him for sainthood, if that were the truth of it, but thinking it over I saw as it wasn't likely that the whole plan had been made that long ago. Not many's the man that keeps the same mistress *and* the same wife so long as that. Besides, the governor had only been married two years at that point, which seems a tad hasty in tiring of a wife. No, my guess was that the governor's agreement with the captain was merely that at some time the governor would set the captain a task to discharge his debt and that this was the task he'd come up with.

And a task worthy of Jack Dancy's talents it was, too, kidnapping a witch. Even *he* hadn't attempted it before.

I wished Jack Dancy were still alive to do it.

So the fire was accounted for, and the letter—but how did the freight wagon fit in? And the parrot?

Had we taken the wagon on board or left it on the dock? I couldn't for the life of me recall just at that moment, though I didn't recollect any order to bring it aboard, nor seeing it anywhere but the dock. I hoped it didn't matter, but I feared it did. Seeing as the captain had said the wagon was to be there at midnight, and as the fire was to be set near about midnight, I judged as we should already have done something with that damned wagon, either taken it aboard or done something with it back at the dock.

"Beggin' your pardon, Mistress Coyne," I asked, "but would you have any notion as to what to a freight wagon might be in this little enterprise we're attemptin'?"

She considered that for a moment and then said, "No."

"I feared as much," I told her. "What about a parrot?"

She looked at me as if I were daft and asked, "What *about* a parrot?"

"Ah," I said. "Never you mind." It was plain that the captain hadn't told her any more than he had us, as to the exact details.

There wasn't much more to be done on deck until we reached the caves, so Bernie and I made some polite chitchat with Mistress Coyne for a moment, and then I slipped away to see just what might be happening elsewhere aboard the *Bonny Anne*.

First off, I saw as the freight wagon wasn't aboard. We'd left it sitting plain on the dock.

I looked into the fo'c'sle, to see the parrot for myself. There it was, on Peter Long's hammock, giving me the beady eye. I called to it, but it wouldn't say a word.

Next I betook myself down to the surgery, where Doc Brewer was sitting cross-legged, naked to the waist and painted like a savage, with black candles burning and a great clutter of skulls and suchlike about him.

He looked up when I came in, and his face was red and puffy, and the sweat was rolling down his chest like rainwater running down the masts. "Hello, Billy," he said.

"I'm not interruptin', am I?" I asked.

He shook his head. "No," he said. "It's of no use. I can't find a trace of him." He got to his feet and leaned against a bulkhead. "It's wearying, it is, calling like that."

I nodded and tried to think of something sympathetic to say, but before the words came he asked me, "Where are we bound, Billy? I feel the ship moving. Did you find out what the captain was up to?"

"In a manner of speaking," I admitted. I took a moment to gather my nerve, and then I asked him, "Tell me, could you be handlin' a witch, if we took one prisoner?"

He blinked. "A witch, you say? Are we to capture a witch?"

I nodded. "That we are."

He turned and poked at a canvas bag that hung on the bulkhead. "That would explain this, I suppose."

"Would it, now?" I asked. "And what might that be?"

"Oh, the hide of a salamander and the bones of an eel and a variety of other things. The captain told me the day before yesterday to find what I'd need for making a geas, the strongest I knew how. I suppose he meant for me to put a geas on her not to harm us, or some such a requirement."

"And you have it all?" I asked. A thought struck me. "You wouldn't need a parrot, would you?"

"A parrot?" He stared at me. "I've no use for a parrot, not for this spell nor any other I know."

"Oh, well," I said, "I was just askin'. So, do you have what you need for this geas, then?"

"Oh, of course," he said. "Save for the hair of the victim."

"Well," I said, "I don't suppose 'twill be any great feat to cut a lock of her hair for you. How long will it take, once you've the hair?"

He pursed his lips and considered that, and I commenced to worry, as I had hoped he'd be telling me 'twould be no time at all. Instead he said, "Well, it would depend on just when I began, but four to six hours, most likely."

"Ah," I said, thinking about what it would be like trying to hold an angry witch prisoner for six hours, with no magic against her. I wondered what the captain had planned—had he gotten a hank of Madame Lee's hair, somehow, that Doc Brewer should have already had?

I thought he might, at that. I told Doc to get ready to start his spell, and then I went back up on deck.

Peter Long met me there and asked, "Mr. Jones, what's to be done with that blasted parrot?"

"Hold onto it," I told him. "We'll no doubt know soon enough." Then I went on to the quarterdeck. Hasty Bernie and Annabelle Coyne were still talking.

"Mistress Coyne," I asked, "did the captain, by any chance, mention anything to you about Madame Lee's hair?"

She stared at me. "Now how did you know about that, Mr. Jones?" she asked lightly.

"About what, mistress?" Bernie asked.

"About the hair. I fetched him a handful of hair, taken from Madame Lee's brush—I don't know why. I guessed he was planning to have a wig made for some part of his deceptions."

"And what became of that hair?" I asked.

"Oh, I haven't the faintest notion," she replied. "I gave it to Captain Dancy yesterday."

I closed my teeth hard to hold back a curse. "Mr. Abernathy," I said, "I'm going below, to take a look at the captain's condition."

"Very good, Mr. Jones," Bernie said.

The moment I stepped through the cabin door, Miss Melissa demanded, "What's this about that woman's hair?" She stepped down from the stool under the skylight and glared at me.

"Doc Brewer needs it for a spell," I told her. "To put Madame Lee under a geas."

"Oh," she said.

"It's most likely somewhere in this cabin," I said.

"Do you think old Wheeler would know?" she asked.

That hadn't occurred to me to wonder, and I allowed as how it hadn't. She went and rousted the old man from his hammock, whilst I began opening cabinets and drawers.

Jack Dancy's old servant wasn't at his best just then, roused in the middle of the night, but at last we managed to explain that we were looking for a hank of a lady's hair that the captain had probably hidden somewhere. I hadn't found anything of the sort in my search—though some of the items I *had* found stirred my curiosity a tad. Whatever did the captain need with a playbill for an opera in Southampton? Or a shell carved to the shape of a herring? And where did he get some of those pictures?

Of course, I recognized a few of his souvenirs, like the tip off the narwhal's tooth and the green pendant he'd got from Madame Kent after Cushgar Corners.

Well, wasn't none of that important just then.

"A lady's hair?" Wheeler asked, and we both nodded, and Miss Melissa shouted at him a little.

He paid her no mind; instead he crossed to a cabinet I hadn't tried yet and reached around the side and opened the cabinet door and then reached in to the hinge and opened that same door again—the door was made in two layers that folded out.

And between those two layers were pinned a hundred locks of hair, each one tied in a ribbon.

And weren't none of them labeled or tagged.

6.

I stared at those damned locks of hair for a moment, and then I said words that I'd never have said in the presence of Miss Melissa had I remembered she was there. She said some of the same sort herself, though.

A thought struck me, then. Those hundred hanks were all the colors in which one might expect a lady's hair to be found, from ash to black with a bit of a side trip out to red along the way. I've known men as would only take a blond lassie or a redhead, but never let it be said that Jack Dancy put any such arbitrary limits upon his interests.

"And what color, then," I asked, "would Madame Lee's hair be?"

There wasn't a soul there who could answer, so I betook myself back to the quarterdeck and put the same question to Mistress Coyne.

"Brown," she told me. "A middling brown."

And wouldn't you know that full forty of those lovelocks were of a middling brown?

Naturally, Madame Lee wasn't one of the four redheads, nor the lone ash blonde.

And then we were anchored below the caves, and I saw the night was growing old, and there wasn't more time to worry about it. If we were to spirit Madame Lee from the palace before her maids were up and about, we'd to do it right soon.

I gathered up a few things I thought might be of use, and then I stood on the quarterdeck with Bernie whilst the call went round for volunteers for a shore party, and the men began to gather on the halfdeck, and Hastings Abernathy and I eyed each other a bit, each hoping the other would speak first.

Hasty Bernie was the senior, though, so it was his place, and at last he sighed and said, "One of us must go ashore, Mr. Jones, and the other keep the ship."

"Aye, sir," I said, not letting a thing show.

"I don't see," he said, "as there's any necessity as to which of us takes which post."

"No, sir," I said, "nor do I."

"D'you want to lead the shore party, then?"

"'Tis your decision, sir."

"Do it, then. As senior, my first responsibility is the ship. And besides . . ."

He didn't finish the sentence, but then I don't suppose he had to. We both knew as I was better at this sort of affair. Hasty Bernie was twice the seaman I was and a finer hand with the sextant and chart than ever our poor dead captain could have hoped to be, but he weren't quite as fond of improvisation, nor as quick with a cutlass, as I was.

So I was glad of the duty because I thought I'd a better chance of pulling it off—but at the same time, I reckoned that chance to be pretty pissing poor, and I'd have been fair relieved if Bernie had taken it upon himself.

I went to the rail and looked over the men I'd be leading. There was Peter Long and Black Eddie and Ez Carter and Goodman Richard—I'd no complaints about who was there and who wasn't, save that Doc Brewer might come in handy.

He was nowhere to be seen, though, and I decided against sending for him. Instead I made a little speech.

"All right, boys," I said. "The captain's gone and gotten us into another one, and we'll just have to get ourselves out. I'll tell you what it's about on the way, not that I know meself."

And then we were climbing up the ropes to the cave mouth, and I was trying to think if there was anything more I should have brought, besides the lantern and matches and the cutlass and the brace of pistols and the powder and shot and the dagger and the sack of biscuit and the flask of rum and the fifty feet of line and the cosh in my pocket.

A little gold might have been nice, in case any bribery were called for. I had three shillings in my purse, and that was all.

Well, it didn't seem worth going back for.

The caves were dark as the Dungeon Pits on Little Hengist until I got the lantern going. Then I had to remember the route without the captain leading the way, which took me a little bit of a moment.

I managed it, though, with only the one wrong turning, and despite what he said to me between oaths, I swear that Black Eddie's foot was still a good ten feet from the brink of the pit when I realized we'd have done better to have turned left than right at the big pillar.

We came out in the palace wine cellar and stopped to catch our breath and look the matter over.

"Well, now," I said. "Here we are in the palace, and ahead is the stair to the kitchens, and from there we're to find Madame Lee. Being the hour that it is, I'm thinking she'll be in her chamber. Now, where would that be?"

Black Eddie and Peter and the others stared at me like as if I'd just ordered them hanged.

"Don't you *know*?" Peter asked.

"There's no need to be takin' that tone with me, Peter Long," I told him. "No, the fact is I *don't* know. How would I? Nor would any man aboard the ship, for that matter."

"Any man, no," Good Richard pointed out, "but what about the women? Or Jamie?"

I didn't think Miss Melissa knew even as much as I did, but I saw as how he could have a point where Jamie McPhee and Mistress Coyne were considered.

"Well, it's too late now," I said. "We're here and they're not and we've to make the best of it. Be ready, but no pistols—we don't want to rouse the whole palace. Come on, then."

I drew my cutlass and led them up the stairs with the blade naked before me, and the four of them followed at my heel with their own swords out.

At the top we gathered tight together whilst I worked the latch, and then the door opened and we all tumbled out into the kitchens, blades at the ready.

There were two people there, a man and a girl, and I judged them to be the palace baker and either his assistant or a scullery girl. Ez and Peter ran up to them and had steel at their throats in a trice.

I put down my lantern but kept my sword ready as I walked over, a bit more leisurely than Ez and Peter had. I tried to behave as if I burst into places like this an hour before dawn, taking prisoners, as a regular thing.

"Tell us truth and no harm will come to you," I said.

They said not a word but just cowered there, mouths agape. I took it for acceptance.

"Where is Madame Lee's chamber, then, and how do we get there from here?" I demanded.

The baker, if such he was, looked at me with even greater astonishment, but the scullery girl piped up, "It's in the north wing. You cross the hall to the stairs, go up two flights, and around, and then down the corridor to the right, and it's the last door on the right."

A fine girl, that—would blab anything to anyone. "Thank you, lass," I said, and then I looked the situation over and felt some misdoubt about it.

If we left these two free, they might raise the alarm. If we bound them, they might be found—and besides, I thought we might need all the rope we had for other uses.

"Eddie," I said, "you stay here and watch these two and make sure neither of them tells a soul we're about."

Eddie opened his mouth to say something, most probably to protest being asked this, but then he took another look at the girl and changed his mind. "Aye aye, Billy," he said.

"Good, then. You others, come along, and try to be quiet about it."

With that, I led them along the course the lass had described.

We crossed the hall and found the stairs, climbed the stairs and found the corridor, and then we stopped, for the wench hadn't mentioned that a guard was posted outside the door of Madame Lee's chamber.

And what was worse, he saw us before we saw him.

I was wavering there between giving it all up as a botch and fleeing back down the stairs or charging ahead, since we did outnumber him four to one and perhaps if we were quick we could convince him not to rouse the palace, when he called in a loud whisper, "*There* you are! My Lord, you're two hours late!"

I blinked at him and then grinned, and I led the lads down the passage. I saw Ez Carter sheathe his sword, but the rest of us kept ours ready.

"Hurry up," the guard said. "My relief is due soon, and nobody bribed *him*."

We scurried up to the door beside him, and none of us had said a word yet.

"What kept you?" he asked me. "And where's your captain?"

"The captain had a bit of a mishap," I said. "A whack on the head. He's in his bunk aboard ship."

"Is he all right, then?"

"Oh, as right as he'll ever be," I said, which was true after a fashion.

He nodded, and then he took a glance at a window at the end of the corridor, which I had not until that moment noticed. "The wagon's ready?" he asked.

"Um," I said, and I heard Ez Carter swearing under his breath.

The guard insisted, "Is the wagon below the window there, ready to catch her?"

"Well, no," I admitted. "If the truth be known, it's not. We had a little mishap—the same one as hit the captain on the head, do you see."

At least, I thought, now I knew what the wagon had been intended for.

The sentry looked disconcerted, as if he'd just seen a tax collector smile, but before he could say anything more, the bedchamber door opened and a woman's head thrust out, long hair hanging free, not decently put up.

"What're the lot of you doing here whispering outside my door at this hour?" she said.

Good was the first of us to react. He dropped his sword and grabbed for her and caught her round the neck with one arm and pulled her out into the hallway. She was a tall wench, and thin, with hair the color of mahogany, and I thought me I knew the face from somewhere. She wore a black nightdress trimmed with lace, a pretty thing and clearly not meant to be seen in public. When Good Richard laid hold of her, her arms flew up to either side, and she made a noise like a spitting cat.

And Goodman Richard shriveled down away from her and was turned into a toad, right before our eyes.

Whilst the rest of us were still staring, Ez Carter caught her across the back of her head with a belaying pin he'd had in his belt, and witch or no witch, she went down in a heap.

"That's her?" I asked the guard.

He nodded, staring.

I had me a thought, wagon or no wagon. I took a quick few steps to the window at the end of the passageway and looked out.

I could see all of Collyport from there, spread out before me, and the harbor beyond. The warehouse fire had died down some but still glowed orange. All the same, I could see that some of the ships had put back into port; the *Armistead Castle* was back at her berth, but I couldn't put names to the others.

I looked down, then, to where a wagon might have waited, if we'd have had one.

Sure enough, there was a road down there—but it was a hundred feet down and the wall was sheer stone.

The captain might have planned to take Madame Lee out that way, but I wasn't about to try it. I'd brought rope, but not enough, and I hadn't brought any tackle to secure it. Nor did I know where the road went, and men on foot, carrying a woman, would be slower and more likely to attract notice than a freight wagon would have been.

We'd have to go back out the way we came—for one thing, aside from the rest, we'd left Black Eddie in the kitchen. I turned back.

"Come on, then, this way," I called to the others, snatching up the toad and tucking it in my pocket with one hand while my other retrieved Good's cutlass. "Pick her up between you and come along!"

"Wait!" the guard called. "You can't . . . You owe me five guineas for this!" With a start, I remembered Captain Dancy's last words. I also remembered the three shillings in my pocket and frowned. "And besides," the man continued, "when they find me . . ."

Ez Carter gave me a look, and I nodded. He let go his side of the woman, and while Peter Long hoisted her up across his shoulder, Ez walked up and whacked the guard soundly across the pate with his belaying pin.

He sat down suddenly against the wall, and a moment later, when I glanced back from the corner, I saw him reach up to rub his head. I could see the lump from there.

We none of us worried about him; with an eye on the witch, who was already beginning to stir, we ran for the kitchens.

Black Eddie was waiting, with the baker and the maid. The baker had his hands tied behind him and was perched on a stool, facing a wall; the wench wasn't tied at all.

"Come on," I told Eddie, and he buttoned his pants and came on. The girl got to her feet and looked around, and at the sight of Madame Lee her eyes widened.

"Maybe we'd best bring her along," Eddie suggested.

"Please yourself," I told him, not caring to waste time arguing. "As long as she doesn't slow us down."

He grabbed her wrist, and Ez grabbed the lantern, and we all trampled down the stairs to the wine cellars, Ez first, then Peter with Madame Lee over his shoulder, then me, and then Black Eddie, dragging his girl along by her wrist.

I saw as how leaving the baker as we had meant that the secret route through the caves would be a secret no more, but I didn't see any way that could be helped, since we'd no wagon outside the window to escape in, as the captain's plan had called for, and I'd no stomach for killing the baker in cold blood. A corpse in the kitchen might well tell the tale in any case.

Madame Lee raised her head from Peter's shoulder and looked at me, and I began to wonder what flies tasted like.

"Madame," I called, with my best manner, "before you act rashly, remember there are four of us left, and if you enchant another, the rest will kill you in self-defense." I lifted the cutlass that was still in my hand. "We mean you no harm, I promise."

I was none too certain that cold steel would kill a witch as easily as that, but I hoped.

And I was more certain than ever that I knew that face, though with the long hair flying loose about it, and all of us bouncing giddily down the stairs, I couldn't place it just then.

We reached the bottom and ran through the cellars, through the door into the caves, where we found ourselves in gloom relieved by only the single lantern—it seemed worse, somehow, than it had on the way in. I looked and saw the glass was a trifle smoked, as the wick needed trimming. I wished I'd brought more than the one, as we'd no way to trim the wick there.

Well, a man can't think of everything, and we had the one, and it was still enough to see by. I tucked the cutlass in my belt—I had two there now, my own and Goodman Richard's. "This way," I said.

"Mr. Jones," Peter said, "might I put her down for a moment? Or could someone else carry her?"

"Is she heavy?" Ez asked.

"Not so you'd notice," Peter said. "but it's awkward, carrying a woman about that way, all on one side."

"I can walk," Madame Lee said, and she raised her head again, and when I saw her face in the lantern light and heard that throaty voice again, I recognized her at last.

"Oh, my good Lord in heaven and all the saints and angels," I said, staring. "It's the Caliburn Witch herself."

7.

She blinked at me and then smiled like a cat stretches. "Billy Jones," she said. "You've a few more gray hairs than when last we met, haven't you?"

"By God I do," I agreed. "And you're the cause of a few of them!"

She just smiled at me again as Peter set her on her feet.

"You've sworn not to harm us," I told her. "For as long as Jack Dancy lives, you're sworn not to touch a single man of the *Bonny Anne*'s crew."

"Well do I know it," she answered, still smiling. "And where *is* Captain Dancy?"

"Aboard ship," I said. "He's feeling poorly."

The smile winked out like a blown candle flame.

"My Jack?" she said. "My Jack's ill?"

"I'll say no more," I told her. "It's not my place."

The other men were staring. Ez and Peter hadn't yet joined the crew six years before, when we'd tangled with the Witch; Eddie hadn't gotten a good look at her face in the dash down the cellar stairs and hadn't been in the passageway when she came out of her room. And poor Good, of course, was a toad—I could feel him squirming about in my pocket—so he couldn't have said anything if he recognized her.

They'd all heard of the Caliburn Witch, though. Everyone in the islands had heard of the Caliburn Witch. Sometimes we'd wondered why none had heard anything *new* of her these past years.

In a way, though, dangerous as she was, I was glad to see her there, for she *had* sworn not to harm us and wouldn't likely flee at the first chance. We might not need Doc Brewer's geas at all.

And of course, against the likes of her, the best geas Emmanuel Brewer could concoct might not be any more use than trying to bail the ocean dry with my hat. The Caliburn Witch was not to be held lightly.

It occurred to me that Captain Dancy hadn't known which witch he'd been sent after, or he'd not have bothered about a geas. That was something that might bear a little more thought when I had time.

Just then, though, the toad in my pocket was still squirming, and that squirm reminded me. I pulled Good out of my pocket and held him out. "Can you change him back now, if you please? You *did* swear not to harm him."

She smiled that cat smile again. "Surely I swore that, but I don't see that he's been harmed. He looks a fine, fat, healthy toad to me."

I frowned at her. "I'd reckon it harm to turn a man to a toad, and I think so would the captain. He's lost the use of his voice, hasn't he? Don't you reckon that as harm?"

She shrugged. "It might be said so," she admitted. "Alas, I can't turn him back here and now. I keep a spell ready to hand at night, against just such as you, but I'd never any need before for the cure, and I haven't got it with me."

I was about to argue, when Eddie said, "Billy, shouldn't we be getting back to the ship?" He pointed at the lantern, which was burning low and smoking more than ever.

I looked and saw that he had a sound argument. "Come on, then," I said, tucking the toad away, and we wound our way back through the caverns to the sea.

I feared we might have to tie the Witch up and lower her down hand over hand, but she gave us no trouble about scampering down the lines, as if climbing ropes were something she did every day between the governor's audiences.

Then again, for all I knew she might have been able to fly down, but she didn't.

The kitchen wench rode down pickaback on Black Eddie, arms about his neck and legs about his waist, and he damn near lost his hold a time or two on account of the added weight.

At the last, though, we were all down safely and back aboard the *Bonny Anne*, and the moment I came up the side, bringing up the rear as befit my position in command of the party, Hasty Bernie gave the order to up anchor and take us back to Collyport.

He was safe up on the quarterdeck, seeing to the ship, and the rest of my party was scattering to their posts in the rigging, whilst I found myself on the halfdeck with the four females.

"Which one is Madame Lee?" Miss Melissa asked, puzzled, though how she could think a lass as young as that serving maid could be the governor's wife of five years I don't know. Governor Lee had his faults, but I'd never heard any say pedophilia was one of them.

"Who's that?" Mistress Coyne demanded, jabbing her thumb at Eddie's wench.

"Mistress Coyne!" the girl said, staring at the governor's woman. "What are *you* doing here?"

"Who are *these* two?" the Caliburn Witch asked suspiciously.

I sighed and tried to decide where to begin.

A croak from my pocket decided me.

"Madame Lee," I said. "Allow me to present Mistress Melissa Dewhurst, who's aboard the *Bonny Anne* at Captain Dancy's personal invitation."

The two women glared at one another, but before either could speak I turned to the next. "And Mistress Annabelle Coyne," I said, "who came aboard to assist us in certain matters and who had the misfortune to be caught on board when a fire on the docks compelled us to depart."

She smiled graciously at Madame Lee, though with a little more tooth showing than might be strictly necessary.

"And I'm afraid," I said, "that I didn't catch the name of the young lady who came aboard with Black Eddie."

"Susan Bowditch," the wench said, and she dropped a curtsy.

"Mistress Bowditch," I said with a bow. "Welcome aboard. And you, too, Madame Lee, of course."

Madame Lee paid me no heed. She was staring at Mistress Coyne with that cat smile on her face again. I'd never seen it until an hour or so before, but already I was growing sore weary of that expression.

"I begin," she said, "to understand. Rouse Jack Dancy out here, I've something to tell him."

I exchanged a glance with Miss Melissa.

"I'll see if he's to be roused," Miss Melissa said, and she turned away and trotted to the cabin.

The ship was heeling over as we rounded the Seal Stones, and I could see Mistress Coyne shifting as she tried to keep her balance. Poor little Susan Bowditch had to grab for the rail, and I guessed she'd be seasick soon.

The Witch, of course, didn't notice. It would take more than a ship's motion to bother *her*.

"Ladies," I began, thinking we might go below, and then I stopped.

I couldn't take them down to the cabin, not with the captain's corpse still stretched out there. The wardroom that I shared with Bernie was hardly a fit place for them, the fo'c'sle even worse. The black, airless depths of the hold would hardly be an improvement.

The gundeck, perhaps?

I decided we'd do best to stay where we were.

I looked about. The sky was lightening in the east; Bernie had a good lot of canvas spread, and we were making way nicely. I judged we'd be back in Collyport within an hour, if the wind didn't turn foul.

An hour on deck in such mild weather would do no harm. "Excuse me for a moment, ladies," I said, and I trotted over to the starboard shrouds, where Black Eddie had just descended to the deck.

"Eddie," I said, "what were you thinking of, bringing the wench along?"

"I'm sorry, Billy," he said. "She just got the better of me for a moment."

"Will it trouble you any if we put her ashore when we make port?" I asked.

He thought about that for a moment. "She's a pretty little thing," he said, "but I suppose it'd be best."

That was one problem solved—and as I watched Mistress Bowditch lurch against the rail and spew over the side, I didn't doubt that she'd want to be put off the ship.

I knew what the wagon had been for, now—that was another problem solved. The captain had meant for us to come in through the caves but go out through the window, so that the route in would remain a secret, safe for later use. He'd probably have told the baker that we crept in earlier and hid in the wine cellars.

And we'd done what the governor wanted—another problem gone.

Now there were just three more that I saw left to us.

First, now that we had the Witch aboard, what were we to *do* with her?

Second, how were we to keep her from discovering that Jack Dancy was dead and that her oath not to harm us was thereby void? She'd sworn long ago that the *Bonny Anne* and all aboard would be hers when Jack Dancy died.

And third, what was the parrot for?

Well, I judged that solutions would either present themselves or not, and in the meanwhile there were things to be done.

I glanced over and saw Mistress Coyne and Madame Lee exchanging words, and with them looks meant to freeze the heart. Little Susan Bowditch was still sick at the rail.

And here came Miss Melissa back again.

"My apologies, Madame Lee," she said, "but the captain's in no state to be seen, nor will he be for some time yet."

The Witch gave a smile worse than any I'd yet seen on her face, and I thought my heart would stop.

"Mistress Dewhurst," she said, "I've seen Jack Dancy at his worst."

Miss Melissa threw me a puzzled and angry look, and I told her, "Madame Lee once held the captain prisoner for a fortnight, six years ago."

The Witch grinned. Jack Dancy had been her prisoner, right enough—but not in the dungeons with the rest of us.

I could see that Miss Melissa didn't know what to make of that, but she could hardly ask for explanations just then. "All the same," she said, facing up to the Witch with a courage I didn't know she had, "Aboard his own ship, he'll not be seen at his worst."

I tried to distract them all by saying, "Mistress Coyne, we'll be back in port shortly, and we'll be sending you ashore there."

She was about to reply when a cry came from the masthead, "Sail ho!"

We all looked up, and I called, "Where away?"

"Dead ahead!" the reply came.

We looked, and sure enough, there was a frigate rounding the point ahead, just where we'd been headed. We were closing on her quickly, and she was turning broadside to rather than continuing on her course. She was scarce a quarter mile away—the headlands had hidden her—and we were bearing down on her.

"What colors?" Hasty Bernie called from the quarterdeck.

"She's flying the governor's flag," the reply came. "She's the *Armistead Castle!*"

That was all right, then—we all knew the *Armistead Castle*. We'd seen her in port that night, seen her ahead of us when we put out to sea, and I'd seen her back at her moorings from the palace window. She was the governor's own ship that he called out to chase away any pirates foolish enough to venture into Collyport without his permission, and as we were on the governor's business, so to speak, we'd naught to fear from her.

We were just beginning to relax when she opened fire.

8.

It wasn't a full broadside, just a warning shot, but the ball whistled overhead and scared the bloody hell out of us all.

"What the hell?" I asked, and that was the mildest remark I heard on that deck. Miss Melissa and Mistress Coyne said far worse; Madame Lee and Mistress Bowditch didn't bother with words.

"Heave to!" Bernie called, and the men hurried to obey,

while the women and I stood there amidships, all of them talking at once, trying to figure out what was happening.

"Hail her," Bernie ordered the man at the masthead, but the lookout called down, "They're lowering a boat!"

That meant a parley, I judged.

I began to have an idea what was happening. I couldn't be sure, though, and I thought I'd best cover every possibility I could. I pulled the rope from my waist, that line I'd taken into the caves and not used.

"Your pardon, ladies," I said, and I proceeded to bind their hands behind them—first Madame Lee, and then Mistress Coyne, and just to be sure I went on and tied Mistress Bowditch and Miss Melissa as well.

Miss Melissa started to protest, but I whispered, "Bear with me, mistress, please."

She shrugged and let me tie her hands.

Then I drew one of the two cutlasses on my belt and waited for the parley boat to arrive.

A few minutes later—which seemed like half of eternity— the boat bumped up against the side. A couple of the men secured it, and Peter Long, who was one of them, called, "Officer coming aboard, Mr. Jones!"

As the officer's cocked hat appeared in the entry port, I lifted the sword to Madame Lee's throat.

The man's face was shocked when he saw me standing there behind a row of women, all with their hands bound, and one with my blade against her neck.

"My Lord, man," he began, and then stopped.

"Speak your piece," I told him. "Why'd you fire on us?"

He blinked and then said, "I'm here at the governor's orders, sir. He'd heard that the crew of the *Bonny Anne* had abducted an innocent woman from Collyport, one Mistress Annabelle Coyne, and he came down to the port and sent us out after you."

I blinked back at him, much relieved. The governor hadn't double-crossed us, then, and wasn't going to sink us for kidnapping his wife. Instead, he'd thought we were double-crossing *him* and stealing the wrong woman.

"Governor Lee's aboard your ship?" I asked.

"Yes, sir, he is," the officer replied.

"Well, then, you can tell him he's been misinformed. Mistress Coyne was not kidnapped; she came aboard of her own free will and she's free to go, any time she chooses." I turned the cutlass about and used it to cut the cords on Mistress Coyne's wrists. Then I cut Mistress Bowditch's, as well—this was as good a time as any to get her out of the way. I pushed them both toward the officer. "Here she is," I said, "and another as well, and you're welcome to take them back with you."

The officer stammered for a moment, and then asked Mistress Bowditch, "You're Annabelle Coyne?"

"No," Mistress Coyne said angrily, "*I* am."

Mistress Bowditch was still too seasick to say anything; she just nodded.

"And those other two?" the governor's man asked, pointing.

"Spoils of war," I said, "and none of your concern."

I thought that the Witch would betray me, and I think for a moment she thought so, too, but instead she grinned.

"They don't speak English," I added.

The Witch nodded eagerly. Miss Melissa glowered at me but kept silent.

The officer—a lieutenant, he was, by his uniform—looked about, and then decided to take what he was given and see what happened. "This way, ladies," he said, and he helped Mistress Coyne and Mistress Bowditch down over the side.

Then the boat pulled away, and Miss Melissa shouted, "Get these ropes off me"

Madame Lee didn't say a word, but the ropes fell away from her wrists.

I set to untying Miss Melissa and spoke up cheerfully. "There, now, ladies, we've settled that! We're rid of those two, who would have been nothing but trouble, and we still have you. I take it from your silence, ma'am, that you had no particular wish to be sent aboard the *Armistead Castle*?"

I looked at Madame Lee, and she looked back.

"Mr. Jones," she said, "I've known for some time that my husband was tired of my company, and I've no more love for him. I enjoyed playing the governor's lady and being mistress of Collyport, but it's not worth the grief if he's going to such extremes as this to get rid of me!"

My mouth fell open.

She sneered—a harsh word to use of a lady, but she did. "Come now," she said, "did you think I didn't know, when I saw Annabelle Coyne on this deck, that it was George Lee who had sent you to kidnap me? And furthermore, do you think I didn't know why? He's trying to rid himself of two problems at once—Jack Dancy and myself. Jack didn't know who I was, but my dear Georgie did. So he sent you to capture me, and Jack agreed, thinking he could handle an ordinary witch—Doc Brewer's surely prepared a little spell of some sort! But then Jack was to find himself with no mere hedgerow enchantress, but the infamous Caliburn Witch aboard, the same who he had scarcely escaped six years ago. Georgie knew I'd rather stay aboard the *Bonny Anne* with my Jack than in his palace with him, and he was right!"

"*Your* Jack!" Miss Melissa burst out.

"Aye," the witch told her, "*my* Jack, or he was once, at any rate, and long before he was *your* lover. But what's it matter now that he's dead?"

My mouth fell open, and Miss Melissa's snapped shut.

"Dead?" she said.

"How did you know?" I asked—for I knew better than to lie any more to the Caliburn Witch.

She gave me a bitter smile. "I know my Jack," she said. "If there was still breath in his body, he'd have come on deck when someone fired on his *Bonny Anne*."

We could scarce argue with that, for it was the plain truth.

"How did it happen?" the Witch asked.

"He slipped and hit his head," I said. "In the alley behind Old Joe's Tavern."

Her eyes widened. "Is that all? It wasn't the Black Sorcerer? Nor Bartholomew Sanchez? Nor the Pundit of Oul?"

"No," I said. "Just a fall and a broken neck."

She shook her head.

It was at that moment that the frigate fired a full broadside at us.

The roar swept over us, and the balls tore through the rigging; I heard lines snap and canvas tear and shot howl through the air. We all spun in astonishment.

"Man the guns!" Hasty Bernie cried from the quarterdeck, and men swarmed to the gundeck.

"*What?*" the Witch cried. "He *dares*?"

"Dares what?" I shouted back over the pounding feet and the rattling of the gun tackles. "Who?"

"That worm who called me his wife! That little bitch from the kitchens told him I was aboard, and now he means to sink us!"

"How do you . . ." I started to ask, but then I remembered whom I spoke to. Instead I asked, "Why didn't he just sail away?"

"And let everyone aboard his ship know he was leaving his lady in Jack Dancy's hands? He couldn't do that. How could he ever hold his head up again if he sailed away and left his own wife in the hands of an adventurer like Jack Dancy?"

"But then why didn't he send a boat to parley . . ." I began.

"You bloody *fool!*" she shrieked, turning on me, just as the frigate's second broadside thundered out at us. "He doesn't want me back, he wants me *dead*! He's trying to sink us! He can't just sail away, but if I die accidentally in the fight, who's to say he's done wrong? And die I might—even a witch can drown in twenty fathoms of salt water!"

I heard the crunch of a ball hitting the side and saw a fore mainsail sheet flying free where a shot snapped it, and then our own guns roared out, raggedly. Doc Brewer tottered up from below, the canvas bag of unused arcana in his fist, looking about wildly.

I knew we had no chance; the *Bonny Anne* carried eighteen guns to the frigate's thirty-two, and smaller guns at that. We had scarce thirty seamen aboard, what with having left port so hurriedly, while he surely had two hundred. "Strike!" I called to Bernie. "He can't sink us if we strike! Better a dungeon than drowning!"

"*No!*" shrieked the Witch. She staggered across the deck and snatched the bag from Doc Brewer, then tore it open.

She looked up at me with a grin of triumph on her face and snatched out something long and thin and yellowish. She lifted it above her head, stretched between her two hands, and shouted out something.

What she shouted was in no language I had ever heard before, nor any I ever wish to hear again.

The frigate's third broadside roared out, but when I looked at the governor's ship I saw that it had heeled back and that most of the balls would pass over us, too high to do any damage.

And our own ship was heeling back, as well, and the sea between us seemed to be rising up, and I tried to guess what trick of the tide or the gunfire could cause that, and then I realized it wasn't any natural trick at all.

The wave rose up higher and higher, above the level of our decks, and then still higher, above the spars; the frigate was hidden from sight now behind a rising wall of surging green water.

The Witch was standing, arms raised and spread, like a statue; wind whipped her hair about her as if she stood in a hurricane, but elsewhere the air was almost dead calm now, the sails hanging limp. Her eyes blazed with a green fire.

The water rose up until it seemed to cover half the sky—and then it fell.

On the frigate.

The backwash sent the *Bonny Anne* rocking and bouncing, yawing wildly, and I grabbed for the rail and saw others doing the same—everyone but the Witch herself grabbed for a hand-hold somewhere.

Spray burst up over the side and caught me in the face.

When I was able to clear my eyes and look again, there was no trace of the *Armistead Castle* anywhere, only the rocks and the tossing waves.

The sea calmed gradually, and I heard Bernie sending the men to repair the damage we'd taken in the battle. I didn't concern myself with that; instead I paid attention only to the Caliburn Witch.

The light had faded from her eyes, and she lowered the yellowish thing and tossed it to Doc Brewer. I finally got a decent look at it, and saw that it was the skeleton of an eel.

"*That* should teach the man not to mistreat his wife!" the Witch snapped. She turned. "Mr. Abernathy!" she called, "set a course for Drummond Isle; we'll be putting Mistress Dewhurst ashore there, in her hometown!"

Miss Melissa started when she heard that and glanced at the Witch, but didn't say anything.

"Aye aye," Bernie called back, in a puzzled tone.

I was just as puzzled. "Your pardon, ma'am," I ventured, "but what is it you're planning?"

I remembered well how, six years before, she had sworn to see me and my mates dead.

So did she, I judged.

Was she planning to set Miss Melissa shore first and then sink us or burn us?

Such scruples hardly seemed likely, given that she'd had no hesitation in sending Mistress Coyne and Mistress Bowditch to the bottom, along with everyone else aboard the *Armistead Castle*. True, Mistress Coyne had been her husband's mistress, and Mistress Bowditch had tattled to the governor, but Miss Melissa was her dead lover's woman, so she'd grounds for a grudge there, too.

"Well, Mr. Jones," she said, turning back to me with the least malicious smile I'd yet seen on her face, "I've had my fill of the governor's palace and for that matter all of Collyport. I'd seen all I cared to of Caliburn Island five years ago, or I'd not have left it. I think the time has come to roam a little, to wander about—and it seems to me that a ship and crew have just fallen into my hands that would suit me fine for that wandering. There's the little matter of your deaths, yours and a dozen others, a sentence I handed down back on Caliburn six years ago. Well, I'm willing to commute that sentence to a few years of penal servitude—aboard this ship, under my command." She made the smile into another of her cat grins. "Or I could hang you. It's your choice, Mr. Jones."

It took me no time to decide *that* one. "Aye aye, Captain Lee," I replied, saluting.

We put Melissa Dewhurst and five crewmen who asked ashore on Drummond Isle eleven days later, where for all I know they're all living peacefully to this day. John Hastings Abernathy, who after all had never angered the Witch and hadn't been with us those six years before, was retired three months after and put ashore in Collyport, where he took a post with the new acting governor as portmaster. I was promoted to first mate.

Captain Dancy we gave a fine burial at sea the very afternoon after the sinking of the *Armistead Castle*. Captain Lee turned the toad back into Goodman Richard, using Doc Brewer's paraphernalia, that same night.

As for the rest, Captain Lee says she'll set us free when she grows bored. She's no worse a master than was Jack Dancy, for the most part, and as she's taken a fancy to me, I've no need now to wait until we're in port to find a woman to share my bunk.

As most of Captain Dancy's plans, the whole affair had all worked out well enough, if not the way we expected.

I see how it was meant to work—the fire for a distraction, the entry through the caves, the escape in the wagon below the window, the geas to hold the witch under control until we could put her ashore somewhere. Captain Dancy hadn't planned to have Mistress Coyne aboard, nor to have the governor think that Mistress Coyne had chosen Jack Dancy over himself and come out to get her back. He hadn't known that Madame Lee was no ordinary witch, but the Caliburn Witch.

It's pretty much all clear now.

But we never did find out what the damn parrot was for.

AFTER THE DRAGON IS DEAD

*I stepped out onto the western terrace and stopped to mar-*vel at the blaze of glory that the setting sun had spread across the sky for our enjoyment. Golden light streamed around the clouds, edging them with fire, while the sun was a crimson oval on a background of pinks and blues more delicate than the finest court painter could ever concoct.

In the village below, the townspeople were lighting torches for their celebration, and by those distant flickers I could make out a thin black line in the square with a thickening at the top, the pole on which the usurper-tyrant's head was impaled.

A serving girl, one of those we had so recently freed from the tyrant's harem, knelt beside me and offered a goblet of pomegranate juice, iced with snow brought down from the mountaintops. As I accepted it, she looked up at me, and from the expression in her lovely brown eyes, I knew that she was offering more than this mere sweet.

I brushed the hair that spilled down over her shoulders and smiled at her. "Will you bring something to my chamber when I retire tonight?" I asked.

She nodded, speechlessly.

I left her kneeling there and crossed to the rail, where my young comrade Algarven stood admiring the view, the Princess Loriana at his side.

"Never have I seen so prosperous and beautiful a land," he said, as his arm found its way around his beloved's waist.

"And free of the usurper and his monster now," she replied. "Thanks to you two."

Algarven smiled an acknowledgment and hugged her to him.

246

"The people adore you, you know," she said.

"They do now," I said, "but it never lasts. If we stay, one day we'll hear them grumbling about us, just as they did about old Kendrik the Oppressor, there."

Algarven stared at me in surprise. "You're joking," he said. "We're their saviors! We'll always be loved."

I shrugged and did not press the point.

Algarven said, "I'll be glad to grow old here, with my love at my side."

I shrugged again.

I knew that I, at least, would be packed and gone before the year was out. I've done this before. This was Algarven's first stint as a hero, though, and he still believed in happy endings.

Maybe he was right; maybe he would stay there without getting bored or wearing out his welcome. Some people manage it. I smiled and resolved to do my best to enjoy the glory while I could.

"A beautiful evening," I said, with a wave at the western sky.

"A beautiful evening," Algarven agreed. "A beautiful evening, a beautiful bride, a palace, my people, the dragon dead and its master beheaded—ah," he sighed, lifting his tankard of ale in salute. "It doesn't get any better than this!"

About the Author

Lawrence Watt-Evans was born and raised in eastern Massachusetts, the fourth of six children in a house full of books. Other details of his childhood may be found in the introduction to this collection.

He dropped out of Princeton University in 1977. Being qualified for no other enjoyable work—he had discovered working in ladder factories, supermarkets, or fast-food restaurants, and selling door-to-door, to be something less than enjoyable—he then began trying to sell his writing, and eventually produced a fantasy novel, *The Lure of the Basilisk*, which sold to Del Rey Books, beginning his career as a full-time writer.

He has gone on to author novels and short fiction in the fields of science fiction, fantasy, and horror. He is best known for the Ethshar fantasy series, consisting of, so far, *The Misenchanted Sword*, *With A Single Spell*, *The Unwilling Warlord*, and *The Blood of a Dragon*.

He married in 1977, has two children, and lives in the Maryland suburbs of Washington, D.C.